WHEN I FALL IN LOVE

WHEN I FALL IN LOVE

LYNN KURLAND

THORNDIKE PRESS

An imprint of Thomson Gale, a part of The Thomson Corporation

THOMSON

GALE

Detroit • New York • San Francisco • New Haven, Conn. • Waterville, Maine • London

THOMSON

GALE

LIBRARY OF CONGRESS CATALOGING-IN-PUBLICATION DATA

Kurland, Lynn.
   When I fall in love / by Lynn Kurland.
     p. cm.
   ISBN-13: 978-0-7862-9862-4 (hardcover : alk. paper)
   ISBN-10: 0-7862-9862-6 (hardcover : alk. paper)
   1. Time travel — Fiction. 2. Large type books. I. Title.
PS3561.U645W47 2007
813'.54—dc22   2007022670

Published in 2007 by arrangement with The Berkley Publishing Group, a member of Penguin Group (USA) Inc.

Printed in the United States of America on permanent paper
10 9 8 7 6 5 4 3 2 1

To my family

ACKNOWLEDGMENTS

First and foremost, briefly, heartfelt thanks must go to my agent, the lovely and talented Nancy Yost. She'll know why.

To my editor, Kate Seaver, for being such a joy to work with.

To my publisher, Leslie Gelbman, for her many kind words, her accessibility, and her gracious, continued support.

To Gail, because I wouldn't be where I am today without her.

To my cousin-in-law Claire for introducing me to the RTO, and her husband, Bjarne, for giving us the pleasure of listening to a professional violinist make the instrument truly sing.

And last but not least, to my family, who puts up with my crazy hours, crazy characters, and the general chaos that reigns the closer I get to a deadline. They are my joy and delight. I can't imagine life without them.

CAST OF CHARACTERS

JENNIFER MACLEOD MCKINNON
Victoria McKinnon MacDougal, Jennifer's sister
Connor MacDougal, Victoria's husband
Megan MacLeod McKinnon de Piaget, Jennifer's sister
Gideon de Piaget, Megan's husband
John McKinnon, Jennifer's father
Helen MacLeod McKinnon, Jennifer's mother
Mary MacLeod, Jennifer's grandmother

NICHOLAS DE PIAGET
Robin de Piaget, Nicholas's brother
Anne de Piaget, Robin's wife
Amanda de Piaget Kilchurn, Nicholas's sister
Jake Kilchurn, Amanda's husband
Miles de Piaget, Nicholas's brother
John de Piaget, Nicholas's brother
Montgomery de Piaget, Nicholas's brother

9

Rhys de Piaget, Nicholas's father
Gwennelyn de Piaget, Nicholas's mother
Joanna of Segrave, Nicholas's grandmother

KENDRICK DE PIAGET, EARL OF SEAKIRK
Genevieve Buchanan de Piaget, Kendrick's
  wife

THE BOAR'S HEAD TRIO
Ambrose MacLeod
Hugh McKinnon
Fulbert de Piaget

PROLOGUE

Manhattan
Present Day
I did lock that door when I left this afternoon, didn't I?

Jennifer MacLeod McKinnon stood in the hallway of her charming Upper East Side brownstone and looked at her apartment door. It wasn't secured with the four deadbolts that she locked religiously no matter what side of the door she was standing on. It wasn't even shut tight in a way that might have encouraged her to lean on it and rely on its strength.

It was ajar.

Ajar in a way that suggested strongly that someone had been inside. Someone who wasn't her.

Jennifer frowned. That was not the kind of thing a girl wanted her deadbolt-encrusted door to be suggesting when she was out alone in the hallway well after midnight with only Mrs. Delinski and her brace of terriers across

11

the hall to help her.

She leaned in a little closer, on the off chance that she might have been mistaken, and heard nothing. Well, that wasn't quite true. She could hear Mrs. Delinski's television, a police siren outside, and someone having a fight upstairs. But in her apartment?

Silence.

It was possible that she had forgotten to lock the door. Possible, but not likely. It was Manhattan, for heaven's sake. She locked the door when she talked to Mrs. Delinski out in the hallway.

She considered her options. She could call the police, but this was the third time this month her apartment had been broken into and she wasn't sure she could face the thought of filling out another police report. She could leap inside and bean her potential intruder over the head with her violin case, but her violin was worth a lot of money so the odds of her being able to really put some *oomph* into the beaning were not good. Or she could call her sister Victoria and see if Victoria's very intimidating husband might be willing to come take a little look-see inside to make sure that her apartment was thug-free.

Now, that was an appealing idea. Connor MacDougal loved trouble. Intruders were his favorite kind of trouble, though he was willing to settle for muggers and petty thieves when he had to. He'd done damage to all sorts of lowlife, to the endless despair of her sister, who was continually trying to convince him that swords, and just fake ones if you please, were better reserved for the stage. Connor did use swords on stage in his flourishing acting career, but Jennifer suspected it grieved him slightly that no real blood ever flowed.

And it probably wouldn't matter to him that the odds of there being anyone still inside were very slim. He liked the role of protective older brother. There was no sense in not giving him the chance to play it. She pulled her phone out of her evening bag and called her sister's cell. Victoria picked up on the first ring.

"We're almost to your place," she said without preamble.

"You are?" Jennifer whispered. "Why?"

"Connor had a bad feeling."

"Wow, he's good," Jennifer murmured. "Why can't I find myself a guy like that?"

"You're looking in the wrong place. So, why did you call and why are you whispering?"

"My front door's open."

"Again? Did you forget to lock it?"

"Of course not!" Jennifer exclaimed, then she paused. "At least I don't think I did."

"Wait for us downstairs."

"I —"

Victoria hung up.

"Was planning to," Jennifer finished. What did her sister think she was, nuts? She had an intimidating brother-in-law to do her dirty work for her; she wasn't going to do it herself.

She put her phone back in her purse, picked up the hem of her beaded gown, and walked carefully down the stairs. She had to walk carefully so she didn't scratch the shoes that could have passed in a pinch for glass slippers. They had seemed like the appropriate accessory to match an evening that had promised to be nothing short of a fairy tale in the making.

She'd been asked at the last minute to fill in for the fabulous Victor Bourgeois who had been slated to play Paganini's Violin Concerto no. 1 in D Major with the Wildly Terrific Orchestra, an edgy group that wasn't nearly as famous as the New York Philharmonic, but in her opinion almost as good. She could thank her agent, the fabulous and very long-suffering Charles Salieri, for the chance. He'd happily taken her on while she'd still been a student at Juilliard, ignored her complaints of burnout after she'd graduated top of her class in violin performance, and only sighed lightly as she'd jumped into business with her mother instead of leaping into the musical pond as he thought she should have.

Fortunately for her, his nagging and Victoria's hounding had resulted in her spending a great deal more time practicing over the years than she'd let on. That had resulted in the invitation that she'd thought just might be the start of a new direction for her.

So, she'd donned her Cinderella duds and headed toward the concert hall where the evening had been as glorious as she'd hoped it might be. She had played flawlessly, even by her own exacting standards. Clicking her glass heels together a time or two had resulted in yet another fairy tale happening, mainly the very talented, enormously gorgeous Maestro Michael McGillicuty, WTO's brilliant conductor, asking her after the concert if she might like to share a cab home. It had seemed too good to be true.

Unfortunately, it had been.

Being forced to plant your fist into your Prince Charming's nose because he had been less than a gentleman was not exactly the stuff dreams were made of.

She stepped out into the frigid March evening and wished for something more substantial than her flimsy shawl. She leaned against the iron stair railing and breathed as deeply as she dared. There she was in a fairy-tale gown with fairy-tale shoes; where was her knight in shining armor, riding up on his white horse to rescue her from all the creeps?

A cab screeched to a halt in front of her apartment and interrupted her gloomy ruminations. Victoria and Connor piled out and hurried over to her.

"How open was your door?" Victoria began without hesitation. "A lot? A little? Just your imagination imagining the extent of its openness?"

Jennifer scowled at her. "The door was open in a way that strongly suggests that a thief had recently been inside and had his arms too full of my stuff to really close it properly on his way out." She looked at Connor. "Do you want to go up and check?"

Connor flexed his fingers. Jennifer thought he might have chortled as well, but she was shivering, so that could have been her teeth chattering.

"Aye," he said enthusiastically. "I'll ascend and see."

Jennifer watched her brother-in-law bound up the stairs and into the building. The door shut behind him. She stared after him thoughtfully for a moment or two, then turned to her sister. "Vic?"

"What?"

"Why did Connor have a knife stuck into the waistband of his jeans?"

"Damn it," Victoria said in exasperation. "I really should have a metal detector installed on the front door."

"How can you ride across town in a cab with a man and not know he's packing an enormous knife in the back of his pants?"

"I was distracted."

"Were you worrying about me?"

16

Victoria actually blushed. "Not exactly. I was otherwise occupied."

Jennifer laughed. "Vic, you're married. It's okay."

"It's humiliating. I was trying to put my arms around him so we could make out properly in the back of that cab, but he kept grabbing my hands and kissing them."

"Romantic," Jennifer noted.

"Ha," Victoria snorted. "He said my hands were so beautiful and expressive, he couldn't let them go. Now I see he just didn't want me finding something better left under his pillow."

"He's good," Jennifer said.

"He would definitely agree. He might also make use of that knife if we're not there to stop him." She took Jennifer by the arm. "Come on. We'll follow at a discreet distance."

"You know, there's probably no one inside."

"I know," Victoria said with a wink. "I'm humoring him."

Jennifer smiled and walked with Victoria back inside, up the flight of stairs, and along the hallway with the exposed brick until they stopped in front of her now wide-open door. Connor appeared suddenly in the doorway.

"Empty," he said, sounding very disappointed.

"What do you mean by empty?" Jennifer asked. "Empty as in no stuff, or empty as in

17

no thief?"

"No thief," he said glumly.

"Better luck next time," she said, giving him a sympathetic pat on the shoulder. She walked inside her luxurious 400 square feet of apartment and looked around. At first glance it didn't seem like anything was missing, but considering the state of things, it was a little hard to tell.

Her apartment looked like a fabric shop, with material she used in her mother's business stacked on every available surface and most of the floor. She did have a bare spot over by the window where she practiced and an exposed bit of kitchen counter on which she stacked take-out. The rest of the place, however, was a disaster.

Victoria put her hands on her hips. "Why does someone keep breaking in? You don't have anything to steal."

Jennifer shrugged. "Who knows? My building seems to be prone to it. It's annoying, but at least no one ever seems to get hurt. Maybe it's just Fate trying to tell me something."

"*Get another apartment* would be my guess," Victoria said.

"I'm beginning to think the same thing," Jennifer said. She started to work on a dangerously listing pile of fabric. "Maybe I need to get something a little bigger."

"Smaller," Victoria countered. "You'll have

less room for all Mom's junk that way. Oh, and speaking of junk, guess who we saw on our way over?"

"I hesitate to ask."

"Michael McGillicuty."

"Did you indeed?"

Victoria smiled. "Yes, we did indeed. He was stomping back down your street, directing an unseen orchestra playing a symphony of disgust."

Jennifer pursed her lips. "How poetic."

"His nose was dripping blood."

"That's poetic, too."

"We rolled down the window and asked him what had happened to him." Victoria smirked. "He said he'd run into a wall."

"He ran into my fist," Jennifer said shortly. "And that wasn't because he was trying to grab my violin."

"Stop dating musicians," Victoria advised.

"I wasn't dating him. I was contemplating dating him."

Victoria looked her over. "Then he's an idiot for blowing it. You look like Cinderella. Why can't you find a decent guy to match that dress?"

"I have no idea."

"You should go to Scotland," Connor said. "Your Gaelic is flawless. You might find a braw lad there in the Highlands."

"It's very tempting," Jennifer said. "Do you think Granny would mind me marrying a guy

19

who packed a sword?"

"That would probably be a prerequisite," Victoria said. "Call her tomorrow and I'm sure she'll tell you as much. Now, do you have anything to eat in that little corner masquerading as a kitchen, or are we going to have to order take-out again?"

"Take-out," Jennifer said. "Mr. Chin delivers all night. The number is —"

"Probably the only thing listed on your speed dial," Victoria interrupted. "I'll take care of it." She paused. "By the way, you were fabulous tonight."

Jennifer smiled. "Thanks."

Victoria smiled in return. "Go see what's really missing this time."

Jennifer nodded. She no longer had a toaster or a microwave, courtesy of the first break-in. The second go-round had resulted in the loss of all her electronics. Victoria was right; there really wasn't much else to steal. She walked over to her small armoire, looked inside, then swore.

Everything was gone. All her clothes, all her jewelry, all her shoes. Not even her ratty flip-flops from last summer or her matted and quite disgusting sheepskin slippers had been left behind. She put her hands on her hips and frowned fiercely. What was she supposed to do now, run around looking like an extra from a kid's fairy tale theater production?

20

Maybe Fate *was* trying to tell her something.

She sighed, then turned around, sat down in her empty closet, and gave thought to her sorry, clothesless, shoeless life. There she was, a successful designer of baby clothes who was preparing to leap headfirst into the kind of music career people would have killed to call their own.

Somehow, the thought of it just wasn't as satisfying as it had been that morning.

She looked at her sister talking on the phone, then at that sister's husband. Connor was leaning against the now-closed front door, watching Victoria with a small smile on his face. Jennifer smiled to herself. He might try to disguise it with jeans and a sweatshirt, but anyone with eyes could see he was Hollywood's idea of the perfect medieval Scottish laird.

And he loved her sister to distraction.

Jennifer watched Victoria hang up the phone, turn, and catch sight of her husband watching her. She smiled as well, the satisfied smile of a woman who was adored by a magnificent man.

Jennifer had to look away. She was closer to tears than she wanted to admit. She realized with startling clarity that what she wanted was what Victoria had. How in the world was she going to find that when her choice of Prince Charmings included the likes of Michael McGillicuty?

She sat there in her cramped, cluttered apartment and suddenly felt more discouraged than she ever had in her entire life. She didn't want to be alone anymore. She didn't want that door to close behind Victoria and Connor. She didn't want silence to descend inside, silence that would be not quite silent because she was surrounded on all sides by people and stereos and televisions. She didn't want to spend any more nights pacing, tripping over stacks of material and feeling the walls close in on her.

She didn't want to be wearing the perfect dress, with the perfect shoes, and find that there was no hope of a happy ending to go with it.

This was not the life she wanted.

She pushed herself to her feet and started to pace. She looked around desperately for a distraction and found herself suddenly staring down at the extra phone she'd bummed off her mother after the second break-in. The light was blinking.

Blinking in a very significant way.

Jennifer reached out to turn on her messages, then realized her hand was shaking. She took a deep breath, flexed her fingers, then pushed the button. Her other sister's voice filled the room.

"Jenner, it's Megan. I know this probably isn't possible, what with the way your career has suddenly taken off —" Megan laughed a little. "And yes, Victoria told me so. Anyway, we're going to be at Artane next month and it just popped into my mind to call and invite you to come along. We're having a little de Piaget family reunion and I need you to keep me company. You will come, won't you?"

Jennifer caught her breath.

She could see rolling hills covered with forests and sheep and bordered by charming stone fences. She could hear the sound of endless waves against the beach and feel the damp, medieval stone beneath her fingertips as she wandered Artane's hallowed halls. How would it be to have room to walk for miles and not see another soul, or have the space to actually touch raw earth and see unobstructed clouds? What would it be like to have peace and quiet where she could actually think?

And who knew that she might not find a bit more than she was looking for? Vic and Megan had found their heart's desires in England.

"Hey," Victoria said suddenly, "you look far too contemplative for your own good."

Jennifer looked at her sister. "I need a change."

"A new apartment? I agree."

"No," Jennifer said, standing up slowly, "I mean a *big* change." She smiled suddenly. "I'm going to England."

Victoria looked at her in shock. "But you're embarking on a new stage in your career."

"It'll keep. This is Fate."

"This is post-performance letdown," Victoria corrected. "Besides, Dad will have a fit. You know he doesn't like his offspring heading across the Pond. It means that if you find a reason to stay, he'll have to head across the Pond as well and he doesn't like chips and peas with his fish."

"Artane has a great chef."

"He won't care." Victoria looked at Jennifer seriously. "This is just a vacation, isn't it?"

"I'll take my violin with me."

"It's a sixty-thousand-dollar Degani, Jenner. You take it to the bathroom with you." She peered at Jennifer for a moment or two, then sighed. "You've already made up your mind."

"Vic, there are sometimes you sound like a stage mother."

"And there are sometimes you sound like Paganini."

Jennifer laughed. "In my dreams. I appreciate the vote of confidence, but right now I want to go land on Megan's doorstep and feel the sea breeze in my hair." She looked at Connor. "What do you think?"

"When change is in the air, you should follow it," he advised. "Change was in the air when I met your sister."

The look he shot Victoria almost singed

24

Jennifer where she stood. She laughed.

"There's my answer. Vic, you don't dare argue with him."

Victoria looked a bit faint. In fact, she fanned herself. "I won't."

Jennifer smiled, then rubbed her hands together briskly.

"Do you know any guys?"

"I know lots of guys. What do you want them for?"

"To bring some boxes for a couple of things, then carry everything left over to the nearest Dumpster."

"And then what?"

"I'll go crash with Mom and Dad for a few days," Jennifer said. "The less stuff I have to put in the back of a cab, the better off I'll be."

"True enough," Victoria said. "I'll find you guys tomorrow. We'll stay tonight and help you pack up."

"Don't you have rehearsal tomorrow?"

"Tomorrow — or today, rather — is Sunday and even Evil Stuart Goldberg takes a day off now and then."

"What are you rehearsing again?" Jennifer asked.

"Connor and I are starring in *Taming of the Shrew,* which you knew already," Victoria said severely, "so don't make any jokes about it."

"Me?" Jennifer said with a smile. "Never." She winked at Connor. "Fun for you."

"It shows Victoria's fire in all its most attractive lights," he said solemnly. "How can I resist?"

Jennifer whistled. "You *are* good."

"And you're about to lose your help packing," Victoria said pointedly. "Where's dinner?"

"Give Mr. Chin a chance."

Jennifer erased the message, then went to pull her Murphy bed down. She was relieved to find her pink flannel pajamas still under her pillow. Her thief might have had no standards when it came to shoes, but he also had apparently been too lazy to see what might be tucked under bedclothes. She went into the bathroom and changed out of her gown.

Maybe she would go to Scotland first and roam through the heather. Then she would head south and catch up with Megan. It would be wonderful. The calm before the storm. The big breath before leaping into the deep end of the musical pool. A chance to decide once and for all if performing was really for her. That wasn't an unreasonable thing to do, despite all of Charles Salieri's text messages and his promise of a full schedule of concert dates in the near future.

Besides, for all she knew she might find a fairy godmother waiting for her. Maybe she would find her knight in shining armor there as well.

One who would actually like to listen to her play. One who had an ounce of chivalry in his soul. One who would love her forever.

It could happen.

But it wouldn't until she'd gotten herself out of her present situation. She would call Charles in the morning and let him know about her trip, dump her few belongings on her mother's doorstep, then head for the airport. It was the right thing to do.

She took a deep breath, then left the bathroom, put away her gown and glass slippers, and got down to work.

CHAPTER 1

Artane
Present Day
Ambrose MacLeod flattened himself against the wall that led to the kitchens and wondered if he'd made a terrible mistake.

It wasn't that he hadn't found himself in like situations before. One could not be the laird of a mighty clan like the MacLeods and not find himself encountering the odd, dodgy situation or the occasional brush with death. He had gone through more than his share of perilous predicaments and lived to boast of their success.

Still, old habits died hard, as the saying went, and a canny sixteenth-century lad out for a lark in someone else's castle didn't simply walk down the passageways as if he had a right to. When assaulting the bowels of someone else's keep, subterfuge and stealth were always the order of the day.

He held his breath as a stout, plain-faced woman of advancing years came down the

29

passageway, rubbing her hands and complaining to herself about the price of fish. He waited until she'd passed and disappeared the other way before he stepped away from the wall and continued down the passageway, his kilt swinging about his knees in a saucy fashion and his mighty sword slapping against his thigh as it always did.

He walked into the kitchen and looked about him for lights that he might see to. He lit a handful of torches of his own making and found that even here at Artane, the kitchen could be counted on for a shiny black Aga holding court. He conjured up a chair, pulled a mug of ale out of thin air, and sat down with a sigh. Perhaps there were some comforts that could be enjoyed, no matter the location.

He had just settled back to enjoy those comforts when the sound of a cat being strangled assaulted his ears. The front two legs of his chair hit the floor with a thump as he leapt to his feet. His sword came from its sheath with the kind of hiss that bespoke serious business intended.

He waited, bouncing on his heels a time or two, as the sound approached. Who knew what it boded? Was he to be reduced to rescuer of large, very loud felines now? It wasn't beneath him, of course. Chivalry was chivalry, after all, and no damsel in distress was beneath his notice — be she of the feline kind or not —

He stared, openmouthed, as the sound — and its maker — entered the kitchen. The point of his sword clanged against the stone of the floor. He thought that he just might have to sit down soon.

Or at least stick his fingers in his ears.

"Hugh," he said weakly. "What, by all the saints above, are you doing?"

Hugh McKinnon, laird of the clan McKinnon near the turn of a particularly medieval century, took the violin from under his chin and made Ambrose a low bow. He straightened, swished his bow through the air a time or two in a manly fashion, then smiled a gap-toothed smile.

"I'm practicing," he announced proudly.

Ambrose resheathed his sword with difficulty, then felt his way down into his chair. "Practicing what, pray? Terrifying the locals?"

"The violin," Hugh said indignantly. "Can't ye see that?"

"Of course I *see* that," Ambrose said. "What I don't see is *why*."

"I was thinking that perhaps my wee granddaughter Jennifer McKinnon might play a duet or two with me when she arrives."

Ambrose was very rarely without some sort of kind word, or a bracing suggestion at the very least, but he found that, in this instance, all he could do was nod, mute. The thought of a musician of Jennifer's caliber playing

31

with this tormentor of ghostly strung steel was almost beyond comprehension.

Hugh pulled up a chair and sat down with a satisfied sigh. "I've already had my first performance, you know," he said.

"Have you?" Ambrose asked.

"Aye, for that Mr. Victor Bourgeois." Hugh paused. "He didn't much care for it, I daresay."

"Victor Bourgeois?" Ambrose echoed. "The violinist Victor Bourgeois?"

"The very same," Hugh said with a nod. "Of course, I told him that if he didn't like my playin', it meant he was just lackin' in a bit of good taste." Hugh scratched his head. "I don't think he took it well. He checked himself into a madhouse that very night."

Ambrose suspected Hugh's playing might drive any sensible soul into madness. He fingered his mug thoughtfully. "And that led to Jennifer's playing in his stead," he mused. "I had wondered how that had come about." He looked at Hugh approvingly. "Well done, Hugh."

"Shall I serenade you as I did him?" Hugh asked, his eyes alight with pleasure.

"Er, perhaps later," Ambrose said quickly. "Let us await the arrival of our other comrade in this adventure —"

He would have said more, but he was interrupted by a horrendous clanging coming from inside the Aga. He leapt to his feet, his sword coming from its sheath with a hiss, and tensed, prepared to meet any sort of foe. He noticed that Hugh had tucked his violin under his arm and taken a firmer grip on his bow. Aye, they were both as ready as could possibly be expected —

The door to the oven suddenly burst open and something popped out onto the floor.

Ambrose looked at it in surprise. It was, and he could hardly believe he was about to identify it as such, a genie's lamp.

Ambrose looked at Hugh. He was staring at the thing with an expression of surprise that Ambrose was sure matched his own. What to do now? Hack at it with his sword?

The genie's lamp began to wiggle as it sat in front of the stove.

Hugh hopped up on his chair.

" 'Tis a lamp, not a mouse," Ambrose said sternly. He stood and looked down at the brass lamp. "I'll grasp it quickly and we'll see what lies within —"

The stopper flew off the top of the lamp and a black, choking smoke poured out. Ambrose used his sword to fan it away. All too soon, the smoke dissipated and all they were left with was Fulbert de Piaget standing there.

Dressed in purple silks.

"Fulbert!" Ambrose exclaimed in horror. "Where is your proper garb, man? Hose, tunic, boots!"

Fulbert scowled fiercely. "Artane is *me*

33

ancestral home. I thought me entrance deserved a bit of flair."

"Flair, perhaps. Genie flounces, definitely not," Ambrose said, resheathing his sword. "This is serious business here."

Fulbert folded his arms over his chest. "I'm experimentin' with a new persona." He straightened his silks importantly. "Fairy godfather."

"Och, but in different gear," Hugh pleaded. Then he paused. "How does a body dress for that sort of assignment?"

"Not thusly," Ambrose said. "You can still act the part without dressing in . . . well, in things that would better suit a beautiful woman. Which, I might add, you are not."

Fulbert grunted, then in a blink of an eye, he was wearing his usual attire of hose, doublet, and sensible boots — more pedestrian, sixteenth-century fashions befitting his station as a nobleman. He pulled up his own comfortable chair and sat down. After satisfying his thirst in the depths of his mug, he dragged his tunic sleeve across his mouth and belched.

"Good to be home," Fulbert said, looking about the kitchen as if he reflected on pleasant memories. "Second son though I was."

"But second sons tend to be the cannier of the two, don't they?" Ambrose said. "While the lord's heir has all to look forward to, the second son must often make his own way and rely on his wits. As you did."

Fulbert looked at him in shock at the unexpected compliment, but regained his composure quickly enough. "Aye, there is truth enough in that. Indeed, consider the second sons in just me own illustrious family. Nicholas, Kendrick, Gervase, Christopher, and, well, Fulbert," he said modestly. "Today even Gideon de Piaget comes nigh onto surpassing his elder brother, what with him bein' the CEO of an important international conglomerate." He paused. "As it were."

"Do tell," Hugh said. "I've heard the name Kendrick nosed about, but I thought the lad bearing that name was the current lord of Seakirk."

"He is," Ambrose said. "Interesting coincidence, isn't it?"

Fulbert looked at him from under bushy eyebrows and snorted. "There is no coincidence, but that is a tale better left for another time. Give me a name besides his and the burden will rest upon me to do his exploits justice."

"What of that first lad?" Hugh asked. "Nicholas de Piaget?"

Ambrose was tempted to leap in, but he forbore. After all, this was Fulbert's ancestral home and 'twas right that he have all the glory of it. Besides, he suspected that his ability to jump into much of anything on this caper was going to be sorely limited.

That, too, was something to be thought on at a later time.

"Ah, Nicholas," Fulbert said, warming to his subject, "Nicholas was, as you might expect, the very epitome of all knightly virtues, things perhaps a Scot would know nothing about."

Hugh growled.

"Hugh," Ambrose said patiently, "you're clutching your bow, not your sword."

Hugh looked down, swore, then set his bow and his violin down on the floor. He then put his hand on his sword hilt and shot Fulbert a look of promise. "I am skilled in many knightly sorts of things," he boasted.

Ambrose blew out his breath and looked heavenward.

"And so was Nicholas," Fulbert said. "Women adored him, men were forced to admire him, kings lusted after his strength of arm and keen wit. He spoke half a dozen languages, traveled extensively, hobnobbed with kings and peasants alike, and burnished his reputation more with each year that passed. He lived a life any man might envy mightily." He looked at Hugh. "Why did ye want to know?"

Hugh shrugged. "Just curious."

"Speaking of curious," Fulbert said, setting his mug aside and rubbing his hands together, "who is it we are set to see settled? Kin of mine?"

"*My* granddaughter," Hugh said. "Jennifer —"

"MacLeod," Ambrose added.

"McKinnon," Hugh finished. He picked up his bow and pointed it threateningly at Ambrose. "And the lad had best be a fine one, else I'll have something to say about it."

"Who is the lad?" Fulbert said. "And why is it I find meself in these pleasant quarters when I could be back at the inn watching you have yer wee parley with the fetching Mrs. Pruitt?"

Ambrose squirmed. "Jennifer is arriving here tomorrow. I thought it would be easiest to see her if we were on site, as it were."

"Leaving ye," Fulbert said with a glint in his eye, "comfortably far from our good innkeeper who'd like to do more than just *see* ye."

Ambrose wanted to avoid the subject, and indeed he had been avoiding Mrs. Pruitt, the innkeeper at the Boar's Head Inn, for several months. She had somehow gotten it into her becurlered head that he was the man for her and she was going to woo him, come hell, high water — or present incorporeal status.

Of course, he hadn't left the inn simply to elude her. He had business at Artane. He needed to watch over his granddaughter, several generations removed of course, and aid her when necessary.

"The lad," Hugh prodded. "I say a Scot."

37

Fulbert shook his head. "A lad from Artane. One with the spine to survive her headstrongness —"

"She isn't headstrong!" Hugh bellowed.

"Aye, ye have that aright," Fulbert groused, "that would be yer *other* granddaughter, Victoria. Young Jennifer is merely opinionated."

"I daresay she isn't that, either," Ambrose said mildly, forcing Hugh back into his chair by means of a pointed stare alone. "She's passionate and kind and intelligent —"

"All the more reason for an Artane lad," Fulbert said. "Someone who will appreciate her."

"And a Scot wouldn't?" Hugh huffed.

"She deserves someone with courtly manners," Fulbert said, casting Ambrose an arch look. "Wouldn't ye agree?"

"For a change, I daresay I would," Ambrose said slowly. "An Artane lad might suit her very well."

"What of Stephen?" Fulbert asked. "The current lord's son? He's a fine lad, if not a little too fond of his texts."

"Aye," Ambrose agreed, "I daresay his time will come, but he is not for Jennifer. She deserves someone who will appreciate her music —"

"Her sweet temperament," Hugh interjected.

"Her ability to recognize a fine man when she sees one," Fulbert finished. He paused.

38

"Though I hear that isn't her strong suit."

Ambrose smiled. "We'll see to it this time for her." He stretched, quite satisfied about the events about to be set in motion. "A fine lad, full of chivalry and good humors."

"Does such a lad exist these days?" Hugh asked.

Ambrose rose and tossed his mug into the fire. "I daresay he doesn't." He smiled at his companions. "I'm off for a walk on the roof. Until tomorrow, gentlemen."

"I'll accompany your leave-taking," Hugh said quickly. "On me fiddle."

Ambrose hurried.

Truth be told, he bolted, but with dignity, of course.

He wasn't sure what was louder in the noises that floated along behind him, Hugh's vile playing or Fulbert's screeching.

He paused at the edge of the great hall. He could see it as it had been in times past, full of music and beautifully garbed souls. Surely it was a place that a woman of talent and beauty would be comfortable in.

Surely.

He smiled and continued on his way.

CHAPTER 2

Jennifer suspected that despite her excellent map-reading skills and the fact that she had a very good sense of direction, she was completely lost.

There was no reason for it. It wasn't jet lag. She'd been in Scotland for the previous month and was well acclimated to the change in time. It also wasn't that she wasn't well rested. She had spent that wonderful month in Scotland basking in the simplicity of a lifestyle that could have been re-created from former times. She'd gone on lots of nature walks, spent lots of time socializing with cousins, and had the luxury of time to practice and play just for pleasure. No, she was rested and awake, just really turned around.

She hit the brakes when she saw a sign for Wyckham Castle. Well, at least there she could sit in the car park and figure out where she was on the map. With any luck there would be a visitors' center as well and she could get a snack. Considering the superior nature of British chocolate, she had every reason to hurry up.

She turned off onto a small road and drove through rolling hills and woodlands. She continued on until the road dead-ended in the car park. She turned off the engine and reached for the map. It took her quite a while to find Wyckham Castle on it, but when she found it, she realized her mistake. She was too far south.

She wasn't sure how that had happened, but now that she knew where she was, it would be an easy thing to get herself to Artane. She set the map down, leaned back against the headrest, and looked out the front windshield.

And she froze.

The next thing she knew, she was standing outside her car without really knowing how she'd gotten there. She locked the car by feel and started toward the front gates in a daze. She walked into the courtyard, clutching her keys and willing herself to feel the metal in her hand. Somehow, that just didn't help the incredible feeling of déjà vu she was having.

She had been here before.

Yet she knew she hadn't.

She shivered as she looked around her, trying to fix on something that would explain why she was suddenly so flipped out.

The keep itself was large, with several walls

remaining. The courtyard was quite spacious as well, with the stone footings for several outbuildings still visible in the grass. She could almost see the buildings as they had looked in times past. The stables had been there, the chapel over there, the blacksmith's hut over in that corner —

She rubbed her arms at the sudden chill in the air. It was crazy. Obviously she'd been in Scotland too long and the rain and the surroundings had had a deleterious effect on her common sense. She'd never been to Wyckham before; her imagination was just getting the better of her.

Still, as she walked across the courtyard, she couldn't shake off the impression that she was floating instead of walking. She didn't dare blink for fear that if she did, she would find herself thrust back in time hundreds of years.

She walked around the end of the keep proper and came to an abrupt halt. She had to reach out and hold on to the corner of the keep to steady herself as she looked at the stretch of ground in front of her.

The garden had been there.

It took her a moment to realize that it was only natural to suspect such a thing — it wasn't a sign of otherworldly activity going on. The patch of ground was the best location for a garden, given its proximity to what had no doubt been the kitchen in times past.

It would have been convenient for the cook that way. It was also easy to imagine how it might have looked with a pretty path meandering through herbs and bushes and trees.

It was spooky how well she could see just how it had looked.

"And ridiculous," she said aloud, turning away suddenly. She just had a great imagination; it was currently running away with her.

She stopped in front of the keep itself and found that she just couldn't tear her gaze from it. She also couldn't help the wrench at her heart just looking at it gave her. There was no reason for it. It was just a pile of stones.

Yet somehow it was just dreadful that such a beautiful place should have fallen into disrepair.

She walked up the stairs and over the threshold, then continued on over grass that had been recently mowed. There on the left was an enormous fireplace set into the wall. She walked over to it and sat down on a large stone that seemed to have been placed there for just such a purpose. She stared into the hearth and wondered about the families who had passed their evenings next to it. Had there been music? Laughter? Children? Had they all been happy together?

She speculated on that for much longer than she should have. She looked up at the sky, finally, and realized that the afternoon was passing and she had no answers, nor even any good theories. Castles were expensive to maintain. Maybe the last family to live there had run out of money. Maybe they'd found themselves on the wrong side of a war. Maybe they had moved.

She didn't know. What she did know was that she'd stayed far longer than she'd intended. By the time she managed to crawl to her feet, she was very stiff. She groaned as she hobbled over to the front door and went outside. At least the pain of a stiff back was enough to distract her from her troubling thoughts. Wyckham wasn't hers; she didn't have to stress over what had happened to it over the years.

Of course, the distraction of sore joints only lasted until she left the front gates and had a good look around her.

All right, so it was a little silly to get teary-eyed over a view, but if ever there had been a view made for it, the one in front of her qualified. The countryside was idyllic: rolling hills covered with trees and meadows and fences made of stones. From where she stood, she could see a little stream that meandered toward the castle, then turned away before it reached the walls.

She wandered a little, finding that the sight was almost too beautiful to take in. She loved the ocean, but this land . . . it was full of life and dappled shade and possibility. It was exactly what she'd dreamed about, standing in the middle of her cramped, cluttered apartment in New York. How fortunate Wyckham's inhabitants had been to have their home in such a place.

She made herself move, finally. She rounded the south end of the outer castle walls and came to a sudden halt. There, just peeking out of a little grove of trees, was a cottage, snug and charming.

Maybe it was a National Trust office and she should have paid to tour the castle. She would now and get a guidebook while she was at it. If nothing else, she could look at it when she was back in a new closet of an apartment in Manhattan, trying to find some silence.

The cottage was locked and seemed to be empty, obviously not a National Trust office. Whoever owned it certainly hadn't gotten around to furnishing it, though it didn't look untended. It would have been a charming place to live, right there where the castle could be seen every day.

How would it be to own it?

The thought came out of nowhere and left her breathless. It was very tempting to figure out a way to buy it herself. After all, she did have a pretty decent savings account. And she had a very valuable violin. Maybe between the two, she could scrounge up enough money to buy a small cottage near a ruined castle —

She shook her head. What was she thinking? She had a career to go back to. Her life was full of noise, busyness, lights, city smells. She didn't have time for an idyllic castle in the charming English countryside.

Or for a little house that sat just outside idyllic castle walls.

No matter how much she suddenly wanted to.

She turned away before she thought about it any more. She didn't look at the castle as she passed by it. She didn't dare. It had affected her more than was reasonable and the sooner she put it behind her, the better off she would be. She walked back to her car only to find that she wasn't the only person who apparently thought Wyckham was a great place. An older British couple had parked next to her and were unpacking gear for a picnic. She smiled.

"Lovely spot," she offered.

"Yes, quite," the older woman agreed.

Jennifer started to get in her car, then hesitated. "You wouldn't know who owns this, would you? Did I miss it on the National Trust property list?"

"Oh, it isn't National Trust, miss," the man said with a smile. "It belongs to the Earl of Seakirk. 'Tis said he owns the cottage as well." He looked at his wife and lifted a shoulder in a half shrug. "Perhaps it was once in his family."

"Whatever the case," the wife added, "he doesn't seem to mind the odd picnic hamper cluttering up the courtyard, so we come now and then." She smiled at Jennifer. "A good day to you, then."

"And to you, too," Jennifer managed.

She looked only at her car as she got in and started it up. She backed out and looked only at the road in front of her as she got under way. She just couldn't bring herself to look back at the castle. It had been too unsettling the first time.

She turned back onto the regular road and headed east. She would catch the A1 and head back up the coast. If she hurried, she would be at Artane well before dark and she might actually get some dinner.

It took her a good hour and a half to backtrack and reach the village. She promised herself several visits to the local fish-and-chips shop later, then continued on her way up to the castle itself. She was stopped at the gate, but allowed to drive inside.

She parked her car where she saw others clustered, then grabbed her violin and her suitcase and headed across the courtyard and up the stairs to the front door. Megan opened it before she could knock and threw her arms around Jennifer.

"Where have you been?"

"Lost in history," Jennifer admitted, hugging her tightly in return. "I took a wrong road and ended up where I hadn't intended to go. But I got to see a great castle, so I can't complain."

Megan took her suitcase from her. "Tell me about it later. For now, let's get you settled." She smiled. "You look like you've just had a month in the Highlands with nothing to do but endure the MacLeod version of medieval boot camp and occasionally play for your supper."

"How did you know?" Jennifer asked with a laugh.

"Rumor," Megan said, "not personal experience. I have no desire to learn medieval survival techniques, though I will admit that Gideon's been tempted a time or two. Endless days in the Highlands, pretending you've gone back in time hundreds of years. It's pretty tough to resist."

"It's impossible to resist, especially if you make the mistake of walking inside Jamie's gates," Jennifer said dryly. "I just went up for a nice family visit. Instead, I learned how to ride a horse and eat weeds — courtesy of Patrick MacLeod, the man all wild greens in Scotland fear." She paused. "I think I'm hungry."

"We're having steak for dinner."

"Thank heavens," Jennifer said, with feeling. "I was hoping for real food."

Megan took Jennifer by the arm. "I'm so

glad you came. I have lots of company, but there's nothing like a sister."

"I understand completely. Now, where's that gorgeous daughter of yours?"

"Snoozing in her father's arms. Let's get your stuff put away, then we'll go see her."

She followed Megan to a very nice guest room that looked out over the ocean, dumped her suitcase on the bed, then propped her violin up between the armoire and the wall. Megan handed her a key. Jennifer took it with a smile.

"You know me too well."

"I know how much your violin cost," Megan said dryly. "Lock it up and let's go."

Jennifer locked the door behind her, then walked with her sister down a maze of hallways, down more stairs, then down a short passageway to a very old doorway.

"We're in the lord's solar tonight," Megan said as she put her hand on the door latch. "You've been in here before, haven't you?"

"I've peeked in," Jennifer said, "but that's it."

"Lord Edward doesn't use it very often," Megan said. "He has an office and another family room where we usually gather, but tonight I think he's trying to impress you."

"I'm impressed already," Jennifer said, then followed her sister inside to a good-sized but incredibly medieval-looking room. There was a hearth to her left in which currently roared

49

a substantial fire. Behind a very, very antique-looking table was a window with a deep casement that showed just how thick the walls were.

But after that, things took a decidedly modern turn. There was an obviously expensive rug on the floor. Half a dozen overstuffed, faded chairs were placed strategically for conversing, and a chessboard and pieces were set up in one corner with two hard chairs ready there for those so inclined.

Jennifer held out her hand to Lord Edward, the current Earl of Artane, and made him a curtsey, which made him laugh.

"Good evening, Jennifer, my dear," he said, patting her hand.

"And to you, my lord," Jennifer said with a smile. "And to you, my lady," she said turning to Helen, the Countess of Artane. Then she looked at Gideon. "My lord."

Gideon smiled. "Genuflecting will win you a turn with Georgianna anytime."

"Why don't you call *me* 'my lady'?" Megan asked pointedly.

"I remember you trying to stuff peas up my nose when I was two," Jennifer said with a snort as she took Megan's daughter Georgianna into her arms and sighed in pleasure. "I've forgiven you for it, but it ruined any hope of you having any genuflecting from me." She sat down and snuggled the sleeping baby close. "She is beautiful."

"She looks like her mother," Gideon agreed. "Hopefully all our children will be so fortunate."

"She is indeed beautiful," Edward said enthusiastically. "And so good-natured. And that is just the beginning of her fine qualities."

Jennifer listened to the four of them discuss the numerous perfections of Georgianna de Piaget and felt a rush of gratitude that Megan had found such a wonderful family to marry into. It wasn't easy having Megan in London, but it wasn't such a bad flight from JFK to Heathrow. At least Gideon's family was lovely and they obviously thought Megan was wonderful. If she had to live across the deep blue sea, it was best that she be with people who loved her.

Eventually a discreet tap sounded on the door. Lady Helen rose and led them into the family's private dining room. Jennifer found herself eating a hearty meal that she certainly wouldn't have found out in the wilds of James MacLeod's pasture and she was grateful for it. Artane's chef was indeed without peer; even her father admitted that.

She fully expected to be asked to play after supper and she willingly fetched her violin from her room without hesitation. It was a small price to pay for the luxury of staying in the ancestral seat. Jennifer knew she was getting to touch things that the National Trust folks probably despaired of ever getting their hands on, so she was more than happy to humor Lord Edward.

She put her violin case on the lord's table at the back of the great hall, took out her violin and tuned it, then joined Megan and her in-laws as they sat near one of the enormous hearths set into the wall.

"Any preference?" she asked Lord Edward.

He sat with his Schnapps and only shook his head. "I'll leave the choice up to you, my dear. We'll just be grateful for the free concert. I imagine there aren't many so fortunate."

Jennifer considered briefly, then began. She chose Mozart mostly because she knew that Lord Edward had a particular fondness for his music. After that, she just played what she liked and was happy to have such a great hall to perform in.

Until she realized that things were starting to feel a little odd.

It wasn't every piece, and it wasn't a consistent thing, but the déjà vus that washed over her were becoming increasingly hard to ignore. She had never brought her violin to England before, having preferred to leave it behind in the round-the-clock care of her mother's older sister, so it couldn't have been that. She closed her eyes and concentrated on letting her instrument sing, but even at that she wasn't completely successful. She wasn't accustomed to not being able to block out absolutely every sort of distraction that could be thrown at her.

But now, she was cold.

As if she stood in a medieval great hall — not one that had been softened over the years until it was a relatively comfortable place.

She had to open her eyes periodically to make sure she was still standing there in a modern hall in a pair of month-old shoes and casually dressy skirt and sweater, playing for the current lord of Artane.

Well, sort of playing.

She stopped in the middle of her favorite encore and found that tears were running down her cheeks. She looked at Megan, then at Megan's in-laws.

"I'm sorry," she stammered. "Let me try that again."

She tried again.

She didn't make it eight measures into the piece before she found that she simply couldn't play it. She tucked her violin under her arm and found that she was shaking.

"You know, my dear," Lord Edward said kindly, "you've been traveling for a pair of days now. Perhaps it's catching you up."

Jennifer nodded, forcing a smile. "I'm sure that's it. I'll try again tomorrow."

"We'll look forward to it, but tonight was brilliant as it stands. I've never heard anything I enjoyed more. But now, children, I'm for bed. Gideon, lock up if you would."

"Of course, Father," Gideon said cheerfully.

Lord Edward rose, collected his lady, said his good-nights, and left the hall.

Jennifer looked at Megan after they left. "I think I'm scaring myself."

"You're tired," Megan said, getting carefully to her feet with a baby who had fallen asleep again. "Get a good night's sleep and don't worry." She smiled. "You haven't lost it."

"I'll say," Gideon said, standing and rubbing his hands together. "Father's right. I haven't heard anything to equal it."

"Flattery of that sort will get you a performance every night," Jennifer said with a smile. Then she looked at her sister. "I think I do need a good night's sleep."

"Want me to wait for you to pack up?"

Jennifer shook her head. "I'll be fine."

"The front door's bolted," Gideon said, putting his arm around Megan, "and the kitchen is secured. I'll come back down and see to the lights."

"Thanks," Jennifer said. She hugged Megan around the baby, gave Gideon a hug, then pretended to focus completely on putting her violin away.

In reality, she thought she just might be losing it — really. First that very weird afternoon at Wyckham, and now this. She'd never not gotten through a performance, not even that disastrous recital she'd finished by sheer willpower alone when she'd been five.

She cleaned her violin, loosened her bow, and closed up her case with a sigh. Maybe a good night's rest was what she needed. Everything would no doubt look better in the morning and she would be back to normal.

She started for the stairs, then paused. She turned slowly and looked over the great hall. She could see it suddenly, peopled with women in glorious medieval gowns and men in finely embroidered tunics. There, on one side of the hall, she could see a collection of skilled medieval musicians, playing a lively tune for the dancers. The rest of the hall was filled with servants, pages, squires, and onlookers. She could hear the music and smell the smoke from the fire.

Then she blinked.

And the hall was as it had been. Empty, very old, and steeped in history.

She shook her head wryly. Definitely too much time in Scotland. Apparently being at Artane was going to be just as hard on her common sense. She looked at the hall one last time. It must have been glorious to be in a place where there was money for fine clothes and skilled musicians. Gideon's ancestors had been fortunate indeed.

But it wasn't for her. She turned away and walked up the stairs to her twenty-first century bedroom, leaving the hall and its glorious past behind her.

CHAPTER 3

Artane
Spring 1229
Nicholas de Piaget sat at the lord's table in his father's keep and wondered why it was that the bloody hall before him couldn't have been empty for a change. He was just as able as the next man to appreciate a beautifully dressed woman, or a fine cup of wine, or a well-played ballad, but there was a limit to the number of times he could be expected to appreciate the like. If he had to endure another evening of food, wine, and capering about to even the admittedly excellent music being played currently, he would lose what few wits remained him.

Unfortunately, there seemed to be no end to the torture in sight. His grandmother, Joanna of Segrave, was determined to fill Artane's great hall with maidens of marriageable age and attractive dowries to tempt him, lure him, vex him, or befuddle him to the altar.

Presently he was being tormented by five of his grandmother's findings. There was a child of no more than twelve summers who he actually hadn't seen completely as she seemed determined to hide behind her mother's skirts. Another wench sat in a chair near one of the hearths, watching him with a calculating look that made him want to go hide behind *his* mother's skirts. A third was speaking to his grandmother in a voice so shrill that even the excruciatingly proper Joanna of Segrave was looking about for a means of escape. Nicholas would have led her to one, but he was sitting between the final two ladies and politeness demanded that he not leave the table until they did. He suspected that, given the way they were working their way through their meals and his, too, they would not be leaving anytime soon.

"What a fine hall your father has, my lord," remarked Adelina of Cladford, the fair-haired woman on his right. She looked over said hall with a practiced eye. "So richly furnished. And what a fine table he sets."

"Ah," Nicholas began, but found that his thoughts on the matter were unnecessary.

"Aye, I agree," said Herleva of Kirton, the equally lovely black-haired woman on his left. She reached over him to stab a particularly succulent piece of meat on his trencher with her knife. "Though it seems to be rather thin here before us, don't you agree, my lord?"

58

"Um," Nicholas said, wondering if she might stab him next if he answered amiss.

Fortunately, whether he agreed or not did not seem to matter. The two began a very thorough and detailed assessment of the supper, the wine, and the desserts that were coming now from the kitchens. Nicholas half feared the women would turn to him and then spend the rest of the evening deciding how best to divide *him* between them.

Actually, the longer he sat there, the more he suspected that such would not be his fate. The ladies of Cladford and Kirton talked over and around him as if he hadn't been there. And once all the food had been seen to and they were left with their goblets of wine, he learned a great deal about the proper cut of sleeve required at court, how best to determine how far the hair should recede off the brow to give a suitable look to the headdress, and which mistresses of which lords had moved on to richer coffers and better laid tables.

Adelina tapped him suddenly on the arm.

"We've run out of wine," she announced.

Nicholas caught the eye of one of his father's pages who ran off immediately toward the kitchen. He smiled politely at Adelina.

"Not long now."

She considered him. "You're not enjoying this overmuch, are you?"

"Are you?" he countered.

Adelina shrugged. "I am here to humor the lady of Segrave and my father both. Enjoyment is not the desired result."

"Nor for me," agreed Herleva.

"And you're here for no other reason?" Nicholas asked, amused.

"Oh, you are handsome," said Adelina.

"And rich," added Herleva.

"But, you're not for me," Adelina finished. She looked at him unflinchingly. "You have a murky past, my lord."

"Some would consider that an asset," he said lightly.

"Aye, if you want a lover," said Herleva, looking at him in much the same way she had the boar not an hour ago, "but not if you'd like a husband."

"Tsk," said Adelina. "Too much time at court, Herleva. That wasn't polite."

Nicholas waved away her words. "I've a thick skin," he said easily. "But no need for a lover at present." He stood up, pushed his chair back, and made way for the wine. "If you ladies will permit me, I have a message to carry to my father."

Aye, that I've bloody had enough tonight and 'tis his turn to come make an appearance at the table with these vultures.

The women waved him on while holding out their cups to be refilled.

Nicholas turned and walked into his elder

60

brother before he saw him. He could tell by the set of Robin's jaw that he had heard the last exchange. Nicholas clapped a hand on his shoulder and turned him around.

"Ouch, damn you," Robin said in annoyance, prying Nicholas's fingers off him. "I was going."

"Good. I'm following."

And he did, pushing Robin ahead of him until they had reached the entrance to the passageway that led to their father's solar. Then Robin stopped and looked at him, his eyes glittering in the torchlight.

"Stupid, thoughtless —"

Nicholas shook his head with a smile. "How gallant you are, brother, to defend my abused honor."

"Murky past, my arse," Robin snorted. "I'd be more worried about *their* pasts. Were they maids, do you suppose?"

"I try not to speculate on that sort of thing."

"Wise," Robin agreed. Then he paused. "Shall we go? Stare at them from the shadows and discuss their flaws? That might pass the rest of the evening most pleasantly."

Nicholas suppressed the urge to roll his eyes. The only thing possibly more irritating than his grandmother's enthusiasm over the prospect of seeing him wed was his elder brother's delight in inspecting what goods arrived as inducements.

"I think I've looked enough," Nicholas said,

"but if you've the stomach for it, I won't stop you."

"Alone?" Robin said with a delicate shudder. "Thank you, but nay. I just came to rescue you. You know, you look hungry."

"I am," Nicholas said, but Robin had already trotted away with the lightness of step only a man safely wed and free from Joanna of Segrave's piercing gaze could possibly manage. Nicholas turned back to look out over the hall, wondering how best he might have something to eat without returning to the festivities. If his grandmother saw him, he was doomed.

Not that all her sojourns to Artane had been so unpleasant. Indeed, he'd been a bit surprised at all the beauties she had been able to produce over the past year. Some of them had even been old enough to be considered women and not children.

Unfortunately, even the children had been far more interested in the state of his purse than the condition of his heart. Was it possible to find a woman who could actually see *him,* not his riches, nor his titles, nor his reputation?

He remembered his sister complaining about the same thing. At the time, he'd thought her complaints to be too many and too loud. Now, he understood completely. Fortunately for Amanda, she had found a man who hadn't cared less about her dowry.

He was beginning to fear he wouldn't have such a happy ending to his own tale.

"Ah, Nicky, love," a weathered voice said smoothly. "Come and be sociable."

Nicholas cursed under his breath. Caught, and so easily, too. Unfortunately, he couldn't glare at his grandmother; she would have pinched his ear at a most inopportune moment as repayment. He also couldn't glare at her because she was a delightful old woman who had always loved him unreservedly; there was little she could not prevail upon him to do. So he sighed, put on his best courtly manners, and offered her his arm.

Joanna put her hand on his sleeve and smiled up at him. "Come and look what I have brought you to choose from."

"Grandmère, I've already looked and I'm not interested."

"How can you deny an old woman her wish to see her favorite grandson wed?" She squeezed his arm with a grip that would have frightened a man of lesser spine. "And you'd best make up your mind quickly, Nicky, before I'm dead. Ah, look you here," she said suddenly, and quite loudly, "there is the lady of Clyffe and her lovely daughter who has overcome her shyness to make you a curtsey. Here is my grandson, Nicholas, lord of Wyckham. Nicholas," she muttered under her breath, "smile, damn you."

Nicholas did.

She pinched his ear anyway.

It took another hour, but he finally orchestrated an escape. He had spewed out in one evening more insincere compliments than any man could reasonably have been expected to voice during the course of an entire year, then pled a bit of manly business as his excuse and fled without a backward glance. Supper could wait. He strode down the passageway to the lord's solar and burst in, slamming the door behind him.

His family was there, looking comfortable and content. Nicholas scowled, booted his youngest brother out of a chair, then sat with a curse. He glared at his father.

"I told Grandmère you were anxious to come and see to her guests."

Rhys looked faintly panicked. "Surely I cannot. It would be unchivalrous of me to leave your mother here."

"Take her with you."

"The company would weary her."

Nicholas scowled. "Feeble excuses, Father. Admit it. You're afraid."

"Terrified," Rhys admitted promptly. "And I hesitate to decide what frightens me more: the ladies or your grandmother." He shivered. "The saints be praised I am safely wed."

"You are fortunate indeed," Nicholas grumbled.

"You should find a wife," Robin suggested.

"Your humors will improve."

"I would," Nicholas said through gritted teeth, "if I could find a woman who didn't hide each time I looked at her!"

"There are many women who look forward to the sight of you," Anne said, smiling at him.

"Ah, but those aren't the kind of wench Nick dares show to his mother —"

"Robin!" Anne exclaimed.

"Nicholas," Rhys warned.

Nicholas was halfway across the chamber, his hands outstretched to throttle his brother. Robin merely sat in his chair, grinning evilly. Nicholas straightened, smoothed down the front of his tunic, and resumed his seat with as much dignity as possible. He looked at Anne. "Your husband is a dolt."

"Robin, do not," Rhys warned.

Robin waved his father away. "That was but a weak insult; not even worth getting up for. But I think it illustrates the deeper problem here. His humors are unbalanced — likely a result of still being unwed. Obviously, we must renew our efforts to find our lovely Nicky a bride."

"He'll find the right woman at the right time," Gwen said placidly.

"Apparently not without help," Robin said. " 'Tis baffling, isn't it? Surely there is at least *one* wench in England to suit him."

Nicholas had to sit on his hands to keep

from throwing something at his brother.

"You would think," Robin added.

"As usual, you shouldn't," Nicholas said shortly. He turned to his mother. "I can bear this madness no longer. I must escape. Perhaps I will go to Wyckham and make repairs."

"Not the roof again," Robin groaned. He rose and reached down to pull Anne to her feet. "Let us leave him before we must listen to yet another endless list of all the activities his stone masons have been about. This is why he is not wed. He bores his potential brides with tales of stones and mortar."

He flicked Nicholas companionably on the ear as he passed. Montgomery, John, and Miles soon followed, taking Isabelle with them.

Rhys sighed and rose from his chair. "I suppose I should go attempt to appease Lady Joanna."

Gwen smiled up at him. "You know she loves you well."

"She has never forgiven me for bringing you so far north. My meals at her supper table are proof enough of that."

"She thinks rich fare is unhealthy for a warrior."

Rhys grunted. "And so she feeds me oats and carrots as if I were a horse." He leaned over and kissed his lady. "I'll go humor her yet again and see if it earns me at least a sweet upon our next visit."

"I'll come in a moment or two," Gwen said with a smile. "To save you from her, if necessary."

Rhys muttered something Nicholas was just certain wasn't complimentary about his lady's mother under his breath as he left the solar.

Nicholas watched his father go, then turned to look at his mother. She was studying him gravely.

"What?" he asked with a faint smile.

"I wish you were happier," she said.

"I am happy."

Gwen shook her head. "If it were merely a bout of foul humors, I would not worry, but I fear it is more than that." She paused. "I wish you could find what your heart seeks."

"A dry spot in front of my own fire?"

"You will not be serious about this, but I vow, Nicky my love, that there is a part of your heart that needs tending that none of us can provide."

He shook his head. "I am merely weary of the endless parade of females that do not interest me."

"What are you looking for?"

That was the question indeed — and one he'd never truly given thought to until his grandmother had begun her siege. Now, he had a list.

He wanted a woman who could appreciate

a finely tuned lute, a well-crafted bit of poetry, a beautiful tapestry. He wanted a woman who had a thought in her head besides what was put there by her sire or the asps at court. He wanted a woman who could see him, not his wealth or his reputation. Even the women who had tempted him slightly had looked at him with the sort of calculation that said he'd best be *damned* rich for them to overlook his *murky* past.

Of course, he could tell his mother none of that, so he settled for a smile.

"I have had the good fortune of knowing many strong women —"

"Or the misfortune," Gwen put in mildly.

Nicholas shook his head. "You know you do not mean that. You and your daughters are without peer. Poor fool am I to want the same kind of woman for myself."

Gwen rose, leaned over to kiss the top of his head, then put her hand under his chin and lifted his face up. "When you fall in love, it will be with someone extraordinary, someone much more remarkable than anyone your grandmère can produce. I have no doubt you'll find her."

Nicholas nodded, but he couldn't answer. He couldn't agree and he wasn't going to argue with the sentiments of a woman who loved him.

"Did you have supper, son?"

"I couldn't bring myself to fight my table

companions for it."

"Poor Nicholas," Gwen said with a rueful laugh. "I'll see some sent in to you."

"Thank you, Mother," Nicholas said. He watched her walk out the door, then turned toward the fire.

In one thing she spoke truly and that was that he would never find a woman to love in a great hall peopled by women of his grandmother's choosing. He was beginning to despair of finding a woman in any other country. If the ladies Joanna had found were any indication of what he could hope for, he would be better off contenting himself with merely being uncle to his nieces and nephews and father to none.

It was, he decided grimly, a rather gloomy thought.

Fortunately, food arrived before he could fully wallow in misery. He thanked the servant and set to a hearty meal without delay.

Once he was finished, he pushed back from his father's table and nodded to himself, his decision made. As soon as it was polite, he would bid his family *adieu* and make for Wyckham. At least there he would face nothing more remarkable than getting rained on in his own hall. With any luck, he could have supper without having to fight for it.

He banked the fire in his father's solar, then blew out the candles and left the chamber.

Peace, quiet, and nothing out of the ordinary.

It was just what he needed.

CHAPTER 4

Jennifer leaned on the casement of the deep, medieval window and stared out over the sea. The bed had been comfortable, the surroundings first class, and dinner the night before so good that even her father would have considered it worth the trip, yet still she was restless. Her dreams had alternated between a ruined keep at Wyckham and a luxuriously appointed Artane sporting medieval nobility. Both had been so vivid that she suspected she hadn't truly slept at all.

Obviously, being in a castle that was that drenched in history was having a very deleterious effect on her poor, overworked brain.

She straightened and turned to look for her keys. What she needed was to get out of the house. Maybe she would take another trip to Wyckham and get that out of her system. That and a hearty order of fish and chips in the village would no doubt cure what ailed her.

She made certain her violin was tucked

between the armoire and wall, locked her room behind her, and headed down the hallway to look for Megan.

She paused in front of another doorway and knocked softly. Her sister opened the door and smiled.

"Come on in and enjoy nap time with me," Megan said.

"Only for a minute," Jennifer said, slipping inside. "I don't want to wake Georgianna."

"I love it when she's awake, but there are times —" Megan shook her head. "Peace and quiet is very nice."

Jennifer laughed softly. "I'm sure it is, even if she is quite possibly the most perfect child ever spawned."

"And Duncan isn't?" Megan asked with a grin. "Thomas wouldn't like to hear that about his firstborn."

"Duncan MacLeod McKinnon is trouble and Thomas knows it," Jennifer said promptly. "But he's a dreamy baby as well. You both are very lucky."

Megan nodded. Jennifer didn't have to hear the words to know what she was thinking. *When is it going to happen for you?* It was a good question, but not one she wanted to answer right then. She smiled at her sister.

"I'm going to take off and go do a little sightseeing."

"Really? But you just got here."

"I know," Jennifer said, "but I'm restless."

"If you say so," Megan said with a smile. "Are you looking for anything in particular?"

Jennifer paused. Megan would probably think she was crazy — then again, maybe she wouldn't. Her sister wasn't unfamiliar with things of a supernatural nature.

"On my way down yesterday, I stopped at this castle called Wyckham," she admitted. "I felt like I'd been there before, but I'm pretty sure I haven't. Weird, huh?"

"Trust me, nothing strikes me as weird anymore. What happened exactly?"

"Nothing really. I just can't seem to get the place out of my mind." She paused. "You wouldn't know anything about it, would you?"

"Actually, I would," Megan said. "It belonged to Nicholas de Piaget, the second son of Rhys de Piaget, Rhys being the man who built Artane. I think it was given to Nicholas as a gift for his knighting."

"That's a pretty good present."

"Rhys was apparently a pretty generous guy."

"You're a veritable font of de Piaget genealogical facts, aren't you?" Jennifer teased.

"It's serious business here. It wouldn't do to miss any details."

"Anything else I should know?"

"Nothing about Wyckham," Megan said, "but I do know a little about Nicholas. I suppose you should take it with a grain of salt, but from what I understand, he was just about the most perfect knight in existence during his day. Name your knightly virtue and he had it. And he was gorgeous as well."

"What a paragon."

"He sounds like one, doesn't he," Megan agreed. "He's had a lot of competition over the years from his cousins, but no one seems to have topped him. How does his castle look?"

"It's a wreck," Jennifer said. "But I'll think kind thoughts about him while I'm there, just for you. And I'll be back in time for dinner."

"Do. Gideon's . . . uncle will be here with his family. You'll like him."

Jennifer had started for the door, but she turned back around. "I think I heard an *um* in there."

"Well . . ."

"Megan, I just spent a month with James MacLeod," Jennifer said. "Really, how much more *um* can it get than that?"

Megan smiled. "Meet Kendrick tonight and decide for yourself."

"I will." She paused, then suddenly found herself turning back to give Megan a quick, tight hug. "I'll be back soon," she said, suddenly blinking hard.

"Jenner," Megan said in surprise, "are you all right?"

"Not enough sleep," Jennifer said confidently. "I'm sure of it."

She was so sure of it, she bolted from Megan's room and ran through the castle and out the front door before she did anything else ridiculous, like burst into tears. She was just going for the day, not the rest of her life. The sudden desire to hang on to her sister like she'd never see her again obviously had something to do with one too many of Patrick MacLeod's wild green salads.

She left Artane, made a quick trip for some gas and a snack, then headed on her way to Wyckham. She drove back down the A1 and turned off onto the proper road as if she'd been doing it all of her life. She supposed she must have recognized landmarks from her trip the day before. She didn't remember, though, seeing the sign for Ledenham Abbey.

Why was it just the sight of the sign made her shiver?

Maybe Lord Ledenham had been one of Nicholas de Piaget's foes; it might be useful to take a look at his abbey while she was there. Maybe she would learn something new to add to the de Piaget lore and win Megan a few brownie points.

She stopped near the ruins and parked. She put her cell phone, keys, and ID in various pockets, had a brief swig of Lilt, and got out of the car. The place was deserted, but she locked the car anyway.

She wandered over to what was left of the walls. She wondered what it had looked like finished. Actually, she couldn't say she cared; the place was giving her the creeps. She stepped over one of the low walls, then found out why.

"Yer keys, miss, if ye please."

Jennifer turned around and gaped at the would-be thief. All right, it was one thing to get robbed in Manhattan. But in jolly old England?

It was just plain wrong.

Jennifer looked at him, considered, then jammed her hands in her pockets.

"No," she said.

"No?" he repeated, looking a little stunned.

"No."

He pulled out a knife from the back of his jeans. Jennifer knew she shouldn't have been surprised, but she was, and surprised enough that she stumbled backward. In fact, she stumbled backward several steps. When she stopped, she realized that perhaps she shouldn't have.

She was standing on a time gate.

There was no point in wondering how she knew that. It was all that MacLeod blood running through her veins, courtesy of her mother. All sorts of otherworldly things went on in that part of her family tree.

Take her grandfather, by means of a very convoluted family tree, James MacLeod. It was a poorly kept family secret that he was actually a fourteenth-century Scottish laird who had fallen in love with a woman from the future and come forward through time to live with her. It was also no secret that on the wall above his desk in his thinking room was a map that boasted scores of red Xs with names scrawled next to them. Byzantium, Ancient Greece, Colonial America. Seventeenth-century Barbados had been underlined several times, as if it had particularly pleasant meaning.

She wished she could only speculate, but unfortunately she knew what they all meant. They were gates from present-day Scotland and England back to an ever-growing list of other time periods Jamie investigated as often as possible.

His poor wife.

"Oy, let me go!"

Jennifer pulled her gaze back to her would-be assailant. He was being held on to by three older gentlemen: two Scots and an Englishman. Jennifer recognized them as well: Ambrose MacLeod and Hugh McKinnon, her ancestors several generations removed; and one Fulbert de Piaget, of the Elizabethan de Piagets.

Ghosts, all three.

She looked a little more closely, then blinked in surprise. Gone were the lethal-looking swords they usually carried. In their places were . . . well . . . wands.

Fairy godmother wands.

"What," Jennifer managed in the least garbled tone possible, "are you doing here?"

"Oh, just out for a little — oot — jaunt," Ambrose huffed, struggling to keep his choke hold on her would-be attacker and hold on to his sparkling silver wand at the same time.

"Traveling keeps ye young," Hugh offered enthusiastically, wrapping himself around the young man's leg. His wand was pink with a sparkly star at the end and scads of curling streamers. She wondered if he'd poached it from some poor little girl at Disneyland.

She wouldn't have been surprised.

"Madness, this," Fulbert grumbled, waving his jet-black wand around in a manly fashion. "By the saints, ye young knave, be still!"

"But," Jennifer began, and started to step forward. The ground beneath her became unsteady enough that she went down onto her hands and knees. She looked down in surprise. She had sunk a good two inches into mud that hadn't been there a heartbeat before.

Then she looked up.

Well, apparently more conversation with her ghostly fairy godfathers was going to be unnecessary.

And impossible.

They were gone. In their places were several men in rather authentic-looking medieval peasant garb, gaping at her as if *she* were the ghost.

Oh, and it was raining.

"Nope," she said, heaving herself back to her feet. "No, this isn't going to happen to me." She wiped her muddy hands on her jeans, planted her feet on the very muddy ground, and wished herself back to the arms of her would-be assailant. "No time traveling," she announced to Fate.

Her only answer was a drizzle.

Before she could say anything else, she found herself dragged off by Middle Age goons, resisting as best she could, to a place well away from the time gate. She tried to break away, but her captors jerked her arms behind her and tied her hands together.

A man stepped out of the pack. She supposed, based on the quality of his clothes, that he was their leader. He looked at her, then barked at one of his flunkies who started to gather up wood. Jennifer frowned. Was he cold? Admittedly the weather was rather nasty and the morning wherever, or *when*ever, she'd landed was gloomy enough for a good blaze, but did it merit the kind of fire they were kindling?

She couldn't help but notice how the leader continued to look at her as if he'd just found an endless box of something special under the Christmas tree.

Things went downhill rapidly from there.

Though her command of French was not good, and her command of what she supposed was the medieval Norman version of it was even worse, she suspected she was hearing brief instructions concerning herself. She understood quite clearly that they were going to have a little frankfurter roast.

And she was going to be the hot dog.

"I'm not a witch," she offered.

Apparently her opinion was not needed. Peasant types continued to feed the fire and Mr. Inquisition continued to look at her as if he couldn't wait to do a little experimenting and see if she burned.

Well, not if she could help it.

She slumped to her knees. When her captors loosened their grips in surprise, she leaped to her feet and bolted. It seemed like as good a plan as any.

She made it farther than she thought she would, but not far enough. She was grabbed by one arm and spun around. She managed to knee one man in the groin and head-butt the other in the nose, but that only made her captors very angry — and her very lightheaded. Within moments, she found herself back where she'd started, only this time the leader of the pack was looking a little annoyed, her guards were definitely annoyed, and she knew she was in trouble.

Who would have thought a little sightseeing could be so dangerous? Damn it, where was that knight in shining armor when she really needed him?

Mr. Inquisition held a long, thin branch out in front of him like a sword and started toward her. His smile was twisted; obviously whatever he planned to do, he planned to enjoy.

Jennifer wondered briefly just exactly what part of her he would set fire to first, then she dismissed the thought as unproductive. She started to blow at the end of the branch in hopes that she might get lucky.

And then came the sound of a voice from her left. It was a commanding voice. It was a voice that her tormentor apparently recognized because he cursed viciously and whirled around to face the newcomer. Jennifer looked as well, supposing that maybe her captor had a boss who wanted to reserve the fun for himself.

Then again, perhaps not.

She looked across the glade and felt her jaw drop. There at the edge of the clearing, sitting atop an enormous horse, was the most handsome man she had ever seen. He was blond, powerfully built, casually dressed, with a face that would have been considered too chiseled if it hadn't been for a refinement that took the hardest of edges off his features. He was sitting on a pale horse, which might have been called white if she had really used her imagination, and he looked like a knight. Well, he wasn't wearing armor, but he was carrying a sword. That sword wasn't pointed at her.

This was definitely a step in the right direction.

Mr. Inquisition started toward the newcomer with his burning stick in his hand. Before Jennifer could open her mouth to call out a warning, the knight had slid off his horse and used his sword to calmly bat the stick out of her captor's hand. He picked up the flaming brand, tossed it back on the fire, and casually ground a few smoking embers under his boot.

Jennifer's mouth went a little dry. Gorgeous and a good citizen. Did it get any better than that?

He then pointed his sword at her captors. They dropped her arms and ran away.

Well, apparently it could.

Mr. Inquisition either thought more of his abilities than his men did of their own or he was just dumber, because he drew his sword with a flourish and took up a fighting stance. Jennifer fumbled around behind her and tried to untie her hands. She felt someone undo the rope and whipped around to see who, just in case she needed to follow up the thanks with a quick elbow to the nose. To her surprise she saw a teenager, probably sixteen or seventeen, standing behind her, watching her with absolutely enormous eyes. Though he was dark-haired, in all other aspects he looked so much like the blond man that she knew they had to be brothers.

"Thanks," she said.

He looked at her blankly.

What the hell, she thought with abandon. "Thank you," she tried again in Gaelic.

"You're welcome," he answered without hesitation.

Jennifer would have taken the time to be surprised, but the clang of swords made her jump. She turned back around to watch the swordfight. Actually, there really wasn't much to watch. Mr. Inquisition was making a nuisance of himself in the style of an irritating terrier while her gorgeous rescuer was trying but failing to keep his yawns in check. Sheer boredom apparently got the better of him because he slapped Inquisition's sword aside and punched him in the nose. Inquisition clutched his face and howled. Her rescuer sighed, then caught him neatly under the chin.

Inquisition crumpled like a length of fine silk, slithering to the ground with an elegance she wouldn't have expected.

The rest of his flunkies, who were hovering under the trees — undoubtedly to watch the bloodbath — fled without a backward glance.

Jennifer managed to swallow as her knight in no armor but possessing an almost-white horse came across the glade toward her. She wasn't short, but he was at least a hand taller than she was. He had a set of shoulders just made for a girl to lean her head on and a belted waist any bodybuilder would have killed to call his own. She cast about quickly for something intelligent to say before her mind went completely south.

"Um," was all she could manage.

Spectacular.

And that was the word for his face, not her witty repartee.

He said something to his brother, his brother answered, but Jennifer didn't even bother to try to decipher. She was just too damn busy staring at male perfection and feeling fragile.

And then she realized where she was. She was standing in the Middle Ages, with mud slathered on her hands, knees, feet, and jeans, with her hair falling into her face and no doubt curling madly everywhere else thanks to the drizzle, and she had only one decision to make.

How fast to get back over to that time gate and get home.

She took a deep breath — damn, he even smelled good — and turned to look at his brother.

"I have to go home."

The young man nodded, still as wide-eyed as before.

Jennifer smiled. "Tell your brother thanks for the rescue."

He dutifully translated. Jennifer made the mistake of thinking she could just add her own smile to the words and be on her way. She looked up into her rescuer's pale eyes and had a moment's hesitation.

Why was it she couldn't find a guy like this in Manhattan? At this point, she would have settled for a guy like this in England.

Life just wasn't fair.

She pulled herself together, smiled, then turned and walked away before she indulged in any more useless speculation. She went to stand next to the fire. Fortunately for her, the precise spot where she'd been standing hadn't been covered by the wood and she had no problem placing herself on it and getting down to business. She had no doubt the gate would work and take her back to the correct place. It was what Jamie always said. *Think about where you want to go and the gate will take you there.*

She took a deep breath and concentrated all her thoughts on getting back home.

She waited.

Nothing happened.

Well, no reason to panic. She would just have to try harder.

I want to go home.

Jennifer frowned. Still nothing was happening. Well, perhaps that was to be expected. After all, she was a little distracted by the fire and a lot distracted by the gorgeous man behind her who probably thought she was out of her mind. She closed her eyes, blocked out everything except thoughts of three grandfatherly ghosts holding on to a shrieking thug and her car, which was locked 200 feet away from where she was standing. In it was that bottle of Lilt and a Kit Kat she'd bought at the gas station. There was nothing like British chocolate to really make a girl feel like the calories were worth it.

A hissing sound almost made her jump out of her skin. She looked over to see that the fire beside her had been put out courtesy of a bucket of water. The blond man set down the bucket, held up his hands, and retreated to the far side of the glade. He stood there with Brother Gaelic and another brother who had to have been Brother Gaelic's twin. They were all watching her with expressions ranging from disbelief to, in the case of her rescuer, not much expression at all.

She wondered if now would be a good time to feel really, really stupid.

She waved.

Brother Gaelic waved back, but his twin slapped his hand down. A fight ensued. Their elder brother ignored them. He merely watched her with his arms folded across his chest. She noticed that he'd put away his sword. That probably meant that there weren't any more witch-hunters in the area and she could get down to business without

86

worrying about being attacked. Very nice of him to give her that luxury.

She turned her back on all of them. She put her fingers in her ears and concentrated on the job at hand.

Home.

Please.

Time passed. In fact, enough time passed that the mud dried on her hands. She unstuck her fingers from her ears. There was silence. She sighed a huge sigh of relief, then froze. Silence really didn't mean anything when she was standing next to a pile of smoldering sticks.

She felt a light touch on her shoulder and jumped at least half a foot. She turned around, her heart beating at her throat. It was Brother Gaelic.

"Lady," he said hesitantly, "we wondered, my brothers and I, if you would care to come with us?" He looked back over his shoulder. His older brother made no move, but simply remained there, watching silently. Brother Gaelic turned back to her. "My brother's hall is not far from here."

Jennifer considered her options: stay or go. The gate obviously wasn't working for her, but why not? She quickly reviewed everything James MacLeod had ever told her about gates in the grass, gates in compost heaps, and gates in clutches of rock. Powerful gates, less powerful gates, one-way tickets, and fickle fairy rings — Jamie had used them all. She suspected that whatever time gate lay in what she could now see was the beginnings of Ledenham's abbey was one of the fickle kind.

She supposed she could have camped there until it gave up and let her go home, but who knew how long that would take? And who knew how long Mr. Inquisition would remain unconscious? Probably not long enough for her to have any meaningful conversations with Fate.

Maybe a little visit to a local castle until she could get her bearings and give the gate some time to get itself together wasn't such a bad idea.

She smiled at the wide-eyed young man standing in front of her. "Yes, thank you," she said. "I would be very grateful for that."

He nodded, then turned away.

"Wait," she said. "What's your name?"

"Montgomery de Piaget," he said, turning back and smiling a little. He pointed toward his brothers. "That is my brother John. And my older brother Nicholas."

Nicholas de Piaget.

Nicholas de Piaget?

She could hardly believe her ears. What were the odds of running into the very guy in the past that her sister had been singing the praises of in the future?

"We're for his castle," Montgomery added, no doubt blissfully unaware at just how freaked out she was. " 'Tis called Wyckham."

I know, she started to say, but she found she couldn't say anything at all.

"Can you ride?" Montgomery asked. "Lady . . . ?"

"Jennifer," she said faintly. "My name is Jennifer McKinnon."

"Of course, my lady," Montgomery said. "Now, if you'll allow it, you shall have my horse and I'll ride with John."

"Sure," Jennifer said. "Great."

She forced herself to follow him across the glade. What she desperately wanted was for all the craziness swirling around her to stop just long enough for her to get a handle on what was happening, but she supposed that was impossible. All she could do was ride to Wyckham and hope for the best. Maybe she would have a chance there to sit and think. Maybe her visit would include an opportunity to observe Nicholas de Piaget, owner of Wyckham and the embodiment of all knightly virtues, at close range for a few days.

Purely in the interest of adding to the store of de Piaget genealogical lore, of course.

She realized, feeling a little light-headed, that such had been her thought in stopping at the abbey. She supposed that maybe she should let Megan do her own dabbling in her husband's family history.

It was safer that way.

Then, blessing James MacLeod for insisting that she learn to ride during her stay, she accepted the reins to Montgomery's horse. She started to put her foot in the stirrup only to realize that a pair of cupped hands was there for her use. She looked up in surprise to find Nicholas de Piaget standing not a foot away from her.

Well, the historians hadn't exaggerated his handsomeness, at least.

Jennifer fanned herself with the reins as if she'd planned to all along.

He waited for her, possessing a seemingly endless amount of patience. Honestly, Jennifer couldn't have cared less about his patience. She was too busy being dazzled by his looks.

Oh, this was just so bad on so many levels.

She had no time for a distraction of this magnitude. She had a future to get back to. Her earlier Manhattan wishes aside, she did not want a guy who carried a sword. Victoria had nothing but trouble with Connor and his insistence on secreting weapons on various parts of himself. And that was one huge sword Nicholas was wearing at his side.

And then there was the rest of him. Too handsome by far. Definitely too buff. How did a girl have that kind of perfection hanging around every day and get anything done? Nope, he was not for her. She had a career to return to, a new apartment to find, new restaurants to scout out near said new apartment, noise and exhaust fumes and congestion to ignore. She had an appointment with Charles Salieri in a month to discuss her soon-to-be crushing performance schedule. Yessiree, she had lots to do and no time for medieval nobility.

Nicholas only waited.

Well, she wasn't going anywhere anytime soon except up on that horse, so she put her foot in his hands and found herself tossed up into the saddle as if she'd been a rag doll.

Nicholas stroked the horse's mane briefly, paused as if he intended to speak, then shook his head and walked away. Jennifer didn't dare look at him for fear she would embarrass herself by wheezing.

Nicholas de Piaget.

It was just too much to be believed. Unfortunately, the medieval boys doubled up on the medieval horse in front of her, and the medieval reins she was holding in her own hands wouldn't let her do anything else but believe it. She closed her eyes briefly, then let out a shaky breath.

Well, she'd wanted to see Wyckham again. She hadn't expected to see it — and its owner — in all its medieval glory. Maybe there was a method to Fate's madness.

She certainly hoped so, because she didn't want to think about what was in store for her if Fate had gotten it wrong.

CHAPTER 5

Nicholas rode along with his hood pulled up over his head to ward off the renewed drizzle and cursed under his breath. His day had just radically deviated from what he'd been planning.

He had the sinking feeling it wasn't going to right itself anytime soon.

He'd set out very early that morning from Artane, happy to escape his grandmother's clutches and content to be on his way to doing something useful. He'd anticipated an uneventful journey to Wyckham with the only highlight being a brief pause at Nigel of Ledenham's building project to see if progress was being made. It wasn't often that he bothered to observe the king's justice being meted out, but watching Ledenham be forced to build an abbey as penance for calling a man a warlock was certainly such an opportunity — and one to be enjoyed.

Especially since the accused warlock was his sister's husband, Jackson Kilchurn.

Of course it was utter rubbish, that accusation, but Ledenham had made such a spectacle of himself spewing it out that the king had finally thrown him out of his presence with the command that he use his time in some useful endeavor, such as building an abbey, if he ever wanted to enjoy royal favor again. It had been fitting and Nicholas and his brothers had enjoyed it immensely. The only thing that chafed was that the abbey was to be built but a hearty day's walk from Wyckham.

Nicholas had expected to see Ledenham making his masons' lives miserable. He hadn't expected to find him preparing to burn a witch.

He would have rescued the woman sooner, but he'd been too astonished by her beauty to do aught but stare at her in amazement.

He regarded her presently from the comfort and privacy of his hood. To say she was lovely didn't do her justice. She was radiant, with cascading red curls and the face of an angel. He watched her ride in front of him and wished that he wasn't having such a difficult time catching his breath. It had been one thing to have merely caught a glimpse of her before he'd set to the pleasurable task of plunging Nigel of Ledenham into unconsciousness; it was another thing to have stood and looked at her thoroughly as she stomped about on a muddy patch of ground as if she expected it to do aught but squelch under her shoes.

He'd never seen anyone like her.

He knew, with a feeling deep in his gut, that he never would again.

Who *was* she? He'd heard her give Montgomery her name, Jennifer McKinnon, which he supposed could mean she was Scottish. She spoke Gaelic, which meant that she could have come from the Highlands. But if that were the case, why did she find herself a hundred leagues from her home, without escort, family, or gear?

Perhaps she had merely been out for a bit of a jaunt and lost her way. Perhaps she had been traveling with a company and wandered off.

Perhaps her beauty had rendered him witless as well as speechless.

He shook his head to try to clear it. There was likely a very reasonable, logical explanation for her sudden appearance so far from where she should have found herself. In time, he supposed he would learn what it was.

If she remained with him long enough for him to do so.

He cursed again. Damnation, but this wasn't what he'd wanted. He'd just managed to escape a keep full of wenches; he certainly hadn't intended to find himself saddled with another one so soon. He had a roof to repair, then a future to contemplate, a future he was sure held such delights as sitting in his great chair before the fire, turning to fat, grumbling about the fare, and complaining about the rain that made his knees ache. He didn't want the distraction of a woman who was so mesmerizing that he couldn't look away from her even when he knew he should.

"John," he bellowed suddenly, "make haste!"

John kicked his horse into a gallop. Jennifer followed without hesitation. Nicholas brought up the rear, cursing in as many languages as he could and finding satisfaction in none of them. He cursed until he was interrupted by the sight of Wyckham rising up before him. It wasn't a large keep, and it was nothing compared to the fortress in France that was his by right of his title of Count of Beauvois, but it was close to Artane and for that reason alone he found it tolerable enough.

The afternoon sun had broken through the clouds and was shining down upon the pale stone of the walls and turning them quite a lovely color. That was, unfortunately, the only thing that he found pleasing about the sight of the place.

It was difficult to believe that after well over a year of regularly sending his steward gold to make repairs, the keep was still missing its front gates. Of course, it was also missing the portcullis and other necessary defenses such as a garrison and a blacksmith to make them swords, but since he didn't have any serfs, defenses weren't much of a concern at present. Unfortunately, no peasants meant no one to till his fields and that meant that he had had no crops planted that spring and would have no harvest come fall.

It was tempting to turn around and ride for France.

But he was no coward, so he pressed on.

He pushed his hood back off his face as he followed his little company from the gates and up the way to the modest stables that stood across the courtyard from the not unsubstantial great hall. He looked about him narrowly. The stables were in disrepair, the garden was full of weeds, and the rest of the courtyard looked as if no one had lived in there in, well, at least a year. Aye, his steward would have much to answer for.

But first things first. He swung down off his horse and went to take hold of the bridle of Montgomery's. He waited, but Jennifer McKinnon made no move to dismount. She merely looked about herself as if she could not believe what she was seeing. Finally, she seemed to have seen enough and turned to look down at him. Something on her cheek glistened.

Ah, by the saints, not tears. Was the place in so terrible a condition? Or did she grieve over something else?

He didn't dare speculate.

Instead, he held up his hands for her. She looked at him in surprise, as if she wasn't quite sure what he intended. He imagined she didn't. It was possible that chivalry wasn't the order of the day where she came from.

Eventually, she leaned over and put her hands on his shoulders. He helped her off the horse, set her on her feet, then released her immediately. He took a step backward. He didn't want to touch her. He didn't want to hold her. He most certainly didn't want to think about the fact that she smelled like sunshine and wild flowers and that her hair where it had touched his hands and face had burned him like fire.

He turned to Montgomery. "Show her into the hall," he rasped. "I'll remain without and see to the horses."

"As you will, Nicholas," Montgomery said with wide eyes. He went over to Jennifer, spoke to her kindly, and offered her his arm. He led her off toward the great hall.

Nicholas didn't want to watch them go, but he couldn't stop himself. She was tall, that McKinnon lass, and slender, but not frail — though he had to admit she wasn't all that steady on her feet at present. She was oddly dressed, in blue, heavy hose and a tunic finer than anything he'd ever seen.

Clothing he suspected was not to be found in the wilds of Scotland.

He turned away before he could think on

that further, scowled at John just on principle, then took the two horses and led them into the barn. He might have wished for a stable master, but it wasn't an ill thing to be forced to tend to the beasts himself. At least it gave him something to do besides think.

He finished, retrieved the appropriate saddlebags, then waited for John to see to his own mount. He watched his younger brother, still a little surprised that the lad was capable of managing a horse so large. Then again, John was ten-and-seven, surely old enough to do many things Nicholas had managed at that age.

John finished, retrieved his own gear, then pulled up short. "What is it?" he asked in surprise.

"You've grown," Nicholas remarked.

John rolled his eyes. "And you're daft. Of course I've grown. With any luck, I'll have my spurs in a pair of years — if Father can see his way clear to find someone to see to it — and then perhaps I will be even taller and more skilled than you."

Nicholas smiled. "Do you think?"

"I'm a hopeful lad," John replied promptly. He looked Nicholas up and down. "I don't suppose you'd want to finish my training, would you?"

Nicholas was rarely surprised, but he found himself so now. It was an effort to not show it. "It would be an honor."

"Done, then," John said. "Assuming Father will allow it. 'Tis possible he might not want me being soured by your vile humors."

Nicholas started in surprise, then realized that John was teasing him. He grunted. "I'll attempt to check them."

"*Can* you?" John asked, scratching his head in an exaggerated fashion that was so reminiscent of Robin, Nicholas had to suppress the urge to throttle him. "I wonder."

"Do you *want* me to leave you weeping in agony on the field tomorrow, or not?"

John only grinned at him, then strode on ahead. "I hope supper is ready."

"I have the food!" Nicholas called after him.

John only waved and continued on his way. Perhaps he wanted a seat by the fire. Or perhaps he wanted a seat next to Jennifer McKinnon. Nicholas supposed he could understand that.

He followed his brother across the courtyard toward the hall, but was interrupted by his steward running up breathlessly to him.

He suppressed the urge to put the man to the sword. He should have rid himself of Gavin of Louth long ago for the thievery he'd perpetrated over the past pair of years. Nicholas supposed he would be fortunate to find anything at all left in the larder or in his coffers. And to think he'd come so highly recommended.

"I wasn't expecting you," Gavin said with a

fawning bow.

"And yet still everything is just as I left it," Nicholas said, pointedly.

"I know you don't care for change, my lord."

A few weeds pulled in the garden and perhaps the acquisition of a cook who could produce something edible were changes he could have lived with. And when had he ever given the impression that he did not like change? The whole bloody place needed a change — in the form of a renovation from top to bottom.

"I should tell you," Master Gavin began uneasily, "that we've nothing prepared for supper."

"We brought things with us," Nicholas said. "I'll sort out the larder in the morning."

"It has been a very lean winter, my lord," Gavin warned quickly. "The larder is not as full as I would like."

No doubt because most of its contents found themselves deposited in Gavin's ample belly.

"Nor are the coffers," Gavin added.

"I'll sort that out as well. Not to worry."

Master Gavin heaved a huge sigh of relief, obviously thinking he had escaped justice. He smiled happily, then leaned forward. "Now that we've settled that, if I might inquire about the woman —"

"Or you might not," Nicholas suggested.

"I heard her speaking Scots to your brothers," Gavin continued on heedlessly. "I assume she is a wench of that breeding, no doubt quite wild in her ways —"

"She is lost," Nicholas interrupted firmly, "and in need of refuge."

"She is beautiful," Gavin said, smacking his lips.

"She is *my* guest," Nicholas said sharply, "and not to be studied thus." Never mind that he'd spent the past pair of hours studying Jennifer McKinnon himself. At least when he admired a woman, he didn't leave everyone around him feeling as if they desperately needed to bathe. "I think we won't leave the ledger until tomorrow. Bring the accounts to my solar now."

"But, my lord!" Gavin squeaked. "It has indeed been a very difficult year —"

"The accounts, Master Gavin."

Gavin looked at him and seemed to consider. His fingers worked, as if he couldn't stop himself from counting gold that had ceased to flow through them. He squeaked a time or two, then turned suddenly and bolted for the front gates.

Nicholas knew he shouldn't have been surprised.

He strode after his steward and caught him just outside the castle walls. He stopped him long enough to trade him a handful of gold coins, the clothes he was wearing and his life in return for the key to a trunk that Nicholas suspected would find itself in Gavin's chamber, full of everything of value that Wyckham possessed. Once he had the key in hand, he booted Gavin in the backside and sent him sprawling.

Too kind a fate, truly.

Gavin scrambled to his feet and fled. Nicholas watched him until he had disappeared into the trees, then turned and walked back into the courtyard, cursing in disgust. He suspected that whilst he might find a few things in Gavin's trunk, he wouldn't find the bulk of his funds. No doubt they had been spent on food and drink, things he could never recover. Well, there was nothing to be done about that now. All he could do was move forward.

He turned around and walked across the courtyard, ignoring the stables that needed refurbishing and continuing on to the lists. He found his stone masons finishing their work for the day and setting up their own cooking fire. At least here he might have pleasant tidings.

They were a diligent lot, which he knew from his time spent working with them on Amanda's keep, Raventhorpe. Actually, the keep belonged to Amanda and her husband, Jackson, warlock extraordinaire. Nicholas had learned, over the past year, not to hate his brother-in-law as intensely as he had at first.

And to think his family complained about his sourness. He'd been passing polite.

He wondered what it would have been like to have been a mere mason. It would have been a good life. Simple. Uncomplicated. Lacking some of the things that he rather enjoyed, such as fine food, French wines, and beautiful music.

He stopped next to the head mason, Petter, and smiled. "Making progress inside, are you?" he said.

"Aye, of course," Petter answered with a smile. "But this is a difficult case."

"Less chilly than Raventhorpe, I daresay."

"That, my lord, is truth indeed." Petter looked upward. "It is the roof that troubles me. It wasn't done properly the first time."

"And your solution?"

Petter smiled. "Do it properly this time."

"And what you mean by that is 'replace the entire roof.' "

"You've no furniture inside to be ruined or moved out," Petter said.

"That is an aye, then."

"It is."

Nicholas sighed deeply, watching more of his gold disappear into the bottomless well called Wyckham. "Very well," he said. "Be about it as you see fit."

"I could attempt to save the most of it."

"Think you?" Nicholas asked, hardly daring hope. "And will it be sturdy enough, do you think?"

Petter seemed to consider. "I imagine not, actually. What you might consider is an arch in the hall to support the roof, and a fine gallery on the second floor. Open to the hall below." He paused. "Aye, gallery all around, with arches and fine details. You could place musicians in that gallery, and have their sweet music waft down to please your discriminating ears." He smiled. "Very lovely."

"Very expensive."

"Elegant."

"Time-consuming."

Petter laughed. "I'll sketch it out and show you before we begin. It would give you a se'nnight to decide where you'll stay whilst I'm renovating."

Nicholas pursed his lips. "Perhaps I should see to the stables sooner rather than later, that I might have a dry place to sleep."

Petter smiled. "That would be my suggestion."

Nicholas grunted and walked away. He liked Petter, not only for his unvarnished opinions and inventive mind, but for the practice of Gaelic when the mood took them both. They had spoken it exclusively at Raventhorpe, which had pleased Jake and annoyed Amanda. Petter was polite about it, though. He would only speak it if Nicholas spoke it to him first. That would be useful, considering he thought that perhaps he might not want Jennifer knowing he could understand her tongue.

He ignored the subterfuge and the fact that he would likely overhear nothing that would serve him.

He picked up his saddlebags from where he'd dropped them to pursue Master Gavin, slung them over his shoulder, and made his way up the steps and into the great hall. He hadn't managed to get halfway across it before he came to an abrupt halt.

Montgomery had found a stool for Jennifer and was currently handing her a cup of heaven knew what. Jennifer accepted it with a faint smile.

A smile that almost brought him to his knees and he wasn't even the recipient of it.

By the saints, she was lovely. Lovely and lost and the saints only knew what else. He'd forgotten, whilst he'd been outside, just how lovely she was. He'd forgotten, for those few moments, what he'd been given.

Er, been saddled with, rather.

She drank, then set the cup down next to her on the floor. Even from where he stood, Nicholas could see that her hand trembled. She turned to the fire and hugged herself. She smiled again for Montgomery, but it was a strained smile.

Nicholas knew he should have gone over to her and offered her his aid, but he didn't dare for a variety of reasons he didn't want to identify.

He realized, quite suddenly, that his brother Montgomery had come to stand in front of him. That he hadn't noticed him right off said much about the state of his wits.

"Nick," Montgomery began, looking supremely uncomfortable, "not to be too familiar, but . . . well . . . don't you think . . ."

"I try not to," Nicholas said dryly, "but you're full of thoughts, apparently. I imagine you're going to share them all with me whether I care to hear them or not, so you'd best be about it."

Montgomery took a deep breath. "I daresay the lady Jennifer should, well, I think she might be more comfortable if she had other . . ." Montgomery had to take another deep breath. "Other clothing," he finished miserably.

"Montgomery, did you by chance bring any other clothes with you?"

"Aye."

"Then offer them to her."

"Aye," Montgomery agreed, then he paused. He looked far too serious for his own good. "Nick, you don't think —"

"I don't."

"But she has no French, Nick. And look at how she's dressed! Surely that means —"

"It means nothing. Give her clothing, Montgomery, and leave it at that. And bid

106

her take Gavin's chamber. He won't be using it anymore."

Montgomery shot him a look of uneasiness, but did as he was told.

Nicholas turned away. He didn't think. He thought nothing about Jennifer with the flame-colored hair, nothing about her clothing, and nothing about her lack of French. He thought nothing about the fact that she had no horse, no gear, and no kin nearby — nor did she seem to be looking for any of them.

He supposed he could hope that Ledenham had it aright and she was a witch. She might remain for a meal, then fly away.

Unfortunately, thinking on Ledenham reminded him that Ledenham had thought his brother Jackson Alexander Kilchurn IV was a warlock. Jake wasn't a warlock, but he was definitely from a place that was strange.

And a time that was not their own.

Nicholas looked at Jennifer McKinnon, then closed his eyes briefly and winced. When he opened his eyes, she was still there. Still dressed in those strange trews that Jake called jeans. Still dressed in a tunic that looked so costly that even he might have hesitated to have it fashioned. Still dressed in shoes that were far beyond the art of any cobbler he knew, and he knew the finest in London and Paris.

Nay, she was not from Scotland.

At least not the Scotland of his time.

He dragged his hand through his hair and cursed briefly. He had passed the last year and a half snorting at every private conversation in which anything of Jake's travels through time had been discussed. He'd mocked his brother-in-law for his fanciful imaginings, his departure from good sense, his delusional dreamings. He had vowed that he would never believe that a man could travel hundreds of years from the Future back into the past. He had sworn that it simply was not possible and anyone who believed the like was nothing short of mad.

That he now should have a woman of Jake's ilk under his protection was almost more irony than a man should ever be called upon to endure.

It was enough to make him think he just might have to sit down.

But that would have made him look weak, so he decided that the next best thing was to repair immediately to the kitchens where he could rummage through the saddlebags and see if he could produce some sort of supper before they all fainted from hunger. He could reasonably be expected to perhaps sit whilst he was doing that.

He crossed the back of the great hall and escaped into the kitchens before he had to look any more on a woman who was most definitely not from his time and therefore most definitely not for him. Fate was behind all this; he was almost sure of it, poking her nose in his affairs just like his grandmother. Perhaps Fate was a female as well. He wouldn't have been surprised.

Damned nosey women, the both of them.

Unfortunately, he suspected that Fate was even more tenacious than his grandmother and that was a frightening thought indeed. Who knew what her tenacity would give him?

A woman from the Future placed in his care as if she'd been meant to be put there. A woman he couldn't look away from when he was within a hundred paces of her. A woman so damned beautiful he couldn't catch his breath when he was around her.

Just what in the hell was he supposed to do now? Ignore her and hope she went away? Ignore her and hope her kin came looking for her? Ignore her and hope his good sense returned before he did something foolish like offer to allow her to stay as long as she liked?

Nay, he could do none of those, especially the last. He would see that she was fed, clothed, and housed. And when she decided that she wanted to return to the Future, then he would let her go willingly and have no regrets.

But until then, he would ignore her.

It was the only thing he could do.

CHAPTER 6

Montgomery de Piaget stood on the steps of his brother's hall, looked out over the court-yard, and contemplated the number of things he had seen over the course of his ten-and-seven years of life. He supposed it could have taken him quite some time to consider them all, but at the moment he was only concerned with one thing in particular.

Faeries.

He clasped his hands behind himself and rocked back on his heels. He'd heard the tales, of course, from the time he'd been small. 'Twas said that faeries lived in a world beneath his own, a world of wonders and magic. Now and again, they were known to leave their world by means of a gate in the grass. There was no shame in admitting that from time to time he'd wondered if such a creature might actually exist. That had been when he was young.

Now, he was older.

And he knew.

He'd met his first faery two years earlier: his brother-in-law, Jake Kilchurn. Though initially he hadn't realized where Jake had come from, he had at one point seen him simply spring up from the grass. Though his sister had fallen in love with him and wed him, his faery parentage aside, Montgomery had never ceased to believe that he had seen what he'd seen.

And now another.

He'd been riding ahead of Nicholas and John on their way from Artane a se'nnight ago, feeling adventurous and a bit restless. He'd reined his horse in at the edge of the clearing near Ledenham's abbey because he'd known Nicholas wanted to stop there. It was there that he'd seen it happen.

A faery springing forth from the world below.

An exceptionally lovely faery, truth be told.

He'd watched her be captured. He had half expected to see her break free of her bonds and escape back into her world, but she had been overcome. When Ledenham had kindled his fire, Montgomery had worried, but then he'd realized Nicholas was right beside him and known all would be well. There was none to equal Nicholas in matters of battle, save Robin of course, so Montgomery had had no fear for the faery's safety.

Nicholas, however, instead of leaping forward to offer aid as was his wont when faced with wenches in distress, had merely gaped at the faery with an expression that Montgomery understood completely.

Wonder.

Montgomery paused. He supposed Nicholas might have also been appreciating the fairness of her face, but who was he to judge in these matters? His brother was continually surrounded by beautiful women, so perhaps one more didn't move him. But a beautiful faery? Aye, that was something indeed.

"Hey, Montgomery."

Montgomery turned and saw the faery in question standing next to him. By the saints, she was lovely. Somehow, even dressed in his clothes with her strange faery shoes still on her feet and her hair piled on top of her head in a manner that he couldn't begin to understand, she was stunning. He found that all he could do was smile stupidly at her.

It seemed to be the condition of most of the men in the keep, actually.

Then he frowned. Hay? Why did she say that? Was it a word from her world? He supposed it might have been. He would have to ask her when next he had the chance.

He supposed the chance would come soon enough, considering that he generally found a way to pass most of his time with her. It had become his habit over the past se'nnight, as he had unfortunately endeavored with his brother John to teach her French — unfortunately, for he would rather have had her all to himself. John, though, seemed just as much under her spell as he was.

Her mastery of his tongue was improving by unnaturally large leaps, even given her tendency to utter the occasional Faery word. It was a testament to her wit, though, that she had been able to learn so much so quickly. Once heard, she never needed to have a word told to her again and she never seemed to forget what she had learned. He suspected that with another se'nnight, she would be conversing easily in French on any number of subjects. Her Gaelic, as well, was excellent, far better than his.

Did they speak Gaelic in Faery?

It was something that he perhaps might also dare ask her at some point.

"I'm off to the garden again," she said. "Come along if you like." She put her hand briefly on his shoulder, smiled at him again, then went on her way.

Montgomery nodded knowingly to himself. Faeries were rumored to be powerfully fond of gardens. Her destination was proof enough of that.

She had passed most of her time in that garden, tending it with the love only a faery could have for such a place. He had worked alongside her, simply because he couldn't bring himself to be anywhere else. She was beautiful, true, and otherworldly, aye, but it

113

was her smile that kept him near her. There she was, no doubt very far away from her world, yet still she could be content.

She hadn't told him much of her world, save that she had family there and that she was a musician. She said she had played for hundreds. What else could he assume but that she was an important member of the Faery Queen's court?

He watched her walk around the edge of the keep, then he turned back to the courtyard. He jumped in surprise. Nicholas was standing directly in front of him. Nicholas, though, wasn't watching him. He was watching Jennifer.

Montgomery understood.

"How is her speech?" Nicholas asked, dragging his attention back to his brother.

"She's doing very well," Montgomery said. "*Unnaturally* well, if you will."

Nicholas pursed his lips. "Have you any other useful observations?"

Montgomery hesitated. This was certainly something he didn't want to reveal, but perhaps he needed to. He took a deep breath. "She has asked how far away the abbey is." He paused for quite a while. "I daresay she has great desire to return there."

"Does she," Nicholas said flatly.

"I fear she wants to return home," Montgomery blurted out. "You know, to *her* world. To Faery."

114

"Montgomery, she is *not* from Faery."

"I think she is. Think on the clothes she was wearing —"

"Scottish gear," Nicholas said. "Who knows what else they do up in those barbaric Highlands?"

Montgomery looked at him miserably. "But, Nick —"

Nicholas put his hand on Montgomery's shoulder. "Montgomery, there are many things in this world that are beyond the understanding of even the most intelligent of men. I know what you think you have seen in the past —"

"Faeries," Montgomery said promptly. "Springing up out of the grass. Like —"

"Like no one," Nicholas said firmly. "Jennifer is not a faery. She is lost. She comes from Scotland where the customs are far different from ours."

"But the way she fights —"

"She's canny."

"She fights like Jake," Montgomery said firmly. "You know that to be true."

Nicholas started to speak, then shut his mouth. He looked heavenward for a moment or two, cursed, then looked at Montgomery. "Has she said how soon she wants to go to the abbey?"

Montgomery shook his head glumly.

"Perhaps her family will come fetch her," Nicholas mused. "Or —"

"You won't just send her away, will you?"

Nicholas cuffed him. "Imp, I do remember how chivalry behaves, even if mine is rusty."

"I don't want her to go," Montgomery blurted out. "Won't you ask her to stay?"

Nicholas dragged his hand through his hair, then blew out his breath, but that seemed to provide him with nothing to say.

"She might stay, if you asked," Montgomery pressed. "You haven't said two words to her, Nick, not even in Gaelic —"

"I don't want her to know I speak it," Nicholas warned.

"So you've said, but I don't understand why not."

"I like to keep my secrets," Nicholas said grimly. He shook his head. "She won't stay, Montgomery. I can't ask her to stay." He turned away. " 'Tis best I keep well away from her until she goes."

Montgomery watched Nicholas walk off. He suspected his brother was more interested than he wanted to admit.

He could understand that. There was something about Jennifer McKinnon that was mesmerizing, bewitching, and so very lovely that it was hard to look away from her and harder still to think of her sunny self not being nearby.

Such was the lure of a faery, he supposed.

Nicholas started for the front gates, then hesitated and turned back. Montgomery watched him wander about the courtyard, then come to stand in the shadow of the great hall. It was, as it happened, the perfect place to see into the garden without being seen.

Montgomery couldn't blame his brother. He hadn't been able to blame his brother over the past se'nnight as he'd kept his distance from Jennifer yet watched her as often as he could whilst being about the business of his keep. Why he just didn't go have speech with her, Montgomery didn't know.

Perhaps he feared Jennifer would leave and he didn't want to have his heart break when she did.

Montgomery could understand that as well.

But she wasn't going today. Montgomery took the opportunity to trot over to the garden, nodding happily to Nicholas on his way by. Nicholas reached out to cuff him, but Montgomery ducked and continued on. John was apparently sharing his thoughts for he was on his way there as well. Montgomery had to elbow his twin aside so he could arrive first and be the beneficiary of Jennifer's welcoming smile.

Faeries.

What wasn't to like about them?

CHAPTER 7

Jennifer stood at the edge of Wyckham's garden and admired the now-tended beds and the lovely paths meandering through them. This was what she had seen when she'd stared at the place hundreds of years in the future. Pruning trees and rosebushes with a knife had been difficult, but she'd given the job to Montgomery, who had seemed to like it. She'd almost suggested he go get Nicholas's sword, but she suspected that probably wouldn't have flown.

What had flown had been time. Two weeks had gone by almost in the blink of an eye, two weeks of gulping down as much medieval Norman French as humanly possible. It helped that she spoke Italian. It helped that she had a very good ear. It had also helped that she'd needed a distraction from the reality of living in a keep she'd seen ravaged by time in the future. She'd been happy for anything to keep her mind busy and off a few questions such as why the gate hadn't worked, what the hell she was doing in medieval England, and, the perennial favorite, why Nicholas de Piaget had to be so ridiculously handsome.

She had no answers for any of them, so she'd done the only thing she could do — keep herself busy until an opportunity to try the gate again presented itself. Besides, it was probably foolish, but she couldn't help but feel a little connected to Wyckham. If she did nothing else but tidy up the garden, it might be just enough of a change that someone would want to take care of it.

It could happen.

She wandered down one of the garden paths, bending down occasionally to pluck out the stray weed, and considered her situation. Thanks to a few casual conversations with Montgomery and John, she'd determined that she was indeed loitering in 1229. Henry III was sitting quite happily on the throne. The Magna Carta was in full force and courtly knights were in full fashion. Gregorian chant reigned supreme. Violins hadn't been invented yet. James MacLeod hadn't even been born yet.

She was in trouble.

Well, at least there were some things to be grateful for. She had Doc Martens on her feet, which were sturdy and didn't look all that obtrusive. She had been given the steward's room, which had a bed and a candle.

She'd learned to take a torch to the bathroom and not have it fall over onto her while she was about her business. She had scoured the nearby forest for leaves, solving the toilet paper problem. The downside was that she hadn't seen any feminine protection products, but she would deal with that when she had to.

Though she had to admit she hoped she wouldn't have to. Despite the comfort of her own room and the pleasure of the twins' company, she had determined that two weeks was probably the extent of her tolerance for hanging out in other time periods not her own.

She'd asked Montgomery about the abbey. She'd learned that it was being built by Nigel of Ledenham as penance for doing something that was apparently so terrible that Montgomery couldn't bring himself to talk about it.

Montgomery was, however, very willing to talk about other things, as was John. She liked Nicholas's brothers. They were open and art-less and quite opinionated about almost everything from royalty to fairies. Montgomery, in particular, had opinions on the latter and he tended to look at her pointedly when he discussed them, as if he expected her to have some special knowledge about them. Maybe it was her Doc Martens. They probably inspired all sorts of speculation in medieval teenagers.

All in all, medieval England had turned out to be a very tolerable place for a brief visit.

The only small fly in the ointment was Nicholas de Piaget himself, that paragon of chivalry who had no idea that inhabitants of Artane 800 years in the future still talked about him. She saw him often, but only from a distance. She supposed he spent a good portion of each day trying to feed them, which Montgomery said he wasn't particularly happy about but had to do, given Gavin of Louth's decimation of the pantry. He showed up at night, but immediately retreated to the kitchen as if she had cooties and he was afraid he'd catch them if he sat too close. He was obviously a good hunter, though, and a very good chef. She wasn't a huge fan of wild game, but hunger was the great culinary equalizer and Nicholas was good with spices. She had tried to provide mushrooms and green edibles for him and though he used them, he never said anything to her about them.

The cootie thing again, obviously.

She didn't consider herself particularly thin-skinned, but it was actually starting to get to her a little. What, was she a complete beast by medieval standards? Was it the red hair? Did she have too many freckles? She had five, by last count, which was pretty good considering her coloring. She'd wondered at first if he was trying to get his keep ready for a bride. Montgomery claimed Nicholas's disagreeable mood actually came from their grandmother trying to marry him off. He had looked at her pointedly during that conversation, too, as if he'd wanted her to audition for the part.

She shook her head. No, there was no point in that. She'd tidied up Nicholas's garden for him. She'd learned a vast amount of medieval Norman French. She'd taught the boys how to forage for wild greens. There was nothing else to be done. It was time to go home.

In fact, she'd decided that tomorrow was the day. She would get up, give Montgomery back his clothes, then get on with getting back home.

She took one last look at the garden, sighed deeply, then turned and walked back around the side of the castle. Montgomery and John were hanging out there, looking hungry.

"Is it time to eat yet?" Montgomery asked hopefully.

Jennifer squinted up at the late afternoon sun. "I suppose it might be."

"Is there supper?" he asked.

"Have you made any?" she countered with a smile.

John scowled. "You know we haven't and Nick isn't back yet. We will likely perish from hunger before he arrives."

Jennifer pointed toward the front gates that

actually had no gates but were just a hole in the wall where the gates should have been. "Go find greens," she ordered.

"But we need to tend the horses," Montgomery said.

"I'll tend the horses," she said. "You two go forage for food."

John's face brightened. "In truth? Are you able? Willing?"

"I am able and I'm happy to do it," she said, smiling. "You find something to eat, I'll pitch some hay, then we'll meet inside in half an hour and have a feast."

John bowed so low, he almost fell over. He straightened and bestowed a brilliant smile on her. "You, lady, are marvelous —"

"Oaf," Montgomery said, giving him a shove. "Rather you should insist on doing the stable work in her stead, as I will. Mistress Jennifer, I will —"

"No, you won't," she said, turning him around. "I can shovel horse manure as well as the next girl. Go look for something to put in a salad."

"But —"

"Go, and don't bring back anything poisonous."

Montgomery hesitated, but she gave him a push in the right direction. He and John trotted off obediently and Jennifer turned to face the stables.

She wasn't a connoisseur of horse housing,

but it was obvious that Nicholas's stables needed spiffying up. Her only frame of reference was what she'd seen at Camp MacLeod, and those were pretty fancy. Jamie and his family took their horses even more seriously than they did their very expensive, very fast cars. Nicholas's stables had potential; they just looked like they hadn't been tended to in a while. In fact, the entire keep looked like it could really use some work. Either Nicholas didn't have the money, or he didn't have the time.

But she had the time, at least for the rest of the afternoon, so she would do what she could.

She resolutely pushed out of her mind what she knew the keep would look like in 800 years.

Montgomery and John's horses were contentedly standing in their stalls. She wasn't sure she dared feed them, but she could clean out their stalls. Then again, just where was she supposed to put them while she was doing that? She'd learned to ride at Jamie's, true, and she had learned something about the care and feeding of horses, but Jamie, Patrick, or Ian had always done all the real dirty work. Presently she didn't have a Scottish uncle or cousin to catch Montgomery's horse if she let it go, so she supposed she should leave the current occupants for later.

Nicholas's horse wasn't there so maybe that

was the place to start. Jennifer found a pitchfork, then paused and leaned against the stall door. She looked inside the empty stall and let herself, in the privacy of hay and manure, wonder about the man who owned the stable.

So his grandmother was trying to set him up. Why hadn't it worked so far? Was he too picky? Too controlling? Too handsome? Surely such a paragon of all knightly virtues should have found himself with a string of beautiful women trailing after him.

She had to admit that he was completely out of her experience, and she wasn't unused to intimidating men.

Her father, for instance, was a tall, handsome, very intelligent man. Her brother, Thomas, had all those characteristics and had added something more in the acquisition of the ability to take a very sharp sword and do business with it. Victoria's husband, Connor, might have been mistaken for one of those medieval Scottish lairds whose lives had depended on their skill with a six-foot broadsword and a mind that effortlessly thought in warfarish circles around lesser mortals. If one believed in medieval Scottish lairds finding themselves in the twenty-first century.

Which, as it happened, she did.

Connor MacDougal and James MacLeod both were of that medieval bent. Jamie's brother, Patrick, who had over the past month taught her more about wild edibles than she'd ever anticipated wanting to know, radiated that same sort of thing. Their cousin, Ian MacLeod, ran a training school where men from all walks of life came to learn how to wield a sword in a most intimidating fashion from Ian himself who, as it happened, had grown to manhood with a sword in his hands. Lots of his students were very, very afraid by the end of day one.

So all those men, relatives of hers, carried that same whiff of medievalness about them. They were rough, formidable, and left anyone who looked at them with the impression that it was better to walk away than engage. Their skill was an in-your-face sort of thing that announced its presence the moment you met them.

Nicholas, to her mind, was a different animal entirely. Since he was a de Piaget, he was medieval nobility, though it wasn't obvious from his relatively clean, well cut clothes. Unfortunately well cut, if anyone wanted her opinion on the matter, because they had hinted at a physique that was truly drool-inducing. But they didn't look expensive.

Still, despite that smooth, unassuming exterior, she had seen what he could do with just a few swings of his sword. He'd been yawning while he was at it. She could only speculate on what he could do if he really meant it.

She suspected that she should have been glad that she'd only seen him in passing for the past two weeks. If she'd had to look at him much more than that, her eyes might have caught on fire.

Like right now.

She clutched her pitchfork as she realized Nicholas was standing in the entrance to the stables, leaning against the door frame and watching her with his arms folded over his chest. He looked at her pitchfork, then lifted both his hands in a gesture of surrender.

She caught her breath on a half laugh, then remembered herself and frowned as best she could. No sense in letting him think that a friendly gesture would make up for having avoided her so pointedly. She put the fork tine-down into the dirt and looked at him.

She was actually a little relieved that she had something to hold on to.

All right, so he hadn't been that friendly. So he probably thought she was a fairy right along with his youngest brother and had decided that staying away from her was the wisest thing to do. So he hadn't trotted out all his chivalric moves and used them on her. Maybe he was shy.

Or maybe he was just the most arresting man she'd ever been in close proximity to and nothing else mattered.

His hair was a beautiful blond, streaked by sunlight and blown by whatever riding he'd just done. It was a little on the long side and some of it hung into his eyes, eyes that were clear and beautiful and very intense. He wasn't smiling, but that was probably a good thing. She supposed if he'd smiled at her, she just might have had to sit down.

She was tempted to look the rest of him over, but that would have been gawking and she didn't think she was up to any of that. So she took a firmer hold on her pitchfork and attempted a smile.

"Hi," she managed.

He pushed off from the door frame and walked over to her.

Jennifer clutched the pitchfork. She suspected she should have been glad he'd been gone so often. She wouldn't have gotten anything done otherwise.

He stopped a couple of feet away from her. "The lads say your French has become very good," he said.

"Thank you."

"You learn quickly."

"Your brothers are good teachers."

He looked at her for another moment or two, then reached out and put his hand on the pitchfork. "I'll take that."

"I think I need it," she managed.

He tilted his head and frowned. "Why?"

"I'm not finished with my work." *But my knees are finished with holding me up.*

She thought it might be best not to say that.

"My mother taught me it wasn't chivalrous to allow a lady to muck out stalls when a man is there to do it for her."

"Did she?"

"Actually, she didn't," he said gravely, "but I suppose she trusted that I would come to that conclusion on my own." He gently pulled the pitchfork away, then pointed at a bale of hay against another wall. "Sit, lady, if you please, and let me see to it for you."

Oh, why hadn't she gone that morning while he'd been out doing whatever it was he did? She managed to get herself over to the aforementioned bale of hay and sit down before she fell down. And then she had the undeniable and unaccustomed pleasure of watching a medieval guy take care of his horse. It really shouldn't have been that big a deal. She'd watched her Scottish kin take care of their horses before. Somehow, though, watching an attractive man that you were unaccountably attracted to take care of some essential stable work was something entirely different.

He pitched hay as if it cost him no effort at all. His arms strained a little under the weight, but in a way that left her fanning herself.

When had it gotten so hot?

He finished far too soon and led his horse into the stall. He took off its gear, put it away neatly, then shut the stall door. He took both

Montgomery and John's horses and put them outside. Jennifer supposed the beasts didn't dare run away.

Nicholas returned and made very quick work of mucking out their stalls. Jennifer frowned. Why couldn't she have found this kind of guy at home?

Because he probably wouldn't have been living in Manhattan where there weren't all that many stables to muck out.

Nicholas finished, put all the gear away, then turned and looked at her.

"Dinner?" he asked.

Then he held out his hand.

She looked at his hand for a moment in surprise, then up at him. "Um," she began.

He only continued to hold out his hand toward her. Jennifer closed her eyes briefly, then put her hand into his and let him pull her to her feet.

His hand was warm and dry and rather callused. She supposed that came from using a sword. Jennifer looked up into those fathomless eyes of his and felt herself growing just the slightest bit faint. His breathing seemed just a little ragged. She knew that because it matched hers.

Oh, this was just so bad on so many levels.

Then he suddenly released her hand as quickly as he'd taken it.

"Supper," he said roughly. "You must be hungry."

"I'm fine," she managed.

He nodded toward the keep. "Cold, then," he said. He grabbed his saddlebags and walked away.

He did look over his shoulder, though, to see if she was following, and he paused to let her catch up to him.

She had to trot to keep up with him as he walked across the courtyard and she was accustomed to the quick pace of Manhattan sidewalks. She ran with him up the stairs and into the great hall. He came to an abrupt halt and looked down at her.

"Dinner," he said.

"You've said that before."

He looked at her, swore, then looked at her again. "I'll see to it," he said.

He walked away from her as if he simply couldn't bear to be anywhere near her. She watched him stride across his great hall and disappear into the passageway that led to the kitchen.

She wasn't quite sure what she was supposed to think about what had just happened.

She *was* sure, however, that she would be much, much better off to just get back home while she had her common sense, and her ego, left somewhat intact.

She was almost run over by John and Montgomery who tumbled in through the door. Montgomery slung his arm around her shoulders in his normal brotherly fashion.

131

"We found greens," he announced happily. "Do you care to inspect them?"

"I'll trust you," she said weakly.

"We'll take our findings to Nick," John said. "Let us be about it, Montgomery, so supper won't be late."

Jennifer watched them disappear into the kitchen. Yes, she had to go home. Medieval England had been great. There was peace and sky and room — all those things she had longed for while she'd been pacing in her minuscule apartment, but it wouldn't do her any good to have those things if she was alone.

And it sure as hell wasn't looking like she was going to have any company anytime soon.

She didn't understand Nicholas de Piaget and she hadn't come back in time to be his girlfriend. The man obviously didn't *want* a girlfriend — at least if that girlfriend was her. She was tired of men who didn't know what they wanted. She was ready for a man who was ready to settle down and have a family.

She wanted what Megan had, what her parents and Victoria and Thomas had. She wanted a husband and children and chaos that revolved around family, not fabric and concert schedules.

Maybe she would get back to the future and have a chat with the Boar's Head Trio. Surely those grandfatherly ghosts who had set up Megan, Thomas, and Victoria could set her up with equal success. Where was that Manhattan attorney with a slim briefcase and a closet full of expensive Italian suits when she needed him?

Yes, it was home for her.

As soon as she could get there.

In spite of Nicholas de Piaget's pale eyes or his warm hands or his beautiful face.

Or the way he had looked at her in the stables, as if he didn't particularly want her to go.

CHAPTER 8

Nicholas looked at what his brothers had collected in the woods and wondered just what in the hell he was supposed to do with it. Make it into soup? Feed it to the horses? Plant it in the garden and hope it would turn into something else come next spring?

He cursed fluently. A fortnight with a very empty larder had proved to be a very inconvenient and expensive venture. He'd hunted, true, and managed to keep his company from starving, but that had grown tiresome. He'd traveled to Seakirk Abbey several times and paid them handsomely for their meal to make porridge, but he'd had his fill of that as well. Not even the dried vegetables and cured meat he'd been able to buy had made much difference to the variety of his supper table.

It was possible that he might have done damage for a loaf of bread.

Obviously, feeding the inhabitants of his keep was not what he did best. He needed someone else in charge of that business so he could be about the business of attending to the affairs of his estate.

Or the other compelling business of doing his damndest not to fall under Jennifer McKinnon's spell.

A sudden ruckus coming from the great hall interrupted his ruminations. He happily tossed his spoon onto the work table and went to see what madness was being combined. Perhaps this was something he could see to with his sword.

He walked out into the hall and came to a sudden halt. The sight that greeted him so surprised him that he couldn't move. His younger brother, Miles, was standing inside the hall, trying to listen to both John and Montgomery at the same time. Miles had been followed inside by a pair of lads carrying in things that looked to have been transported by wagon.

Nicholas sighed with unrestrained relief. He sincerely hoped that his mother had sent along something to eat as well.

It likely should have galled him to need such aid, but he supposed if it had galled him in truth, he would have packed up his brothers and sailed a fortnight ago for France where the larder was always full and his cook was without peer.

He frowned thoughtfully. Perhaps a small journey at midsummer wasn't out of the question.

But for now, he would be grateful for whatever he stood to receive. He would also stretch himself and endeavor not to kill his next-youngest brother for immediately setting his sights on Jennifer McKinnon.

It was, after all, something he should have expected.

He knew the exact moment when Miles noticed her. John and Montgomery were left babbling into thin air as Miles deserted them to cross the hall without delay. He reached Jennifer, took her hand, then bent low over it. He straightened and gave her his most charming smile. Nicholas had no doubt that his brother was girding up his loins for a lengthy siege of her common sense.

He scowled. Perhaps it didn't serve him to have spent so much time with his family. He knew his brothers far too well for comfort. Miles could be tremendously charming, but Nicholas was fairly sure he wasn't truly interested in finding a wife. He would woo Jennifer until he was faint from the effort, but he would not desire to win her heart truly.

Then again, and more terrifying still, perhaps Miles *was* in the market for a bride.

That Miles's intentions might have changed was alarming enough to make Nicholas leave off with his casual observations. He strode over to the hearth and glared at his brother.

"Stop drooling on her," he said shortly, "and tell me you brought food."

Miles smiled pleasantly. "A good e'en to you as well, brother. Aye, I brought food. And a bit of furniture," he added pointedly, "which is well since all I see in your hall is a stool. A beautiful woman should have a chair with a cushion to sit upon, don't you agree?"

Nicholas struggled to unclench his jaw. "Did you perchance bring a chair with a cushion?"

"I did."

"Then why don't you go fetch it?"

"I'll keep our lovely lady here company while *you* go fetch it."

"I'm unfamiliar with how the wagon is packed," Nicholas growled.

"The men will acquaint you."

Nicholas didn't dare look at Jennifer. Well, he did dare, but only from the corner of his eye. She was looking from him to Miles and back with an expression of slight confusion, as if she couldn't understand why in the bloody hell they would be arguing about chairs. Nicholas scowled at Miles, but his brother only stared back at him, a hint of a smile playing about his mouth.

Nicholas knew he had no reason to feel possessive of Jennifer. She was no doubt counting the hours until she could return home. He had no desire to have her leaving affect him. Then again, he supposed that if Miles fell in love with her, *his* heart would be shattered when she left.

There. That was a happy thought.

Nicholas glared at Miles, glared at Jennifer just on principle, then walked over to the hall door, keeping himself company with a few curses.

Why was it that his brother could walk into his hall, see the same beautiful woman that Nicholas had been looking at for a solid fortnight, and begin to woo her before he even removed his cloak or unbuckled his sword belt whilst Nicholas couldn't bring himself to spew out three kind words in succession her way?

Because Miles didn't know where she was from and what she would be giving up if she didn't return home.

The Future.

What a bloody terrible place.

He loped down the steps to the courtyard floor and tried to distract himself with the very large wagon full of goods that were apparently intended for him. It was his mother's doing, that much he knew. His father would have let him sit on the floor for a decade before he would have stirred himself to send along a stool.

Nicholas had to smile at that. He had learned to rely on himself from his sire and how to accept aid from his mother. It had been a very good combination.

And aid was what he would gladly accept now. Chairs, blankets, bedding, a bed, fabric, and sacks of things he would have to investigate at a later time were all unloaded and carried inside. He found makings for supper and took those himself back to the kitchen. He did his best to hide behind the large sack he carried. It was safer that way. He was quite certain that if he'd had to watch Miles and Jennifer together, blood would have been spilt.

He assumed someone would come to help him, but he apparently assumed incorrectly. He sorted through the things his mother had sent along, yet still no one came to his aid. Finally, when his disgust exceeded his patience, he cursed and walked through the passageway that linked the kitchens to the hall itself. He peered around the corner.

He was unsurprised to find that Jennifer had been placed in the most comfortable chair nearest the fire and that his brothers were seated in a little half circle in front of her, hanging on her every word. Even the men his father had sent along as Miles's escorts were standing nearby — and Nicholas would have wagered Beauvois that it wasn't because they were cold and wanted to make use of the fire.

He grunted and turned back to the kitchen. Perhaps Jennifer would notice him when he brought her something to eat — though he was certain that he would not care if she did. He busied himself instead by finding a keg of ale and jamming a spigot into it. It was somewhat satisfying, that pounding, but he would have been the first to admit he almost crushed the lid.

Truly, this had to end. At this point, he wasn't sure he cared how it would end. He just wanted it to be over, he wanted her to go so he could get down to the business of wallowing fully in his miserable future.

He looked up suddenly when he sensed that someone had come into the kitchens. He supposed it was Montgomery come to offer aid. He was wrong.

It was Jennifer.

He caught his breath before he could help himself. By the saints, what *was* it about her that was so fascinating? That she was lovely? That she was intelligent? Unafraid of hard work? That she looked more beautiful in his brother's clothes than any woman had a right to?

He scrambled for something to say. Finding nothing, he latched onto the first thing he could think of.

"I've no idea what to do with the weeds the boys gathered," he said curtly.

She blinked, then smiled faintly. "I'll make a salad."

"A what?"

"A bowl of greens to eat. It's good for you."

He wasn't so sure, but he didn't stop her as she sorted through the weeds, then put them into a bowl. That said, he had no intention of eating them when there was real food in the hall. He laid out dried fruits, cheese, bread, and meat on the work table.

"I'll fetch the lads," he said, then walked away before he had to either look at her or speak to her. He couldn't stop himself, though, from glancing back casually over his shoulder to see what she was doing.

She was simply standing there at the table, looking down.

Nicholas cursed himself. He was a hard-hearted whoreson and deserved whatever unhappiness came his way. 'Twas obvious even to his jaundiced eye that she suffered. He should have been offering her his aid. Instead, all he could manage to offer her was nothing at all. By the saints, he couldn't keep a decent woman when she was plunked down into his castle —

He stopped short. Was that the case? Had she been sent back for him?

"Supper?" Montgomery said, skidding to a halt in front of him. "I can smell it from here!"

"Smell what?" Nicholas demanded, then staggered as all three of his brothers pushed past him and hurried into the kitchens. "Don't eat it all!" he bellowed after them. It was a good thing he hadn't laid out every-thing. It would have been gone within moments.

He turned and looked back into the kitchens. The lads were storming the tables, forcing Jennifer to step back to avoid being trampled. She watched them with a half smile, standing there with her arms wrapped around herself. Nicholas shook his head. Had he been in her place, he would have been urging his brothers out of the way with his foot against their backsides, not waiting patiently for them to remember their manners. Yet there Jennifer simply stood, smiling a bit wistfully.

Or perhaps it was a bit sadly. Nicholas winced. She looked very alone, in spite of the confusion going on around her. No doubt she was missing her kin and worrying if she would see them again.

He pursed his lips. His mother would have had something to say to him about his disagreeable behavior where Jennifer was concerned. He put his shoulders back, turned, and walked back into the kitchens. He could be polite. He would be kind yet aloof. He could keep his heart uninvolved.

Or so he hoped.

He lifted Montgomery off the only stool, then looked at Jennifer and gestured. "Sit," he said. He paused. "If you please."

Jennifer looked at him in surprise, but she sat.

Nicholas cursed silently. Was she so astonished that he could actually be pleasant?

He slapped his brothers' hands away until he'd given Jennifer the best of everything there. He even fetched a cup and poured her ale. Only then did he see to his own meal.

He ate and drank, but tasted none of it. He couldn't take his eyes off her, that glorious McKinnon wench, who was bewitching him as easily as she had his brothers.

Her laugh was like water tumbling over smooth stones, her face like a perfect flower in spring sunshine, her eyes as warm as an intimate blaze on a chilly night. Nicholas watched her smile at his brothers, tease them, be interested in their conversation, compliment their chivalry. She was arrestingly beautiful and terribly charming. Even with her hair falling off the top of her head, her clothes less than clean, and her hands showing the extent of her toil, she was simply spectacular.

The lads basked in her approval. They only half concentrated on their food, no doubt fearing to miss yet another smile or gesture that might make them preen even more.

Nicholas wanted to slap them all smartly on the back of their heads to dislodge a bit of sense.

He suspected they might think him mad if he did the same thing to himself.

When everyone had eaten, Nicholas bid Montgomery inquire after the state of the men Miles had brought with him. Petter and his lads were self-sufficient; Nicholas assumed his father's lads were the same. John went with Montgomery, but Miles was not so easily gotten rid of. He sat on the edge of the table and smiled at Jennifer.

"At least Nicholas had provided you with a bed," Miles said. "I wonder that he hasn't seen you provided with something more comfortable to wear than Montgomery's clothes."

Nicholas started to open his mouth, but Jennifer answered first.

"He didn't need to," she said easily with half a smile. "I was very grateful for the loan of Montgomery's things."

Nicholas looked at her in surprise. He wasn't sure that even his mother would have been so patient. He was positive his sister Amanda would have at least demanded another pair of hose by this point.

"You are too accepting," Miles said, tossing Nicholas a brief frown. He turned back to her and smiled. "I will see something else found for you, if Nicholas will not."

"Oh, don't trouble yourself," Jennifer protested. "I probably won't be here much longer."

Nicholas didn't mean to clench his jaw. Somehow he just couldn't help himself. He'd known it all along, of course, but he'd grown accustomed to ignoring her each day. What would he do now?

Whatever Miles and Jennifer conversed about after that he couldn't have said. He busied himself storing the food that his mother had sent him, then, despite his earlier vow to be solicitous, ignored Jennifer a final time and walked from the kitchen before he had to listen to anything else or see Miles fawning over a woman who couldn't possibly be interested in him. At least *he* had a pair of keeps to his name. All Miles had to offer a wench was his surly disposition.

He strode out of the great hall and saw to the putting away of the wagon and the stabling of the cart horses. That didn't take nearly as long as he would have liked, even though he was particularly careful about it. When he had finished with his father's horses, he tended his own again and more thoroughly than he normally did.

Finally, he rested his hand on the stall door and blew out his breath. She would go and there was nothing he could do to stop her.

A woman from the Future.

What in the bloody hell would he have done with her anyway?

He turned to leave the stables only to find Miles standing at the entrance, looking at him gravely. Nicholas suspected he had jumped half a foot, but he tried to cover that with an itch or two that he had to reach over his back to address.

Miles was apparently not fooled.

"She's lovely," he said.

Nicholas grunted and looked about himself for something else to do. Unfortunately, it was all done and to perfection, else he might have had a task to repeat and thereby ignore his brother a bit longer.

"By the way, you're missing your front gates," Miles added.

Nicholas looked at him crossly. "Did you come all this way just to remind me of that?"

"I was just being helpful."

"Go be helpful elsewhere."

"Perhaps inside," Miles said thoughtfully. "I could procure another pair of shoes for Jennifer. Hers are a bit odd, don't you think?"

"I hadn't noticed."

"I can understand that," Miles agreed. "She is so fetching that her shoes are the last thing a man in his right mind would pay heed to. Do you know she is a musician?"

Nicholas looked at his brother in surprise. "How in the bloody hell did you find that out so quickly?"

"She has beautiful hands. I wondered." Miles looked at him with wide eyes. "Surely you took the time to ask her a question or two. Nay, it isn't possible that you've been *ignoring* such a creature."

"I've been busy," Nicholas said through gritted teeth.

"I find I always have time for a beautiful woman."

"I'm quite certain you do. I daresay, though, that this woman is not the one for you."

"Do you think not?" Miles asked, furrowing his brow in an exaggerated fashion. "Why not?"

"Because you want to crusade. You said so."

"I have thought about it," Miles admitted.

"Perhaps you should think about it more now, lest you find yourself falling in love with a woman who would not have you."

"Why wouldn't she have me?"

"She has two eyes and a decent collection of wits," Nicholas growled as he pushed away from the stall door and past his brother.

He was half surprised Miles didn't demand some sort of satisfaction for that nasty comment. That he didn't led Nicholas to believe that he was contemplating Jennifer far more intensely than he should have been.

"Nick."

Nicholas stopped on the steps leading up to his hall and turned to look at his brother. "Aye?" he said wearily.

"She's of Jake's . . . sort. Isn't she?"

Nicholas considered denying it, but decided that there was no point. Miles knew Jake better than he did. It followed that Miles knew quite a bit more about Jake's origins than he did. He nodded. "Aye, I suspect so."

"What will you do?"

Nicholas snorted out a laugh that contained no humor at all. "Do? What in the bloody hell is there *to* do? She will return home to her life and count this a pleasant adventure, nothing more."

Miles looked at him searchingly. "I think you fancy her."

"For all the good it does me," Nicholas said darkly.

Miles smiled. "Perhaps if you were pleasant to her, she might not want to go."

"Obviously, you have spent too much time with Grandmère and have begun to think that romance alone will win the day. In reality, brother, that simply isn't so."

"Hmmm," Miles said thoughtfully. "I think I see."

"I imagine you don't," Nicholas said. He nodded toward the hall. "Find a comfortable place on the floor inside and seek your rest before speculation unbalances your delicate humors."

"Nick, if you asked her to stay —"

"Go," Nicholas commanded. "And leave me to my own business."

Miles hesitated, then sighed and walked past him up the steps and into the hall.

Nicholas remained outside and considered.

Would she stay if he asked?

He almost couldn't bear the thought of it.

He supposed he could refuse to aid her. It was an unpleasant thought for it went strongly against what he'd practiced from the time he'd first thought chivalry an ideal worth pursuing. To not aid a woman when she needed it? He wondered if he might be able to manage such a refusal.

But the thought of her remaining was so compelling, so irresistible . . .

'Twas too tempting by half.

He walked into the hall. Fortunately, Jennifer had apparently already gone to bed. At least he wouldn't have to look at her again that night.

Or, rather, he wouldn't have the pleasure of looking at her again that night. He rolled his eyes. Obviously, he had been too long without a decent meal. He wished that Robin was there, for then at least he could have worked out his frustrations in the lists.

That he was longing for such torments from his brother said much about his state of mind.

The saints pity him.

Nay, she would return to her time, and he would let her. That bloody abbey . . . it had all started with Ledenham accusing Jake Kilchurn, which led again back to the Future. A place he was learning to loathe with a passion.

Aye, she would go and there wasn't a damned thing he could do about it. After all, it wasn't as if he could refuse to aid her.

He paused.

Could he?

He turned away from that thought before it

became far more appealing than it should have.

CHAPTER 9

Jennifer stood at the doorway of the steward's bedroom and looked at it one last time. It had been a pretty decent place as far as medieval accommodations went. Not quite as fancy as the hotel in Elizabethan England she'd stayed at with Connor and Victoria while they'd been rescuing her grandmother, but she wasn't going to complain. The room had been very nice, she was very grateful, and now she was very ready to get home. With any luck, she would be back at Artane before sunset and then she could have a shower, a Kit Kat, and go to bed on a mattress that didn't crunch when she rolled over.

She left Montgomery's clothes folded on the trunk, then turned and walked into the great hall. She felt better already, being back in her jeans, with her cell phone in one pocket and her keys in the other. Even her credit cards were a comforting thing in her back pocket. *Modern life, here I come.*

Now, all she had to do was hitch a ride back

to the abbey.

She walked into the kitchen. Nicholas was sitting there on a stool near the fire, looking like Cinderella at her most bummed. He didn't acknowledge that he'd heard her come in, so she simply stood there at the end of the table and allowed herself the luxury of a last look.

She almost wished she hadn't.

Why did the man have to be so handsome? Why did he have to keep showing her little bits of something very chivalrous underneath all those grumbles? Why couldn't she just go sit down next to him, take his hand, and talk about nothing like normal people did?

He looked up suddenly from his contemplation of the porridge kettle. When he saw her clothes, all expression disappeared from his face.

"Are you off, then?" he asked.

She nodded. "Yes. I need to get back to the abbey."

"Do you have kin meeting you there?"

"It's entirely possible," she said.

He said nothing. In fact, he wasn't even moving. He just sat there, staring at her silently. Jennifer sighed. Obviously, chivalry was back on hiatus.

"Would you help me get there?" she asked.

He hesitated, then turned to look back at the fire. He was silent for quite a while and seemed to be struggling with something.

Finally, he spoke.

"Nay."

She felt her mouth fall open. "What?"

He shot her a look that just about singed her where she stood. She wasn't sure if it was anger, irritation, or possessiveness. It had come and gone too fast for her to decide what it had been, though it made her wish desperately for a stool.

"Nay," he said hoarsely. "I will not help you."

Jennifer wasn't sure if she felt flattered or foolish. Did he want her to stay or did he want her to go?

Did it matter?

She let out a shaky breath. "All right. Well, thanks for all your help."

He didn't answer.

She turned around and walked unsteadily from the kitchen. Maybe she could get directions from Miles. After all, how far could it be? Even if it took her eight hours, she would be to the abbey well before dark. She could drink from streams and eat quite nicely things Patrick MacLeod would have enjoyed.

Besides, what did it matter what she ate when she'd be at Artane by nightfall?

She walked through the great hall, out the front door, and down the steps. Montgomery, John, and Miles were talking to Petter. Jennifer walked across to them. Montgomery stared at her in surprise.

"Your clothes," he said faintly. "You've changed."

"I'm going home," she said with a cheerfulness she didn't feel. She turned to Miles. "You said the abbey was a little north and a lot east. Is that right?"

"Aye, but isn't Nick taking you?" Miles asked, looking even more surprised than Montgomery.

"No," she said simply. "He's busy."

Miles's expression darkened. "Did he say you nay?"

"It's okay," Jennifer said. "He's got things to do."

"Then I'll take you."

"Nay, you will not," a deep voice said from behind her. "You will not, and neither will Montgomery nor John."

Jennifer was unsurprised. She only would have been surprised if Nicholas had allowed his brothers to help her. Epitome of chivalry? Yes, occasionally, but would she have several things to say about the rest of his history when she arrived back at Artane that night. She smiled at Miles.

"I'll be fine," she said.

Miles put his hand on his sword, but Jennifer quickly shook her head.

"Really. I like to walk."

And before Nicholas could say anything to stop her, she gave his brothers quick hugs, then walked away. She didn't dare look back.

Then again, maybe it wouldn't have mattered if she had looked because her eyes were so full of tears, she couldn't have seen anything anyway.

She did manage a glance at the nonexistent gate as she walked through it and wondered if Nicholas would be so grumpy over the course of his lifetime that he just wouldn't have the wherewithal to put a gate in, or if his descendants were so irritated with his grumpiness that they wouldn't bother.

Maybe a little light reading in the Artane library was called for after all.

"Be warned," Nicholas called after her, " 'tis a goodly distance — oof!"

Jennifer dragged her sleeve across her eyes, then looked behind her to see Nicholas not twenty feet away, in the midst of being tackled by John and Montgomery.

"Go with her Miles!" Montgomery shouted.

Nicholas managed to shake off his younger brothers and grab Miles before Miles could get through the gates. Miles slugged him in the stomach. Nicholas doubled over, but straightened and treated Miles to the same pleasure, though not with nearly as much enthusiasm as his younger brother had used.

The burden of being the elder, apparently.

Jennifer was tempted to stay and watch the brawl, but after Miles, John, and Montgomery piled on top of Nicholas, she suspected it wouldn't be very interesting for very long. She waved, then turned and walked off. She would miss them.

She walked quickly. It made her feel purposeful. It also might have the added bonus of keeping her from getting eaten by a wild animal, though she didn't think there were all that many wild animals around — with the exception of Lord Ledenham.

She walked until the sounds of battle faded and all she could hear was the sound of her own footfalls. It was very easy to believe that she was just out for a stroll in the woods on a very quiet day. Why couldn't that day be in modern England? She could imagine it so —

Until she heard the crunching of a branch a fair distance behind her.

She spun around. Nicholas was thirty feet behind her. His hair was mussed and his clothes askew. He hunched over with his hands on his thighs, apparently trying to catch his breath.

"What do you want?" she asked shortly.

He heaved himself upright. "You must go east," he said, panting lightly. "Then bear north after several leagues."

"I appreciate that."

And with that, she turned and continued on her way down the road. She looked down at her shoes. Such normal, modern-looking shoes. She could have been going anywhere in those shoes: hiking in the English countryside or preparing to return to her car and enjoy that Kit Kat and Lilt she'd left in the front seat. Was it possible that her car was still there, or had Megan come and gotten it? Megan would find that hard, considering Jennifer had the keys in her pocket.

She slowed to a stop, feeling as if she wasn't alone. She looked over her shoulder.

Nicholas was still following thirty feet behind her.

All right, this was starting to get a little ridiculous. She turned around and put her hands on her hips.

"What are you doing?"

"Following you."

"You could help me, you know, instead of just trailing along after me."

"I don't want to help you," he said, through gritted teeth.

"Why not?"

"I just don't."

"Then get lost."

He tilted his head. "I beg your pardon?"

"Unless you're going to walk with me the entire way, why don't you just go back home and leave me alone?"

He folded his arms over his chest and glared at her. "It goes against my grain to leave a lady unaided."

"Then help me!"

He hesitated, then shook his head. "I cannot."

She threw up her hands in frustration. "I

don't understand you!"

He only glared at her and said nothing.

"Jerk," Jennifer muttered under her breath as she turned and walked away.

"How was that?" he called.

"Jerk!" she bellowed over her shoulder, then stomped off.

Half an hour later, she looked behind her, but there was no sign of him.

It was just as well. It was obvious to her now that Artane genealogists had been completely wrong about him. Paragon of chivalry? Ha! She set her face forward and stomped off enthusiastically.

She stomped for quite some time. In time, though, she found that stomping was too much of an effort, so she settled for walking. She wasn't a slow walker, but it was late afternoon when she finally found her way to the abbey — and she supposed she was lucky to have managed it. East and then a little north was not exactly an accurate set of directions. It was nothing but dumb luck that she wound up at the right place.

But that was okay. All she had to do was get there, stop on the X that marked the spot, then she would be back in the future where she belonged.

It was for damn sure she didn't belong in the past.

She walked right into the abbey construction site, then came to a screeching halt.

The abbey was there.

But the gate wasn't.

Jennifer could hardly believe her eyes. The patch of ground where she had come through was completely dug up. She felt a little queasy as she wandered over to the enormous pit that had once been her time gate. She stared down at it in horror.

Just what in the hell was she supposed to do now?

She wasn't one to panic, but she found herself very near to it. She took several deep breaths and tried to think rationally. The exact patch of dirt was gone, but who was to say that the gate wasn't part of some cosmic well that would extend down several hundred feet?

Before she could second guess herself, she jumped.

She realized, as she landed, that she had only gone down about six feet. Maybe Ledenham hadn't finished digging yet. She climbed over a very uneven floor and went to stand on the spot where she'd found the gate before. At least she thought it was the right spot. Too bad it didn't feel like anything but dirt.

She tried several more spots, but with the same result each time.

She stood in that pit for a very, very long time, hoping against hope that something would change, that she would feel that tingle in the air, that a magic red X would appear on the appropriate spot.

She realized, after even more time, that someone was watching her. She looked up, half expecting to see Nicholas.

It was Ledenham.

"Ah," he purred, "the witch has returned. What rituals will she perform this time?"

She decided immediately that it had been better when she hadn't been able to understand him.

"None," she said shortly. "Why don't you go away?"

He looked at her in astonishment. "You didn't speak my tongue before."

"I was torturing you," she said briefly.

He smiled coldly. "Perhaps I should return the favor. Shall I light a fire in that pit there, or shall you come back out and we'll see to it here?"

That wasn't much of a choice. Well, at least if she was out of the pit she could perhaps try another spot and maybe find her way home again. She held up her hands.

He pulled her up. She almost thanked him, but before she really found her feet, he had wrenched her arm behind her back and jerked one of her fingers out of joint.

The pain was so intense, she couldn't even gasp. All she could do was stand there, her mouth hanging open, and try to stay conscious.

Ledenham urged her forward. She went, only because each time she hesitated, he wrenched her finger again to inspire her.

The only plus was that her dislocated finger was on her bow hand. When she was back home, that would be a good thing. A little physical therapy and she would be good as new.

Ledenham handed her over to his goons, then went off to do his usual bit with wood. Jennifer stood there with one man holding her by the arm and another holding her by her dislocated finger. She could do no more than try to hold on to reality.

She didn't think she was doing a very good job.

Maybe she was in shock. Pain did that to a person, didn't it? She would have given that more thought, but Ledenham began to swear and that distracted her. She looked up.

Nicholas had ridden into the clearing.

"Oh, great," she managed, "*now* the calvary has arrived."

Her captors immediately dropped her arms and scurried away. Ledenham, as usual, was not as wise. He ran at Nicholas with his blazing piece of wood. Nicholas kicked it out of Ledenham's hand.

Ledenham produced a crossbow and shot a bolt at Nicholas. It stuck in his upper arm. Jennifer winced as Nicholas jerked it free, threw it across the glade, then leaned over and backhanded Ledenham across the face. Ledenham stumbled, hopped around, then fell backward into the pit of his own making.

Jennifer wondered if he'd broken his neck. She didn't wonder long, though, because curses soon floated up from the hole. She looked blearily at Nicholas and saw that he was riding toward her with his hand outstretched. Oh sure, *now* he was going to ply some of that infamous chivalry on her —

She shrieked as he grabbed her by the hand and pulled her up in front of him on his horse.

"What —" he began, then he held up her hand. He swore. "Hold on," he said, as he kicked his horse into a gallop.

"Do I have a choice?" she gasped.

"Do you want a choice?"

"Not really," she wheezed in a voice that sounded a little unhinged even to her ears.

Nicholas only tightened his arms around her. Jennifer concentrated on staying conscious. It was, she had to admit, a most unpleasant trip. She wanted to enjoy the ride, but her hand felt like someone had smashed it with a sledgehammer and it was starting to rain again. Oh, and she was apparently stuck in medieval England.

With a man who really didn't seem to like her very much.

It seemed only a short time later that they were thundering into the courtyard. Nicholas stopped his horse in front of the stables, then swung down and held up his hands for her. Jennifer made the mistake of putting her hands on his shoulders so he could help her down, but since she was halfway to the ground before the pain went from her finger to her brain, she continued on her way.

She only realized she'd fainted after she'd come to and found herself in Nicholas's arms, being carried into the great hall.

"Tend my horse," he threw at Miles, who had come to open the door.

"What befell her?"

"Something you can cross swords with me for in the morning," Nicholas said shortly.

"Brother, you are a horse's —"

"My horse!" Nicholas bellowed. "Montgomery, fetch me wine. John, go stoke the fire."

Jennifer heard their questions, heard their exclamations of dismay, but she couldn't respond. She also couldn't bring herself to think about what sort of methods of healing were popular in medieval Wyckham.

In fact, considering that she was stuck, unwanted, and now unwell, she decided it was best to just not think at all.

She closed her eyes and didn't think about the tears that seemed determined to ooze from underneath her eyelids. The gate was destroyed. Gone. Unrecoverable. She would never get back home, never see her family again, never touch another violin.

She suspected it might qualify for the worst-day-of-her-life award.

Nicholas set her down carefully in the comfortable chair with the cushion, but she just didn't care. She buried her face in her good hand and wept.

She cried for a very long time.

There came a point when she found that her finger hurt too badly to allow her the luxury of any more tears. She realized at the same point that a hand was gently stroking her hair. She lifted her head up and found that Nicholas was sitting on a stool he had set down right in front of her. He was watching her with a very grave expression.

He was also the one stroking her hair.

"I should have accompanied you," he said quietly.

She dragged her sleeve across her face and had a better look at him. "Why didn't you?"

"Because he is a horse's arse," Miles offered.

Jennifer would have smiled at Miles but she caught the look Nicholas gave him. Miles held up his hands in surrender and backed away.

"I'll check on the horses. Again."

"You do that," Nicholas said curtly. Then he turned back to look at her. "Perhaps I'll tell you later, but not now." He paused, and there was pity in his eyes. "Your kin were not there."

"No."

He nodded slowly. "I see." He hesitated, then reached for her hand and took it in both his own. "I'm sorry for this."

"It wasn't your fault," she croaked. She looked down at her hand, then squeezed her eyes shut. There was something very unwholesome about staring at a finger that wasn't bending the right way.

"Will you let me tend it?"

She opened her eyes to look at him. "Can you?"

"Aye."

"Is it broken?"

"I daresay not. Pulled out of joint more likely. I've seen worse. On myself, actually. It won't be pleasant to put it back into place."

"You know, that's more than you've said to me the entire time I've been here."

He pursed his lips. "Aye, well, as my brother will tell you, I am a horse's arse."

She almost smiled. It figured that the very moment when she would have killed for something strong to drink and her hand hurt so badly she wanted to cut it off, Nicholas de Piaget would be charming.

It just wasn't fair. There she was, stuck hundreds of years out of her own century, just itching for another round of bitter weeping and desperate for some painkillers, and all she had to look at was a man who was so damned beautiful, she could hardly catch her breath.

"You know," she said, "you have very beautiful eyes."

He blinked. "What?"

"They're gray."

He almost smiled. She was almost sure of it.

"Aye, I suppose so," he agreed.

"I think I might be delirious," she said, putting her good hand to her head.

"Think you?" he asked. "Pain will do that to a person, I suppose. And I fear that the pain won't cease until I —"

She shrieked, then found that her finger suddenly felt much better.

"Oh," she said, looking down at her hand. "That's better."

"Aye, I imagine it is. Don't move it overmuch yet." He looked around him. "Damnation, but is there nothing in this hall that might be used for a bandage?" He turned back to her. "Stay here."

"We'll watch over her," Montgomery offered.

It was only then that she realized that Montgomery and John were standing on either side of her chair, looking rather protective. She was grateful for it. She smiled weakly.

"I'm not having a good day," she offered.

"Nay," Montgomery agreed. "I daresay not."

"We tried to go with you," John said grimly. "We almost had Nick overpowered, you know, but he is older than we are and a man fully fashioned. And he has spent the better part of his life training with our eldest brother, Robin, who is the best swordsman in England save our sire."

"Nick never bests Robin," Montgomery said reverently.

"I never best Robin," Nicholas said, resuming his place on his stool, "because his ego would never survive it."

"Think you that you could?" Montgomery asked in surprise.

"I'll attempt it when next we meet if you both will go attend Miles in the stables and leave me in peace."

Montgomery and John left without hesitation.

"Now, I'll bind your hand, lady —"

"My name is Jennifer."

He went still, then nodded briefly and started to tear cloth into strips. "Aye."

"But you knew that already."

He paused, then nodded. "Aye."

She continued to watch him work. "My sisters call me Jenner," she said. "My grandmother, whom I love, calls me Jen, but only when she's feeling particularly affectionate."

He laid the strips over his knee, taking quite

a bit of time at it. He paused, but did not look up at her. "And what am I to call you?" he asked, finally.

She pretended to consider for quite some time. "You may call me Mistress McKinnon."

He looked up in surprise. She could have sworn he almost smiled.

Then he bent his head again and fussed with strips of cloth that looked perfectly arranged to her. "Indeed. Well, Mistress McKinnon, let me have your hand so I might bind it for you."

She gave him her hand and tried not to tremble as he took it.

It wasn't from pain.

Not at all.

It was from utter madness, she decided quickly. Nicholas de Piaget was a medieval knight from a noble family and she imagined that even his flings were girls with titles and medieval kinds of trappings. And what was she thinking, to even contemplate the condition of his flings? She didn't fling. She *certainly* didn't fling with a guy who was 800 years older than she was.

Besides, she didn't want to stay in medieval England. She had a life to get back to.

Somehow.

"My lord," she began.

He looked up at her very briefly. "Nicholas."

"My lord Nicholas —"

"Nay, just Nicholas." He paused. "My brothers call me Nick." He continued to wrap cloth around her hand. "My grandmother calls me Nicky, but then so do my sisters and my mother, on occasion when they're feeling particularly affectionate."

"And what," she managed in an alarmingly garbled tone, "am I to call you?"

He did look up at her then. "You choose. Pray, do not make it worse than any of those."

Nicholas. Nick. Nicky. Was it possible all those names, with all their colors attached, could possibly find home in the man sitting so close to her that their knees touched?

Unfortunately, she suspected they could indeed.

"Nicholas is a beautiful name," she said finally.

"Then call me that." He finished tying the cloth around her hand and carefully held it in both his own. He looked up at her. "If it pleases you."

She had the most ridiculous urge to go into his arms, put her head on his shoulder and close her eyes. Maybe she was just lost in a dream. Maybe she would wake up and find that he was just a regular guy working at the local barrister's office in the village near Artane. Maybe she would meet him in the local fish-and-chip shop, they would exchange phone numbers, and he would actually call. Maybe Gideon had a cousin who looked just

169

like him and she was destined to meet and fall in love with him at the family reunion.

All of which had to happen in the future.

She realized that tears were streaming down her face only because she couldn't see him anymore.

"You must be hungry," he said quietly, rising. "I'll fetch you something and return quickly."

"Great," she managed.

But she suspected it would take a great deal more than food to cure what ailed her.

A medieval lord who had been kind to her.

A time gate that hadn't.

She put her good hand over her face and cried.

CHAPTER 10

Nicholas fetched bread, cheese, and rather wrinkled apples from the larder, then paused by the kitchen fire. Unfortunately, he could remember in perfect detail his short, unpleasant conversation with Jennifer there that morning. He closed his eyes briefly. He should have told her that he didn't want her to go. He never should have ignored her in the first place —

Then he shook his head. Nay, there was nothing he could have done differently. He couldn't have offered to aid her when all he'd wanted to do was keep her; he couldn't have told her that he wanted her to stay when he'd known she needed to go home. It was, in all respects, an untenable situation with no good solution.

But now the situation had changed.

He left the kitchen, then paused at the edge of the great hall. Jennifer was sobbing into her sleeve, her injured hand resting on her knees. Nicholas grimaced at the sound. How terribly lost she must feel. Lost and frightened and in pain. The pain he could ease, but the fear?

Not without telling her far more than he wanted to about things he shouldn't have known.

He stepped out into the hall and stumbled, almost dropping his burdens. He cursed silently. His arm was beginning to ache abominably. He would have to see to the arrow wound sooner or later, which he wouldn't enjoy. He would also have to see Ledenham sooner or later, which he would enjoy very much.

That thought kept him warm as he crossed over to the fire.

He sat down on the stool in front of Jennifer. She dragged her sleeve across her eyes and looked at him. Nicholas winced. He should have aided her; he could have spared her much of what she suffered.

Though he suspected that he couldn't have spared her all. He had wit enough to have seen that her gate had been dug up. Did that mean it was ruined? He supposed it could mean nothing else.

"Do I look that bad?"

He studied her and hesitated. Her eyes were puffy, her nose red, and she looked more miserable than any woman should have the misfortune to.

"Well," he said, casting about for something

polite to say, "you've had a rather trying day."

"Thank you for that. I think." She sat back in the chair. "I'd have to agree."

He nodded silently. He could only imagine how terrible that must be, to have home and hearth unreachable.

Unfortunately, there was nothing to be done about it that night. What she needed was sleep and food, and not in that order. He held up his findings.

"Can you eat?"

She shook her head. "I don't think so."

"Have you eaten today?" he asked. "Something besides those bitter greens you've been foisting off on me?"

"No," she said and her eyes teared madly, "but I'm not hungry."

"I'm hungry," Montgomery offered suddenly.

Nicholas realized that his youngest brother was standing behind Jennifer's chair. He was looking just the slightest bit fierce, as if he wanted to protect Jennifer, but wasn't sure he dared.

Nicholas rose and handed him cheese, bread, and fruit. "Go find Miles and John and *share*. I will care for Mistress McKinnon well in your absence."

Montgomery hesitated.

"Go," Nicholas commanded, pointing toward the door.

Montgomery went. Nicholas sat down,

poured Jennifer more wine, then forced the cup on her. He made sure she had at least drunk a few sips before he turned his attention to his bloody sleeve. Damn that Ledenham —

"Are you going to do something about that?" Jennifer asked uneasily.

"Eventually," he said grimly. He should have gone with her. He could have saved them both a great deal of aggravation. If he had, perhaps her gate through the centuries would have worked and she would have been safely home, not sitting in his drafty hall, drinking from a cup he'd borrowed from his mother.

Pitiful.

"When?"

He looked up. "When, what?"

"When are you going to fix that?"

He blinked. "Oh, my arm. Well, I'll need to soon." He paused, then looked at her. "Can you sew?"

"Quite well, actually," she said. "Why?"

"Wait for me." He made his way to his solar, dug through his personal gear and came up with a wallet of needles. One never knew when some sort of sewing might be required. He liked it better when that sewing was limited to his saddle.

He returned to the hall, resumed his place on the stool, and handed the leather wallet to Jennifer. She looked at him in shock.

"You want me to sew *you?*" she asked incredulously.

"Someone must," he said easily. " 'Tis either you or one of my brothers and believe me when I tell you that they do not sew well."

She blanched, but unfolded the leather containing his needles just the same. Her hands were shaking. Nicholas spared a brief moment to wonder just how it was they took care of wounds in her day, then let the thought continue on. She was, for better or worse, now in his day and she was limited to what he could provide. He poured her more wine.

"Drink that," he said. "You'll feel better."

"I imagine not," she said politely. But she drank the entire cup in one long pull just the same, then dragged her sleeve across her mouth. She handed the cup back to him. "Thank you," she said with a gasp. "Better."

"In truth?"

"No," she admitted unsteadily. "I'm trying to give you a feeling of confidence in me."

"I trust you."

"See what you say after I'm finished."

He smiled, then set her cup down. He stood up and took the knife out of his belt, unbuckled his sword belt, then set all his gear down on the floor next to him. He stripped off his tunic, cursed at the pull of his arm, then sat down again. He watched impassively as she threaded the needle with what he'd brought

175

her. He was, he had to admit, somewhat relieved by the expert, unthinking way she did it. Obviously, she did indeed have experience with the art.

He watched as she leaned over and held the needle against the flame of the fire. He knew he should have been surprised, but he'd watched Jake do that a time or two and knew that she was burning off something. Germs, gems, he couldn't remember what Jake had called them. What he could remember was the inventively vile comment he'd tossed at his brother-in-law for his foolishness.

How ironic that he should be the recipient of such ministrations now.

He vowed then never to tell Jake about it. The onslaught of laughter at his expense would have been unbearable.

Jennifer wiped the needle off on a clean bit of her jeans, hesitated, then reached for the wine.

She didn't bother with the cup this time.

"Save some for me," he said dryly.

She put the bottle down and smiled. "If I must."

He was rather glad his backside was firmly placed upon a stool. He realized then that he had never been the recipient of one of her easy smiles.

No wonder his brothers were completely under her spell.

"You have more need of it than I," he managed. "At least for now."

She shook her head. "I can do this." She held up the needle. "I think."

At least the needle was the smallest and thinnest, which he appreciated. But her hands were trembling visibly. She took a deep breath.

It didn't aid her, apparently.

Nicholas reached out and took her hands in his, avoiding her injured finger. He looked at her seriously.

"I am accustomed to this," he said. "You will not pain me."

"You wouldn't have this if you hadn't come to rescue me."

"And you wouldn't have needed rescuing if I'd agreed to help you in the first place. We are at an impasse, so let us leave it behind us."

She looked down at their hands folded together. "Why didn't you help me?"

"I like your salad," he said, her term for those bitter greens feeling foreign on his tongue. He would not, even under pain of torture, give her the real reason.

"Liar."

He blinked, then realized that she was saying it gently. He smiled briefly, then released her hands. "Be about your work, Mistress McKinnon, and perhaps I'll have another salad before I retire. I'm sure it would be strengthening."

"Hmmm," she said, then she took her needle in hand. "Ready?"

"Aye."

"Do you fight often?" she asked, taking a strip of cloth and soaking it with wine to press against the wound.

"When necessary. I generally walk away unscathed."

"Do you?"

"I do," he said simply. "My father is Rhys de Piaget and he is a master swordsman."

"And you would best your brother if you didn't think it would destroy his fragile ego."

Nicholas snorted. "Meet Robin and judge for yourself. His swordplay is his life."

"And you?" she asked, looking at the wound and becoming very pale indeed. "What is your life?"

"I don't know," he said quietly. And he realized that he didn't.

But he knew what he wanted.

Why did he have to meet a woman he couldn't look away from only to find that she was hundreds of years out of his reach? If he hadn't been a more cheerful soul, he might have suspected that Fate was punishing him for some misdeed he couldn't remember.

He started to give his usual vague answer about repairing his castle and filling his coffers, but Jennifer had set to work on his arm and he found that speech was impossible.

She wasn't a poor needlewoman. She was

actually quite a bit better than anyone else he'd had sew his poor flesh together. She was a damned sight better than Robin and vastly superior to Miles.

Still, sweat broke out on his forehead.

He couldn't believe it was from pain, for the pain was nothing.

He realized Jennifer was looking at him. He grimaced.

"I am well."

"You don't look well."

"I am well," he repeated.

"I'm almost done. Then you take the chair and I'll go get you something to eat."

He didn't argue. He closed his eyes as she leaned forward and bit off the last bit of thread. He bowed his head and blew out his breath as he listened to her pack up his gear and pour wine.

"Nicholas."

He lifted his head and looked at her. She was a bit blurry, but he supposed that was to be expected. He took the wine, downed it, and almost fell off his stool.

He felt her hands on his bare shoulders. If the rest of the evening's events hadn't finished him, that certainly did. He put his hand over hers briefly, then rose. He wasn't happy with the sudden weakness that struck him, but he couldn't seem to do anything about it. He didn't protest when she put her hands on his waist and guided him into the good chair. He

179

sat, closed his eyes, and leaned his head back against it.

"Thank you," he said hoarsely.

"You look dreadful."

"Thank you for that, as well."

"Montgomery, watch him," she said, sounding particularly concerned. "I'm going to find him something to eat."

"I'll come help," Miles offered. "You might need a man's strength of arm in your labors."

Nicholas realized then that he hadn't noticed his brothers. How long had they been there? At least they'd had the good sense to be silent. He concentrated on breathing for several minutes, then finally forced his eyes open so he could look down at his arm. The stitching was done quite well, actually. It burned like hellfire still, but he knew that would pass. He leaned his head back against the chair again and closed his eyes. Perhaps a small rest wasn't out of the question.

"Nicholas."

He woke to find Jennifer leaning over him. He nodded and straightened. "I feel better."

She sat down on the stool in front of him and held a wooden trencher on her knees. It was full of things that should have looked good, but didn't.

"You should eat."

He focused on her with an effort. And once he looked at her, he found that he could do nothing else. By the saints, she was lovely.

Firelight had surely been created to caress her porcelain skin and deep red hair. Nicholas thought he might have smiled in pleasure at the sight. Or he might have slept.

That he wasn't certain was very unsettling.

He opened his eyes to find Jennifer looking behind him with an expression of concern. Nicholas frowned and glanced behind him, too. Miles was standing there. He wasn't doing his damndest to woo Jennifer, which was disconcerting somehow. Nicholas drew his hand over his eyes.

"Are you unwell?" he asked Miles.

"I'm not, but I think you are," Miles said gravely. "How do you feel?"

"Fine." Nicholas turned back to Jennifer. "I am well."

"Eat something, then."

"Didn't I already eat?"

"No, you didn't," she said, shooting Miles a look of concern. "Here, try the bread to start with."

Nicholas did, but it tasted gritty and stale. He tried dried fruit, but it was too much effort. He settled for a cup of wine.

He wondered, briefly, if any of it would come back to haunt him.

"To bed, I think," he announced.

Then he frowned. Were his words slurring?

He rose, drawing his hand over his eyes. "I think I need air."

Jennifer set the trencher down behind her

and leaped to her feet. She put her hands on his arms.

"You look terrible."

"You keep saying that," he slurred. Aye, those were his words and they did sound quite garbled.

He felt hot and very, very ill.

"Please let me help you," she said, from very far away.

Nicholas shook his head, but that made the hall spin violently so he stopped.

But, by then it was too late.

He felt himself falling and couldn't stop it.

CHAPTER 11

Jennifer tried to catch Nicholas as he fell, but it was impossible. He was too heavy and he had fallen too fast. She knelt down next to him and started to roll him over on his back, but she stopped in surprise. She looked at Miles who was kneeling on the other side of him.

"Feel him," she said.

Miles put his hand on his brother's back, then whistled softly. "He's burning with fever."

"What is it?"

"Poison," Miles said succinctly.

"You can't mean that," she said in disbelief.

Miles bent over and looked closely at the wound on his arm. Jennifer looked at it as well. It didn't look any worse than she supposed any other medieval arrow wound would look, especially given that Nicholas had ripped it out of his flesh with no particular care. It was a smallish wound, no more than an inch wide, but it had been deep. She would be the first to admit that a proper suture needle would have been a better tool, but she'd done the best with what she'd had.

"Poison?" she repeated. "Why do you think so?"

"Because it was Ledenham," Miles said simply, "and because my brother didn't complain. Had it been merely a bout of foul humors, he would have felt it coming on long before this and likely wailed like a babe over it."

She frowned at him. "Are you joking?"

Miles smiled. "I might be."

"How can you joke at a time like this?"

"Because he is senseless and will remember nothing of it," Miles said. "If I cannot jest at his expense now, then when?"

"Miles!"

He waved his hand dismissively. "I am trying to ease your mind, of course. Nay, this is poison and it isn't beyond Ledenham to do such a thing."

"But what kind of monster poisons an arrow?"

"One with a particular grudge against my family," Miles said. "I'll tell you of it later, but first we must put him to bed. He'll catch his death out here in the hall." He paused. "Montgomery says you know much about herbs."

Jennifer swallowed with difficulty. "I know a little." She paused. "You know, it's one

184

thing to make up a good salad or soup; it's another thing entirely to heal someone."

"But you can," he said. "Can't you?"

Jennifer thought back to the hours she'd passed with Patrick MacLeod and all his lessons on all the properties of herbs she might find useful in another century. She'd learned it all because it had felt good to be outside in the fresh air and because his enthusiasm for weeds was infectious. She'd never dreamed that the knowledge might be the difference between life and death.

She looked at Miles. "Do I have a choice?"

"I could ride for the abbey at Seakirk," he said slowly. "They have healers there." He paused. "Of a sort."

"What would they do?"

"Bleed him, no doubt, to balance the humors in his form." Miles paused. "I've never thought that a wise idea."

Bleeding? She wasn't an expert, but she'd seen her share of movies set in medieval times. Even in Hollywood, bleeding was a pretty gruesome practice. She had no faith at all in its efficacy. She shook her head. "No. No bleeding. We'll just do what we can."

Miles reached out and put his hand on her shoulder. "I trust you. Now, do you have what you need or must you make a search?"

Jennifer thought of all the herbs she and Montgomery had already collected. She had what would serve, but she could use more and since she knew what to look for, it was best that she do the searching. She looked up at Montgomery who was standing behind Miles.

"Get a torch and you and I will go. Miles, you'll take him to the steward's room?"

"Done," Miles said.

"John, can you boil water?"

"Um," John said hesitantly.

Miles rolled his eyes. "Go with Jennifer and Montgomery and I'll see to the water as well."

Jennifer took the torch Montgomery was holding and hurried across the great hall and out into the night.

Patrick had only given her one concoction to try in case of poison. Apparently the herbal remedy had been a possibility in medieval Scotland or he wouldn't have known about it. Maybe the same thing held true for medieval England.

Half an hour later, she walked back into the steward's room with handfuls of herbs and the twins at her heels. Miles had his brother stretched out on the bed, only partially dressed. Jennifer promised herself a good long look later, when she thought Nicholas might survive.

She handed the herbs to Montgomery and looked at Miles. "Hot water?"

"Aye," he said simply and left the room.

Jennifer sat down on a stool by the bed and looked at Nicholas lying there. Her stomach was in such knots, she couldn't even gawk at him as she should have. Maybe later, when he wasn't still as death and she couldn't feel the heat rolling off him like a wave. She glanced down at her bandaged hand and realized that it was aching abominably. Well, she would think about that later, too. It was just a dislocated finger, not a life-threatening wound. Not like what Nicholas was suffering.

She swallowed hard. There was something terribly unforgiving about life and death in the Middle Ages.

"Here, lady," Miles said.

Jennifer turned to him and nodded. "Sure," she said, putting her shoulders back. "We need cool water and clean cloths as well, if you can find them. We'll try to flush the poison out of him with as much of my tea as possible. If his fever goes too high, we'll try to bring it down." She took a deep breath. "That's all I know how to do." She looked at Miles.

He smiled encouragingly. "It will be enough."

She took another deep breath. "All right. Tea first."

She wished she'd had dried herbs, but she did the best she could with fresh and steeped them as long as she dared. She looked at Miles while they were waiting.

"This won't taste good. Do you think we'll be able to get it down him?"

"I'll see to it," Miles said grimly. "What about the wound?"

"I suppose we could open it and try to draw out the poison, but I think it's gone all the way through his body by now." She took a deep breath. "I know the type of herb to heal all kinds of things, but poison . . ." She shivered. "It's his life at stake."

"Shall I ride for the friar?"

She looked up at him. "Do you trust those monks?"

"With my soup? Possibly. With my life? Never."

"Do you pray, Miles?"

He smiled grimly. "Aye. But first let's see what your herbs can do. He's a strong lad and has much to live for."

"Revenge on Ledenham?"

"Among other things."

Jennifer looked at Montgomery and John, standing in a corner of the small chamber, looking grave. "Montgomery, do you have another candle? I'd like more light."

He nodded and ran from the room. John only stood there, grim-faced. Jennifer looked back at Nicholas. If he died, it would devastate his brothers. She could hardly believe she was even thinking about the possibility, but she was so far out of her depth at the moment, she wasn't quite sure what to think. All she knew was that she wouldn't manage very well in her own life either if Nicholas died, knowing that she had been partially responsible.

"This isn't your fault," Miles said quietly.

She looked up at him and blinked back tears. "Are you reading my thoughts now?"

He tapped his forehead meaningfully. "My terrifying intellect coming to the fore."

"Frightening."

He smiled deprecatingly. "Actually, I put myself in your shoes and wondered how I would feel. You must realize that it was Ledenham's choice to strike out at Nick. It was Nick's choice not to aid you initially as he should have. Your only choice was to walk out the front gates and leave us all bereft behind you."

She smiled briefly. "You're very kind."

"I always tell the truth." He leaned back against the wall. "I don't suppose you could stay, could you?"

"Stay?"

"Stay here with us."

Jennifer felt the breath be knocked out of her.

"Then again, perhaps your family is waiting for you."

"Yes," she managed. "I'm sure they are."

"Hmmm," was all he said.

She turned back to Nicholas. Stay?

Never mind that he wouldn't want her to. The simple fact was that she had a life in another time, a life she wanted to get back to. She couldn't stay.

She also couldn't think about the future, or the Future or anything else but doing all she could for the man lying in the bed in front of her, shifting restlessly as he burned.

Montgomery returned with more candles, which John lit. Jennifer drew out a cup of her brew and looked at Miles.

"Can you help me hold him up?"

"Hold him down, you mean?" Miles asked mildly.

She smiled. "I'll laugh about it with you later."

"We'll poach a bottle of Nick's finest for the occasion," Miles promised.

"Does he have a finest?"

"Hidden somewhere, no doubt. If it's here, I'll find it."

Jennifer sipped the tea, winced at the bitterness of it, then looked at Nicholas's brother.

"It's vile. But it's also now or never."

She could only hope *never* would be something Nicholas would bellow at her in conjunction with *again* when he woke and complained about the taste of her tea.

It was a very long night. At one point, during that very long night after they'd tried to get tea down Nicholas for the fifth time and ended up wearing most of it, she wished she had a first-aid kit with her. Or some dried herbs ready-made in tea form. All she had was the knowledge Patrick MacLeod had given her and the most rudimentary of tools with which to make that knowledge work.

She suspected that might not be enough.

She sat there far into the night, feeling very inadequate. Obviously that was yet another reason why she shouldn't be anywhere but in the twenty-first century with a drugstore and emergency room down the street. She was not good with poisons inflicted by disgruntled medieval barons.

But she did the best she could.

And hoped it would be enough.

It was barely dawn when Miles convinced the boys to go curl up on the floor in the great hall and took himself off to do a little guard duty. Jennifer was almost too tired to think. She had to, though, to digest what had gone on that afternoon and what it meant.

Her gate was destroyed. The ramifications of that were enormous. She couldn't say that she was a vastly experienced time traveler, but she did have a few centuries under her belt. She didn't know all the rules, but she did know that it was only possible to follow another person to wherever a time gate had taken them by using the same gate.

And only if the destination side of that gate were functional.

Her family couldn't come along behind her

and arrive at the place she had because her side of the gate was destroyed. And since they couldn't follow her, they wouldn't have any clue where she'd gone.

She bowed her head. She could only imagine what would happen at home.

Megan would panic, first when she didn't come home, then when they found her car abandoned near the abbey. Her parents would be devastated. Someone probably would attempt a rescue only to have it fail as many times as they might attempt it because Ledenham had dug up her side of the gate.

She was, for all intents and purposes, stuck.

She sat up, then slowly pulled her cell phone out of her pocket. Her wallpaper was a picture of the Manhattan skyline. She stared at it, hearing the sounds, smelling the city smells, seeing the snow in winter, feeling the press of people on the subway in the summer.

Yet where she sat, there was absolute silence.

Well, except for the ragged sound of Nicholas's breathing.

She looked at her phone for quite some time, then let out a deep, shuddering breath. Slowly, she turned off the power. It beeped once, then the light faded and the phone went silent as well. She put it back in her pocket.

She closed her eyes briefly. She wanted to believe that she was there for a purpose.

Maybe Nicholas would have been wounded by Ledenham anyway and she was there to save his life. She turned that around over and over in her head until it gave her a headache, then she stopped. She reached out and took Nicholas's pulse another time. It was still racing and he was still burning.

She put her head down on the bed. She would rest for a minute, then go make more tea and try to get it down him.

It was all she could do.

She realized she had fallen asleep with her head on the bed only because her back hurt so badly she could no longer ignore it. She straightened with a groan. The candles had burned low again. She propped her chin up on her fists and tried to remember how long she'd been there. Two nights? Three? She rubbed her face with her good hand. Three nights already. She supposed, based on the light trying to get in through the crack in the shutter, that it was day again. Day number three.

She rose, gasped at the pain in her back, then limped over and lit another candle with the one that was threatening to go out. She hobbled back over to the bed and sat down on her stool. She looked at Nicholas.

His eyes were open.

She suffered a momentary flash of panic until she saw that he was breathing. Then she put her face down on the bed and let out a shaky breath.

Thank heavens.

"I feel terrible," he croaked.

She lifted her head and smiled for the first time in three days. "I imagine you do."

"What in the hell did you pour down me?"

She couldn't help it. She laughed. "You're so welcome, gracious lord. I worked very hard on that tea."

"It was dreadful."

"And here I was afraid you wouldn't remember it."

"I had hoped it was but a nightmare." He coughed. "Woman, you make appallingly bitter brews."

"Tell Ledenham the next time you see him. He thinks I'm a witch."

Nicholas snorted weakly. "No witch of any skill would make such vile stuff." He let out a shaky breath and closed his eyes. "What was it?"

"We think poison. From the arrow."

He took a deep breath, then coughed again. "Fever?"

"Yes."

"How long?"

"Three nights," she said quietly. "Today is the third morning."

He was silent for several minutes, then opened his eyes and looked at her. "In truth?"

"Yes. But I didn't worry about you," she

said lightly. "Miles said you had much to live for."

"Did he," Nicholas said. "And what would that be?"

"An extensive cache of very fine French wine that you hadn't come close to finishing yet," she said. "He said you hoard things."

"He would."

"He suggested that if you lived, you might want to share."

"With him, no doubt."

"Well, yes, actually," she said.

He took a deep breath, then coughed. Then he merely breathed in and out raggedly for several minutes. Jennifer reached out and briefly touched his arm. His skin was cool, for a change. She would have to tell Patrick MacLeod that his recipes were good ones.

Somehow, she suspected he probably already knew as much.

"Did I behave?" Nicholas asked suddenly.

"Ha," Jennifer said, before she could stop herself. Then she smiled. "You're a terrible patient."

"Patient?"

She bit her tongue. She was going to have to stop mixing English with medieval Norman French.

"One who is treated by a healer," she clarified. "You're a rotten one."

He turned his head to look at her. "Was I indeed?"

"You were indeed, but I suppose I could blame that on the fever."

"I fear to ask what I did."

"Oh, I'll tell you without you having to ask," she said, settling herself more comfortably on her stool. "You spoke to people who were not here, you cursed, you spat out your tea on me and Miles, you threatened to kill all your brothers including Robin, who you vowed to track down and kill as soon as you were able, and you almost gave me a black eye."

"Did I?" he asked quickly, starting to sit up.

"I said almost," she reminded him. "I was too quick for you."

He fell back against the bed. "Forgive me."

"I did, already." She didn't bother to tell him that he'd also slept like the dead and been so pale, she'd been certain on several occasions that he *had* been dead.

She watched him as his eyelids fell and he began to sleep again. She looked up as Miles came into the chamber. His expression was grave, then he looked at her.

"The fever is broken?" he asked quickly.

"It is," she said with a smile.

"And he is himself?"

"He complained about my tea."

Miles smiled. "Ah, then all is as it should be." He came and sat down on the end of the bed. "He owes you his life."

196

She shook her head. "You're trying to make me feel better, but none of it would have been necessary if he hadn't come to rescue me."

"Trust me, Ledenham would have found some other opportunity to harm him. Instead, content yourself with knowing that you were here to tend him when he needed you."

"I suppose," she said, feeling somewhat better. She looked at Nicholas for a moment or two, decided she was just too tired to really appreciate him, and turned to Miles. "Well? What shall we do now?"

"Let us discuss him whilst he's senseless," Miles said, making himself more comfortable on the edge of the bed. "Shall I begin with his faults or his virtues?"

"Which list is longer?"

Miles laughed. "I daresay you're not rested enough for the faults. You tell me what you want to know and I'll give you the brief answers. We'll save the more interesting details for another day."

"All right," Jennifer said. Nicholas was asleep again and Miles looked ready for a good gossip. She was feeling a little punch-drunk from lack of sleep and it seemed like as good an idea as any. She would ask her questions and see what sorts of answers she could get. "Why isn't he married? He has to be, what, almost thirty?"

"A score and eight," Miles said. "As to why he is not wed, there is no good answer. He has looked at every eligible maiden my grandmother has been able to produce. He will have none of them."

"Are they ugly? Bad tempered? Not frugal?"

"Not that I've seen."

"Then what's his problem?"

Miles shrugged helplessly. "I have no idea." He paused. "Well, I have an idea why he wouldn't be interested *now* —"

Nicholas's foot jerked so hard, it almost sent Miles off the edge of the bed. Jennifer looked quickly at him, but he was snoring.

"Bad dream," she surmised.

"No doubt," Miles said dryly, resuming his place. "Now, what of you, my lady? Are you wed?"

"No," she said. "I suppose your brother and I are in the same situation. I've met many men, mostly musicians, and I just haven't been able to find one I like." She smiled briefly. "I'm getting old, I suppose."

"Surely not," Miles said. "You look barely past your childhood days."

She laughed. "Very diplomatic of you."

"I'm always that, at least," Miles said, his eyes twinkling. "Now, do I dare ask your age?"

"I don't have anything to hide," Jennifer said with a shrug. "I'm twenty-eight."

"Nick's age," Miles said. "Yet not wed? How is this? Is it your music that has kept you from it?"

"Partly, I suppose. Mostly I think it's because I just couldn't find the right man."

"I'm available," Miles offered.

Nicholas kicked him so hard that he landed on the floor in a sprawl. He crawled to his feet and glared at his brother.

"That was no dream."

"You're disturbing my rest," Nicholas muttered. "Go tend the horses."

"I already tended the horses," Miles said. "I've been tending the horses for two bloody days. I came so our good lady might go take her rest in your bed that I put together for you yesterday, you ungrateful wh—"

"Careful," Nicholas said, opening his eyes and looking at his brother narrowly.

Miles rubbed his abused backside. "I don't know that I'll sit with you after all. But I will send Mistress McKinnon upstairs."

"Feed her first," Nicholas said weakly. "I'll come fetch something for myself later."

"Of course you won't," Jennifer said, rising. "I'll go make something. Miles, don't irritate him. Nicholas, don't kick him again." She rolled her eyes. "Your poor mother."

"And we are the well-behaved ones," Miles said. "You should see him with Robin."

"I can only imagine." She limped toward the door, then turned briefly and looked back at Nicholas.

He was watching her gravely.

At least he was alive to do so.

She was very, very grateful.

She smiled at him, then left the room and went to the kitchen for something edible. There was an abundance of rather wilted greens on the table, but she wasn't going to be choosey. She sorted things into piles, then set to chopping and mixing up a salad. There were flowers there as well. That was Montgomery's doing, she was certain. She would have to thank him later, for they were lovely and she suspected he'd picked them to please her. She took the blossoms that were edible and sprinkled them in a ring around the edge of her salad bowl.

And then she froze.

Flowers in the grass.

Fairy rings.

She felt her way down onto the kitchen's lone stool. She couldn't believe she hadn't thought of it before. There was a fairy ring in Mr. Farris's potato field near the inn Megan owned. The Boar's Head Inn was a little over an a hour west of Artane, which meant it couldn't be all that far from Wyckham. Certainly something she could get to by horse.

The gate was one she had used with Connor and Victoria to get back to Elizabethan England to rescue their grandmother. Jamie had said, after having tried it himself, that it was a very powerful gate. Thomas had suggested once that Farmer Farris put up a fence around it before someone really got lost.

Then something else occurred to her. Thomas had used a gate as well, one he had claimed was north of Artane in a clutch of rocks. Did that gate still exist as well?

Maybe she wasn't as stuck as she had thought.

She looked down into her salad bowl. Why hadn't either of those options occurred to her in the past three days?

Oh, right.

Nicholas.

She bowed her head and thought about it all for far longer than she should have. Oh, why had he held her hand? Why had he stroked her hair?

Why did she have to meet a decent guy hundreds of years before she'd been born?

She sighed deeply. There was nothing to be done, no matter how much she wished things could have worked out differently. He was a medieval lord. He needed a medieval lady. She was not for him and he was not for her.

She would have to try again to get home.

She took a deep breath and looked blearily at the things on the work table in front of her. She would take Nicholas something to eat, then go crash upstairs in his bedroom. Maybe she would watch over him until he was well and try not to spend any more time with him than she had to so she wouldn't become any more fond of him than she was already.

It occurred to her briefly that such had possibly been his strategy that first fortnight she'd been at Wyckham, but surely it hadn't been for her reasons.

No, she would do what was necessary to see him get back on his feet, then run like hell for Farris's potato field. She knew for herself that *that* gate worked. Surely it had a stop in the Middle Ages, sort of like a subway station. Who knew how many places she could have gotten off if she'd had the right sort of map?

She stood up and gathered together dinner. Yes, she would stay as long as was required, then get home.

And then she would spend quite a bit of time in the future trying to forget the way a medieval lord had looked at her when he'd woken from a fever.

As though he'd been glad to see her. As though he wanted her to stay.

She shook her head firmly. She had to go home. She had no choice.

No choice at all.

CHAPTER 12

Nicholas paused at the doorway of Master Gavin's chamber and put his hands against the door frame. That he needed such aid was unsettling indeed. He took a moment to make certain his legs were steady beneath him, then made his way with trembling limbs down the passageway to the great hall. He hoped he would arrive at a chair before he fell down.

Two more days had passed in which he hadn't been able to even rise from his bed. Today, though, he'd been determined to dress himself and be about his business.

He steadfastly refused to think about the fact that what motivated him the most was the thought of seeing Jennifer.

If she was still there.

She hadn't tended him after that first morn when he'd woken. Perhaps she had left to seek another way back to the Future . . .

He looked across the hall to see Jennifer sitting in front of the fire, deep in discussion with Miles. He felt an unwholesome sense of relief course through him. He leaned against the wall and tried to catch his breath.

He watched Jennifer catch sight of him and leap to her feet. He would have been gratified by that had she not hastened over to him with the sort of look on her face that was better reserved for giving to toothless dotards on the verge of tumbling into their stew.

Nicholas scowled at her as she stopped in front of him. "I am well."

"You don't look it."

He frowned. "And here I thought you were going to offer me your arm, or perhaps carry me across the floor."

"I would," she said seriously, "if I thought you'd let me."

He grunted, but didn't protest as she put her arm around his waist and drew his arm over her shoulders.

"You're shaking," she said, looking up at him with a frown.

He wasn't going to tell her that it was her touch that was undoing him at present. "I am eager to get on with my day," he lied.

"Whatever," she said with a smile.

Whatever? What sort of word was that? He muttered it under his breath several times as he allowed her to help him across the hall, and thought that it might be something useful to have at the right moment.

He sat in the good chair, waited patiently

whilst she brought him something with which to break his fast, then did his best to eat what he was given.

He felt like hell.

But he knew the fastest way to rid his body of the rest of Ledenham's gift was to sweat it out. He sat for quite a while, steeling himself for the task of getting up and walking out to the lists.

Of course, that steeling took more time than usual, likely because Jennifer was sitting on the stool in front of him and he thought it best to have a good look at her whilst he could.

It would have been so much easier if he'd disliked her. It would have been easy to ignore her smile, her laughter, her sparkling eyes.

He shook his head. When had it happened, that he was the one wanting but not being able to have? He began to have sympathy for a whole host of people he'd never felt sorry for before —

Then he paused. Perhaps he was being too hasty. Perhaps he might have what he wanted in the end. What if Jennifer had no choice but to remain in his time?

He would have chortled with happiness over that thought if he hadn't been so weary.

And then he abruptly stopped mentally chortling. He realized that even if her gate hadn't worked, that didn't matter.

Because he knew where another one was that *did* work.

He leaned his head back against the chair and closed his eyes. Damnation, but knowledge was a bloody awful thing. Aye, he knew that another gate existed and he knew just exactly who would be able to tell him precisely where it could be found.

Jackson Alexander Kilchurn IV. His bloody brother-in-law.

Damn him. Nicholas had always known he had good reason to hate him.

"Nicholas?"

He heaved himself to his feet. "I must go train," he said hoarsely.

She was on her feet instantly as well. "I'm not going to tell you what to do —"

"Don't," he said. He reached for her uninjured hand, squeezed it briefly, then walked away whilst he still could. "I am in perfect health."

"Of course."

Well, at least she wasn't going to coddle him until he wanted to bolt like a cornered hound.

He refused to think about the fact that he might rather have enjoyed that coddling.

He walked out of his hall and made for his stables. He made his way inside, then spent an appallingly long amount of time clinging to a stall door and fighting the way his head felt as if it were spinning. Not even the lovely

206

smell of horse manure aided him at present.

In time, he gave up and turned away. It would be the lists, apparently, that would do for him what he needed. He started to walk over there, then caught sight of Petter. Better yet, a bracing bit of discussion about the expense of seeing to his roof to stir his blood. He'd almost managed to get all the way over to Petter when he was startled by a bit of thunder.

He looked up.

There wasn't a cloud in the sky.

It took him a moment to realize that the thunder he heard was coming from his own great hall and that it wasn't thunder at all.

It was his roof collapsing.

He stood stock-still for a moment or two, staring at the hall in horror before he managed to make himself move. He flung himself into a stumbling run toward the front door.

"Wait!" Petter exclaimed, leaping toward him. He caught him by the arm. "You can't go inside!"

Nicholas flinched. It was his stitched arm. The pain made it all the more difficult to pull it away.

His brothers were inside.

So was Jennifer.

"I must find them," Nicholas snarled.

"Nicholas, Miles is right here," Petter said, turning him toward the lists. "Look!"

Indeed, Miles was running toward him.

Nicholas closed his eyes briefly in thanks. He heard Montgomery and John shouting. He bowed his head and blew out his breath. The saints be praised, they were all were accounted for —

Jennifer.

The knowledge caught him like a score of fists in his gut. He gasped, then jerked away from Petter. He stumbled across the rest of the courtyard, choking on the dust that was pouring out of the hall from the falling timbers that had spanned his roof and the stone that had held them in place along the edges. He tried to wave away the dust, to see inside the hall, to see how he might get himself inside. One half of the door was still intact. Perhaps that was a way in. He drew his sword and raised it over his head to use as an ax —

"Nicholas?"

Nicholas heard her voice, but thought perhaps that she was now an angel and had come to comfort him.

"Nicholas, what happened!" she exclaimed.

He heard his sword clang against the stone of the stairs as he dropped it. He himself went down to his knees there on the top step. He hadn't meant to. He knew that he would look like an old woman to his brothers and his men, but he was just too overcome to do anything else. He knelt there, panting, and could see nothing past the darkness that had clouded his vision.

"Miles, take his sword," Jennifer said quietly.

Nicholas felt her hand on his shoulder. "Nicholas, come away from the door," she said, sounding very concerned. "Please. I don't think it's safe."

He heaved himself back up to his feet by sheer willpower alone. He turned. He didn't think, he merely pulled her into his arms and clutched her to him.

"You're shaking," she said, her voice muffled against his tunic.

" 'Tis the fever," he managed.

She patted his back. "Please come away from here," she said, pulling back to look up at him. "Please."

He closed his eyes briefly, then released her. "Forgive me. I was overcome."

"It was torture, really," she said with a grave smile. She took him by the arm and pulled him down the stairs with her. "Miles, is everyone accounted for?"

"I'll see," Miles said.

Nicholas managed to focus on her. "Where were you?"

"Grubbing in the garden," she said with a smile that wasn't any more steady than his knees. She sat down next to him. "Lucky for me, I suppose."

He bowed his head and blew out his breath. By the saints, he could not stand this. He didn't know the wench, didn't want the wench, didn't even like the wench. Surely, he shouldn't be this undone by the thought of losing her.

He had to get her home. It was the only thing that would save his sanity.

He sat there, shaking far longer than he should have, and waited for Miles to return. He couldn't bring himself to touch Jennifer again, though he was acutely aware of her sitting next to him on the step. He lifted his head when he heard Miles returning.

"We can't be sure," Miles began slowly, "but we think one of Petter's lads was inside. I'll go through the kitchens and see what of the roof is left —"

"You will not," Nicholas said immediately. "I will."

"I will go," Petter said, coming to stand next to Miles. "He is my lad, after all, and my responsibility. Besides, I'll know if what's left is stable."

"Perhaps he wasn't in the great hall," Nicholas offered. "The bedchambers and the solar are still intact, aren't they? And the kitchens?"

Petter shook his head. "Impossible to tell. I'll see, then return and tell you what's left."

Nicholas nodded. Perhaps it was unmanly to allow his head mason to investigate whilst he waited, but Petter had it aright. He would be the one who knew what of the remaining roof was stable and what was not.

"Can I get you something?" Jennifer asked softly. "Is there some way I can help you?"

Nicholas looked out over the courtyard, wrestled with his common sense for a moment, then surrendered. She would leave; he knew that.

But not that afternoon.

He held out his hand. "Your company is enough," he said quietly.

She put her hand into his.

It was her injured hand, so he held it very carefully. It would be, he decided, very easy to become accustomed to such a thing.

He held her hand, but he didn't dare look at her.

He couldn't.

It wasn't long before Petter had returned. Nicholas took a deep breath.

"Aye?"

"Mark was in the great hall," Petter said grimly. "He is the only one."

Nicholas sighed deeply. "Poor lad. Had he a wife or children?"

"Not that I know of," Petter said. "Perhaps just aged parents. That doesn't lessen the sorrow, but it doesn't increase it, either."

Nicholas nodded. "Of course." He paused. "Was it just the great hall?"

"It was," Petter said. "The roof should have been repaired a year ago."

"It *was* to have been repaired a year ago," Nicholas said grimly. "Damn that Gavin of

Louth. If I find him again, he'll feel my displeasure. Well, I suppose this gives you reason enough to build that gallery."

"An unfortunate reason," Petter conceded, "but reason enough."

Nicholas nodded, then looked at his brothers. "We'll dig the poor man out, bury him here, then go to Seakirk Abbey and buy him prayers for his soul, as is right. But we'll need a priest here to bless the burying. Miles, will you ride to Seakirk and fetch us one?"

"Of course," Miles said. "Anything else whilst I'm away?"

"Tell the abbot we will be there before the se'nnight is finished. He'll be happy to see me for my gold, at least."

Miles smiled. "If you want to believe that, do."

Nicholas scowled. "I am not so unwelcome at Seakirk."

Miles only lifted one eyebrow, then turned to look at Jennifer. "Don't let him overdo."

"Can I stop him?" she asked.

"Use your feminine wiles," Miles suggested. "I'll be back in a pair of days, then we'll lay the man to rest."

Nicholas nodded and watched him walk off, then looked at Jennifer. He was just so damned grateful that she was there next to him, not buried under piles of rubble and wood, that he hardly knew what to say. He stroked her hand gently, then finally sighed and released her.

"I need to train."

"I'll see what's in the kitchen."

"Nay," he said quickly, then took a deep breath. "Please do not go inside. Allow me to aid you there later."

"You couldn't have kept the roof from falling, Nicholas, any more than I can keep you out of the lists."

"You underestimate me," he said seriously. He heaved himself to his feet. "I beg you find some shade and have yourself a rest. I'll fetch you later."

She looked up at him. "You'll be all right?"

That day? Or a month from then? He didn't dare ask what she meant, but he was quite sure he wouldn't have a good answer either way.

"I'll be fine," he said with more enthusiasm than he felt. "I was the one sleeping for the past five days, remember? You need to catch me up."

She smiled briefly. "All right. I'll go."

He held out his hand and pulled her gently to her feet. "Thank you."

"I won't tell you to rest."

"Thank you for that as well."

She looked at him searchingly for another moment or two, then smiled briefly and walked away. Nicholas realized then that she had put Montgomery's clothes back on. He wasn't sure how he should take that. Was she resigned? Was she trying to blend in?

Had the fever rendered him completely wit-less?

He turned toward the lists and hoped he would find sanity there.

He didn't hold out much hope.

The afternoon waned and Nicholas waned right along with it. He had to admit there was something unwholesomely welcome about ceasing crossing swords with John to find Jennifer standing at the edge of the lists, waiting for him. He resheathed his sword, walked across the field, and accepted the bottle she handed him. He drank, then dragged his sleeve across his sweating fore-head.

"Better?" she asked.

"Exhausted," he admitted. "But, aye, bet-ter. And you?"

She smiled. "I had a very long nap. I feel wonderful."

And you look spectacular. He nodded toward the hall. "We should see what's left of the kitchens. We couldn't be so fortunate as to have anything left to eat."

"I have greens."

"Aye, I was afraid of that," he said, with feeling.

She laughed. "They're good for you."

"So you say, but I can't say my belly agrees. But if you insist, I'll try to bear up manfully and eat them."

"You won't regret it."

Perhaps not, but he suspected he would regret quite a few other things, beginning with the decision to come to Wyckham. He should rather have gone to France. He could have been there now, enjoying fine food and fine wine with his feet up on a very fine table.

Without Jennifer.

"Nicholas?"

He looked at her quickly. "Aye?"

"You groaned."

"Too much swordplay," he lied. By the saints, he wasn't equal to deciding if having her in his life was torment or bliss.

He pushed all thoughts of her possibly being out of his life aside and walked with her around the keep and through the garden. The kitchen was unharmed and Petter had assured him the roof was indeed sound. Nicholas hadn't argued with him. After all, Petter had told him almost a month ago he was unsure the great hall roof could be saved.

He should have listened.

"Nicholas?"

He looked up from his contemplation of food on the work table. "Aye?"

"I hesitate to ask this, but I would like to go with you to the abbey." She paused. "Actually, I need to go past the abbey and I'm not certain I can get there on my own."

"Go past the abbey . . ." It took him a moment to realize what she was saying. "Oh," he said. "Of course."

Of course, indeed. She likely had another gate or two to try. How was it that these time travelers seemed to have so many opportunities to traipse through the centuries? He was certain he'd never met another one.

He frowned. Then again, how would he have known whether he'd met one or not? He'd encountered many forward-thinking souls over the course of his travels. Who was to say they hadn't been not only forward thinking, but from a forward time?

He would have pondered that a bit more, but it made the space between his eyes begin to pound. He rubbed it absently and looked at her.

"Of course," he repeated. "I'll take you wherever you want to go."

She looked pathetically grateful. "Thank you."

"Will you find your kin there?" Nicholas asked.

She shifted. Well, whatever else she might have been, she was not a very good liar. He watched as she put her shoulders back, giving herself courage apparently, and looked him full in the face.

"I expected to be able to find my kin at Ledenham's abbey, but I think the digging there disturbed them."

"They sound like faeries," Montgomery

said from behind her.

Nicholas sent him scurrying off with his fiercest frown. He turned back to Jennifer and made an effort to lighten his expression. "Think you?"

"I think so," she said. She took a deep breath. "I can think of two more places where I might find them."

"Two more?" he asked. "Two more meeting places?"

"One that I'm fairly sure of. The other, I've only heard tell of."

Nicholas wanted to sit down, but he realized his youngest brothers were hovering at the garden door, watching him, and he couldn't appear weak in front of them.

"Where?" he asked quietly. "Where must you go?"

"I'll know it when I see it. It is north of Seakirk Abbey."

He grimaced, hardly able to believe that he was in the midst of such madness. He'd shunned everything to do with it when his sister had fallen in love with a man who was . . . who was not of their time.

By the saints, even thinking the thought made him want to sit down.

Jennifer looked at him gravely. "You know, on second thought, I think I will be all right on my own, if I can just go with you to the abbey."

Nicholas blinked. "I didn't say I wouldn't

aid you."

"You were swearing."

"Was I?"

She smiled suddenly, an understanding smile that he surely didn't deserve. "You've had a hard day."

"Aye, but it could have been worse."

"Your brothers could have been inside," she said softly.

Or you, he thought to himself. "Aye," he said aloud.

"Why don't you sit, and I'll make supper."

"Thank you," he said, with feeling. He sat down and watched as she prepared a hearty meal for them.

It was a good thing that she was going back home. He nodded to himself. Having her in his life was entirely too troublesome. Her beauty distracted him, her laugh mesmerized him, her hair made him want to bury his hands in it. The thought of something happening to her made him feel a terror he'd never in his life felt before.

Aye, he would accompany her and be glad to see the last of her.

He supposed if he told himself that enough times, he might someday begin to believe it.

CHAPTER 13

Nigel of Ledenham stood in the shadows of the forest near Wyckham and watched the party leave the keep. Unfortunately, there were more alive in that party than he cared to see. Obviously he would have to have a word with the lad who had sold him that poison.

He cursed under his breath. Damn that Nicholas de Piaget. Damn all the de Piaget brats. The lads were handsome, skilled with a sword, and had deep coffers. The gels were no less canny than the lads, and equally as rich. They were all also seemingly able to consort with witches without harm. Amanda de Piaget, their sister of astonishing beauty and terrifying independence, had proved that by wedding herself to a warlock. Ledenham was certain of it. He'd seen the man's gear. He'd tried to convince everyone who would listen of the truth of that.

Unfortunately, trying to convince the king had landed him in his current straits — pouring all his gold into a damned abbey that would probably not stand fifty years.

Not that he cared either way, not being a religious man himself.

He returned to his list of particular grievances against the Artane lads. The list was long but satisfying, so he didn't hurry himself. He frowned and stroked his chin.

He took to rubbing his nose for more inspiration and there hit upon something else to hate them for. He was fairly certain the last time he'd seen Nicholas de Piaget was the second time the whoreson had broken his nose.

Yet another reason to harm him in return — and succeed.

He cast about for something that might serve. Immediately, a vision of the flame-haired witch came to his mind. He considered the possibilities there. If de Piaget had any feelings for her, which he must have given that he'd rescued her, he would be grieved by her loss.

If she were captured, her gear would serve as proof of her evil nature. Ledenham was certain her gear was the same sort of stuff he'd stripped off Jackson Alexander Kilchurn a pair of years earlier. He hadn't managed to put Kilchurn to the fire, but he would be damned if he didn't find a way to see that Scottish wench there.

And if he could prove she was a witch, he

might be able to redeem himself with the king. Then he could return to London where there was trouble more to his taste.

He would have to give thought to how to capture her. It would have to be when de Piaget was not about. The man had no personal guard, but he didn't seem to need them. Ledenham's own men were all cowards, as the encounter a fortnight before had amply shown. Obviously, he would need to find other more hardened lads to aid him.

Then he would somehow manage to separate the wench from her protector, and he would spirit her away and take her to the king.

He would watch and follow. After all, he was a very patient man and he was willing to wait for his revenge.

He was willing to wait quite a while.

CHAPTER 14

Jennifer stood just inside the doors of Seakirk Abbey and tried to blend in with Nicholas's brothers. She had braided her hair and tucked it into the back of Montgomery's tunic so it didn't show so much, her Doc Martens were filthy and probably nondescript enough, and she was wearing John's cloak pulled close around her face. Who would know she was a girl? And if they knew, who would care? She hoped no one, because she wasn't sure she could move.

She was listening to Gregorian chant performed in the original setting by a choir of medieval monks. It was like rain after a very long, very hot dry spell.

She had forgotten.

She closed her eyes and leaned against Montgomery, letting the music wash over her. It was glorious beyond description and she could hardly catch her breath. Who would have thought that something so simple could be so enthralling?

She stood there forever, drinking in the sounds, wishing it would never end.

"Jennifer?"

She smiled. When was the last time she'd heard her name pronounced with that soft, French J? All Nicholas's brothers did it. Nicholas, though, didn't. He called her Mistress McKinnon if he called her anything. She supposed it was for the best. If he called her by her given name, she might not survive.

She dragged herself back to the present and opened her eyes. She realized that her cheeks were wet from tears and Miles was peering into her hood. He smiled gravely.

"The music?" he asked.

She nodded.

"Then come with me," he whispered. "We'll go closer."

Jennifer nodded and followed him to where the nave was separated from the rest of the chapel by an iron-barred partition. She stood at the gate and clutched the bars. The music blew through her soul like a bracing bit of chill autumn wind. She was accustomed to Rachmaninoff bringing tears to her eyes; she never thought medieval chant would do the same.

Obviously, she'd been in the Middle Ages too long.

She longed for her violin in a way that made her catch her breath. Why had she ever thought to put it aside for even a moment?

All those years, when she could have been concertizing, spent designing and sewing baby clothes that anyone else could have done a thousand times better . . .

Regret was a terrible thing.

She vowed that when she got back to the twenty-first century, she would pick her violin up and never put it back down. She would practice until her fingers bled. She would accept any gig, no matter what podunk town it found itself in, and she would give Charles Salieri very, very expensive Christmas gifts every year to make up for all the times she'd said no to dates he'd tried to get her to take in the past.

If she could get back.

But for now, the chant was enough. At least it was music.

She listened until Miles touched her arm. Then she opened her eyes and looked at him. "Yes?"

"Can you pry yourself away yet? I think Nick's almost done."

She nodded, then looked to find Nicholas whispering furiously with a man she assumed was the abbot. "He doesn't look happy."

"Seakirk Abbey is not his favorite place," Miles said. "I daresay they aren't overfond of him here, either."

"What did he do?" she asked.

"It's all part of a long list of secrets he has. I'll tell you a few, if you like."

"I'm not sure I want to know any of them, do I?"

"You might find the conversation interesting. I didn't have the chance to tell you much whilst he was senseless." He looked at his brother and smiled grimly. "It is far past time he ceased to let his past have power over him."

"Why do I get the feeling that you're about to do something you shouldn't?"

"Is it the glint in my eye?" Miles asked.

"No, it's the chills I'm getting down my spine," she said honestly. "Those sort of don't-go-there chills I get every time I'm on the verge of making an enormous mistake."

"I never get them," Miles said promptly. "You know, Nick is usually the sunny one in our family. You might like to see what's buried under all that frost. I imagine with the right sort of inducement, he would show it. What say you?"

"Forget it," Jennifer said, shaking her head firmly. "He's angry enough as it is — even I can see that. If you push him, he just might kill you."

"He loves me too well to do me any serious harm."

"You know, one of my father's favorite sayings is *let sleeping dogs lie*. My grandmother has one she likes even more: *the cesspit doesn't stink till you stir it.*" She paused. "Or words to that effect."

"I like the last one."

"I thought you might. So, take Granny's advice and leave him alone."

"Hmmm," he said, then linked his arm with hers. "Let us go outside. I think I need some air."

"Miles, really," she protested, but she suspected he wasn't going to listen to her. She looked at Nicholas as they slipped out the front door. He was standing there with his arms folded over his chest, his expression so cold she was tempted to rub her arms. She wondered how the abbot managed to not cower. Then again, the man was probably used to dealing with nobility. "Well," she said, "at least the abbot isn't yelling at him."

"When Artane is your father, you find that no one yells at you."

"Do you find that?" Jennifer asked.

Miles smiled. "If I caused less trouble, I might. Here, let us seek out a comfortable place and I will tell you all sorts of appalling things. We will see what sort of reaction it produces."

"Miles," she warned, "I honestly don't care if I ever see Lord Sunshine."

"Oh, I think you would care, if you knew what you were missing." He looked over his shoulder. "Ah, Nick," he said easily, "finished so soon?"

"Finished so soon?" he echoed in disgust. "Gouged so quickly, rather. And we have but begun the negotiations. But I will endeavor not to ruin the gift by complaining." He looked at Jennifer, then started in surprise. "You've been weeping." He glared at Miles. "Did you torment her?"

"The music moved her. We've decided now to go outside so I can tell her all your secrets."

Jennifer watched as a muscle in Nicholas's jaw twitched. "Is that so?" he asked.

"Shedding blood on the abbot's front stoop would only worsen his opinion of you," Miles said, sounding supremely unconcerned. "And I haven't told her anything yet. Oh, I know. Why don't *you* tell me which ones she should know and I'll round them out a bit with all the details."

"Secrets are only powerful when the one they concern cares if they're told," Nicholas said, through gritted teeth.

"Which is why telling yours will bother you so," Miles said smoothly.

"Think you?" Nicholas asked in a very dangerous tone.

"Let's reveal them and see, shall we?"

"Shut up, Miles."

Miles rubbed his hands together. "I say we begin with the secret that you're least willing to reveal. I wonder which one that might b—"

Nicholas drew his sword so quickly, it made a hissing sound.

Jennifer backed up quickly. She realized

227

Montgomery and John were behind her only because she knocked them over and landed on top of them. She would have scrambled to her feet and run, but she had a hard time untangling herself from Nicholas's youngest brothers.

Nicholas flung his cloak at her. "Hold that," he growled.

Miles tossed her his cloak as well. "If you don't mind," he said politely. "And I think it best that you move. Now."

She didn't have to hear that twice. It wasn't easy to get up and protect her sore hand at the same time, but she had incentive. She struggled to her feet, hauled Montgomery to his and left John to fend for himself. He seemed to realize the precariousness of his situation because he leaped up and ran after her. She stopped a safe distance away, clutched the cloaks in her arms, and watched with wide eyes as Nicholas tried to kill his next youngest brother.

"By the saints," Montgomery said weakly, "I've never seen him in such a temper."

"I daresay Nick wouldn't be so irritated if he wasn't at Seakirk," John said. He smiled at Jennifer. "Not his favorite place, you know." He rubbed his hands together. "Finally, now we'll have some decent sport. Who will walk away unscathed, do you think?"

Jennifer could hardly believe her ears. She gaped at John, but he only shrugged sheepishly. She turned to Montgomery. "Why in the world would Miles do that?"

"Provoke him?" Montgomery asked. "Who knows? I think it bothers Miles to see Nick so dejected —"

"I am not dejected!" Nicholas bellowed from across the garden.

"Of course not," Miles agreed. "And why would you be? After all, it doesn't trouble you that you lost Anne to Robin."

"Anne already loved Robin, which you *know* damn well I knew all along," Nicholas snapped. "I was pushing Robin to make the decision he should have years before. I knew she did not love me as anything but a brother."

"Ah, now speaking of being a brother," Miles continued placidly, "what of Amanda? Let's examine that, shall we?"

Montgomery and John backed away. Jennifer decided that they knew more than she did, so she backed up with them.

"I will not discuss that," Nicholas said icily.

"You should. You should let it go and let your heart heal."

"Who are you," Nicholas spat, "my mother to give me such advice?"

"Nay, I am your brother and I love you just as much as she does."

Nicholas took a vicious swipe at his brother. "Why are you doing this?" he demanded.

"Why did you choose this moment to do this?"

Miles shrugged. "I thought I might seek sanctuary inside if you became too feisty."

Nicholas attacked. Miles retaliated. Jennifer watched them in mute horror, then found herself surrounded by a handful of wide-eyed monks. Nicholas snarled curses at them and they scurried back inside.

Jennifer flinched each time their swords crossed, jumped a little each time Nicholas tried to stab his brother, and gasped at the horrible names Nicholas was calling Miles.

She shivered as well. It was one thing to watch a choreographed sword fight in a movie. The swords weren't sharp and the actors had practiced. Here there were no such safety nets. Nicholas's sword *was* sharp and he wasn't doing some preplanned fake fight.

She was very, very glad she wasn't in the hot seat, as it were.

Nicholas de Piaget in a temper was an impressive sight. He fought with a cold detachment that should have sent Miles running the other way with his tail between his legs. Maybe Miles was accustomed to it.

Jennifer doubted that she would ever become so.

Finally, Nicholas jammed his sword back into its sheath, turned to her, and glared at her with his chest heaving.

"Will you hear my secrets?" he demanded.

She wanted to say no, but she couldn't manage anything but an inarticulate stammer.

"I loved my sister," he snarled. "I loved her from the time we were small. And I am a bastard. There. There are all my secrets."

And with that, he sent Miles another scathing look, then turned and strode back into the abbey.

Jennifer stood, holding his cloak, and wasn't quite sure what to say. She looked at Miles.

"He forgot his cloak." She paused. "He'll be cold inside."

"Do you think so?" Miles said, dragging his sleeve across his sweaty forehead, then resheathing his sword. "I daresay he's furious enough to keep himself warm for quite some time." He put his hand to his ear. "Listen. I can hear him bellowing from here."

She handed him his cloak. "I don't think that accomplished what you meant it to." She paused. "And it was unkind."

Miles looked at her briefly, then looked behind her. "Ah, here is a good friar to aid us. Might we have a meal while we await my brother? We'll eat out in your garden, if you like."

"As you will, my lord," said the man. "A small meal."

"I believe my brother is making a substantial contribution to your coffers," Miles said pointedly.

"A large meal then," the monk said with disgust, then he stomped off.

"Now that's seen to," Miles said, putting his arm around Jennifer's shoulders, "let us find somewhere to sit and I will explain to you why I did what I did."

Jennifer walked with him over to a bench. They sat down with John and Montgomery on the ground at their feet. Miles made small talk with his brothers, critiqued Nicholas's swordplay, and gave no sign that he had been in a terrible fight not five minutes earlier. He waited until a tray of food had been deposited on the ground before them by a monk who departed as quickly as he'd come, then looked at her.

"Will you know it all?"

"I suppose I might as well, given all the trouble you went to for it."

Miles had a long drink of wine, then set his cup aside. "I suppose to understand what drives Nicholas, you should understand a bit of our family history."

Jennifer suppressed a smile. Those de Piagets and genealogy. And from the horse's mouth, no less. This was certainly something she could share with Megan the next time she saw her.

"Go on," she said with a smile. "I'm all ears for that at least."

Miles nodded. "Without giving you details that Nicholas actually might prefer to give you himself, let me just say that through an unusual series of events in the past, my elder siblings have a unique parentage. Nicholas belongs to my father alone, my brother Robin belongs to both my father and mother, and my sister Amanda belongs to my mother alone."

"So Nicholas and Amanda do not share the same blood."

"Nay, they do not," Miles agreed.

Well, it was one thing to be in love with your sister when you were related; it was another thing when you weren't. "I see," she said.

"So you do. Now, the rest of us, my sister Isabelle and I, and the little twins here, were born to my parents after they wed. Robin, Nicholas, and Amanda were adopted by my parents after their wedding. That doesn't, however, change the fact that both Robin and Nicholas were born bastards."

"I see."

"It is also true that Nicholas and Amanda did love each other for years, which only I seemed to notice, but in the end, she wed with another." He paused. "I suppose that it was nothing more than the love of a brother and sister for each other, but it was a deep love, for Amanda had been his most ardent champion for years. She wed a year ago."

"Nay, Miles," Montgomery said. " 'Twas a year and then half a year again."

"You have it aright," Miles agreed. He looked at Jennifer. "Before that time, Nicholas was the most pleasant of us all. He is perfectly versed in all the courtly arts of love. He can sing and dance, speak many languages, and is cheerful and good-humored at all times."

"So, what happened to make him — oh, never mind, Amanda married someone else."

Miles nodded. "Aye."

"And that led to Nicholas's unhappiness?"

"That and my grandmother trying to find him a wife." Miles paused. "The wenches have not been kind."

"But why not?" she asked, surprised. "He seems like any woman's dream."

"Being a bastard is not necessarily an asset," Miles said dryly.

"But you said being Artane's son was enough."

"For everyone else, perhaps, but not for Nick." He looked off toward the abbey thoughtfully. "I had hoped that if I forced him to spew out his secrets, if he saw that a beautiful woman didn't care about them . . . well," he said, turning back to her, "it was obviously an ill-conceived thought." He paused. "Do you care about the condition of his birth?"

"I don't," she said quietly. "But I don't think my opinion matters."

Miles looked at her for a moment or two,

then smiled faintly. "You never know. And you'll also not know how delightful this repast is unless we eat it before the little lads finish it off. John, this meal is not all for you!"

Jennifer helped herself while she could and listened to the friendly bickering between Miles and his younger brothers. After what she'd just witnessed, it seemed very mild and very normal. She was also finding it very normal to be eating stuff that was just this side of Dickensian gruel, chatting with medieval nobility in a medieval monastery's garden, and speculating about the future of a certain medieval lord.

She was just too damned adaptable, apparently.

"Well," Miles said as they finished, "where to now, Mistress Jennifer?"

She took a deep breath. "I think I need to go north and a little west. There is . . . um . . . a field."

"A field," Miles said, sounding unconcerned. "As you will, then."

"Shouldn't we wait for Nicholas?"

Miles smiled. "If you have any affection for me at all, then nay, we shouldn't. I imagine he isn't overly pleased with me."

"You deserved it."

"A brother's love," he said offhandedly. "Let us go. He'll find us."

"Will he?" she asked seriously. "Or will he go back to Wyckham?"

"Does it matter to you?"

She looked at the abbey before she could stop herself, then back at Miles. "I would like to thank him for his help."

"He'll follow. When his pride and his business here will let him."

"I wouldn't worry about Nick," Montgomery put in. "He's a marvelously skilled tracker. He can follow anything, if he wants to. He'll find us."

"I hope he takes his time and allows his fury to subside," Miles said dryly. He looked at his younger brothers. "I almost made him lose his temper, didn't I?"

"Almost," John said seriously. "But not quite. I vow he twitched but a time or two. What say you, Montgomery?"

"He was mostly unmoved," Montgomery offered.

"He didn't look unmoved to me," Jennifer said uneasily.

"Think you?" Miles asked. "For myself, I would just like, once in my life, to see him in a towering rage. His neck bulging unattractively. His eyes rolling back in his head. A bit of froth at his mouth." He shook his head. "He's too bloody pretty, even when he's annoyed. Now, take me for example. When I am angry, I am quite a sight."

Jennifer snorted. "You're all terribly handsome and hopelessly charming. And I think you should just leave him alone."

"I cannot. I miss the Nick I grew to manhood admiring. The man who calls himself my brother is far too gloomy and unhappy. And that has made me sentimental. Come, my lady, and let us be on our way. You'll take Montgomery's horse and we'll discuss our destination as we ride."

Jennifer took Nicholas's cloak, folded it, and laid it over his saddle. She stroked his horse's nose for good measure, then walked back over to her little company. She held the reins of Montgomery's horse and started to put her foot in the stirrup when she chanced to look back at the abbey. Nicholas was coming out the door. He stopped when he saw her and simply stared.

She stared back.

She couldn't help herself.

Nicholas cursed as he walked across the grass. He came to a stop in front of them and dragged his hand through his hair.

"This is going to be more complicated than I thought," he said wearily. "Apparently Mark does have kin. The abbot told me of them himself."

"No doubt," Miles murmured.

Nicholas shot him a dark look. "I'm in no position to argue with him, am I? I'll ride to the village, see if they exist, then see to them. 'Tis the very least I can do."

"Do you want company?" Miles asked.

"Yours?" Nicholas said in disbelief. "Thank

you, but I believe I've had enough of your company today."

Miles only shrugged, apparently unoffended. "I had to offer."

Nicholas gave him a look of fury before he took a deep breath, then turned to Jennifer. His expression was anything but furious.

She thought it might have been a little bleak.

"You're on your way, then," he said quietly.

She nodded. She didn't bother to try to speak. It would have been impossible past the lump in her throat.

"A safe journey to you then," he said. He took her left hand, bent low over it, then straightened. "Fare you well, lady."

And with that, he strode over to his horse, swung up onto its back, and rode out the abbey gates. Jennifer stared after him until she couldn't see him anymore. Actually, that didn't take very long. Her tears were definitely getting in her way.

"Come, Jennifer," Miles said softly. "We'll away as well."

She nodded and let him boost her up into the saddle.

She followed Miles out of the gates and turned north. She was grateful that he seemed content to let the horses meander for a bit; she was completely unequal to determining where Farris's potato field might find itself. Perhaps in another hour or so, when she could see again and when her heart didn't hurt so much.

She wished she'd thrown her arms around Nicholas and hugged him for an eternity. She wished she'd said anything to him.

She almost wished she could have stayed behind with him.

But that was impossible. She had to go home. She pulled John's hood up around her face and let her tears fall unimpeded.

Yes, home was her only choice.

Chapter 15

Nicholas walked his horse across the meadow toward Miles's camp, cursing. Damnation, when were his troubles with abbeys going to end? He'd found Jennifer at an abbey. He'd found himself recently gouged far beyond what a normal set of prayers for a man's soul should have cost at an abbey. He was going to have to endure Ledenham's presence near Wyckham because of an abbey. Perhaps he would do well to avoid them in the future.

At least his recent business at Seakirk had been something of a distraction. He had followed the abbot's directions to the proper village and discovered for himself that Mark did indeed have aged parents, as well as a sister. The family had taken the news of their son's death very hard. Perhaps at another time Nicholas might have been less affected by it, but the entire time he had looked at those poor people, he'd thought about Jennifer's parents, also no doubt grieving for their missing child.

Sobering, indeed.

Nicholas had given them wergeld to compensate them for the loss of their son and offered them a portion to farm at Wyckham as freemen if they so desired. Past that, there had been nothing to do to ease their suffering. Masonry was not without its perils, which Mark had known. Still, the expression on the mother's face had been difficult to look at.

Did Jennifer's mother in the Future wear that look?

Perhaps not, now. He was sure Jennifer had found her time gate, had found that it worked to her satisfaction, and she was now sitting happily before her fire in the Future, enjoying luxuries he couldn't begin to imagine.

He cursed for quite some time.

It did no good to think on it. She was gone and he would be better off without her. He was fairly sure that he would begin to believe that immediately after his heart didn't feel as though it had been ripped from his chest by bare hands.

Some of that pain could be laid at Miles's feet. If Miles hadn't provoked him, he might at least have been able to say good-bye to her properly.

He spent several satisfying moments imagining up all the ways he could kill his brother, then an equal number of less satisfying moments thinking on all the reasons why he shouldn't.

He sighed and dragged his hand through his hair. Perhaps he should have been grateful to Miles. Uncanny was the only way to describe his brother's ability to cut to the heart of any matter and wrench it to his own purposes. What his purpose had been in the bit of business at the abbey Nicholas couldn't have said. Perhaps it had been to force him to face what truly grieved him. Much of his current discontent did indeed spring from the issue of his parentage, something he had passed most of his adult life being unconcerned about.

In his own family, it never came up unless Robin was feeling particularly vile, but since Robin was actually a bastard himself, Nicholas had gleefully thrown the term back at his brother as often as Robin had tossed it his way.

As far as the law was concerned, he was the adopted and therefore legal son of Rhys de Piaget. At court, that had been enough. If anyone spoke of it, they didn't dare do so to his face. He hardly cared what anyone said behind his back. He had never lacked for company of the highest quality either at supper or in his bed. But somehow that had changed once his grandmère had begun to seek him a wife. Perhaps it was one thing to take Rhys de Piaget's natural son to your bed; 'twas another thing entirely to take him to the priest.

At first he had been surprised that such a thing would matter to anyone. After a time, he'd been irritated by it, then amused, then simply weary. Was there no wench in England who wouldn't look at him and think him less than he was for something he couldn't change?

He wondered what Jennifer had thought. He didn't want to think about how much her opinion had come to matter to him. Not that it made any difference now, now that she was gone.

He pushed aside the thought and continued on his way. He'd tracked Miles the day before to a camp near a meadow, then realized that his brothers had turned for the coast. Perhaps Miles was planning to return to Artane. Nicholas would have made the same decision in his place. Given that he had no hall to return to at the moment, he had willingly taken up their trail and followed it as it made its way east. At least at Artane he might have a decent meal or two.

The only thing that had disturbed him had been the other trail he'd seen whilst he'd been following his brothers. It had occurred to him at one point that someone had been trailing after Miles in the same way he had, but then those tracks had eventually veered off to the north. It was unsettling just the same. It had made him realize just how foolish it had been to leave Jennifer in the care of three children, even for a short time.

Nicholas snorted. Children, indeed. Miles would have disagreed strongly with that term.

He sighed deeply and continued on his way to the fire. He stopped outside the circle of firelight, took the saddle and bridle off his horse, then sent his horse off to roam freely in search of supper. The beast would return. He, at least, seemed to find Nicholas tolerable company.

Nicholas walked over to the fire, set his gear down, then stopped short. Miles was sitting there, warming his hands against the blaze. Montgomery and John were stretched out nearby, senseless and drooling.

Jennifer was sleeping on the far side of the fire, dressed in her Future clothes.

He could scarce believe his eyes.

"Something to eat?"

Nicholas wrenched his gaze away from her and looked at his brother. "She was unsuccessful?"

Miles patted the ground next to him. "I'll tell you of it quietly. Eat something first."

Nicholas sat down mostly because he wasn't equal to standing anymore.

"Food?"

Nicholas blinked and looked at his brother. "What?"

"You need to eat," Miles said with a faint smile. "We'll talk after you do."

Nicholas nodded, ate a quick supper only because Miles shoved it into his hands, then drained his cup gratefully. "Thank you."

"You're welcome. For the food as well."

Nicholas pursed his lips. "I will be long in thanking you for the other. Be grateful I've had time since then to convince myself your death wouldn't serve me."

"I am," Miles said. "Truly."

Nicholas snorted. "I daresay you aren't, but we'll leave that for now. Tell me instead of your journey."

"There isn't much to tell," Miles said with a shrug. "We went to a field half a day's ride from here. Jennifer walked around it for an hour, growing increasingly frantic." He looked at Nicholas. "Nothing happened, but you likely could have divined that on your own."

"I should have come sooner," Nicholas said, rubbing his hands over his face. "I should have been there."

"To what end?" Miles asked. "You couldn't have aided her. By the way, why did you take so long? Were you having yourself a goodly pout?"

"Nay," Nicholas said, reaching out to slap his brother sharply on the back of the head. "I was off making peace with Mark's family."

"Then he had one after all."

"Aye. Parents and a sister. I saw to them."

"Of course you did," Miles said quietly.

"I'm sorry, then. That couldn't have been easy."

Nicholas nodded but said nothing more. He couldn't, considering that Jennifer was still with them and her mother no doubt grieved for her centuries in the Future.

A double-edged sword, indeed.

"Of course, you were likely delayed as well by time spent contemplating how best to do me in."

"Aye, that, too."

"I did provoke you terribly," Miles said easily. "Of course, when *I* am provoked, I don't stomp off like an overindulged brat."

Nicholas started to curse him, then couldn't help a brief laugh instead. "By the saints, you are a disrespectful chit of a girl. No one dares talk to me that way."

"Perhaps someone should have long before now."

"Aye, likely so," Nicholas agreed. He looked out into the dark for several moments before he turned back to his brother. "Have I truly been so foul?"

"You know you have."

Nicholas sighed. "When you are a score and eight and have no woman to call your own, nor children to love, then you will understand."

"I have no intention of being a score and eight and unwed."

"And you think I did?" Nicholas demanded.

"By the saints, Miles, I despair of ever finding a woman who doesn't look at me and think *bastard*."

"It disturbs you so deeply?"

"You have no idea. You have no flaw that makes women think twice before they consent to kneel with you before a priest."

"Oh, I don't know," Miles said, stretching lazily. "Perfection does present its problems as well."

Nicholas threw his cup at his brother. "Why do I talk to you?"

"I'm not sure," Miles admitted with a laugh. He set Nicholas's cup aside. "As for the other, I cannot believe you haven't met your share of women who would have had you no matter that fatal flaw."

"Not a one," Nicholas said. "Not a single, bloody one of them."

"Perhaps you should look further afield. Perhaps you should consider a woman from *very* far away."

Nicholas looked at Jennifer before he could stop himself. She was sleeping near the fire, still lovely, still bewitching, still not of his time.

"Nay," he rasped. "I couldn't."

"But what if she is the one for you? What if that is what Fate has decreed?"

"Then Fate has a very vile sense of humor, which I already knew. Nay," he said, shaking his head, "she will go and that will be that.

Now, why don't *you* go and leave me in peace. I think I've had enough speech to-night."

"As you will," Miles said. He rose and went to make himself a place on the other side of the fire. "Don't nap whilst you should be standing guard."

"I don't think I could."

How could he, when there was such loveliness so unexpectedly still there for his enjoyment?

He fed the fire occasionally and spent the rest of the night watching Jennifer McKinnon sleep.

Poor fool that he was.

She woke when the stars were wheeling toward morning. Nicholas wished suddenly, and quite desperately, that he'd had more time to steel himself against the feelings he knew he shouldn't have for her. She would return home. She had no choice, damn it.

She sat up, saw him, then smiled.

He closed his eyes briefly, then looked at her and surrendered. What else could he do?

"You found us," she said, sounding pleased.

"I did," he managed.

"Miles said you would. He said you are a very good tracker."

"My misspent youth," he said with a negligent shrug.

She smiled and drew the blanket around her shoulders. "Is that so?"

Nicholas searched for something else to talk about, but found nothing useful. Was he to apologize for his tantrum? Was he to explain to her things that couldn't possibly interest her? Was he to again spew out all his secrets and expect absolution?

Or should he just hand her his sword and invite her to inflict a fatal wound so he might escape his own foolish thoughts?

"Nicholas?"

He blinked and found that she was looking at him. "Aye?" he said.

"You were cursing."

"Did Miles figure prominently in my slander?"

She smiled. "He didn't, but he probably should have."

Nicholas reached for a cup and poured her wine. He held it out to her. "Do I have any secrets left, or did that babbling fool spew them all out?"

She rose and came to sit down next to him. She took the cup, then seemed to consider her words for quite some time. Nicholas wondered what she was thinking, then found himself distracted by her nearness. It was all he could do not to reach out and touch that flaming hair of hers that cascaded over her shoulders and down her back. It took even more self-control not to stroke the porcelain perfection of her cheek.

He decided that thinking on kissing her was

extraordinarily stupid, so he forbore.

"Nicholas?"

He blinked. "Aye?"

She smiled. "You were very far away."

"Ah, I'm distracted," he managed. "What were we speaking of?"

"Secrets," she said with a grave smile. "Yours, actually, and no, Miles didn't tell me more of yours than you did yourself. And those secrets of yours didn't seem all that startling."

"But I have a murky past," he managed.

"Do you," she said with a smile. "What horrible thing did you do that makes your past so murky?"

He took a deep breath. "As I told you before, I was born a bastard."

She waited. "And?"

He frowned. "Isn't that enough?"

"For what? To force women to run screaming the other way? Of course not. What difference does it make?"

"What difference does it make," he echoed weakly. "It makes a great deal of difference to some."

"Then they are idiots. I mean, look at you. What's not to like?"

He wanted desperately to stop and catch his breath. She had shrugged off his darkest secret as if it were nothing.

He could scarce believe it.

"You're doing it again," she said pleasantly.

He dragged himself back to the present, though it was not easily done. "Forgive me," he managed. "I daresay I think too much at times."

"Don't we all," she said dryly.

"I will be more attentive," he vowed. He paused. "You know, I can actually be chivalrous."

"So I've heard," she said, looking at him with one eyebrow raised, "but I have yet to see it."

"I did rescue you, if you remember. Twice."

"You complained the entire time."

He found himself smiling. "I didn't."

"You did. My ears are still burning. I suppose that's my fault for trying to understand what you were saying."

He refilled her cup and helped himself to it. "I'll try to refrain from it in the future, especially since you took the trouble to learn my tongue when you could have limited yourself to conversing with my brother in Gaelic."

"Miles says you speak several languages," she said, wrapping her arms around her knees and resting her cheek against her forearm. "I don't suppose Gaelic is one of them, is it?"

"I don't suppose it is —" Nicholas stopped short. He realized that she was speaking in Gaelic. More frightening still, he wasn't sure how long she'd been doing it. He looked at

her and came very close to blushing. "Um
—"

"Your misspent youth?"

"Nay, the past year and a half with Montgomery at my heels and Petter at my side."

"You could have told me," she chided. "Did you just want to see if I'd say anything nasty about you?"

"Aye, something like that."

"And what other languages do you speak, just so I'll know?"

"Latin, Spanish, a Germanic language or two, and a little Hebrew," he admitted. "And, well, Gaelic."

"You could have told me and saved me weeks of trying to learn French."

"Miles would have missed conversing with you," he said. "Consider it a favor for him."

"I will," she said. She continued to look at him as if what she saw was not unpleasing. "By the way, did you find Mark's family?"

He nodded, grateful for something else to think on besides the sorry state of affairs in his heart. "Aye. I offered them a place at Wyckham and paid them the price for their son's life." He paused. "The mother was grieved."

"No doubt," Jennifer said quietly.

Nicholas wanted to ask her what she thought her mother was thinking, but he didn't dare. He was horribly torn. On one hand, he was profoundly grateful that her

252

other gate had not worked, on the other he was well aware of what her mother must be feeling.

He steadfastly refused to think about Jake Kilchurn and anything he might or might not know about traveling through time.

He chewed on his next words for quite a while, then sighed. He would have to ask eventually. 'Twas best he had it over with. "You didn't find your kin, I assume," he said quietly.

She took a deep breath, then shook her head. "I didn't," she said, looking at the fire.

"Is there anywhere else?" he asked, though he supposed he knew the answer already. She had said she had two locations to try.

Two damned gates through time.

He supposed there weren't curses enough for all of them.

"Yes," she said. She paused. "One more place that I know about."

"Of course," he said. "I'll take you there."

She looked at him with a grave expression. "I'm sorry," she said quietly. "You probably want to be back home."

"Actually, Wyckham is a rather depressing place right now," he admitted, "save the garden, which you made beautiful. I am perfectly content to see you delivered safely to your kin."

"Thank you."

He nodded, but he didn't deserve her

thanks given that he couldn't say he meant what he'd just said and he would likely spend the next few hours cursing and wishing he'd never rescued her that first time. It was Fate that had brought him there at the right time.

Fate.

A terrible old woman with no heart.

He would have to have a word with her after he'd put the shattered pieces of his own back together.

CHAPTER 16

Jennifer reined in Montgomery's horse, looked at the collection of boulders in front of her, and wondered if now would be the proper time to have a nervous breakdown. It didn't look like a time gate in front of her, it looked like a bunch of rocks. But Thomas had said something was there and Jamie had confirmed it. At the time, she hadn't cared. Now, she cared very much. She had to care; it was her last chance. If this didn't work, she was stuck.

She slipped off Montgomery's horse, waited until her legs were steady beneath her, then looked again at the day. The sky was full of dark clouds, the wind was chilly, and she thought she might be getting a cold. That had either come from camping out the night before or from too much weeping after she had insisted that Nicholas get a little sleep.

Dawn, firelight, and a gorgeous knight to stare at.

Obviously a very bad combination.

She sniffed and tried to get hold of herself. She wasn't a crier. She was more apt to go for a run or scrub her bathroom or pour her energy into playing very fast things on her violin. She'd wept more in the past month than she had in her entire life. It was not a good sign.

She patted the pockets of her jeans. Cell phone, keys, credit cards. All residing where they were supposed to. She looked down at herself. She looked the part of a twenty-first-century gal. In fact, it was really easy to just look out over the ocean she could see a mile away from her and imagine that it was the same ocean that found itself in modern England. Honestly, the countryside just didn't look any different. She half expected to look up and see a plane flying overhead.

But then she made the mistake of glancing behind her.

There, in a little row, stood her escorts. Her medieval escorts.

She wasn't back in Kansas yet.

She led Montgomery's horse over to him and handed him the reins. She smiled as best she could. "Thank you," she said. "Your horse is very well behaved."

Montgomery nodded, mute.

Jennifer hugged him quickly. "Take care of your brother," she whispered in his ear, then pulled back and smiled at him. "You know which one."

"I will," he promised, then smiled shyly. "I wish you could stay."

She nodded, but found quite suddenly that she couldn't speak for the lump in her throat. She turned and hugged John, who actually seemed to be having as much trouble speaking as she was. Then she turned to Miles.

He pulled her into what she could only call a very thorough embrace. She let him hug her far longer than she should have, then pulled back and laughed up at him through her tears.

"You're terrible."

"I wish you could stay, too," he said. "But if not, I think it only right that I kiss you good-bye."

"Only if it is to be your last act," Nicholas growled. "Release the poor wench before she hurts you. And if she doesn't, I will."

Jennifer smiled at Miles, kissed him on the cheek, then pulled away and turned to look at Nicholas. She didn't think she could touch him; if she did, she might not be able to let go.

"I have to go," she said.

He only nodded.

She took a step backward. "You can all ride off now." She hoped she sounded more confident than she felt. "I'm sure someone will be along for me soon."

Actually, she wasn't sure of that at all, but what else was she going to do? Give up? Give in? This had to be the place Thomas had told her about. He'd said it was about two miles north of Artane. Jamie had warned her about the same place when he'd learned she was going to Artane. Jennifer was almost positive this was the same group of big rocks. All she had to do was sit on them and she would be home.

Or so she hoped.

She looked at Nicholas one last time. "Thank you, my lord," she said. "For the rescues."

He only nodded.

"You deserve someone spectacular."

"Hmmm," was all he said.

"You should go," she whispered.

He nodded, then gave his brothers shoves in the right direction. Jennifer watched them walk off, then turned away and walked over to the rocks. She sat down. Immediately, a light rain started up.

She started to swear.

After a while, she wondered if she might be sitting on the wrong rock, so she moved. Actually, she moved several times. There came a point when she realized that she had sat on every single rock there, no matter how small. And she'd felt no hint of a time gate anywhere.

She hadn't felt it in Farris's potato field — or what would someday become Farris's potato field — either. She'd recognized the countryside so she'd known she had been in the right place. Only the place hadn't been right for her.

She started to feel a little short of breath.

She stood up suddenly, then turned around. Nicholas and his brothers were clustered together, fifty feet away. Miles and the boys had their backs turned to her.

Nicholas was watching her.

Jennifer turned away. They probably thought she'd lost her mind. She didn't care. Besides, she was going to be home at any moment. She would leave Nicholas de Piaget safely in the past where he could find himself a medieval gal who would be thrilled to have him. She would go back to the future where she would spend ridiculous amounts of time trying to find someone just like him — and failing.

She forced that thought away. She wanted to go home. She wanted sheepskin slippers and hot chocolate on snowy Manhattan evenings. She wanted central air and a fireplace that wasn't big enough to roast an entire pig on. She wanted clean clothes every day, shampoo, toilet paper, potato chips, and slushies from the local Mini Mart. She wanted loud movies in theaters, her iPod with Rachmaninoff cranked up to the hilt, front-row seats to the New York Philharmonic. She'd had a great time with wide-open spaces and lots of silence in the Middle Ages, but now she wanted the hustle and bustle of her busy, filled-to-the-brim life.

Hell, at the moment, she wanted an umbrella.

She finally sat back down, because she was really tired of standing up. She closed her eyes and imagined she could hear the traffic from the A1.

In time, she realized it was just the roar of the ocean.

And still the drizzle continued. Jennifer felt like she was being misted by an invisible spray bottle that was fiendishly determined to soak through everything she had and leave her hair a frizzy, madly curling mess around her face.

Her stomach growled.

The afternoon continued to wear on. She didn't dare look behind her to see if the boys had gone. It was enough to just look in front of her and realize that the scenery just wasn't changing. Not that she'd needed that as confirmation. The gate here wasn't going to work for her, either.

She was, despite her best efforts, stuck. Stuck hundreds of years out of her time. Stuck with a man who would marry a woman of rank and riches. Stuck in a place where she had no way to make a living, no way to keep herself safe, no way to play anything she loved, no way to let her family know where — or when — she was.

She bowed her head and let the tears drip

down her nose.

Maybe she should have known, when she'd found the first time gate destroyed. Maybe she should have known when Farris's fairy ring didn't even acknowledge her presence. She definitely knew now that she'd found Thomas's rocks to be unresponsive.

She pushed herself up to her feet and walked away. She would live and die in the thirteenth century and no one would be the wiser. Her family would never find her because she wouldn't merit so much as a blip in the de Piaget genealogy, except possibly an entry about a daft wench who had stomped around grassy fields until she'd gone nuts, but Megan probably wouldn't be looking for that —

"Jennifer?"

She closed her eyes briefly. No, he didn't say her name the same way his brothers did. Apparently, he'd listened to her closely. For some reason, it was more overwhelming that way.

As if he knew her as well as her family did.

She was startled to realize he was so close to her. He put a cloak around her shoulders. She felt him pull her braid out from underneath it, then put his hands briefly on her shoulders. Then his hands were gone. Jennifer took a deep, unsteady breath.

"I'm sorry," she managed. "I've dragged you all over for no reason."

"Your kin," he began slowly, "you have missed meeting them here?"

"So it would seem," she said. She would have tried to wipe her eyes, but she was afraid that if she did anything but hug herself, she would shatter.

Music. Modern life. Her *family.*

She couldn't believe she would never have any of them again.

But she couldn't believe anything else.

"Perhaps . . ."

She waited. When he didn't finish, she took a deep breath. "Perhaps?"

"Perhaps you would care to take your ease at Artane."

She turned around slowly. "Artane?" she said breathlessly.

"My father's hall," he said. "We would not be unwelcome there. We would be safe and dry."

"It sounds wonderful," she said. She dabbed at her eyes with her sweater sleeve, but that didn't do much. She used the corner of Nicholas's cloak instead. "Wonderful," she repeated.

He simply stood there and looked at her for so long, she started to get uncomfortable.

"What?" she asked.

He shook his head. "I am simply sorry you have missed your kin. Is there no where else you can search for them?"

The thought of London flitted across her

mind, but her failure at Farris's field was enough to convince her that wasn't even worth trying. For one thing, the streets wouldn't be the same and there was no guarantee she would find the same location she'd used to get home from Elizabethan England. And even if she did find the same location, there would be no guarantee that it would work.

She could see that now.

She shook her head. "My home is very, very far away. I am here for a reason I don't understand." She looked down at the ground for a very long time. "I don't think I'll ever be able to go home," she said finally.

"Then stay with me."

She looked up at him in surprise. "What?"

"Stay with me *at Artane,*" he said quickly. "It is a beautiful hall, right on the edge of the sea. You can see it there to the south."

Jennifer looked toward where he was pointing. Yes, that was Artane all right.

She looked at it for a moment or two, then looked up the coast until she came to another castle on her left, quite far away. "And that?" she asked, pointing. "What is that castle there?"

"Raventhorpe. That is the keep of my sister Amanda and her husband."

She nodded. She'd seen Raventhorpe in the distance before, but it had been just the shell of a keep. She imagined it wasn't just a shell now.

"We could be home by dark, if we ride hard."

She turned around to look at him, but she couldn't see him very well. Her eyes were swimming with tears. "Thank you."

He only shook his head. " 'Tis nothing." He paused. "Perhaps another solution will present itself in a day or two."

"Sure," she managed, blinking rapidly. She doubted it, but she wasn't going to say as much.

"Artane?" he asked, reaching for her hand.

She nodded and walked with him over to where his brothers stood with their horses. He stopped in front of his horse, but kept hold of her hand. Jennifer looked at him, surprised.

"Am I not riding Montgomery's horse?"

"I thought perhaps you should ride with me."

She managed a smile. "Do I look that rattled?"

He nodded gravely.

She shivered. "I think you might be right." She turned and looked at Nicholas's stirrup; it was about level with her belly button — and she wasn't exactly short.

"Allow me to aid you," he said, cupping his hands for her.

She found herself boosted up into his

saddle as if she weighed nothing. How he managed to swing up behind her, she didn't know, but he did. His brothers were already in the saddle, ready to go.

"Home, lads," he said to his brothers. He took the reins from her, put his arm around her waist, and clicked at his horse. "Hold on," he said into her ear.

She shivered, and she suspected it wasn't really from the chill and the rain. She put her hands over his arm that held her and nodded. Once they were on their way, she let herself weep. The wind whipping in her eyes was perhaps cover enough.

"You're getting me wet."

Jennifer dragged her free arm across her eyes. She couldn't say anything.

He didn't seem to expect her to.

They reached the castle just after dark. Men greeted Nicholas as he rode up the way. Jennifer considered worrying about the fact that she was wearing jeans in a medieval setting, but the only light came from torches so she supposed she wouldn't have that much attention paid to her.

Then she found she had no more time to worry. She was too busy being flipped out by the sight of Artane, and a very medieval Artane indeed, in front of her.

She looked at the stairs and half expected to see Megan come bounding down them. It was simply mind-blowing to think her sister was staying inside that same castle right then.

Well, eight centuries from right then.

Nicholas stopped his horse in front of the stables and leaped down to the ground. He held up his arms for her. She let him help her down to the ground, then stood there and tried to keep herself from completely losing it. She had to take several deep breaths.

She wished they had helped.

Nicholas looked at her searchingly. "Are you unwell?"

Jennifer struggled to find something coherent to say. "I'm fine," she said, finally. "Artane is . . . magnificent."

"It makes Wyckham look a little shabby by comparison, doesn't it?"

"No, Wyckham is charming," she said, trying to keep her breathing steady. "You need some furniture, though."

He took her hand and led her toward the hall. "I daresay. Montgomery, you and John see to the horses."

"And me?" Miles asked politely.

"You keep out of my way."

Jennifer walked with Nicholas across the courtyard and up the stairs, stairs that she had walked up before, stairs her sister was probably walking up right now in a different century.

She had to take several more deep breaths.

"Jennifer?"

"I'm fine," she wheezed.

He didn't look convinced, but he didn't press her.

"Food," he said, pulling her arm through his. "Then a decent bed. You'll feel more yourself tomorrow."

She suspected it would take a great deal more than that to feel more herself, but she wasn't going to say as much. She let him open the door for her, then stepped into Artane's great hall.

Another deep breath was called for.

It wasn't as if she didn't recognize the place. Though she couldn't say she'd spent a lot of time there, she had visited a time or two. She knew where the kitchen was, where the lord's solar was, what the great hall looked like.

Only it didn't usually look as it did now — as if it had had a medieval makeover.

Nicholas led her over to the fireplace on the right-hand side of the hall. A dark-haired man sat there, but he leaped to his feet in astonishment at the sight of them. He clapped Nicholas on the shoulder briefly, then turned his attention to her.

"Who is this?" he asked.

"This is Jennifer McKinnon," Nicholas said. He looked at her. "My brother Robin."

Jennifer looked at Nicholas's older brother. *Older* perhaps was misleading. She didn't know the particulars, of course, but to her eye they looked identical, except for their coloring, which they had to have inherited from their mothers. They were obviously the same age.

There were, perhaps, a few more subtle differences. While Nicholas seemed, despite his recent irritations, to be fairly laid back, Robin simply radiated intensity. Jennifer found herself being scrutinized in a dizzying fashion. In a matter of seconds, she knew her clothes had been examined, her looks assessed, and the fact that her hand was tucked in the crook of Nicholas's elbow digested.

Robin smiled.

Well, apparently, she had passed some sort of muster. Robin barked at Miles to vacate the chair he'd just collapsed in and leave it for her.

Jennifer sat, grateful for something that didn't shift underneath her.

"My lady," Robin said pleasantly, "you must be hungry. I'm sure there's something left from supper."

"Wonderful," Nicholas said, sitting down next to her. "Why don't you go fetch it for us?"

"Why don't you?" Robin suggested. "I'll keep her company here."

"So will I," Miles said, dragging up a chair on her right. "She's endured Nicholas's foulness for almost a month, Rob. I daresay she deserves a respite of some kind."

Jennifer watched Nicholas glare first at Robin, then at Miles. Then he slapped his hands on his knees, stood up, and pulled her up out of her chair.

"I don't dare leave you with either of them," he muttered. "Come with me, if you will, and we'll make a brief foray into the larder."

Jennifer went with him, actually rather relieved to be with him instead of facing more scrutiny from his brother. She felt tremendously conspicuous in her clothes. She was grateful for Nicholas's cloak, because it hid at least a bit of what she was wearing, and for the forgiving light of fire and torch that obscured the rest.

Nicholas was greeted enthusiastically by the chef and provided with a hearty meal. He took his burdens and led her back out to the great hall. She tried not to shudder as she sat down next to him at the high table.

It was, as it happened, the same very antique, very rare table that Megan was probably sitting at right then.

"Okay," she said, taking a deep breath and reaching for her wine. "I can do this."

"Do what?"

She looked at Robin who had sat down on her right. She managed a smile. "Breathe," she admitted.

He laughed. "Poor girl. Has Nick been that trying?"

She shook her head. "He's been wonderful, actually."

"Indeed," Robin said, his eyes twinkling. "I can't imagine that."

"Robin," Nicholas warned.

Robin ignored him. "I'll leave you in peace tonight, since you've just arrived, but tomorrow I will pester you with all sorts of questions as to why you're here, why Nicholas is so protective, and why Miles can't take his eyes off you. Oh, and how you've managed to survive what has to have been at least some time in Nick's company without having your humors soured —"

"Rob, shut up," Nicholas growled.

"Don't want to," Robin said cheerfully.

"Do you care for aid in that?" Nicholas asked pointedly.

Jennifer held up her hands quickly. "I beg you both not to fight with me in the middle."

Robin laughed and poured her wine. "I see now that you have indeed passed a bit of time with the lads. Have they misbehaved?"

"Only Miles," she said with a smile.

"Ha!" Miles exclaimed. "I was my usual wonderful self, spreading good cheer and encouraging the sun to shine whenever possible."

Jennifer caught the murderous look Nicholas threw his younger brother and couldn't help but smile. How lovely it must be for them to have each other. She felt that way about her siblings. They were her fans, her critics, her best friends.

Several centuries away.

A few more deep breaths were called for after that.

Nicholas put his hand over hers briefly. "You're tired. Allow me to see you to my sister's chamber."

She nodded unsteadily. "Thank you. I think that might be best."

He rose, then helped her to her feet. Jennifer looked at Robin.

"Thank you, Lord Robin," she began.

He shook his head. " 'Tis just Robin. You may call me Artane if you're feeling particularly fawning."

Nicholas snorted. "He'll not earn that title until our sire is dead and that won't happen for years. Do not flatter him. Artane, indeed."

Jennifer winced as he took her right hand. He stopped and looked down.

"Does it still pain you?"

"Not so much," she said. She managed a smile. "You did good work on it. Another few days and I'm sure it'll be fine."

If only she could have said the same thing for the rest of herself.

She walked up the stairs with him. In time, he stopped in front of a door.

"My sister Isabelle's chamber," he said. "She'll be pleased that you used it."

Jennifer nodded, then felt her eyes start to

burn. "I can't begin to thank you —"

"Don't," he interrupted. "In truth, I did little." He opened the door, fetched a candle, then lit it with one of the torches in the hallway. He handed it to her. "Sleep if you can."

She nodded, then went inside the bedroom. She froze.

She heard Nicholas shut the door behind her, but she couldn't look back. She stood in the middle of the room until she thought she could move without shattering.

She walked across the floor and put the candle down on a table. She leaned on the casement of the window. She didn't need daylight to know what the view would look like. She didn't need a lamp to know that the corner to her left was the perfect place for an armoire or that there was space enough between the armoire and the wall to stash her violin.

There was nothing quite like staying in the same room she'd been staying in before — only almost 800 years earlier.

She kicked off her shoes, shucked off her jeans, and crawled beneath the covers. She had to get back up and blow out the candle, but that wasn't hard. She got back in bed, closed her eyes, and let the irony wash over her and continue on its way.

She didn't have to think about anything, she just had to sleep.

At least she had a bed, if only temporarily. It could have been so much worse.

She didn't want to consider how much worse it could have been.

She suspected she would learn the extent of that soon enough.

CHAPTER 17

Nicholas sat in front of the fire and looked at the gray dress in his hands. It had been Amanda's, but given that he'd found it in his mother's mending pile, he supposed it was something she intended for Isabelle and wouldn't mind if he took for his own use. The gown would have suited either of his sisters, for they shared the same dark hair, fair skin, and aqua eyes of their mother, but he wasn't sure it would do for Jennifer.

He wasn't unaccustomed to marking the color of a woman's gown. He was, especially when it was of such a vile hue that it made her look like a corpse. It would take a truly horrible color to make Jennifer look like anything but an angel.

He rose and held the dress up to himself. It was too short. He hadn't truly thought about how much taller than his sisters Jennifer was until that moment. He leaned over and saw that the hem hit him just below the knees. It would need to be lengthened if it was to serve her.

"It looks lovely on you, truly."

Nicholas lifted his head. "It isn't for me, as you well know."

"A pity," Robin said with a grin. "The color sets your hair off to perfection."

Nicholas contemplated stabbing his brother with his mother's scissors, but decided against it. They were her prized possession and very rare. He'd found them in Rome himself and brought them back to her several years ago. Nay, he would have to settle for a glare, which he indulged in thoroughly as he resumed his seat. He looked through extra bits of material he'd brought with him and tried to decide what he thought might look best at the bottom of the dress.

He decided on a swath of gold silk and set to measuring it so he could cut it.

"That doesn't match."

Nicholas glared at Robin. "Did I ask your opinion?"

"I thought you might be afraid to," Robin said, rubbing a finger over his mouth as if he strove to fight his smile. "So I offered it freely."

"I think I'll manage on my own, thank you just the same," Nicholas said. He cut the material to the right length, then threaded a needle and started to sew.

"Miles told me about your roof," Robin

remarked finally. "A pity."

Nicholas nodded, but continued on with his work. "At least it was only one life lost. It could have been worse."

"Aye, it could have been," Robin agreed.

Nicholas soldiered on. He knew he couldn't have been so fortunate as to have Robin decide to go to bed. He steeled himself for the onslaught he knew was coming.

It came, of course, only after Robin had cleared his throat pointedly several times, shifted in his chair an equal number of times, and crossed and uncrossed his legs until Nicholas suspected he might need a rest.

"So," Robin said, drawing the word out for an inordinate amount of time, "what other mischief have you been combining this past month whilst you've been away?"

"Nothing of interest."

"Nothing?" Robin echoed in mock disbelief. "No sword fights? No enemies routed? No abbots tormented?"

Nicholas looked at him from under his eyebrows. "What has Miles already told you?"

"Unfortunately very little. He said he'd revealed too many of your secrets of late."

Well, at least Miles had found sense. Nicholas despaired of Robin finding the same.

"So you went to Seakirk Abbey," Robin continued. "How did you find it?"

"As I always do."

"And the abbot?"

"The same."

"The weather?"

Nicholas sighed and looked up from his work. "It rained. Now, what is it you want?"

"Is it not enough simply to want to converse with my younger brother? Can I not be interested in his life? In his doings —"

"Let me be interested in yours instead," Nicholas interrupted him. "I take it Anne and the lads are at Fenwyck?"

Robin looked momentarily baffled at the reversing of the attack, but he seemed to recover soon enough. "Aye."

"You didn't go with them."

"Would you?" Robin asked with a shudder. "I can scarce bear Anne's sire's vile self when I leave her there and yet again when I return to fetch her. You'll note, however, that I left my entire collection of lads to guard her. Geoffrey of Fenwyck is incapable of protecting his larder, much less my wife."

"Then I wonder that you left her there at all," Nicholas mused. "Surely you'll want to hurry back and see that she is well."

"I will, after my curiosity is satisfied about you."

"What of the rest of the family?" Nicholas asked. "Mother? Father? Isabelle?"

Robin frowned, obviously frustrated. "They escorted Grandmère back to Segrave."

Nicholas sighed in relief. "At least I am safe from her ministrations for a time."

"Don't breathe too easily," Robin advised. "You know she only left to drop off the current crew and take on another. She intends to return as soon as she can collect them all."

"Surely not."

"Oh, aye," Robin said, rubbing his hands together with enthusiasm. "I daresay she will outdo herself this time. I understand 'tis quite a powerful band she will bring. You should also know that she vows to see you wed by Michaelmas."

"Or?"

"Or one of you dies."

Nicholas blinked in surprise. "In truth?"

"Aye," Robin said happily. "Either you or Joanna will be dead before the Yule log burns, unless you wed. She has sworn it." He paused. "I daresay you don't want to test one of her vows. Then again, perhaps you will have solved the problem for her before that time."

"How so?"

Robin threw up his hands in frustration. "The wench, Nick! By the saints, you are tight-lipped about her!"

"So I am."

"Aren't you going to tell me *anything?*"

Nicholas looked at him evenly. "Aye, here is something: mind your own affairs."

"Your happiness is my affair."

"It isn't."

"She was wearing interesting garb."

Nicholas set his stitching down in his lap. "You won't relent, will you?"

Robin smiled in a genuinely affectionate manner. "I'm curious, Nick. You leave for a pair of fortnights, then return with a gorgeous woman, a woman, I might add, who is wearing clothing that should likely be fed to the fire this very night lest someone look at her askance."

"Hence my labors upon her gown."

"Burn her clothes, Nick," Robin said seriously.

Nicholas grimaced. "I fear she will need them again."

"Is she going home?" Robin asked.

"What do you mean?"

Robin looked at him levelly. "You know what I mean. I've seen clothing like that before and I know exactly where it comes from. When I say *home,* I mean the Future and you know it."

Nicholas started to speak, then shut his mouth. He considered, then sighed. "If you must know, she did try to go back."

"Go forward."

"That's what I meant," Nicholas growled.

Robin only looked at him calmly. "And?"

Nicholas looked down at the gown in his hands. It didn't look dreadful with that strip of gold at the bottom, but it wasn't wonderful, either. His sisters wouldn't have worn it. His mother, that woman of tremendous patience, might even have hesitated. Obviously, he would have to have new clothes made for Jennifer. Robin had that aright; her Future clothes would have to be burned.

"Nick."

Nicholas looked up. "Aye?"

"Tell me all."

Nicholas hesitated only briefly. Robin knew his most atrocious secrets and only laughed at them. He was as ready with his fists as he was with his manly backslaps. Nicholas knew that whatever he told Robin would go no further, not even to Anne. Well, perhaps to Anne, but she was an even better secret keeper than her husband.

He sighed. "She came through a time gate in Ledenham's abbey."

"The abbey he's building?" Robin asked incredulously.

"Aye."

"I can scarce believe it. Of all places."

"Aye, I know." Nicholas sighed. "I rescued her from being burned as a witch. By Ledenham, of course."

Robin whistled softly. " 'Twas fortunate you were there, then. So, you rescued her, then you noticed her clothes."

"Aye."

"And you knew what sort of traveler she was."

"Aye."

Robin looked at him for a moment, then he

laughed.

Nicholas gritted his teeth.

Robin continued to laugh. He laughed so long and so forcefully, that he had to stand up and lean over until he caught his breath. Finally, he sat back down and wiped the tears from his eyes.

"Ah, Nick," he said with a gasp. "You, of all people."

"Trust me, I'm still shaking my head over it," Nicholas grumbled.

"And after all your snorts at Raventhorpe, all your ill treatment of Jake Kilchurn, all your unwillingness to believe anything he said —"

"Aye, I know!" Nicholas exclaimed. "Trust me, I've been living with the irony of it for a month now."

Robin grinned. "Did she fall in love with you right off, or take one look at you and immediately try to return to her time?"

Nicholas scowled at his brother. "She tried to return home, of course, as she should have." He continued with his work. "She tried three separate places. None of them worked."

"But what of Jake's —"

"She tried all the places *she* knew," Nicholas said, cutting him off. "And that is enough."

Robin gaped at him.

"She's weary," Nicholas continued, bending back to his work. "She needs to rest. After she rests, she can try again." He sewed for a moment or two. "If she wishes to."

Robin was silent for so long, Nicholas couldn't stop himself from looking up. Robin was looking at him in complete astonishment.

"But you know where a gate lies that *does* work."

Nicholas looked away. "Rumor. Rumor and hearsay. Who's to say if Jake is telling the truth or not?"

"Nick!"

"Perhaps it only works for him," Nicholas continued. "Besides, 'tis best that she stay here for a time. Until she is rested."

He continued to stare into the fire. Finally, he realized that Robin was silent. He didn't want to, but he knew that he would eventually have to face his brother. He sighed, finally, and turned to look at Robin.

Robin wore an expression of profound pity.

"You poor bastard," he said.

"I despise that word," Nicholas said.

"Why? I'm a bastard, too."

"But your mother and father are now wed."

"They certainly weren't when I was conceived and you bloody well know it's more complicated than that. Besides, I didn't mean the word that way. Bloody hell, Nick, when are you going to let the past go?"

"Ha!" Nicholas exclaimed. "You're a fine one to talk. It took you years to come to terms with quite a few disagreeable bits of your past. Such as how you keep running into children without fathers who look so damned much like you —"

Robin attacked with a growl.

It was the growl that saved them both from being stabbed by a needle. Nicholas had time to set aside his stitching before his brother took both him and his chair backward onto the floor.

It was a glorious brawl. It was lovely to not have any sense of responsibility or restraint preventing him from fully taking his frustrations out on Robin. It was a pleasure, and nothing but.

Half an hour later Nicholas sat on the floor next to his brother and winced as he put his hand to his eye. Robin looked worse, so he couldn't complain.

"I left you with your teeth intact," Robin said, "though you deserved to lose several of them for your cheek."

"You don't want to saddle yourself with me as the eternally unwed uncle to your children," Nicholas said. "Self-serving, as you usually are." He reached over and picked up his stitching.

"You like her."

Nicholas sighed, set the gown in his lap, and looked at his elder brother. "Unfortunately."

"She could prove to be a most disagreeable wench," Robin pointed out. "Feisty. Of a complaining and dissatisfied nature."

"Perhaps."

"And yet you are unafraid."

"As always."

Robin was silent for far longer than was no doubt good for him, then he sighed. "So, you'll let her rest."

"Aye."

"And then?"

Nicholas sewed in silence for several moments, then forced himself to look at Robin. "As I said before, she tried all the places she knew. I have no *proof* that there is anywhere else she might try. You didn't see her standing for hours on a bloody clutch of rocks that was nothing but a clutch of rocks. Another disappointment is more than I can watch her endure."

"So you will keep her here."

"I will offer her the hospitality of my father's hall," Nicholas corrected. "I will clothe her properly, feed her well, and make certain she sleeps in a comfortable bed."

"And hope to hell she falls in love with you before she learns what you know."

Nicholas felt his jaw drop. He wished he could predict when Robin would spew forth those sorts of unerringly accurate assessments. It was so difficult to regain his footing when his brother had things aright.

"Um," he said, casting about for something to say.

Robin only shook his head and crawled to his feet. "Feed the fire with her gear, Nick. You daren't do aught else."

"Rob?"

Robin paused and looked down at him. "Aye?"

Nicholas got to his feet and stood there, Amanda's gown in his hands. "She doesn't realize I know." He paused. "About where she comes from."

Robin looked at him in silence for a moment, then nodded. "I won't say anything."

"I appreciate your discretion."

"You cannot keep this secret forever."

"Which secret?"

"You have many. Choose one."

Nicholas pursed his lips. "Go to bed."

"I will. Happy mending. If ever you tire of the sword, you can hire yourself out as a stitcher. I'd learn to choose my colors with more care, though," he threw over his shoulder as he walked across the hall.

Nicholas resumed his seat and finished his work. He examined the hem, then gathered his mother's sewing things together and left the great hall. He returned his mother's gear to her solar, then made his way to stand outside Jennifer's door. He listened, but heard no sound.

At least she wasn't weeping.

He returned to his own chamber, grateful that his mother still left him such a place to return to. Perhaps she despaired of his ever finishing his own hall — or of finding a woman to share it with. Whatever the case, he was grateful. He set Jennifer's new gown over the back of a chair, then sought his own rest.

He lay awake for quite some time, thinking very seriously about what he was doing.

Aye, he suspected there was another gate. If anyone knew where it was, it would be his brother-in-law. But if he himself didn't know, he couldn't tell Jennifer. And if he couldn't tell Jennifer, perhaps she would want to stay at Artane. And if she stayed at Artane, perhaps she might find him to her liking.

And perhaps by the time she learned the secret he didn't want to reveal to her, she wouldn't want to go.

He couldn't bear to think on what she might do otherwise.

CHAPTER 18

Jennifer woke and sat up with a start. She looked around her and let out a shuddering breath. Well, it was still the bedroom she was accustomed to having, but the very fine goose-feather mattress — topped as it was by an admittedly fine sheet and a luxurious duvet — let her know that she was very much trapped back in the past. That, and the fact that her violin did not find itself propped up in the corner.

At least not in this century.

She lay back down and looked up at the canopy of the bed above her. It was a very fine bed, obviously something made for a woman of rank. She supposed that being a noblewoman in the Middle Ages hadn't been so bad. Unfortunately, she wasn't a woman of rank.

She didn't want to think about what she was going to do, but she knew she had no choice. She couldn't live forever at Artane, daughter of no one, wife of no one, without kin or friend, without occupation or money, with only her cell phone to keep her company. She would have to find something to do, some way to earn her keep, someplace to live. Unfortunately, based on what she knew of the time period, she suspected her life as a medieval peasant was not going to be good.

She sat up, wished desperately for a comb, then swung her legs to the floor and got out of bed. She shouldn't have given Montgomery back his clothes. At least wearing them would have made her less conspicuous.

Having no other choice, she put her jeans on. Checking that her pockets were still full of what they were supposed to be full of, she turned and faced the door. There was no time like the present to be about her future, even if that future was so hopeless, the very thought of it made her want to go back to bed and pull the covers up over her head.

She opened the door, then started in surprise. There was a collection of servants standing in the hallway in front of her. A young, neatly dressed woman, who couldn't have been any older than eighteen, bobbed a curtsey.

"A good morn to you, my lady," she said with a smile. "My name is Marlys. My lord Nicholas thought you might find a bath to your liking this morn."

Jennifer looked at the tub that sat between

two burly guys. "A bath," she said in astonishment.

"He also said that you were from Scotland" — and here Marlys crossed herself briefly — "so we were to understand that your customs might be different from ours and that you would likely wish to bathe in private."

Then, before Jennifer could say anything, Marlys directed that the tub be brought in, saw that it was filled with hot water, then ordered everyone out.

"Call me and I'll wash your hair for you," Marlys said.

Jennifer didn't stop to argue. She shucked off her clothes, rolled them up and put them under the covers, then got into the tub.

It was bliss.

She didn't even mind using soap made from a substance she didn't dare identify, or letting Marlys wash her hair, or trying to convince three other serving girls that she could really dry herself off by herself.

Before she could decide how best to retrieve her old clothes, Marlys had produced a dress and a pair of shoes which they put on her without delay. She was then placed on a stool and Marlys combed out her hair.

"My lord Nicholas awaits you in his father's solar," Marlys said as she finished. "He said that if you wanted to bring your special Scottish clothing with you, he would put it in his father's trunk for safekeeping."

Special Scottish clothing? Well, if that's what they wanted to believe, so much the better. Jennifer nodded, grabbed her rolled up things and thanked Marlys for the bath. She left the bedroom feeling quite a bit more comfortable in medieval gear than jeans, though the lack of bloomers was a little disconcerting.

When in Rome . . .

Jennifer supposed, as she stood in front of Rhys de Piaget's solar a few minutes later, that she should have at least pretended to ask for directions since she wasn't supposed to have been at Artane before. Well, too late now. She lifted her hand and knocked.

"Enter!" came the bellow from inside.

Jennifer took another deep breath, tried to ignore the fact that the last time she'd seen the inside of the room in front of her had been 800 years from that moment, then pulled on the latch and let herself into Rhys de Piaget's solar.

The only thing that helped her remember that she was a twenty-first-century gal was holding on to her clothes. In every other respect, she felt as though she could have been a medieval miss walking into a lord's solar as automatically as if she'd done it the whole of her life. Only she wasn't a medieval miss.

And the two men sitting there looking at her weren't just average medieval guys.

Robin and Nicholas both had their feet propped up on their father's table. The moment Nicholas saw her, though, the front legs of his chair hit the floor along with his feet. He stood and made her a low bow.

Then he smiled.

Jennifer clutched her clothes. Oh, where oh where was Mr. Grump? She knew how to handle him. She wasn't at all sure what to do with the rather contented-looking man in front of her.

"Good morrow to you, lady," he said, inclining his head.

"And to you, my lord." She smiled weakly. "Thank you for the bath. It was wonderful."

He clasped his hands behind his back. "It was but a small thing."

She held up the skirt of her gown. "And I take it I have you to thank for this and the shoes?"

"Small things as well."

"He was up half the night stitching the hem," Robin offered, leaning back in his chair with his hands behind his head. "That's why it doesn't match."

"Ignore him," Nicholas said pleasantly. "I usually do. Now, I see you've brought your gear. Shall I stow it for you?"

Jennifer surrendered her only links to the future and watched as Nicholas locked them in a large trunk. He tossed the key to Robin, then smiled at her again.

"Your things will be there, whenever you want them," he said. "Now, do you care to eat, lady?"

"You're being very polite," she managed.

Robin burst out laughing. "Polite, indeed. I daresay his lack of sleep has robbed him of the energy necessary to be foul. It has also apparently robbed him of the ability to match fabrics."

Nicholas made what Jennifer suspected was a very rude gesture to his brother. Robin only grinned in return.

"I've never had a man make a gown for me before," Jennifer put in. "I think it's very nice."

"See?" Nicholas said pointedly to his brother. "She likes it."

"She's obviously weak from hunger." Robin dropped his feet to the floor and rose to arrange a chair for her nearby. "I'm sure enduring your company for so long has been very draining. Come, my lady, and take your ease."

Jennifer started to sit, then noticed that he had the beginnings of a black eye. Nicholas, she could see, had a matching shiner. She looked back at Robin.

"Did you two fight?"

"Only a little brawl," Robin said with a conspiratorial wink. "It won't stop him from going to fetch us something to eat."

"*You* go fetch it," Nicholas said.

"Show her that you have decent manners,"

Robin said, nodding toward the door. "I will keep her safe enough here for you. And I won't tell her any more of your secrets."

Jennifer smiled at Robin. "Does he have any left?"

"Not any interesting ones," Nicholas muttered, heading toward the door. "Feel free to swat him if he becomes annoying."

Jennifer sat and watched Nicholas go. She wished desperately for a moment to think before she had to converse with his brother, but that wasn't to be. She turned slowly and looked at him.

She couldn't say he looked much like the current lord of Artane — the lord of her day — but she couldn't say he didn't, either. In fact, he looked so much like a dark-haired version of Megan's husband, Gideon, she had to take a deep breath. For that matter, Nicholas looked a good deal like Gideon, but there were so many other complications laid on him that she hadn't really had the presence of mind to make the comparison before.

One thing was certain: Robin de Piaget was very comfortable in his own skin and obviously quite comfortable sitting in his father's chair and taking over his duties as lord of the manor. Jennifer smiled at him.

"Thank you for the hospitality, my lord," she began.

He waved her words away. "I'm just Robin, remember? And I wouldn't think to do anything else. Any friend of Nicholas's is always welcome at Artane."

Jennifer smiled deprecatingly. "I don't know if he would call me a friend. He rescued me from an unpleasant situation and was kind enough to give me refuge. I can't say he's had a choice in the matter."

Robin put his elbows on the table. "Nick always has a choice. He could just as easily have left you in the care of the lads at Seakirk, or given you a horse and sent you on your way. I understand you've missed your kin a time or two."

Jennifer realized then that she was going to have to stay on her toes with Robin of Artane. He was very polite, very handsome, and apparently quite adept at finding out what he wanted to know. His changes of subject were dizzying.

"Ah, yes," she said with a nod. "I have."

"Are you from Scotland?"

"Ah," she managed again, "yes. Most recently." And that really wasn't a lie. She'd just come down from Jamie's a month ago. All things considered, she thought that just might count as someplace to be from.

"Nick would take you back there, if you wanted," Robin said mildly.

Jennifer considered that quickly. Yes, he could take her to Scotland but it would be about fifty years before James MacLeod was born. She would find herself tossed immediately into a dungeon and left there to rot, if something worse didn't happen to her first.

"Or perhaps the distance is too great," Robin mused.

"My home is a very long way away," she agreed.

"I think," Robin began thoughtfully, "that sometimes when we are far from home, it almost feels as if our homes are in another world entirely —"

"Food," Nicholas said suddenly, bursting into the solar and banging a tray down on Rhys's table. "Indulge yourself, brother, and give Jennifer's poor ears a rest."

Jennifer soon found herself with a wooden bowl full of porridge in her hands. She tasted, prepared to bear up under less than ideal culinary circumstances, but found herself pleasantly surprised.

"Has Nick been cooking for you?" Robin asked around a mouthful of breakfast.

"How did you know?"

"You look surprised that this is good," he said. "Artane always has a very fine cook. We've a new one now who's even finer than the last one."

Apparently that was a tradition that would be carried on through the ages, but she chose not to say as much. She merely nodded and continued to eat. She was acutely aware of Nicholas sitting next to her, looking quite comfortable. He had gone from a man who had refused to aid her in returning home to a man who seemed determined to make her feel welcome in his home.

Weird.

Robin looked at them both with twinkling eyes, as if he was turning over in his head a joke so delicious that he simply couldn't wait to share it.

Jennifer took a surreptitious look at Nicholas, but he was merely eating with the relish of a man who had been partaking of his own cooking for far too long. He did look up once at Robin, saw him smirking, and uttered a very succinct and pointed curse.

Robin laughed.

"What is so funny?" Jennifer asked, unsure if she was amused or exasperated.

Robin looked at her and shook his head. "I am merely of a pleasant and cheerful disposition. I can see you are of a like temperament. Perhaps you will cause a sweetening of my brother's humors."

"Hmmm," Jennifer said. "Maybe."

Nicholas turned his head and looked at her with a very small smile.

It was enough to make her very glad she was sitting down.

It also made her realize that she was playing with fire. This wasn't her family, Nicholas was not her boyfriend, and she was not medieval nobility. The sooner she came to terms with that and figured out what she was going to do with her life, the better off she would be.

And the less broken her heart would feel.

It was all she could do to make polite, innocuous conversation during the rest of the meal. She wasn't sure she could do it for the rest of the day. Fortunately, she was rescued by a knock on the door.

"Enter," Robin called. "Ah, Sir Walter. Do you have business for me?"

An older man entered the chamber and inclined his head both to Robin and Nicholas. He made her a bow as well. "My lords, but a few moments of your time."

Jennifer stood up. "I'll go."

Nicholas rose as well and walked her to the door. "I daresay you would be quite safe wandering about the inner bailey. Isn't that so, Sir Walter?"

"Oh, aye," Sir Walter said with a nod.

Jennifer nodded. "I'll take a little tour. Thanks for breakfast."

She left while she still had some control over her polite smile. In reality, she was contemplating that return back to bed. Covers over the head seemed like a very strategic move at the moment.

But she wasn't a coward, so she made her way through the great hall and went out the front door. She hesitated, then walked down a couple of steps and sat down where she could see the goings-on and have a bit of a think.

She looked out over the courtyard. She supposed it had to be the same size as the one at modern Artane, though it was definitely filled with different things. First of all, there were no cutouts in the walls where cannons had been used for defense during the 1500s and no Victorian carriage house that in the twenty-first century housed the earl's fine collection of antique cars and a Range Rover or two. No satellite dish, no floodlights, no modern village stretching out beyond the walls and into the distance.

Instead there were stables and a blacksmith's shop, a chapel, and a garden. There were a pair of other buildings she couldn't identify a use for and to her right were the lists. Men went about their duties. Women carried cloth or food or tended small animals. She could hear horses neighing, the blacksmith pounding, guardsmen calling out to each other. It was very, very medieval.

She wondered, with a detachment that almost frightened her, just what she would be doing in a month's time. She supposed she could become a washerwoman or a seamstress. The gown she was wearing was something professionally done. Well, except for the hem, but that had been an act of kindness so she was willing to look on it with a friendly eye.

She heard the door open behind her, but she didn't dare turn around. Besides, her eyes were so full of tears, she wouldn't have been able to identify the person anyway. The newcomer sat down next to her. She knew without looking that it was Nicholas.

That in itself was a little scary.

She dried her eyes with the hem of her sleeve, then turned to look at him. He was watching her gravely. She returned his look as steadily as she could. There was definitely something different about him. She supposed it probably had something to do with being home. Maybe Wyckham was where he planned to make his home, but it wasn't the home of his heart. Not yet.

Whatever the case, all she knew was that he was much more cheerful here in his father's hall, despite the seriousness of his expression at present.

"Bad news?" she asked lightly.

He frowned. "What do you mean?"

"You look very serious. Miles said you were the sunny one of the family."

He pursed his lips. "Then Miles indeed babbled freely, I take it."

"Did you expect anything else?"

"Nay," he said quietly. "I suppose I didn't."

Jennifer turned away from that subject as quickly as possible. She didn't want to think about how Amanda had broken his heart. And she most definitely didn't want to think about him marrying someone while she stood at the back of the hall, waiting for the duty of sewing his wife's clothes.

"I need to think about my future," she said suddenly, not trusting herself to look at him. She looked out into the courtyard, swathed in all its medieval glory.

"Well —"

"I have relied on your kindness for far too long," she continued, plunging heedlessly into the morass that was now her life's disaster. She had to keep plunging, however. If she stopped to think about what she was saying, she knew she would break down and weep. "I was thinking that perhaps I could become a seamstress, or perhaps even a musician. I'm not sure how I would go about becoming either. Do you think your mother might hire me to do sewing for her until I could earn enough money to make it on my own?"

He was silent for so long, she almost looked at him.

But she had more self-control than that.

"Nay."

She did look at him then. "What?"

"My mother will not hire you because you will not ask her."

Jennifer felt her eyebrows go up of their own accord. "I beg your pardon?"

He dismissed her words with a faint look of

impatience. "You do not need to earn any gold."

"But —"

"I have more than enough for the both of us."

"But I can't take yours," she said miserably.

"Why not?"

"Because," she said, turning to face him, "I just can't. You don't owe me anything and I can't live forever on your charity. I have to make my own way."

He looked down thoughtfully at the bit of stair between his feet. He regarded it steadily for several minutes, as if it contained all the answers he needed. Then he looked at her.

"Give me a fortnight," he said quietly.

She blinked. "What?"

"Give me a fortnight," he repeated. "A succession of days in which nothing warrants a rescue, nothing merits tears, and nothing leads either of us to batter my elder brother."

"But —"

"We will rise in the morning, enjoy a leisurely breaking of our fast, pass the day in pleasant activities, then return each evening to the hall where we will partake of fine wine and fine music."

She felt a tear escape down her cheek. She would have tried to wipe it away, but that might have drawn attention to it and that she couldn't have.

"Why?" she asked.

"Why not?"

"No," she said impatiently, "it's a fair question. Why? Why with me?"

He smiled a half smile. "Can a man not wish to spend a fortnight with a beautiful woman without his motives being questioned?"

"No," she said simply. "He cannot."

He sighed and looked out over the courtyard. "Very well, then, here are my reasons. I have had a difficult pair of years. You have had a difficult pair of fortnights. I daresay we both could stand a stretch of time that is filled with lovely things. Or," he said, turning his head to look at her, "it could be that I find your company fascinating and I am a selfish bastard who selfishly wants to have you all to myself."

"Oh," she said, but no sound came out. She considered for a moment, then shook her head slowly. "But I couldn't, Nicholas," she said quietly. "I can't bear the thought of becoming accustomed to something that could never be mine."

He looked at her for several minutes in silence, then put his hands on his knees. "Wait for me."

And with that, he rose and went back inside the house. Jennifer took a deep breath, then gave in and put her face in her hands where she could really have a good cry.

She cried for quite some time.

Eventually, she felt someone sit down next to her again. She did her best to repair the damage to her face with her sleeve yet again before she looked to see who it was.

It was Robin.

She was so surprised, she squeaked.

"Sorry," he said with a smile.

She shook her head. What was it with these Artane men? Every one of them was more handsome than was good for him — or, no doubt, for any female with decent vision living within a five-mile radius.

"I'm not myself," she managed finally. "I'm not a crier."

"It's Nick," Robin said. "He drives everyone to it. He would drive me to tears, too, if I were that sort of lad. But I'd rather express my displeasure with my fists."

"So I have seen on his face."

"I went easy on him."

"I wonder what he looks like when you go hard on him."

" 'Tis extremely unattractive," Robin said with a grin.

Jennifer couldn't help but smile. "You have a lovely family."

"What of you?" he asked. "Do you have siblings?"

"Two older sisters and an older brother. All married. Two with children."

"Children," Robin said with a wistful smile. "They are a joy."

"I agree."

Robin seemed to consider his words. "Nick is a good lad."

"Is that what you came to tell me?"

Robin blinked, then laughed. "And here I worried."

"Worried about how my foot will feel against the back of your head?"

Robin rose and turned to look up at Nicholas who was standing on the step above him. "Nay, I was worried about this tender lass's heart. And yours."

"I'll protect her heart," Nicholas said.

Robin looked at him for a very long moment, then he looked at Jennifer. "And you?"

"I'll protect my heart as well," she said solemnly.

Robin's jaw went slack, then he laughed. He started up the stairs and clapped Nicholas on the shoulder on his way by. "You, brother, have met your match in that one."

Jennifer rose and turned. "Robin?"

Robin stopped and looked at her. "My lady?"

"I'll protect his heart as well."

"Of course you will," Robin said with a smile. "Brave wench."

Jennifer watched him disappear inside the hall, then looked at Nicholas. "What is it with you de Piaget men and the word *wench?*"

"Term of affection," Nicholas said. He handed her a bottle. "If you will carry that,

I'll carry the rest."

"Where are we going?"

"To the strand," Nicholas said. "Does that suit?"

She looked up at him. "Nicholas, I really think I should —"

"Hurry? I agree. It looks like rain."

"No," she said in exasperation, "I'm trying to tell you something."

"Tell me later."

"I need to tell you now."

He paused on the step below her, turned, and looked at her very seriously. "Jennifer McKinnon, I am asking you to give me a simple fortnight. You grieve for your family. I am weary of the unpleasant lout I've been over the past pair of years. For a fortnight, let us make merry, enjoy the pleasures of Artane, and be at peace."

"And then?" she asked softly.

"And then you will tell me what you need to tell me, I will tell you all my secrets, and then we will see if a morning in the lists is called for."

"The lists?" she repeated. "What, over swords?"

"What else?" he said with a smile.

She closed her eyes briefly. It was so tempting. Two weeks of nothing but Nicholas's company, with the world at bay and reality kept outside the gates. She looked at him, wanting it desperately but sure it would just end so badly . . .

"Please," he said quietly.

She blew her hair out of her face. "You had to say that, didn't you?"

He gave her a quick smile, then turned. "Bring the bottle, wench," he said, loping down the stairs. "We'll have to run if we're to have any dry lunch at all."

Jennifer hesitated.

He turned around and smiled up at her. It was that de Piaget smile all right, though it wasn't Robin's, which was full of good humor, or Miles's, which was full of mischief. It was Nicholas's and for the first time, she could see how he had earned a reputation for wooing dozens of women without an effort. It was a smile that made her feel as if the sun had come out just for her.

How could she not bask in it, even briefly?

"I will regret this," she said with a sigh.

"Not possible," he said. "I didn't cook the lunch."

She laughed in spite of herself.

After all, how much trouble could her heart get into in a fortnight?

She smiled and walked down the stairs to meet him.

CHAPTER 19

Nicholas welcomed the jongleurs into the great hall, pleased with the fortuitous nature of their arrival. He'd hoped he might be able to provide Jennifer with some sort of entertainment, but he'd thought he would need to go find it himself. His father hadn't yet, in all his years as lord of the keep, been able to retain a set of musicians for longer than a pair of months. Perhaps the hall had never been to anyone's liking or perhaps the keep was too far north.

Perhaps Petter's proposed gallery for Wyckham would be suitable inducement for minstrels of his own. He supposed, though, that thinking about that might be premature. After all, it wasn't as if he had a lady to grace that hall with her glorious presence and enjoy music on a nightly basis.

Not yet.

The day had gone well so far. He had passed a very lovely morning with Jennifer on the strand. They had talked of nothing of import and for that he was unwholesomely grateful. He'd been satisfied to discuss the contents of Artane's new cook's basket, the pleasing nature of his father's finest wine, and the potential for rain before they finished both. The very last thing he'd wanted to discuss had been Jennifer's future.

Or her return to the Future.

They were two different things entirely, but neither to his liking.

They had run back to the keep before the rain turned into a storm that had blown in hard from the sea. He had advised her to retreat to Isabelle's chamber and have a rest lest she catch a chill. That she had agreed said much about the strain the past fortnight had put upon her.

Nicholas had immediately set to procuring some sort of entertainment for the evening. When the minstrels had knocked on the front doors, begging for shelter, he'd happily invited them in. He'd shown them the kitchens as further inducement. The agreement had been fixed right there in front of the cooking fire.

Now all that was left was to wait for Jennifer to reappear and hope that she would be pleased.

He waited for quite a while. Montgomery and John arrived from points unknown and began to pace in front of the table, as if they thought making themselves visible might hurry supper along. Miles arrived from outside and sauntered over to where Nicholas stood in the middle of the hall, waiting impatiently.

"I like gold and gray together," Miles offered solemnly.

Nicholas grunted. "If you think that will earn you a dance with her, you are mistaken."

"You can't have her all to yourself," Miles protested.

"Why not?" Nicholas asked.

"At least allow her to dance with Montgomery. You will benefit from the comparison."

Nicholas pursed his lips. "I don't need that sort of benefit. Even at court I manage to put one foot in front of the other and avoid treading on expensive, bejeweled frocks —"

He realized Miles was no longer listening. Indeed, Miles was no longer standing next to him. He looked behind him and saw that Jennifer had come into the great hall. Miles was hastening over to her as if he intended to claim her before anyone else had a chance.

Nicholas might have rushed over and elbowed him aside, but two things stopped him. One, he'd forgotten over the course of the afternoon whilst she rested just how arrestingly beautiful she was. Just looking at her was enough to render him motionless.

Secondly, he wasn't going to tumble over all his younger brothers as they currently tumbled over each other to be the first to reach her. He would simply wait until they had tangled themselves in a heap, then he would step *over* them and reach her first.

Unfortunately, his brothers were less bumbling than he had hoped, for they managed to get Jennifer and themselves to the table. In spite of that miscalculation, though, he did manage to take the seat on her right.

Never mind that he'd thrown Montgomery out of it.

Robin barked for Miles to move out of his seat, then he sat down at Jennifer's left. Nicholas wasn't concerned about that. Indeed, Robin made a fine buffer between Jennifer and Miles, who should have known better than to ply his wooing wiles upon a woman who had agreed to a fortnight with *him.*

"Nicholas?"

He looked at her. "Aye?" he asked shortly.

"I think you should have had a nap as well."

He took a deep breath, blew it out, then gave her his best smile. "Sorry. I was contemplating ways to do in my younger brothers."

"Why?"

"Aye, why?" Robin asked with exaggerated confusion. "I can't imagine what they could have done to merit that."

Nicholas shot Robin a glare, then looked back at Jennifer. "I thought they might be vexing you. Tell me if their attentions weary you."

She shook her head with a smile. "It's very flattering."

"See," Robin said with an exaggerated nod. "Very flattering."

"Rob?" Nicholas said.

"Aye?"

"Be silent before I must silence you."

Robin looked at Jennifer solemnly. "He is possessed of vile humors, as you can see. I try to beat them from him as often as possible, but 'tis an endless labor from which there is no rest for me. Perhaps you can aid me in my task."

Nicholas would have argued the point with his brother, but the musicians emerged from ingesting their early evening morsel and had begun readying themselves near the back of the hall. Nicholas stole a surreptitious look at Jennifer to see how she was reacting. She was watching them with great interest.

He leaned closer to her. "Don't ask them for employment."

She looked at him in surprise. "How did you know that's what I was thinking?"

"You were quite obviously lusting after that one's lute. Can you play the lute, by the way?"

"I never have, but I could try."

"I have one in my chamber. We'll each attempt a song or two tomorrow. For now, you are the guest."

"So I should just enjoy, not try to learn all

their songs so I can perform them at a later time?"

He smiled. "Aye. But, now that you say so, could you learn all their songs?"

"I have a good ear."

"Can you dance as well?" he asked.

She smiled. "No, but I could learn that, too, I imagine."

He inclined his head. "It would be my pleasure to teach —"

"You," Miles finished, hopping over the table and bowing low in front of it. "Mistress Jennifer, allow me to aid you however I might with my modest knowledge of the steps."

"And me," Montgomery said, coming up behind her and putting his hands on her chair. "If you're finished with supper, that is."

"You'd best include me as well," John said with a weary sigh. "In fact, you should likely start with me. I'm the worst dancer of us all."

Nicholas reached for Jennifer, but it was too late. She had been captured and spirited away from the table. He started to protest, but soon decided it was useless. His brothers were determined and he supposed it wasn't such a bad thing. They could trip over their feet whilst trying to teach her the dances, then he would step in and toss them out the front door and have his lady to himself.

As he watched the lads take her out into the middle of the hall, he couldn't help but compare his view at present with the views he'd had recently from his father's high table. How many nights had he sat exactly where he was, enduring the schemes and machinations of his grandmère? How many evenings had he looked over a hall filled with women he couldn't have cared less about? How many times had he wondered if it were even possible to find a woman to love?

He leaned his elbows on the table and his chin on his fists and watched Jennifer as Miles and the twins took turns fighting over who would take the lead in teaching her the dances they were trying to help her master. He was quite certain he'd never seen anyone like her. She treated his brothers with an easiness that was enchanting to watch. She laughed at them, teased them, made them exaggerated courtly bows, and simply enjoyed them. He could not, for the life of him, imagine any other woman of his acquaintance doing the like. Certainly none of his grandmother's offerings would have bothered.

She was magnificent.

After a time, however, the pleasure of watching her with his brothers began to turn to ever-so-slight irritation that they seemed disinclined to release her.

"Miles," Nicholas called. "My turn."

Miles simply turned his back on him.

Nicholas tried to catch Montgomery's eye, or John's, but with equal lack of success. He heard a snort next to him and looked at his brother.

"What?" he asked.

"You might actually have to get off your comfortable perch and go rescue your lady," Robin remarked. "Though I don't see what you're so stirred up about. They're your brothers, for pity's sake."

Nicholas scowled at him. "Don't you have somewhere to go? To Fenwyck, perhaps, to retrieve your wife?"

"I'm not certain I trust you to be alone with your lady without some sort of chaperon," Robin said solemnly.

"Chaperon?" Nicholas exclaimed. "Surely you jest! I have chaperons right there. Three of the most irritating sort. I'll never have the girl to myself."

"It serves you right," Robin said with a smile.

"What does?"

"To fall in love with a woman of her ilk. Especially given how rude you were to Jake about his past."

"Future."

"Whatever."

Nicholas scowled at his brother. "Damnation, what does that word mean?"

"It means you are a dolt and Fate has a sense of humor," Robin said with a chuckle. "I still can't believe it. You with a wench . . .

well, that sort of wench. You know what I mean."

"Aye," Nicholas said with a sigh. "I know, indeed." He looked at Jennifer dancing with his brothers. "It is ironic, isn't it?"

Robin was so silent for so long that Nicholas finally looked at him. His brother was watching him with an expression of something genuine on his face. It could have been affection. It could have been pity.

Mayhap it was indigestion.

Nicholas scowled. "Yet more to spew at me?"

"Nay," Robin said quietly, shaking his head. "Just my apologies. I didn't realize."

"Realize what?"

"That you *do* love the girl."

"After less than three fortnights of knowing her?" Nicholas said, grasping at anything that sounded sensible. "Don't be ridiculous."

Robin smiled gravely. "I imagine it didn't take more than a single glance, did it?"

Nicholas wanted to deny it, but he simply couldn't. He glared at his brother. "You're detestable."

Robin tapped his forehead. "My superior intelligence yet again rendering all within my scope helpless against my perception."

"Shut up."

Robin laughed. "I'll leave tomorrow to fetch Anne, then your lady will have some tolerable company for a change."

"Do that," Nicholas suggested. "It might be even better if you went now."

"And miss the dancing? Never. I love to dance. I love even more to watch dancing."

"You lie," Nicholas said. "You loathe every aspect of every type of courtly entertainment and the only reason you tolerate it at all is for Anne's sake and to avoid censure from Grandmère for avoiding it."

"And yet it doesn't prevent me from wanting to watch you attempt to wrest your love away from your brothers." Robin sat back and smiled pleasantly. "Be about it then, lad. Provide me with some sort of sport."

Nicholas drained his cup, pushed his chair back, and walked around the table to the floor of the great hall. He invited his brothers quite politely to return to their suppers. They protested. He invited more firmly. He supposed they might have been tempted to refuse yet again, but he escorted them across the floor and over to the lord's table where he instructed them to take their ease. He unbuckled his sword belt, laid his sword and his knife on the table, then turned and looked at Jennifer.

She was standing in the middle of the floor in her lovely dress with the less-than-lovely bit attached to the bottom. She clasped her hands behind her back and waited, smiling slightly.

He walked over to her and stopped. He

bowed low, then nodded to his minstrels. They began with a very pleasant tune. Nicholas smiled.

"Did they manage to teach you any of the steps, or were they too busy trying to woo you?"

"I suppose I learned a step or two. Be gentle and I'll do my best."

He held out his hand. "I imagine I'll be the one tripping over my feet."

"I'll try to keep you from falling on your face."

He laughed as best he could for not having much breath to do it. All his had been stolen by the touch of her hand.

He had no idea how many dances they danced. He glanced, at one point during the evening, at the musicians, but they were looking at Jennifer in much the same way his brothers had, as if they simply couldn't drink in the sight of her enough to quench themselves.

He understood completely.

Eventually, when he thought Jennifer looked a little flushed and he felt a little parched, he walked her over to the table then went to see how his minstrels fared. There was no sense in not pampering them a little so they would stay a bit and aid him in his wooing. He looked at the lutenist.

"Weary?" he asked.

"Not when there is such beauty to be

317

enjoyed as your lady," the man said, inclining his head. "Pardon my boldness."

"I share your sentiments. Can you carry on for a bit?"

"Till dawn, my lord, if you like."

"I do," Nicholas said with feeling. And he did. He turned and watched Jennifer standing in front of the high table, sipping from a cup, then laughing at something Miles said.

Her laughter was music. *She* was music. Everything about her from her smile to her visage to her touch was glorious music that left him wanting nothing more than to hear her for the rest of his life.

The saints preserve him, but it was true.

He walked over to the table, accepted a cup of wine from her, then watched her over the rim as he drank. "Tired?" he asked, setting the cup down.

"Never. You?"

"The sun hasn't risen yet."

She laughed and took his hand. "Then, my lord, let us make good use of the night."

"May I not have at least *one* more turn?" Miles asked plaintively.

"You've already had several."

"One last one."

Nicholas looked at Jennifer. "He's had a turn."

"You could consider it repayment for his teaching me the steps."

Nicholas considered. He didn't want to

release her, but then again, he had an entire fortnight of her company to look forward to. He could afford to be gracious. He put her hand in his brother's. It wasn't hard to do given that Miles was shoving him out of the way.

He leaned back against the table and watched Miles dance with his love. Miles was, Nicholas had to admit unwillingly, as handsome as any woman could have wished, he actually danced quite well, and he was full of brilliant wit.

"Father won't like it if you kill Miles," John said from behind him.

Nicholas threw his brother a glare and turned back to watching the dance.

"Patience is a virtue," Robin added.

Nicholas made a rude gesture behind his back which only left Robin laughing. He himself saw nothing amusing about any of it.

Yet, in time, the dance was over, and Miles was escorting Jennifer back to him. Nicholas watched her laugh with his brother and compliment him on his dancing.

And then she caught sight of him.

And she smiled.

He managed to smile back, but the truth had caught him full in the chest and he was finding it very hard indeed to take a normal breath.

By the saints, he was truly, hopelessly, profoundly lost.

His mother had told him once that when he finally fell in love, it would be with someone truly extraordinary. He would have to tell her that she'd been right. Jennifer was everything he could have hoped for, and more.

Now, if only he could see it last forever.

He took her hand and led her out onto the floor.

It was a beginning. With any luck, and perhaps a bit of help from Fate, it would be the beginning of something that would last forever. He pushed aside the knowledge of what he hadn't told her and what he would have to tell her eventually. For now, he would dance with her, drink in her beauty and her smiles.

The Future be damned.

CHAPTER 20

Jennifer braided her hair, tied it with a ribbon, and turned toward the doorway. She'd had a wonderful time the night before. In fact, the whole day had been wonderful. She'd had a lovely lunch on the beach, a decadent nap during the afternoon, an excellent dinner, then the pleasure of an evening spent dancing with four handsome men, one of whom she really, really liked.

It was terrifying.

She let out a shaky breath. The thought of two weeks spent pretending to be medieval nobility, followed by the rest of her life as just an average medieval peasant was just not pretty, especially since she would probably spend the rest of that life longing for the company of the lord of Wyckham.

He was, as Megan would have said, truly the epitome of all knightly virtues.

She smoothed her hand over her dress. It was hard to pinpoint just when he'd unwittingly laid siege to her heart. Maybe it had been that first moment when she'd seen him, sitting on top of his horse, so magnificently handsome that she hadn't been able to draw a decent breath. Maybe when he'd stroked her hair in front of Wyckham's fireplace. She was fairly certain she'd been in trouble when she'd realized that he'd altered a dress for her with his own hands so it would be long enough.

And then there had been the dancing the night before . . .

She sat down on the bed because it seemed safer than trying to stand up. She put her face in her hands and let out a shuddering breath. What in the world was she doing? Playing with fire, that's what she was doing. She was spending days on end with a terribly handsome man paying terribly flattering attention to her, all clothed in medieval finery and accompanied by fine music made by wonderful medieval musicians.

It would not end well.

She had to tell him no. Didn't she?

Yes, she did. She stood up and walked across the room. She would find him while her common sense still had the upper hand. She flung open the door and walked out purposefully into the hallway. She pulled up short and squeaked in surprise.

Nicholas was standing against the opposite wall, leaning back against it with a foot propped up underneath him and his arms folded over his chest.

She felt a little weak in the knees. All right, so she had marched out into the hallway, firm in her determination to tell Nicholas to get lost so she could get right on with her miserable medieval-gal working life.

Now, she wondered if she'd just temporarily lost her mind.

He dropped his hands and pushed away from the wall. He smiled. "A good morrow to you, my lady."

"Ah," she began weakly, "you're awake early."

He smiled. "I thought it best to be here before sunrise."

"Why?"

"I feared you would bolt."

She tried to swallow, but she wasn't entirely successful. "I considered it."

"I imagined you would." He took her hand in his and pulled her down the passageway. "You realize that I'm not going to allow you to renege on your promise, don't you?"

"Well —"

"I will be forced to convince you afresh each morning, you know. What a waste of early hours that could be spent atop the castle enjoying the sea breezes, or out in the lists learning how to express your displeasure with a sword."

She looked at him in desperation. "But I don't fling."

"Fling?" he echoed. "Fling what?"

She would have laughed, but it just wasn't funny. "You fling when you romance a woman, take her to bed, then leave her the next day." She paused. "I don't do that."

His expression was utterly serious. "It never would have occurred to me to ask you to."

She hesitated. She was tempted to mutter *abandon hope all ye that enter here* but she thought Dante probably wasn't appropriate. Then again, Nicholas spoke Latin, so Renaissance Italian wouldn't have been so far off.

He pulled her down the passageway again. "No flinging."

She gulped down a bracing bit of chilly passageway air and surrendered without a fight. "All right."

"Good," he said, sounding satisfied. "Now, let us hurry, before the lads eat everything."

She took another deep breath and followed him down the stairs. Maybe it wouldn't be so bad. She could spend the next two weeks with him and remain unaffected.

She was almost sure of it.

Soon she was sitting at the table with him and his younger brothers and enjoying another in what was becoming a string of very fine meals. She finished, then realized that someone was missing.

"Where's Robin?" she asked.

"He's out in the lists, I imagine," Nicholas said, sitting back in his chair. "He must leave this afternoon to fetch Anne and his lads from their yearly fortnight of torture at Fenwyck. He is no doubt indulging in a few hours of training before he's forced to go be polite to Anne's sire."

"Torture?" she echoed. "Doesn't he get along with his wife's family?"

"I'll answer that," Miles volunteered. "Nay, he does not, though I daresay he has reason. Geoffrey of Fenwyck never liked him and sought any reason to prevent him from wedding Anne. Of course, Robin did his part to provide as many of those reasons as possible."

"Flings," Nicholas clarified.

Jennifer looked at him. "Flings? Before they were married?"

Nicholas nodded. "But given that all his flings were blonde and Anne knew he flung them in an effort to forget her, I suppose she doesn't fault him overmuch."

Jennifer smiled to herself. She would have to be more careful with her words or she would have the entire place messing up future editions of the *Oxford English Dictionary.*

"Interesting," she murmured.

"Interesting is watching Robin and Nick train," Miles noted. "We might, if you like."

Jennifer turned to Nicholas. "Is that what you do after breakfast?"

"Generally," Nicholas said. "When I'm home with Robin. He demands sport as often each day as he can have it."

Jennifer looked at Miles. "And you? What do you do now?"

"Wait until Nick has worn Robin down before I venture into the lists," he said with twinkling eyes. "Today, though, perhaps the little lads will keep you company whilst Nick and I train."

"I won't have time after Robin has gone," Nicholas said, "because Jennifer and I will be in Mother's solar where she will take her ease and I will play the lute for her."

"Might I come?" Montgomery asked. "I like it when you play the lute, Nick."

Nicholas pursed his lips. "We'll see. Be my squire this morning and I'll consider it."

Montgomery leaped to his feet. "Mail shirt or leather jerkin, Nick?"

"How long has Robin been outside?"

"Two hours."

"Leather jerkin then," Nicholas said. "The garrison will at least have the edge taken off him. Do you mind?"

Jennifer realized he was asking her. "Mind what?"

"If I train?"

"Nicholas, I'm not going to tell you what to do with your day. But," she added, "I will listen to your lute playing this afternoon."

He smiled. "I will endeavor to please you. With your permission?"

Jennifer watched him leave with both Montgomery and John bounding after him. She sat back, then realized Miles was staring at her. She smiled reflexively. "Yes?"

He shook his head. "I was just looking."

"What did you see?"

"What Nick sees, I imagine."

"And that would be?" she asked uneasily.

"A woman so far superior to anything he's ever met that it's a wonder he can draw a decent breath."

Jennifer laughed. "You are a flatterer. I'm sure your brother has scores of women trailing after him, trying to catch his eye."

"Oh, he does," Miles said, "but none to equal you." He took her hand and kissed it briefly. "I should be so fortunate." He looked at her for another moment or two, then smiled and rose. "Let us go, shall we? I'd best escort you out now, before Nick comes in to find out why I haven't."

She nodded and rose with him to walk around the high table. She followed him out of the hall and down the stairs into Artane's courtyard. Today, though, it didn't seem so strange and that in itself was a little strange. She walked across the dirt with only a slight jarring of her sense of reality when she heard men swearing in the lists and the blacksmith's hammer pounding in the still morning air. The mist, however, felt familiar, and the smell of the ocean was comforting. She was comfortable with Miles in a brotherly sort of way.

She had on a good dress and she had shoes that fit.

What wasn't to like about that?

Miles produced a cloak and put it around her shoulders. "I'll show you where you might sit and best observe the mayhem."

Jennifer hugged the wall with him and walked along until he stopped her and showed her a stone bench. She noticed that Montgomery and John were standing farther down the wall, watching intently. She sat down, then realized why.

All right, so she had seen Nicholas do a little damage to Ledenham. She'd watched him in the lists trying to sweat out the last of Ledenham's poison. She had even watched him go at Miles at the abbey. But now she realized he hadn't been all that serious before.

She wondered if *she* would be the one to manage to take a decent breath at any time in the foreseeable future.

There was no question that Robin de Piaget was an absolute master. He was aggressive, ruthless, and quite loud in his taunts. He was everything she had expected he would be, given his propensity to grin at things that amused him and needle his brothers at every opportunity. He was strong, fast, and relentless. He reminded her a little of James MacLeod, who intimidated first by his sheer presence, then finished with the killing blow of perfect technique.

But Nicholas . . .

Her mouth went unaccountably dry.

She was no expert in assessing the skill of swordsmen — her stays in Scotland and her association with Connor MacDougal aside — but it looked to her as though Nicholas was every bit his brother's equal.

But the frightening part was, he was quieter about it.

And no doubt deadlier because of it.

It didn't matter how ferocious Robin's attack was, Nicholas gave no ground. It didn't seem to make any difference how many jaw-droppingly rude comments Robin made to him or about him, he ignored them and wore nonchalance like a shield.

"Nicholas is," Miles said quietly, "as you can see, the only one who gives Robin decent sport."

"What of your father?" Jennifer croaked.

"My father taught them all he knows." He smiled at her. "He holds his own still."

"Are they showing off?" she managed.

Miles looked at them thoughtfully, then shook his head. "Indeed, I daresay they are holding back so as not to upset your delicate humors."

She looked at him in surprise, then saw the hint of a smile. "You're terrible."

"Thank you."

She turned back to look at the combatants. "They're very good, aren't they?"

"None better in England or France," Miles said easily. "And they are equally matched, though Robin would prefer death to that admission."

"And Nicholas says nothing?"

"What do you think?"

"I think Nicholas is a very, very dangerous man."

"I know *my* delicate humors are at peace when he's guarding my back."

Jennifer pulled the cloak closer around her, leaned back against the damp stone, and watched everyday life in medieval England go on in front of her. It was no wonder the men were in such good shape. No time at the gym, just time with a sword in a muddy field. She started to wonder if they enjoyed it or if it was drudgery, then Robin said something particularly vile to Nicholas.

And Nicholas laughed.

She was enormously grateful she was sitting down.

Maybe the stories had been true and he was perfect. She could easily see how every man with a son might want Nicholas to train him. She could see how any king with a battle to win might want him involved. She could also see how every woman who ever laid eyes on him would fall all over herself to get him to look at her just once. She could only imagine what a woman would be willing to do to have him look at her twice.

And she had tried to get out of their fortnight?

What was she, nuts?

She watched for quite a while, until the mists thinned and the day began to warm. It could have been an hour, it could have been three. All she knew was that she just couldn't look away from Nicholas de Piaget.

She was beginning to think he'd fully earned his place in Artane lore.

"Wine?"

A midmorning cup was just the thing for her, surely. She accepted a cup from Miles and drank happily. It was probably better than the water and it certainly settled her nerves. She clutched the cup and allowed herself for the first time to look at Nicholas without attaching all sorts of checks for her common sense to sift through.

He was gorgeous. Yes, she had thought that from the start. But now, she noticed different things. She noticed how the mist plastered his fair hair to his head and how it stuck up here and there when he dragged his sleeve across his face to get the sweat out of his eyes. She noticed how his laugh lit up his entire face and made her want to smile reflexively. Robin was astonishing, but there was something so lethally polished about Nicholas. She could understand now why Miles despaired of ever seeing him in a towering rage. Even dripping with sweat and obviously working quite hard, he looked elegant.

"He is beautiful," she said, then clapped her hand over her mouth. She looked at Miles with wide eyes. "Ah," she said quickly.

Miles smiled. "I'll keep your secret."

"Ha," she said with a snort.

"I provoked Nicholas for a reason. I wanted to see the man you're looking at now."

She smiled. "Then I'll admit it was worth it. But don't tell him I said that."

"Said what?"

Jennifer looked up and saw that the guys had apparently finished with their work. Nicholas was standing far enough away that he didn't drip on her, but close enough that he'd obviously heard her.

"I said that it was worth the trip out in the damp to see you two try to kill each other," she said quickly.

Robin waved his hand dismissively. "Light exercise. I didn't want to do him any damage, given that he intends to pass his afternoon indulging in manly labor with a lute."

"Why don't you go," Nicholas suggested. "Now. And be careful."

"I'm always careful," Robin said. He bowed to Jennifer. "I'll bring you better company than this fool here in the person of my Anne. Hold out hope for that." He looked at Miles. "Behave and keep the little ones in line." He clapped Nicholas on the shoulder, then walked back off toward the hall.

Nicholas resheathed his sword, then smiled. "I'd help you up, but you may not want to touch me."

She held out her hand and he took it and pulled her to her feet. "I have a high tolerance for lots of things," she said with a smile. "Just don't think I'm going to come out here and pick up a sword with you."

He looked surprised. "You don't think I would treat you as I do Robin."

"I don't know what you would do," she admitted with a shaky laugh.

He smiled. "You needn't feel you must indulge me. It was an offer made mostly in jest."

"Oh, I would come," she said honestly. "Just don't expect too much."

"I'll expect nothing and simply content myself with the pleasure of your company," he said. "But not today. Today, I think, demands an afternoon of leisure in my mother's solar. And aye, Montgomery, you can come."

"And me?" John asked.

"And me?" Miles drawled.

Nicholas looked at her and sighed. "I see no hope of escape."

"I like your brothers."

"Unfortunately, they seem to be enamored of you as well. Perhaps my playing will soothe them to sleep and then we will be free of them."

"And then what will we do?"

He smiled with a shrug. "The telling of secrets is out, I suppose. We'll think of something."

I'll just stare at you would have been first on her list, but she suspected that it wouldn't be wise to say as much, so she simply walked back with him to the great hall and kept her thoughts to herself. She was acutely aware of him and what she'd just seen in the lists. It was amazing that he could be so lethal one moment and so pleasant the next.

She wondered just how in over her head she was getting.

She supposed that might be a thought she should avoid contemplating too much for the next thirteen days.

Half an hour later she was seated in a comfortable chair in Gwennelyn de Piaget's solar with a fire in the hearth and a freshly washed lord of Wyckham plying his lute.

His voice was as perfect as the rest of him and he played better than any of the men from the night before. He had an enormous repertoire of songs, so many that she thought she might have to listen to them more than once to learn them all.

The rest of the morning passed most pleasantly, with Montgomery having been sent at one point for food. The afternoon was equally lovely, with nothing but music and conversation to enjoy. By the time Nicholas got up to light candles, Montgomery and John were snoring on a rug in front of the fire and Miles was snoring in a chair. Nicholas sat back down and looked at them in disgust.

"Isn't that what you wanted?" she asked with a smile.

"Aye," he admitted. "It was."

She looked at him and wanted to ask him a dozen questions, beginning and ending with why in the world he didn't find himself married already. Surely there had to have been at least one girl he could have proposed to. Surely there had been at least one girl who could have overlooked the matter of his birth.

Then she realized that he was smiling at her. "What?" she asked, smiling reflexively in return.

"You were scrutinizing me. I think perhaps I should be afraid."

"Are you ever afraid?" she asked.

He shook his head. "Not often."

"I didn't imagine so." She paused. "Thank you for a lovely day."

"Ten-and-three remaining," he said pleasantly. He set his lute aside. "What would you do tomorrow?"

She looked into the fire for several moments, then looked back at him. "Is this how all your days go?" she asked. "So easily?"

"Nay," Miles said, smacking his lips a time or two. "Generally his days begin much earlier and end later, with more work between dawn and dusk. One would think he was wooing, what with all the lute playing he's done today."

Nicholas reached over and smacked Miles smartly on the back of the head. Miles only laughed, stretched, and rose.

"I'll see if supper might be ready soon. Don't say anything important while I'm gone."

Nicholas threw him a glare, then turned back to her and his expression softened. "I suppose he has it aright about the earliness of the hour usually."

"Would you mind if I just followed you around tomorrow to see what you do?"

"If you like."

She suspected she would like it far too much. "Yes," she said. "I would."

"Done, then. Let us go find supper."

She nodded with a smile, then let him pull her up. She tripped over the rug at her feet and fell into his arms. Then she made the enormous mistake of looking up into his very lovely gray eyes.

"Oh," she breathed. "Sorry."

"I'm not," he said, holding her gently by the arms. "Steady now?"

"Not entirely."

He laughed, put his arm around her shoulders, and turned her toward the door. "Food. It is our only hope."

She went with him and decided that maybe

she would quote Dante for him. Hope? Hope that she would emerge intact from a fortnight spent in his company? Hope that she could keep herself from falling in love with him?

Impossible.

"You're thinking," he said in a singsong voice.

"Oh, no," she said with a half laugh. "No more of that. I'm convinced."

"Good."

She took his arm as they walked down the passageway as easily as if she'd been doing it her entire life, ate next to him without feeling the slightest bit of discomfort, and finally went to bed in his sister's bedroom without finding it at all unusual.

Convinced? Yes, she was convinced.

Convinced she was in deep trouble.

CHAPTER 21

Nicholas carried a candle with him down the passageway. He wouldn't have bothered with such a thing for himself, but he thought that it might give him yet another moment or two to admire Jennifer before the sun rose. He paused at the door, but before he could knock, the door opened. Jennifer was standing there, very much awake and seemingly prepared to follow him in whatever madness he planned to combine. Her hair was loose today and she was smiling.

She was spectacular.

"You did mean early," she said with a smile.

"But you were ready."

"I couldn't exactly sleep late when you're agreeing to take me on your day now, could I?" she asked. She stepped out into the passageway and shut the door behind her. "Where to first?"

Into my arms was almost out of his mouth before he could stop it. He feared, though, that once he had her there, he would never want to let her go.

"First?" he repeated, dragging himself back to the present. "Well, often I attend mass in the morning. Does that suit?"

"It's your day," she said with a smile. "I'm happy to go where you go."

Oh, that she might always feel thus. Nicholas nodded, offered her his arm in his most gallant fashion, and led her down the stairs, through the great hall, and across the courtyard to the chapel.

Moments later, he was sitting next to her on a hard wooden bench, listening to mass. Well, to be perfectly honest, he was pretending to listen to mass. He was actually excruciatingly aware of the woman sitting next to him with her hands folded demurely in her lap and her eyes fixed on the priest. He couldn't say he was doing the same. He was watching her, simply because he couldn't help himself.

Did they have mass in her day?

Did anyone pay the priest any heed at all if she was there to look at instead?

"Nicholas," she murmured.

"What?"

"Pay attention."

"I am paying attention."

"Pay attention to the *mass.* The friar is glaring at you."

He looked at Friar Osbert and found that that was indeed the case, so he bowed his head. But he smiled. He was tempted to hold Jennifer's hand, but he didn't dare. As she had said, his father's priest was not happy with him and such a thing would have only irritated the man further. So, instead, he sat on his hands as he had done when he'd been ten-and-two, sitting next to Robin and trying not to hit him.

At least for a few moments. Eventually, he couldn't help himself. He extended his little finger and touched a bit of her skirt.

She froze, then looked down. She stared at his hand for several moments, then looked at him from under her eyelashes.

She smiled.

Nicholas smiled weakly in return.

Friar Osbert cleared his throat pointedly.

"Pay attention," Nicholas whispered.

She shot him a glare, then turned her attentions fully back to the priest. But she was smiling, apparently in spite of herself. Nicholas bowed his head and kept his eyes focused on the stone floor between his feet, but he couldn't help a smile as well.

By the saints, what he'd been reduced to.

Several hours later, he realized that attending mass had simply been the start to a spectacularly useless morning.

He had managed to break his fast fairly successfully after escaping the chapel, but things had deteriorated rapidly after that. He hadn't heard anything his father's steward tried to tell him; he'd been far too distracted by the sight of Jennifer sitting before the fire in his father's solar. After embarrassing himself there, he'd added to his stature by almost finding himself slain by Miles in the lists. In his defense, he'd been likewise distracted there by Jennifer sitting on a bench near the wall.

After being profoundly grateful for an unpierced belly, he had attended to all the business of the day, and then hastened upstairs to have a bit of a wash and dress himself for the more important activities of wooing a beautiful woman.

He hurried back down to the great hall to collect Jennifer from where he'd left her. She was alone, simply standing there staring into the fire.

He paused at the edge of the stairwell and looked his fill. She had a very contemplative air about her and he wondered what she was thinking. Did she look at his father's hall and find it lacking? Surely she was accustomed to unbelievable luxuries. He hadn't peeked into his father's trunk and examined her Future clothing, but he had been tempted. Fortunately, he did have some small bit of self-control left.

A very small bit.

And what did she think of him? She'd been kind and even given him the odd compliment, but perhaps she was being polite. After all, he hadn't shown her much to recommend himself so far. He'd been vile, rude, and unchivalrous. He'd housed her in a keep that was falling down. He'd left her with her only security being his younger brothers.

'Twas a pity he hadn't met her in France. She might have even thought his hall there fine enough to tempt her to stay in the past — though he supposed she didn't think she had a choice *but* to stay. He pursed his lips and looked heavenward. He couldn't tell her about a gate until he was certain he knew where a working gate lay. He couldn't do that until he'd talked to Jake. And he wasn't going to talk to Jake that day.

It wasn't wrong to ignore the fact that he might have a way to help her home just so he could keep her near and hope beyond hope that she would learn to love him. Was it?

He couldn't bring himself to examine that.

He sighed deeply and stepped out into the hall. She looked up, saw him, and smiled.

He made it across the floor, but he honestly couldn't have said how. He stopped in front of her and bowed.

"How do you fare?" he asked, straightening.

"Very well, thank you, my lord. What now?"

"I thought perhaps you might like to see the village," he said. "To see how a simple peasant lives."

"I likely should —"

"Nay, not for that reason," he said with a snort. He took her hand and led her toward the door. "I think you should simply because you should know how my father's people live. You won't find this elsewhere in England."

"Why not?"

"Come with me and see."

He walked with her out of the great hall and down the stairs to the courtyard. He tried to look at everything with a fresh eye, imagining himself coming from inconceivable comfort and luxury.

He nodded purposefully at a pair of his father's guards as they walked through the barbican gates.

They'd made their way across the drawbridge before Jennifer looked over her shoulder. Then she glanced up at him.

"Don't look now, but we're being followed."

"I know," he said with a smile. "I asked them to come."

"Really? Don't you usually go into the village on your own?"

"Usually," he answered, "but today I am not alone and having a pair of my father's guardsmen to hand is simply added safety."

She smiled. "Thank you."

"It is my pleasure."

They walked in silence for a bit longer. "Nicholas?"

"Aye?"

"Why don't you have guardsmen of your own? Or a squire?"

He considered. "I haven't really had the opportunity for it. Before Robin wed, we spent so much time traveling it wasn't possible. Then Amanda wed and I went with Petter and his lads to work on Raventhorpe." He looked at her with a smile. "Do you think I should have a clutch of squires and pages dogging my steps?"

"I think their fathers would count themselves fortunate to have you care for their sons."

"Think you?" he asked seriously.

"Don't you?"

He shrugged. "I'm capable enough, I suppose."

"Please," she said wryly. "You can't not know you're much more than that."

"Perhaps," he said with a smile.

He continued on, walking next to her with his hands clasped behind his back, trying to watch her surreptitiously so he might see her reaction. She was looking around her, wide-eyed. He wondered, far less casually than he would have liked, what she thought of it all. Robin had it aright. He should have listened to Jake whilst he'd had the chance.

Then the village was upon him and he had no more time for speculation. He greeted most all the inhabitants by name, though he was the first to admit that there had been several additions in the persons of babes and a spouse or two he didn't know. He talked with men about their crops, picked up a youngling who seemed determined to become too familiar with his sword, and paused to play a game with the lads. The village elders requested a conference, which he agreed to only after Jennifer said she would be fine on her own. He left his father's men with her and went to the village hall to speak with the leaders of his father's people.

It took longer than he'd wanted it to, but when he finally found Jennifer, he realized that his delay had been amply rewarded. He found her on the green, sitting on a stump with a baby on her lap, talking with a handful of young mothers and a pair of old grand-mothers. She looked perfectly at ease and had a way about her that seemed to make others feel equally at ease.

Yet she was no peasant. Her manners were too fine, her grace too apparent.

She was luminous. He decided, as he watched her and lost his heart more with each moment that passed, that her beauty came from inside. She was his mother and her goodness; Amanda and her fire; Isabelle and her love of all things beautiful. She was everything he'd looked for.

She made Joanna's brittle beauties look cold and distant.

He decided suddenly that no matter what

happened, he would see that she lived the life of a fine lady. If she couldn't return to her time yet did not want him, he would see her dowered properly. He could do nothing less.

But the thought of her wanting anyone but him was enough to sober him abruptly.

Then Jennifer lifted her eyes and caught sight of him.

She smiled.

He would have staggered, but he was made of more sturdy stuff than that. He smiled in return, then waited until she had finished conversing with the women. She thanked a mother for the loan of her child, returned the babe gently, then excused herself. Nicholas nodded to the women, then looked at his lady.

"Well?" he asked.

"I have a lot to think about," she said honestly.

"Would you care to see the rest of the village?"

"I would."

"Then let us continue on."

He showed her the houses of the miller, the baker, the village smith. He showed her dwellings that were well fashioned and those inhabited by less prosperous folk. He walked with her past fields and pastures. And all the while, she didn't say aught. She merely watched everything with a grave expression.

He suspected she was trying to put herself in a peasant's place and wondering how she would manage.

He supposed he should wonder the same thing. But for the insistence of Gwennelyn de Piaget on seeing if he existed, he would have been orphaned at six and likely been tilling some piece of earth for another man himself.

'Twas sobering, truly.

Jennifer stopped on the edge of a large field planted with wheat and looked at Nicholas. "It seems like a hard life," she said, finally.

"How so?" he asked.

"Farming is never easy," she said.

"Neither is being a lord," Nicholas said frankly. "There are perils associated with both."

She sat down on a rock wall and looked up at him. "Tell me."

He sat down next to her, lifted his face briefly to the early summer sun, then turned to her.

"My father's villeins work three days a week for him, farming his land. That is a usual amount of time for a man to farm his lord's earth. What is different is my father pays them for their labor as well. Not much," he added, "but something. I don't know another lord who concedes so much. He bears a portion of the cost of grinding their wheat and baking their bread as well. When the girls wed, he sends gifts. When there is a death, he sees to the widows and orphans."

"As you did with Mark's family," she said quietly.

He shrugged. "I did what was needful."

"I never meant to suggest that I thought your father was a hard taskmaster," she said. "Farming just seems a harsh life to me."

Nicholas smiled ruefully. "It is my own defensiveness that speaks. My sire is very, very wealthy and there are those in England who believe he has garnered his wealth from the backs of his peasants."

"They seem to be quite happy to be here."

"For the most part, I daresay they are," he agreed. "To be sure, there is some comfort in knowing that if an enemy approached, they could retreat to the castle and my father would protect them."

"That would comfort me." She paused. "And what of you? You have a keep in France, don't you?"

"Aye."

"Is it large?"

"Very," he admitted.

"And how do you treat your people?"

"As my father treats his."

She smiled. "Do you like it there? In France?"

"Aye," he said. "The wine is perfection and my cook is beyond compare. And the view is lovely as well."

"Why aren't you there?" she asked.

"Fate," he said with a smile. And so it was.

If he had been in France, he wouldn't have ridden to Ledenham's abbey that day and . . . He shuddered.

"Nicholas?"

"A chill," he said promptly. Aye, he wouldn't have ridden to the abbey that day and he would have missed finding the treasure sitting next to him.

He could scarce bear the thought.

"Shall we keep walking," he managed, "or would you care to return to the keep?"

"I'm just following you today," she said, looking not unhappy by that. "What do you need to do?"

Nicholas gazed over the fields and gave it serious thought. He could have trained a bit more. He could have considered his own coffers and made himself a budget for the new keep. He had missives to write, books to read, escape routes to plan before his grandmother returned . . .

Then he saw a collection of wagons traveling slowly up toward the keep.

"Merchants are coming," he said, nodding. "We could see if they have anything needful."

"What would you buy?" she asked. "What do you need?"

"Ah, nothing in particular," he said. *Save your own sweet self.* "But it seems a shame to have them make the journey and not at least be polite enough to look at their wares."

She watched the carts as well, then turned

to him. "Would they have knitting needles?"

"Knitting needles?" he echoed. Future implements, obviously. He frowned. "Ah, I don't think I've seen any in quite some time." Especially if *some time* were to mean *never at all*. "And their purpose, again?"

"To take yarn and turn it into useful things. Socks, tunics, gloves. That sort of thing." She paused. "We could make a pair if we had some straight sticks."

He paused. "Your tunic, the one in my sire's trunk — is it made thus?"

"It is," she nodded.

"Then we will see what can be procured. Otherwise, I'll make what you need."

"Can you?" she asked, rising with him.

The saints pity him, he had no idea. But he wasn't about to tell her that.

"Quite possibly," he said, hoping it would be true.

They walked back to the castle. Nicholas watched her as they walked. She smiled and waved to a few of the women she'd met. She caught a toddler who ran toward her, picked her up, and cuddled her close before she set her down and sent her back to her mother. Aye, she was the equal of any nobly born woman he knew. And he would see that she lived that kind of life. Somehow.

The merchants were already setting up their wares in the courtyard by the time they reached it. Nicholas recognized the cloth merchant. The man, Bertrand, came often to tempt the lady of Artane with his very fine goods. Nicholas hung back as Montgomery and John materialized and spirited Jennifer away to see the baubles and pretties a trinket man had brought with him. He walked over to Bertrand and clasped hands with him.

"Good day, Bertrand," he said.

"A good day to you as well, my lord," Bertrand said with a bow. "I understand your mother is not at home."

"A disappointment, no doubt," Nicholas said with a smile, "but never fear. I will take her place today. I have a guest in need of a new wardrobe. Dresses for court, simpler gowns for everyday, as well as all the other things a lady might need."

"Where is the lady in quest— ah," he nodded, interrupting himself. "The noblewoman over there."

"Aye."

"Fine tastes?" Bertrand asked.

"Very frugal, more than likely," Nicholas said, "but as I am buying, we will not concern ourselves with what she would allow herself to buy."

"Most generous, my lord."

"She deserves nothing less."

Bertrand nodded, bowed again, then set to rearranging his cart. Nicholas could see that already he was laying out things that would suit Jennifer's coloring, as well as simpler, but still quite fine, cloth for undergarments and such. A very intelligent man, but that was his business.

Nicholas turned away and found Jennifer with Montgomery and John yapping at her sides like pups. Nicholas drew her away and steered her to the cloth merchant. She looked everything over, skimmed over the more common things, and caught her breath at the stuff that was of the finest quality. She fingered all of it, making appreciative noises.

"Beautiful," she said finally, smiling at the merchant. "You're very skilled. Do you weave these yourself, or just design them?"

"I used to weave," the man admitted readily, "but now I just tell the weavers what to do."

"It shows," Jennifer said with a smile. "You are obviously a man of very good taste, with an eye for very beautiful things. Unfortunately, I'm not looking for anything right now. Perhaps another time."

Nicholas looked over her head at the man. "All of it," he mouthed.

The man started to cough. He straightened, wiped his eyes, and made Jennifer a bow. "I wish you good health, my lady, and a need for cloth at another time."

Jennifer nodded and turned away without disappointment. She smiled up at Nicholas. "What now?"

"A rest in my mother's solar?" he suggested. "I'll see you up —"

She shook her head. "I can find it. I imagine you have lord of the castle business to take care of now, don't you?"

"Aye," he admitted. "I should see the merchants fed and sent on their way."

"I'll wait for you upstairs, then," she said, sounding not displeased by the necessity. "Thank you for a lovely day."

He nodded and watched her walk into the great hall and considered her reaction for several minutes. He simply couldn't imagine any of his grandmother's ladies being forced to walk away empty-handed without screeching over it. Yet Jennifer seemed unconcerned.

He looked at Bertrand. The man was looking at Jennifer as well, then he turned to Nicholas.

"Remarkable," he offered.

"She is," Nicholas agreed. "Now, if you'll bring what I like along with whatever else you think would suit her to my father's solar, I'll settle with you."

"Of course, Lord Nicholas."

Nicholas quickly looked over the rest of the goods. He found three bobbins of undyed wool, very soft and fine, and he paid for them without haggling. *Knitting needles* were completely beyond his experience, but he found half a dozen long, very thin sticks of straight wood for joining furniture and purchased them without complaint.

He started toward the house, then stopped.

He wasn't one to unnerve easily, but there was something about the feel of the courtyard that he didn't like. He looked for the two guardsmen who had come with him to the village. Both of them were watching the front gates closely, as if they felt the same thing. Nicholas went back down the stairs and stopped next to them.

"Sir Etienne," he said quietly.

Etienne turned immediately. "Aye, my lord?"

"You are uneasy as well."

"Aye, my lord," he said with a frown. "There's no accounting for why, but there you have it."

"I will see to the merchants. Will you watch here and perhaps noise your feelings through the garrison?"

"Of course, my lord. Immediately."

Nicholas sent Montgomery up to his mother's solar with a meal for Jennifer, then made quick work of feeding the merchants and sending them on their way. He made certain his brothers were inside the gates, spoke a final time with Sir Etienne, then retreated to his mother's solar. He opened the door, walked in, and collapsed in a chair.

"You're out of breath," Jennifer said with a smile.

"I've been myself, my brother, and my father all in the past hour," he said dryly. He held up his dowels. "What think you?"

"Perfect," she said. "But thinner and pointed there."

He set to with his knife and turned them into things that looked like very thin arrows without the fletching. She seemed very pleased, though, and that was enough for him. He handed them to her with the bobbins of yarn and was amply rewarded for his efforts. She looked as if he'd brought her a chest full of gold.

She held the yarn and her needles in her arms and smiled at him. "I'm happy now. What else do you have to do today?"

"Kiss you?"

She looked at him in surprise, then blushed a quite lovely shade of red and laughed. "Is that so."

"Hmmm," he said. "But since you don't fling and I wouldn't think to ask you to, I'll forbear."

"Chivalrous of you."

"Aye," he said sourly, "isn't it."

She laughed. "Yes, actually, it is."

The door opened suddenly and his brothers tumbled inside. By the saints, was he to have no privacy with her at all?

But Jennifer looked happy, he could spend the rest of the day looking at her which would make him happy, and there were still many, many days ahead to look forward to.

It was enough for now.

CHAPTER 22

It wasn't often that events were just so remarkable that one needed to stop and admire them for their sheer weirdness. Jennifer decided that such was the case at the moment, given that she was standing on the beach in a medieval gown, crossing swords with a man who could have cut her to ribbons with both hands tied behind his back, and neither seemed out of the ordinary. She held up her hand to ward him off.

"Wait," she said with a half laugh. "Give me a minute."

Nicholas propped his sword up on his shoulder like a rifle. "Tired?"

She didn't have the energy to put her borrowed sword up on her shoulder in that cool, medieval way, so she jammed it into the sand and used it to lean on. "Very. And trying to do this in a dress is impossible."

He tried without success to suppress his smile. "I won't remind you that I suggested you filch Montgomery's clothes again."

"If I'd worn those, I couldn't have walked barefooted in the sand."

"Most knights would consider that an inducement to wear boots."

"Fortunately I am not a knight," she said, using her sleeve to wipe her forehead, "and I like sand between my toes." She looked at him. "This is hard."

"Did you expect anything else?"

"Not really," she said with a smile.

"You have trained some yourself, though, haven't you?"

"A little," she admitted. And she had — two years of fencing, just so Victoria would have someone to practice with. "But it was nothing like this."

"Are you calling for a retreat to camp?"

"Definitely."

He took her sword from her and resheathed his own. Jennifer walked with him back to the blanket spread out on the sand. He cast himself down on it, supremely comfortable and seemingly not at all concerned about his future.

Would that she could say the same thing.

She sat down on the other side of the picnic hamper and turned to look out over the ocean. It was so beautiful and soothing that she found it difficult not to let the peace of it lull her into forgetting the reality of her situation, a reality that she simply couldn't ignore anymore.

She had pushed her concerns aside the day before, in deference to Nicholas's wishes. But going through the village, as interesting as it had been, had been a stark, unyielding reminder of what lay in store for her.

She sighed and dragged her hand through her loose hair. It was time for another bath. Another one or two before she faced her future as an ordinary medieval gal.

"Jenner?"

She closed her eyes briefly. Why did he have to call her that? He'd done it a time or two the day before. It was almost as if he knew her, liked her, thought of her as family. She turned her head to look at him. She attempted a smile, but thought it might not have been very successful. "Yes, my lord?"

"I fear you're thinking," he said, clucking his tongue.

"A horrible habit," she said.

"It is. Have some wine."

She accepted a goblet, then watched him as he made himself at home in the picnic hamper Artane's cook had packed for them. It was full of simply delightful things: pasties, dried meat, fresh greens, very nice bread. She had stood in the kitchen and watched Nicholas charm the man without an effort. Mr. Glum had apparently left the building for good. In his place was the sunny, chivalrous knight whose smile brought men and women both to heel without complaint.

And why not? He was just as kind to the servants as he was to his brothers. The peasant women yesterday had spoken of him in glowing terms. His father's guardsmen were cheerfully deferential. His brothers simply worshipped him. It was almost enough to make her forget that she shouldn't be doing the same.

"Bread?"

She didn't think she could get it down. She shook her head. "I'm fine, thank you."

"You look far too serious for such a lovely day," he remarked quietly.

She turned to look at him fully. It was a little difficult through the tears that seemed to have suddenly taken up residence in her eyes.

She had to talk to him. She had to at least tell him the truth about where — *when* she'd come from. He would find out eventually and when he found out, he would ditch her. There was absolutely no point in not getting it over with now.

As it was, she was living a lie. Unfortunately, it was such a delicious lie, so beautiful and sparkling and perfect —

"You know," Nicholas began slowly, "you begin to make me doubt my ability to please a maid."

"Nicholas," she said, "we have to talk."

He looked into the basket and spoke as if he hadn't heard her. "Let us eat now," he said, "then perhaps we'll train a bit more."

"Nicholas —"

"After that perhaps an afternoon of leisure. I'll play the lute for you —"

She jumped to her feet and walked away while she still could. She started to run. She tripped and went down on her knees.

Strong hands took her by the arms and pulled her back up to her feet. "Jennifer, please."

She didn't want to cry. Somehow, she just couldn't help herself.

"You promised me a fortnight," he said, dabbing at her eyes with the hem of his sleeve.

"Nicholas, I have things I *have* to tell you."

"Tell me later," he said. "For now, let us be merry, let us forget the world beyond Artane's reach, let us be at peace —"

"I can't," she said miserably. "If you knew the truth about me, you'd want to burn me at the stake just like Ledenham. I am *not* going to spend all this time with you, fall in love with you, never want to leave you just to have you dump me — or worse."

"Dump you?" he echoed.

"Yes, dump me," she repeated in irritation. "It means to cast someone aside without a backward glance. Trust me, when you find out *my* secret, you'll want to do that." She backed away. "You will."

She turned and ran before she had to see the look in his eye. It wasn't a pretty run, but she was past caring. She couldn't go on any longer. Every moment she spent with him was torture, torture because she knew that it wouldn't last. It *couldn't* last.

And if she fell any more in love with him than she was already, it would kill her.

She ran until she got a stitch in her side, then she walked. She kept her skirts up out of the waves and continued on so long that she passed Artane on her right and left it behind her. And when she had walked herself out, she simply stopped, turned toward the sea and stared out over it. Tears ran down her cheeks and she let them. She was past wiping them away.

She stood there for a very long time.

After a while, she realized that she wasn't alone.

She turned around. Nicholas was standing ten feet away from her, watching her gravely.

"Are you still here?" she asked, dragging her sleeve across her eyes angrily.

Nicholas looked at her for a moment or two in silence. Then he took three strides forward and pulled her into his arms. He slid an arm around her waist, a hand under her hair, then looked down at her.

And then he bent his head and kissed her.

He proceeded to kiss her until she had to hold on for dear life just to keep from disintegrating into a heap on the sand.

"Nicholas," she said, when he took a breath.

It was only a brief breath — not enough for her to really get in any decent conversation.

And then she found that the thought of conversation wasn't really all that interesting.

She was certain a good chunk of eternity had passed before he finally lifted his head and looked down at her. She had expected to see stormy gray eyes. Instead, she saw eyes that were as clear as an undisturbed Scottish loch reflecting gray clouds above. She was somewhat vindicated to notice, however, that his breathing was not all that steady.

"Give me the fortnight," he said.

"Pretend that I don't have things to tell you?" she whispered.

"Pretend that you've told me already and I don't care."

"They're pretty big things."

"Are you wed?"

She shook her head. "I'm not."

"Do you secretly despise me?"

She managed a miserable half laugh. "You know I don't."

"Then anything else can be resolved," he said. "Anything."

She felt her eyes beginning to burn again. "Why? Why do you want this?"

"Because I . . ." He paused and shook his head. He pulled her close again and simply held her. "Because I just do," he said quietly against her hair. "Please, Jennifer."

"But —"

He kissed her again.

It was in the back of her mind to tell him that kissing wasn't a very good way to fix their problems, but then she found that she couldn't think very well. As time passed, she began to think that perhaps she wasn't able to think at all.

All right, so she'd never dated anyone long enough, or found them unjerky enough, to get past making out. She had the feeling Nicholas had, and probably more than once. She completely understood how a woman being kissed by him might seriously consider a whole lot more than kissing.

When she thought she simply couldn't stand up anymore, he stopped ravaging her mouth and simply kissed her softly, sweetly. He kissed her eyelids, her cheeks, the tip of her nose. When she could pry her eyes open, she looked at him.

"Wow," she whispered.

"Wow," he repeated with a smile. "A Gaelic expression I don't know?"

"Something like that."

"Is it favorable?"

"Oh, yes."

He smiled, a half quirking of his mouth that was so charming she couldn't help but reach up and touch it. He kissed her fingers, then bent his head and kissed her again.

Jennifer hung on for dear life.

When he lifted his head the next time, his

breathing was a little ragged. "Were you saying something?" he asked.

"I think I was trying to remind you that I don't fling," she said faintly.

"I'm not asking you to fling."

"Then what are you asking me to do?"

He looked at her so seriously for such a long time, she thought he wouldn't answer her. Then he took a deep breath.

"I'm asking you to stay with me and see if this life might suit you."

Her knees did buckle then. The next thing she knew, he had swept her up in his arms. She put her arms around his neck in self-defense.

"I can walk."

"Then you'd best carry me, for I'm not at all sure I can."

She looked at him, then laughed. "Sure."

He let her slip down to the ground, then put his arm around her shoulders. "I feel better when you smile. Now, help me back, would you?"

She hesitated, then put her arm around his waist and walked slowly with him back down the beach toward where they'd left their lunch. They walked all the way back to Artane, then past it before she dared look up at him.

"Are you certain about all this?" she asked quietly.

"Are you yet unconvinced that I am?"

She looked out over the sea for quite some time before she turned back to him. "Did you mean what you said?" She paused. "About me staying . . ."

"Aye," he said quietly, "I did."

She let out a shaky breath and tried not to let her heart run away with her. "Then I suppose I can't be anything but convinced, can I?"

"Nay," he said gently, turning her to him and putting his arms around her. "I daresay you cannot."

She wanted to believe him. She had the feeling things would change when he learned all *her* secrets, but there was no point in trying to convince him of that. She stood there in his embrace, rested her head against his shoulder, and considered.

Maybe she was looking at it the wrong way. Maybe she should take the few blissful days she would have in his company and burn them into her memory. It might be what helped her survive all the hours in her future she was certain would be spent making expensive medieval gowns for evil stepsister types.

She pulled back and smiled up at him. "All right," she said, taking a deep breath. "I'm convinced."

He smiled, looking rather relieved. "Finally." He took her hand. "Let's find lunch. I daresay we need it."

She walked with him back down the beach, then caught sight of their picnic hamper being overrun by the locusts he called brothers.

"Damn it," she said under her breath.

He laughed. "What did you say?"

"You heard me. Look at them. There won't be anything left by the time we get there."

He smiled down at her. "I had no idea you were so fierce."

"It's lunch," she said.

"I agree. And though I suppose we'll need to endure them now, later we'll seek privacy in my mother's solar."

"Do we dare?"

He lifted one eyebrow archly. "I have self-control, even if you don't."

She pursed her lips. "I'd throw something at you, but I don't want to shock your brothers."

He only laughed at her and pulled her down the beach with him.

They stopped next to the blanket. Montgomery, John, and Miles were helping themselves to lunch.

"So," Miles said, through a mouthful of pie, "that's how it is."

Nicholas reached out and swatted their hands away from the basket. "Aye, that is how it is and it was so exhausting that we need food. Leave ours be and go find your own."

Montgomery lifted up a basket from behind him. "We brought our own, but it doesn't look as good as yours."

Nicholas nudged his brothers out of his way with his foot, then sat down and pulled Jennifer down to sit between his legs. He removed the good food and put it on the far side of him.

"We didn't ask for company," he said.

"Chaperons," Miles said, nosing about in the other basket with a frown. "You need us, I daresay."

Jennifer suspected that he might just be right about that. They didn't seem to mind, though, that Nicholas stroked her hair, or stole kisses, or had his arms around her continually. Miles watched, with a very small smile playing around his mouth.

Jennifer smiled back at him. "What?"

He shrugged. "It pleases me to see my brother happy."

"Is he happy?"

"Aye," Miles said, throwing a quick smile at Nicholas. "I daresay he is."

Jennifer toyed with her wine. "Surely you've seen him happy before."

"Never like this," Miles said.

She was surprised. "Really? Doesn't he usually bring ladies to the shore and kiss them silly?"

"Kiss them silly, indeed," Nicholas snorted.

Jennifer smiled at Miles. "Well?"

"Never," Miles said, shaking his head slowly.

Jennifer settled herself more securely in Nicholas's arms, then leaned her head against his shoulder and stroked his arm idly. "So, how does he usually woo, then?"

"He woos quickly," Miles said. "One dance, one look, one quirking of his little finger and then the lady is won."

Somehow, she could believe it. "And the next day?"

"Oh," Miles said with one raised eyebrow, "I imagine a few have lasted until the next day."

"Miles," Nicholas growled.

"I asked," Jennifer pointed out, tipping her head back briefly to smile at him.

"Aye, and I should growl at you for it as well. *Must* we discuss this?"

"We'll turn to your other flaws later," Miles said. "This is entertainment enough for the moment. Now, Jennifer, you must understand that my brother is not a monk."

"Miles!" Nicholas exclaimed.

"But, aside from a mistress or two whom he simply would not wed —"

"Miles, if you do not cease —" Nicholas warned.

"I daresay he's never truly been in love."

"Interesting," Jennifer said. And it was. Was it possible that Nicholas was serious about her?

She hardly dared believe it.

She looked casually at Miles. "So, tell me

more about these past wooings of his. You say they never lasted longer than a day?"

"None that I know of."

"And if he were to woo for, say, a fortnight?"

"Unprecedented," Miles said.

"Interesting," Jennifer said.

"Significant," Miles said, leaning forward and waggling his brows. "Have you heard of him planning such a thing?"

Jennifer only smiled and shrugged. "That's my secret, I suppose."

Nicholas's arms tightened around her and Jennifer smiled to herself. Perhaps there were secrets that were best left unrevealed. Besides, there was something very pleasant about having a secret *with* Nicholas for a change. She squeezed his arm briefly and felt him kiss her hair in return. Miles moved on to cataloging his brother's faults, and all was well with the world.

In spite of the uncertainty of her future, which she steadfastly refused to think about while the sun was shining.

Nicholas covered one of her hands with his. "Perhaps Miles will blather on yet awhile," he whispered against her ear. "The weather is lovely and I could sit here quite happily for the rest of the afternoon."

"I heard that," Miles said, "but I'll ignore it. Now, as I was saying —"

Jennifer smiled as Miles went on about

something she only half listened to. The only thing she could truly concentrate on was the feeling of Nicholas's arms around her, his fingers trailing now and again through her hair, the way he pulled her back occasionally to kiss her.

She was *definitely* in trouble.

She sat, several hours later, in Gwennelyn de Piaget's solar with the boys sprawled in various chairs around her and Nicholas sitting across from her, playing the lute. He sang beautiful songs and she knitted happily with the four double-pointed needles he'd made her on a pair of socks that would look ridiculous with everything he owned. Maybe he could wear them to bed.

She glanced up periodically, but not too often. Every time she did, the sizzling looks he gave her made her drop stitches.

Very dangerous.

Finally, Montgomery's yawns became too great to ignore. Nicholas set his lute in another chair and pointed toward the door.

"Montgomery, go to bed. John, bank the fire. Miles, begone. I'll walk Jennifer to her chamber."

"I think not," Miles said, rising and stretching.

Nicholas frowned. "What?"

Miles folded his arms over his chest. "Kiss

her here, brother, *chastely,* then allow me the pleasure of seeing her safely to her chamber."

Nicholas stood up slowly and turned to face his brother. Jennifer wondered if they would come to blows. She set her socks aside and thought briefly about rescuing Nicholas's lute. Miles was every bit as tall as Nicholas, but not quite so broad. She supposed that wouldn't matter enough to prevent them from engaging fully in some sort of brawl.

"I don't think you should do this," she put in quickly. "It's your mother's solar, after all. I can't imagine she'll be pleased if her chairs are broken."

Miles reached out and put a hand on his brother's shoulder. "Nick, she is a maid."

Jennifer wondered how he knew that, but maybe there was a medieval radar of sorts that all these guys had.

"Here," Miles said, releasing his brother, "let me give you a name to cool your ardor."

"Who?" Nicholas grumbled.

"Geoffrey of Fenwyck."

Nicholas flinched. He dragged his hand through his hair, looked heavenward, then turned and pulled Jennifer to her feet.

"He has it aright."

"Anne's father?" she asked. "What does he have to do with anything?"

"That is a very long, sordid tale which I'll tell you at another time," Miles said. "For now, I daresay you should leave your lord happily — or unhappily — and *prudently* here. Kiss her hand, Nick, and let her go."

Jennifer looked at Nicholas, then smiled and held out her hand. He took it, then he lifted it and kissed the back of it.

Then he turned it over and kissed her palm.

Miles groaned and turned his back on them. "I said *chastely.*"

"That was chastely," Nicholas said.

"The saints preserve us all," Miles said.

Nicholas smiled, then bent his head and kissed her very sweetly. And chastely.

"Good night, my lady," he said. "Until to-morrow."

"The saints preserve *me,*" she managed.

He looked like he was going to haul her into his arms, but he took a deep breath, took a step backward, and made her a bow.

"Chastely, damn it," he said with a scowl.

Miles took her hand and pulled her toward the door. "You'll see each other in the morning. Jennifer, I would suggest you bolt your door, but my brother does have his honor. Let's hurry, whilst he still has it."

"Jennifer."

She turned and looked at Nicholas. "Aye, my lord?"

"Are you still convinced?"

She knew exactly what he was talking about. She nodded with a faint smile. "Aye, my lord. I am."

He only looked at her gravely, his hands clasped behind his back.

Miles pulled her out into the passageway, then tucked her arm under his. He walked with her until they had reached Isabelle's bedroom, then he stopped and smiled.

"I'm happy for you," he said simply.

She smiled. She supposed it hadn't trembled all that much. "I'm nervous."

He considered her by torchlight for a moment or two, then nodded. "I can understand that. All I can tell you is that Nicholas has never looked so happy and so miserable at the same time."

"Miserable?"

"A man like Nicholas does not give his heart lightly. I daresay he has never given his heart before." He shrugged. "Perhaps he fears it will not be enough."

And with that cryptic statement, he fetched a candle out of her room, lit it, then handed it back to her and bid her a good night.

Jennifer went inside and shut the door behind her.

Cryptic indeed.

A soft knock in the middle of the night woke her. She lit a candle in the embers of Isabelle's fireplace and went to the door in her borrowed nightgown that was several inches too short.

"Who is it?"

"Nicholas."

She unbolted the door. He was standing there, fully dressed with a cloak around his shoulders. Jennifer looked at him in surprise.

"Trouble?"

He shook his head. "A suddenly urgent errand." He paused. "I had thought to leave it for another se'nnight, but I think it best to be about it today. I will return by evening."

"Are you all right?"

He smiled, took her candle in one hand, and pulled her into his embrace with the other. "I am well," he said softly. "I'm sorry to wake you, but I didn't want to leave without bidding you farewell."

"Farewell?"

"For the day, of course," he said dryly. He smiled and kissed her softly. "Miles will keep you safe until I return." He handed her the candle and stepped back. "Until tonight, my lady."

"My lord," she said softly, then closed the door.

She walked back over to the bed, set the candle down on the nightstand, and looked at it, sure she now wouldn't sleep a wink. Then she leaned over, blew out the candle and, to her surprise, felt herself falling into a peaceful, contented sleep.

Farewell . . . for the day.

Tomorrow be damned; she would take him

at his word.

After all, how long could a single day last?

CHAPTER 23

Nicholas walked into his sister's hall just as she was sitting down to her morning meal. He'd chosen his father's fastest, most uncontrollable horse and he supposed he wouldn't have been undeserving of a bucking off, but fortunately giving the beast his head had resulted only in blistering speed. It was so quick that he'd made what was normally a three-hour journey in less than two.

He thought he just might have to buy that horse from his sire.

Amanda looked up from her breakfast in surprise. "Nicky," she exclaimed joyfully. She jumped up from the table, then ran around the end of it and threw herself into his arms.

Nicholas held her tightly, then set her down and kissed her soundly.

"You look wonderful," he said. "Motherhood suits you."

And it did. Amanda was easily one of the most beautiful women he'd ever seen. Not only were her features flawless and her eyes a most mesmerizing shade of greenish blue, she had fire and wit and spine to match any man. Being wed had only enhanced all her charms. Jake Kilchurn was a fortunate man.

Then again, Jennifer was just as lovely in a mesmerizingly different way. He could only imagine what being wed would do for her. Was it too much to want to see the truth of it for himself?

Amanda took his hand and pulled him around the table. "Jake is changing Rose, but he'll return shortly. Come and sit. Why are you here so early?"

"I need speech with your husband."

Amanda urged him down into the chair next to her and looked at him in surprise. "Indeed? But why?"

"You may listen as well and then you'll know."

"I can scarce bear the wait," she said, pushing her trencher and cup in front of him. "Here, you had best eat, so you won't faint before you spew out your tale."

He had a long, desperately needed drink, then looked up as Jackson Alexander Kilchurn IV came into the hall, cradling his year-old daughter in his arms as if he held the Holy Grail itself.

Jake looked at him in surprise. "Nick," he said easily. "What brings you here?"

"I need to talk to you."

"Really? About what?"

Amanda took Rose from her husband. "He's being mysterious. I imagine we won't hear anything until he's eaten."

"Likely not," Nicholas agreed. "Lovely porridge, this."

"Some things never change," Amanda noted.

Nicholas nodded, but applied himself to his sister's meal. He did periodically look not only at his sister but at her daughter as well.

"Rose is," he said, between swigs of ale, "a spectacularly beautiful babe. Well done, Mandy."

Amanda looked down at her daughter. "I've had her less than a year, but I cannot imagine life without her." She looked at Jake. "Think you?"

"I think you're both magnificent," Jake said with a smile. "A luckier man doesn't exist on the face of the earth."

Nicholas sat back with his cup. "Stop," he groaned. "You're making me dizzy with those looks of love."

Amanda cuffed him smartly. "Should I not love him?"

"You should," Nicholas said frankly. "I think I might love him as well after he answers my questions."

"Then I can hardly wait to hear them," Jake said with a smile. He gave Amanda a calculating look. "Should I torture him first before I tell him what he wants to know? Is there anything you want from him?"

"His happiness," Amanda said without hesitation. She studied Nicholas for a moment or two, then shook her head. "Perhaps you shouldn't torment him, my love. He looks distressed enough."

"You have *no* idea how true that is," Nicholas said grimly.

"Is it love?" Jake asked.

Nicholas hesitated, then shot Amanda a brief look. "It might be," he admitted.

"The saints be praised!" Amanda exclaimed, then leaned over and kissed his cheek. "It is far past time. Did one of Grandmère's lassies catch your eye? She had best be a good one, Nicky, or I won't give you permission to wed with her."

"Nay," Nicholas said slowly. "Not one of Grandmère's lassies."

"Who then?" Amanda asked. "And why do you need Jake?"

"I'll answer both at the same time." He looked at his brother-in-law. "Might we repair to your solar? I fear both the questions and the answers require privacy."

"Should I fetch more food for a long parley?" Jake asked.

"Likely so."

"Then go stoke my fire and I'll bring along a hamper," Jake said. "Cook is particularly skilled, you know."

"He would have to be," Nicholas said with

a snort, "given your wife's inability to keep from burning everything she touches."

"I seem to withstand it," Jake said mildly.

"I wasn't talking about *you,* dolt," Nicholas said, "I was talking about your food."

Jake looked at Amanda. "He has insulted your skill in the kitchens. Shall it now be torture?"

"It should be," Amanda said with a laugh, "and it would be if it weren't true. 'Tis a good thing you didn't wed me for my ability to keep from burning your stew."

"I married you for a whole host of other reasons, which I will be happy to list for you now if you like —"

Nicholas groaned and heaved himself to his feet before he had to listen to anything else. He'd heard enough of that sort of talk during their sickeningly sweet courtship and revolting first year of marriage, a first year he'd been forced to watch from close range as he and Petter had worked on their keep. He couldn't say he'd been particularly happy that Jake had wed Amanda, though he had been resigned. But watching the man woo his sister from dawn to dusk even *after* they'd been wed had almost been too much to bear.

If he managed to wed Jennifer McKinnon, he would make certain they had some privacy.

He retreated to Jake's solar and built up the fire. He cast himself down on the least comfortable chair, but even that one wasn't bad. He would know, given that he'd built all Jake's chairs himself. He shook his head. The things he had done for his sister.

It wasn't long before Jake and Amanda joined him. Amanda sat down before Jake's fire, turned her back to them and started to nurse her daughter. Nicholas winced.

"Must you do that?"

"She's hungry and I'm being discreet." She looked at him over her shoulder. "Besides, she won't be long. Close your eyes for a minute or two."

"Perhaps that's a good idea just in general," Jake said with a smile. "Then you won't have to watch me smirk at you if your questions are ridiculous."

Nicholas bowed his head and blew out his breath. Then he leaned his elbows on his knees and looked at his brother-in-law.

"I need help."

"Wait," Amanda said, "please don't start this now. Give me a quarter of an hour. Couldn't you speak of something unimportant until Rose finishes?"

Nicholas sighed. "I suppose I could take a nap." The saints knew he needed it. He hadn't slept more than a pair of hours the night before. Spending the previous day holding Jennifer McKinnon in his arms had been too much for him. Of course the fortnight had been his idea, but he had begun to wonder about the advisability of it. Fourteen days with her in his arms, then to lose her?

He'd decided in the middle of the night that he had no choice but to find out what Jake knew. At least he would have the knowledge to hand if he needed it.

He couldn't help but wish he wouldn't.

"Jake, play chess with him."

"Nick?" Jake asked.

Nicholas looked up, remembering where he was. "Of course, if you like." He waited until his brother-in-law had set up the game pieces Rhys had given him, then rose and went to sit at the board. He attempted to play with his usual canniness, but found it impossible. Jake bested him quickly, then sat back in his chair and let out a low whistle.

"You *are* in trouble."

"I am," Nicholas agreed.

"Then toddle feebly back over to your chair. I'll put this stuff away."

Nicholas scowled at him, but went to sit back at Jake's table. He watched his brother-in-law put away the chess pieces and return to his seat. He tried not to think overmuch about the questions he had to ask, or the answers he feared to have.

The saints pity him, he was in trouble indeed.

"All right," Amanda said suddenly, turning back around with her sleeping daughter in her arms. "I'm ready. Tell us everything."

Nicholas put his hands on his knees for a

moment, then rose. He paced about the solar for several minutes until he thought he could bear up under the ridicule he was just certain would be heaped upon his head. And he would deserve every moment of it. He had mocked Jake the entire time he'd been working at the man's keep. Snorts, eye rolls, noises of disgust — he'd indulged in all fully every time any mention was made, however slight, of Jake's past or his home.

In 2005.

He finally stopped and sat down. He looked at his sister's husband.

"I apologize," he said.

Jake likely couldn't have looked more surprised if Nicholas had sprouted wings, donned faery attire, and begun to hover in the air.

"What?" Jake asked, clearly stunned.

Nicholas felt his lips tighten of their own accord. "I apologize."

"For what?"

"For disbelieving you," he said.

"For disbelieving me about what?" Jake asked, looking rather confused.

"For disbelieving you when you said you had traveled back in time from the Future!" Nicholas bellowed. He gritted his teeth, then took another deep breath. "Sorry."

Jake sat back in his chair. He still looked rather shocked. "Well, thank you. I think." He shot Amanda a look of surprise, then turned back to Nicholas. "And you rode all the way from Wyckham at this unearthly hour to tell me this?"

"I rode from Artane."

"Whatever."

There was that word again. Someday he would have to master its use. He pursed his lips. "Nay, I didn't come just for that. That is but my opening move."

"I can hardly wait for the others," Jake said, wide-eyed. "Please go on."

Nicholas leaned forward and looked at Jake earnestly. "I need advice."

"But not wooing advice."

"Well, actually, aye, I might need that as well. Advice and . . . directions."

"Directions?"

"To a time gate that works." Nicholas paused. "The one you used, actually."

Jake sat back in his chair. He tried to speak several times, but each time words seemed to fail him. He looked at Amanda, looked back at Nicholas, then shook his head as if he thought he was losing his mind.

Nicholas understood completely.

Jake finally put his hands palm down on his table. "Why the hell for?"

"Aye," Amanda agreed. "Why would you want to know that?"

Nicholas jumped up again and began to pace.

"He's pacing again," Jake said in a loud

whisper.

"Then it must be truly grave," Amanda agreed in an equally loud whisper.

Nicholas came to stand behind his chair. He clutched it and looked at Jake.

"I met a woman."

"Congratulations."

"Nay," Nicholas said impatiently, "not that kind of woman. I met your kind of woman. A woman from the Future."

Jake frowned. "What do you mean?"

"What I mean is that I met a woman from the Future! By the saints, man, how much clearer can I be than that?"

"How would you know?"

"Because I spent a bloody year listening to your madness," Nicholas snarled, "and I knew what to look for."

"Hmmm," Jake said, but he looked skeptical. "Are you sure?"

"Of course I'm sure!" Nicholas realized he was bellowing yet again, but he was hard-pressed to do anything else. He took a deep breath. "Aye. I'm sure and I need directions to your gate so I can give them to her." He paused. "Eventually."

Jake looked at him in astonishment for several moments, then shut his mouth with a snap. "Why don't you tell me everything."

Nicholas walked around his chair and cast himself down into it. "Montgomery saw her spring up from the grass."

"She could be a faery," Jake pointed out.

Amanda laughed. "Jake, you're terrible."

Nicholas gritted his teeth and dredged up a goodly amount of patience. "And to think I apologized. I take it back. You deserved every moment of irritation I provoked."

Jake laughed. "I'm messing with you, Nick." He poured a cup of wine and slid it across his desk. "Drink that, then tell me what happened."

Nicholas drank. Then he took a deep breath.

"I rescued her from Ledenham. He was kindling a fire and preparing to put her to the test of witchcraft."

"So?" Jake said. "A little bonfire doesn't make her a time traveler."

"It does when she was wearing . . . jeans," Nicholas said.

Jake lifted one eyebrow. "Oh," he said.

"Aye, oh," Nicholas agreed. "She spoke in some strange tongue, but she also spoke Gaelic. Had I not noticed her clothes and known whence they came, I might have thought her a Scot."

"Go on."

"I rendered Ledenham unconscious —"

"Painfully, I hope," Amanda put in.

Nicholas smiled briefly. Amanda had her own reasons for detesting the man and he was happy to be able to tell her of a goodly revenge taken. "Aye. I imagine I broke his nose."

"Thank you."

"My pleasure. And after I meted out that well-deserved bit of revenge, I listened to the maid thank Montgomery kindly in Gaelic for the rescue, then hurry back to a particular patch of ground and stand there — as if she expected something to happen." He paused. "Nothing did, of course. When I saw that she wasn't going to be successful, I had Montgomery offer her the hospitality of Wyckham."

Amanda laughed. "If she is still wanting to keep company with you after that, then she must love you truly. Does your roof still leak?"

"My roof collapsed," Nicholas said grimly, "but that is a tale for another day. Jennifer tried the abbey gate a fortnight later, without my aid, which I regret still, and ran afoul of Ledenham again."

"And he ran afoul of your fists again?" Amanda asked hopefully.

"Nay, he fell into a pit of his own making — and that pit was the cause of her trouble." He looked at Jake. "The ground where her gate had lain was dug up. I think it destroyed whatever portal was there. Do you agree?"

Jake considered for a moment or two, then shrugged. "I have no idea. I suppose that the ground being disturbed might have ruined that particular gate."

"She tried others, but they didn't work, either."

"Did your Jennifer — and that isn't exactly a medieval name, is it — tell you what she was trying to do, running around to all these places?"

"Nay, but I knew just the same." He flashed Jake a look. "Having listened to you for so long, of course."

"Really," Jake said with a twinkle in his eye. "How interesting. And now? Are you going to take her to my gate?"

Nicholas sighed and looked down at the floor. Then he lifted his head. "As I said, I will tell her about it. Eventually."

"And?"

"And hope to hell she won't wish to use it."

"Ah," Jake said, sitting back. "I see."

"Do you love her?" Amanda asked seriously.

He looked at her. "Would you mind?"

"Only if she isn't spectacular."

Nicholas had wondered, on his way north, if telling Amanda that he was in love with someone else would grieve her. Then again, she had wanted that for him, so perhaps there was nothing to be done about it. He nodded seriously.

"She is." He paused. "Do you mind, in truth?"

"Nicky," she said softly, "I have only ever

wanted your happiness. I will love you always, which you know, but this is as it should be." She flashed Jake a brief smile, then looked back at him. "I'm happy for you."

Nicholas let out a breath he realized he'd been holding for quite some time. "Thank you, Mandy."

"Fool," Amanda said affectionately. "You know I wouldn't begrudge you happiness."

"I know," he said quietly, "though you certainly have reason to." He took a deep breath, then turned back to Jake. "Can you give me directions?"

"I can," Jake said. He paused. "You know, I wonder if it might be wise to write them down at some point."

"Never let Montgomery find them," Amanda said dryly. "We'd never see him again if he did."

Nicholas wanted to laugh, but he suspected Amanda was closer to the truth than any of them wanted to acknowledge. "Just tell me where to go and I'll remember."

"Does your Jennifer know you know she's from the Future?" Jake asked.

"Nay," Nicholas admitted. "I daresay she wants to tell me, but I forced her to agree to a fortnight with no conversation about anything serious. I'm hoping that by the end of that time, she'll love me enough to want to stay." He looked at Jake earnestly. " 'Tis possible, isn't it?"

"I'm living proof," Jake said. "But, then again, your sister was the prize." He looked at Nicholas with half a smile. "You're not chopped liver, either, I suppose."

"Chopped liver?"

"Nick, my friend, there are a few words you have to learn in modern English if you're going to live with a Future girl."

"Like *wow?*" Nicholas asked.

Jake smiled. "Did she say that? When?"

"After I kissed her."

Jake laughed. "Then perhaps you aren't chopped liver after all. And yes, I'll give you directions and some wooing ideas. You'd probably better plan on staying awhile, though, because I'm sure you'll need *lots* of the latter."

"I can only stay the afternoon," Nicholas said, "and I don't need *that* many wooing ideas. I brought the Black so I'll still be home before nightfall."

"The Black?" Amanda said, her ears perking up. "Is he as fast as he promised to be?"

"Faster. I was here in two hours."

"Is he still saddled —"

"Forget it," Jake said, reaching out to take hold of her free hand. "You will *not* ride that horse."

Amanda looked at him with one raised eyebrow. "I won't?" she asked archly.

"Please, Amanda," he said very evenly, "please do me the courtesy of not leaving me with a baby to raise on my own and years to spend without indoor plumbing and a wide-screen and your own exquisite face to admire endlessly by getting on a horse that should be shot, riding off where I can't catch you, then dashing your brains out against a rock when that damned horse throws you." He paused. "Please."

Amanda winked at Nicholas. "He loves me."

"So I see." He sat back and smiled. "So I see."

In fact, he saw several things that afternoon. Jake sketched for him several Future marvels that Nicholas had snorted at over the past year and a half. He watched, with a new and friendlier eye, the love that flourished between his sister and her husband. And he held their daughter and understood why Robin was so full of fine humors.

He wanted the same for himself.

He stayed longer than he'd meant to, simply because he found for the first time that he was enjoying the warmth of their family. The sun was setting as he took his leave. He walked with Jake and Amanda out of their great hall, then paused on the steps below them and considered. His brother-in-law was a tremendously talented artist and goldsmith. While he hadn't wanted any of Jake's creations when Jake had offered them to him before, he wanted one now.

"Would you make me a ring?" he asked.

Jake smiled. "Of course. What is her coloring?"

"She has flaming hair and sparkling green eyes. I've no skill with jewels and such. Make it how you see fit."

"Such confidence," Jake said with a grin.

"Aye, well I had none in you before and I apologize. Again. At least I gave you horses for your wedding gift."

"Very fine ones indeed," Jake agreed.

"Let's breed the bay mare with the Black," Amanda said, elbowing Jake in the ribs, "and see what comes of it."

"Never," Jake said pleasantly, putting his arm around her. He paused. "Well, all right, if you like. I suppose I can't keep you safe from everything, can I?"

"I'll be careful," Amanda assured him. She looked at Nicholas. "You be careful as well. Don't fall off on the way home."

"I won't." Nicholas turned to Jake. "I think you just might be worthy of my sister."

"Why do you say that?"

"Because you didn't smirk once."

"I will once you're gone."

Nicholas smiled and for the first time felt a feeling of affection for the man. He gave him a manly hug, hugged his sister so tightly she squeaked, then kissed his niece. He left with their promise to come south at the end of his fortnight.

He'd learned what he'd expected to learn, which did nothing to put his mind at ease. There was indeed a way for Jennifer to get home. He supposed Amanda was lucky she hadn't known what Jake was giving up. Nicholas wished he didn't. He didn't lack confidence, but he had to wonder if he might be worth it to her.

A fortnight, he reminded himself. Jennifer agreed to cease thinking on the Future for a fortnight. He could do the same. He would put his knowledge of the gate aside and concentrate on wooing her in lavish, medieval fashion.

And then he would tell her that he loved her, and that he wanted her to stay, but that he knew a way she could return home.

But he did not look forward to that moment.

He kicked the Black into a gallop.

Chapter 24

Jennifer sat on the front steps and looked out over the courtyard. The weather was very nice for England in June, with a slight breeze and rain no doubt in the forecast for later that afternoon. She smiled to herself. One thing she did not miss was inaccurate weather reports. In medieval England, there wasn't any worry about dressing for the weather. She suspected that work in the lists went on whether or not it rained.

She looked next to her. Miles sat there, staring off into the distance. Montgomery and John sat on the step below her. For some reason, it was just terribly comforting to have them there around her. And in spite of her better judgment and sense of self-preservation, she wanted it to last. She was very happy in the company of Nicholas's brothers.

She was even happier in the company of Nicholas himself.

"Well," she said finally. "What should we

do to pass the time?"

Miles smiled as he turned to look at her. "We are a sad lot, aren't we? Nick rides off and we mope."

"Pathetic," she agreed. She reached out and tousled Montgomery's hair. "What do you think, Montgomery? Should we go mope in another location and play cards? Should we take a walk through the village?"

"A walk," Montgomery said, standing up. "We'll protect you, Jennifer."

"I'm sure you will." She accepted Montgomery's help up, then linked arms with him and walked down the stairs and through the courtyard.

He smiled at her shyly. "Nick calls you Jenner. I like that."

"But you will not call her that," Miles said sternly. " 'Tis Nick's name for her."

Montgomery scowled at his brother, then turned back to her. "May I call you Jenner?" he asked in a whisper.

"Of course," she said. "Miles is teasing you."

Montgomery shivered. "I never know. And I'm not overfond of crossing blades with him, though I am much improved over the past pair of years. I squired with Amanda's husband, Jake, for a year, you know."

Jennifer frowned thoughtfully. "Jake," she mused. "An odd name."

Montgomery leaned closer to whisper to

her. "He's a faery."

"Montgomery," Miles said sharply. "He is not a faery and I *will* take you back to the lists and remind you of that if you cannot cease with that foolishness."

Montgomery looked at Jennifer knowingly, but said no more as they walked through the front gates and down to the village. She would have asked him more about it, but quite suddenly he broke away from her.

"Look!" he said, running ahead. " 'Tis Robin and Anne. And Father and Mother as well!"

Miles took Jennifer's hand and pulled her off the main road. Jennifer watched as he brushed off a stump, sat down, and made room for her on half of it.

"This will be interesting," he said dryly.

"Why?" she asked, sitting down next to him.

"Just wait." He looked at her seriously. "Can I offer one piece of advice before the company arrives?"

"Do I need advice?"

He chewed on his words for a moment or two. "Perhaps not advice. A reminder, if you'd rather."

"And what would you remind me of?" she asked.

"That you are without peer," he said simply. "And that Nick loves you."

She wasn't sure she should be counting on Miles's opinion, but she couldn't deny that there was some comfort in hearing that. "Do you think so?"

"Aye, I do, damn him to hell."

She laughed softly. "Oh, Miles, you are wonderful. But why did you feel the need to tell me all that?"

"Just watch." He crossed his legs and clasped his hands around one knee. "I'll identify the players so you'll recognize them later. Now, there in the distance we have my eldest brother, Robin, whom you already know. Next to him is his lovely wife, Anne. The two lads squirming atop their father's horse while his lady wife looks on with horror are his young sons, Phillip and Kendrick."

Jennifer jerked a bit, startled. "Kendrick? What an interesting name."

"He's a brat," Miles said affectionately, "but I adore him."

Jennifer watched as Robin and Anne rode up the way. Robin struggled to hold on to his sons and pull his horse up at the same time.

"Miles, why are you sitting on the side of the road?" he asked. "Where's Nick?"

"Off somewhere," Miles shrugged. "He didn't give details, but he promised to come back."

"He has inducements," Robin said. He smiled at Jennifer. "I see you've survived your time with these ruffians."

"Quite well, my lord," Jennifer said.

Robin nodded toward his wife. "This is my

Anne. Anne, this is Mistress Jennifer McKinnon. I might have told you about her already."

Anne smiled warmly. "You did indeed, husband. Mistress Jennifer, when we have time I would be pleased to hear of your adventures. It sounds as if you have had several."

Jennifer got to her feet and started to curtsey, but Anne shook her head with a laugh.

"Don't you dare," she said. "Here. I'll come down and we'll embrace, as we should." She slid off her horse toward the ground.

Miles hurried around her horse and put his arm around her waist. Jennifer watched as he waited until Anne nodded before he helped her walk over to where Jennifer stood.

"Will you sit?" he asked.

"I beg you, nay," Anne said, with feeling. "My leg pains me enough as it is." She gave Jennifer a quick hug. "I hear you made our Nicky laugh."

"I didn't do anything," Jennifer protested, "though I imagine Miles can't say the same."

Anne looked at him narrowly. "Aye, I heard about that as well. Reprehensible, Miles, truly."

"And yet Nick loves me still," Miles said placidly. He put one arm around Anne's shoulders and the other around Jennifer's. "Now, I have two exquisite ladies to admire. My day has just vastly improved." He looked up at Robin. "I'll see Anne back, brother, if you care to go on ahead."

Robin looked at Anne. "Does that suit?"

"I'll be fine," she said with a smile.

"Then I'll take the lads," Robin said, urging his horse forward with his knees. "Lest they be trampled in the swarm coming along behind us. And I won't lose either of them," he added with a look thrown Anne's way. "I promise."

Anne only smiled and waved.

Miles looked at her. "Are you certain you don't want to sit? I'll vacate my spot on the stump so you and Jennifer can take your ease."

"Perhaps that would be welcome," Anne said. "I daresay I would prefer to sit upon something that doesn't move." She let Miles help her down. "Jennifer, come and sit with me. We may as well be comfortable as we watch the procession."

Jennifer sat next to Anne. "Who's coming?"

"Robin's parents and his grandmother," Anne said.

"And my grandmother's collection of eligible maidens, no doubt," Miles added. "Is that right, Anne, my love?"

"Aye," Anne said, sounding less than enthusiastic about the last.

"Eligible maidens?" Jennifer repeated. "For you, Miles?"

Anne looked at her and bit her lip. "For

399

Nicky, I fear."

"Oh," Jennifer said.

Well, that was going to make things interesting.

"Remember what I told you, Jennifer," Miles said in a low voice.

"What did you tell her?" Anne asked. "Or is it private?"

"I told her that Nick loves her madly."

Anne looked up at him. "Then I'm happy for him. And does she love him?"

"She tolerates him," Miles said confidently. "I'm convinced she secretly prefers me and isn't quite sure how to tell him."

Anne slapped him smartly on the backside. "You're terrible."

"As is, no doubt, the collection of misses coming our way. Who did Grandmère bring this time?"

Jennifer listened to the guest list and felt a little sick. She wasn't a coward and she never ran, but there was something about facing an entire family of medieval nobility, along with their selection of potential brides for their son, that made her just a little queasy.

Especially since she loved the son they were trying to marry off.

She realized with a start that she did love him. Against her better judgment, against the little voice that told her she was crazy, against all rational reasoning.

She hoped he was hurrying.

Then she didn't have any more time for thinking because the parade was right there in front of her. There were horses and wagons and more people than Jennifer thought she could identify in a week.

But as she looked closer, she saw that her first impression wasn't exactly accurate. Nicholas's family wasn't hard to pick out. She saw an older, extremely handsome man who she was certain had to be Nicholas's father, Rhys. Next to him rode an equally stunning, dark-haired woman who had to have been Rhys's wife, Gwennelyn. Behind her rode a younger version of Gwennelyn. Isabelle? Jennifer sent her a particularly warm thought, especially since she'd been sleeping in her bed for almost a week.

Rhys reined in his horse. His wife and daughter stopped with him. He smiled affectionately at Anne, scowled at Miles, then looked at Jennifer with cautious interest. Miles stepped forward and kissed his mother's hand.

"Mother," he said with a nod. "Father. Allow me to introduce Lady Jennifer McKinnon. She is Nick's guest."

Jennifer rose immediately and this time she did curtsey. "My lord," she said. "My lady."

"Miles," Rhys said with a frown, "why on earth do you have her sitting down there in that dust?"

"We came for a walk and did not expect

you," Miles said.

"Where is Nicholas?"

"Off somewhere," Miles said with a shrug. "He'll be back tonight."

Rhys lifted his eyebrow as he looked at his wife. "Very well. A good day to you then, Lady Jennifer. I'll greet you properly at the hall."

Miles smiled and waved to his mother and sister. Jennifer waited until they rode past before she looked at him.

"I'm not a lady," she pointed out. "Why did you do that?"

He looked at her with tranquil eyes. "Because regardless of whether you are or not at the moment, you will be if Nick has his way. It is best that you are treated as Nick would wish to have you treated while he is away and I am in charge of your care."

She smiled faintly. "Thank you."

"It's not entirely altruistic," Miles admitted with a smile. "I fear my brother's wrath if I fail him." He winked at her, then turned back to the road. "Ah, now it comes. Just remember, *Lady* Jennifer, that Nick loves you. Madly. Ah, Grandmère," he called, striding out into the road and taking the bridle rein of the lead horse. "What an unexpected pleasure."

Jennifer looked at the woman who hopped off that horse with agility and realized, with a shock, that she had to have been pushing seventy.

"Grandmère, might I introduce you to Lady Jennifer McKinnon," Miles said smoothly, taking his grandmother's hand and drawing it through his arm. "She is a guest here at the hall. Lady Jennifer, this is my grandmother, Joanna of Segrave."

Jennifer found herself facing a thorough, but not unfriendly assessment by the lady of Segrave. She looked a great deal like Miles's mother and her eyes showed that she was sharp as a tack. There would be no bamboozling this woman.

"Are you Miles's guest?" Joanna asked briskly.

"No, my lady," Jennifer said, with a curtsey.

"She is acquainted with me," Anne said, getting to her feet with difficulty. She put her arm through Jennifer's. "And Nicholas as well, isn't that so?"

"Sure," Jennifer said faintly.

"Hmmm," Joanna said, looking Jennifer over from head to toe. "Very pretty." She paused. "I like red hair. It means you have spirit and no small bit of temper. Is that so?"

"I'm afraid it is, my lady," Jennifer said, with another curtsey.

"Well, then perhaps if you know my grandson, you can persuade him to take a bride very soon." She gestured over her shoulder. "I brought yet another collection of eligible misses. We have very high-ranking women here, so he'd best find one of them to his liking. Montgomery!"

Montgomery shot to his feet as if he'd been singed with a hot poker. "Aye, Grandmère?"

"Walk me up to the keep, lad. I'm weary of riding."

"Of course, Grandmère." Montgomery offered her his arm and escorted her away.

Jennifer looked at Anne. "You didn't have to do that, but I appreciate it."

"It was my pleasure. And don't fear her. She's brisk on the surface, but under it all she's quite a lovely woman," Anne said with a smile. "She convinced Robin to stop dithering and actually woo me. I owe her a great deal."

"Perhaps you shouldn't have spoken up for me," Jennifer said.

Anne shook her head. "I am acquainted with you. Now. 'Tis enough." She looked back down the road. " 'Tis too late to escape at present. Perhaps we should stand and keep our faces out of their dust." She paused. "They won't be kind. I imagine they'll mark all our flaws for a discussion later."

Jennifer looked at Anne, then down at the hem of her dress. "I can't see that you have any flaws," she said easily. "And as for me, I'll stand here happily knowing that Nicholas sewed the hem on this dress himself because I had nothing else to wear. I don't give a damn what they think."

Anne blinked, then she smiled. "I think I will find you much to my liking."

"I think I'll feel the same way. But why do you worry? You're Robin of Artane's wife. I imagine they all envy you."

"Anne is the fairest flower in Artane's garden, as Robin continually tells her," Miles said, coming to stand between them. "Unfortunately, the ladies we're about to see would sooner trample beautiful flowers than admire them."

"No doubt," Anne said with a snort.

Jennifer found herself unaccountably nervous, though she supposed there was no need.

Well, no need except for the fact that she was going to be looking at women that Nicholas's grandmother expected him to marry.

She took a deep breath, determined to watch with disinterest as the company passed, but it only took the sight of the first potential bride to make her realize that she was way out of her league. These were medieval noblewomen and they were a different breed of gal entirely.

She wasn't sure if *pretty* described any of them. There were six, by her count, and all of them were beautiful. One, the last one with the most expensive-looking trappings, was simply stunning. But she couldn't have said she would have felt comfortable talking to any of them. That was probably just as well because apart from the most disinterested of glances, they didn't bother with her.

They didn't bother with Anne, either, and that made her mad. She looked at Miles after the last one had left them, literally, in the dust.

"Charming," she said. "Do you know any of them?"

"I've met all of them at court at one time or another. They are very high-ranking women. Their power alone makes them attractive."

"Are you attracted to them?" Anne asked.

"Nay," Miles said, "but I have two wits to rub together and can imagine how miserable life with them would be, in spite of their gold."

"Do we have to go in?"

"Unfortunately," Miles said grimly. He offered an arm to her and to Anne. "Get up, John," he threw over his shoulder. "You must come as well."

"Saints preserve me," John groaned as he rolled to his feet. "I'm for the stables. I'll be safer there."

Jennifer was ready to join him, but Miles wouldn't hear of it. She wasn't particularly vain, but she would have given quite a bit for her fairy-tale dress and glass slippers. As it was, entering Artane's great hall with a dress that was two different colors, no matter the man who had sewn it, was just not making her list of delightful experiences.

Apparently, lunch was being served. Robin walked across the hall to them.

"Anne, sit with me," he said shortly. "Miles, you'll keep Jennifer with you and sit next to Isabelle. Jennifer, I've already told my grandmother that you're to remain in Isabelle's bed. I fear, however, that my grandmother may be joining you there."

"All right," Jennifer said with only a small gulp.

Miles kept her arm linked with his. "I'll introduce you to Isabelle. She's my twin and rather old for a gel to be not wed. She refuses until she finds a lad she loves. She had one once, but changed her mind, so perhaps she didn't love him after all."

Jennifer let him distract her until they were seated. She made nice with Isabelle and didn't look up. Well, that wasn't precisely true. She did look up a time or two. Each time, she found herself being studied by a different one of Lady Joanna's eligible maidens. She supposed that came from sitting between Miles and Isabelle. She couldn't be dismissed as a servant and she supposed she was enough of an unknown quantity to warrant speculation.

She found herself longing, quite intensely, for that recent stretch of days when she'd just had the boys for company.

The afternoon crawled on unendingly. Jennifer would have given her right arm to have disappeared, but Miles wouldn't let her. He sat next to her and made polite conversation with whomever approached.

The sun did set eventually. Nicholas's minstrels were joined by players that apparently Lady Joanna had brought along. Jennifer enjoyed the music, but not much else. Isabelle had pleaded a headache early on and had gone upstairs. The little twins were nowhere to be seen. The only thing that saved her was that Miles was guarding her as ferociously as she could have wished for.

"Is it time to leave yet?" she murmured.

"Not until Grandmère goes. She told me you're to be sharing Isabelle's bed with her." He lifted one eyebrow. "That's quite an honor, you know. I think even Isabelle's being reduced to a pallet on the floor."

"I'm grateful," Jennifer said faintly. "I'd be even more grateful if she'd go get in that bed. Her stamina is frightening."

He flashed her a quick smile, then resumed his grim and rather forbidding expression. "Aye, so say we all."

"Where is Nicholas, do you think? He said he would be back tonight."

"I wouldn't worry. Perhaps he was unexpectedly delayed."

"Hmmm."

Finally, Joanna yawned. Jennifer almost

cheered. She waited until Joanna had made for the stairs before she followed with Miles. Joanna stopped at the bottom of the stairs and turned.

"Come out from behind him, gel."

Jennifer took a deep breath and stepped out from behind Miles. "Aye, my lady?

Joanna looked her over again from head to toe, then took her by the arm. "I understand you're sharing the bed with me."

"A pleasure, my lady," Jennifer said, shooting Miles a look of mild panic.

"He can't save you, gel," Joanna said sharply. "I won't eat you for supper, you know. I've already had mine and now I'm ready for sleep. Do your feet run to cold?"

"Um, I don't think so, my lady."

"Good. Now, you realize Anne confessed to me that you are here as my Nicky's guest and not hers."

"Did she?" Jennifer wondered if Joanna used thumbscrews or just a really piercing gaze.

Joanna took her by the hand and pulled her up the stairs. She only let go when they started down the passageway. "Why doesn't your hem match? And stop looking at Miles for a rescue. He can't help you anymore."

Jennifer took one last look at him. He shrugged helplessly. She took a deep breath and turned to face Nicholas's grandmother.

"The truth is I became cut off from my

family. Nicholas added the hem on this dress because it was too short."

"Did he indeed," Joanna said, sounding quite a bit more interested. "A chivalrous lad, my Nicky."

"Aye, my lady, he is."

"He's my favorite grandson, you know. I've never denied it."

"Understandable, my lady."

"And you, gel?" Joanna said. "What do you think of him?"

Jennifer gave her the honest truth. "He's perfect, my lady."

"Harrumph." Joanna walked again, then stopped in front of Isabelle's bedroom. "Is your father a lord?"

Jennifer took a deep breath. "Nay, my lady."

"Your mother a titled woman?"

"Nay, my lady."

"Hmmm. But my Nicky likes you."

"So he says."

"Has he kissed you?"

Jennifer gaped at the old woman. "Ah . . ."

"An impertinent question," Joanna said. "Quite right. Well, I'll watch him with you and see. I've brought all these other gels along, you know, so I'll want him to give them a fair look." She paused and looked at Jennifer again. "I like your hair. And your frankness, truth be told. 'Tisn't often to find an honest gel these days."

"Thank you, my lady," Jennifer said.

Joanna made a few more harrumphing noises. "To bed, Jennifer McKinnon. We've a long day tomorrow. I assume you can dance?"

"Just barely, my lady."

"Well, I'll polish you a bit, then. You'd best not have cold feet in bed, though, or I'll renege."

"Of course, my lady." She opened the door and made Joanna a curtsey. "After you, my lady."

"I should think so," Joanna said, but she patted Jennifer's cheek as she sailed by.

Jennifer looked back down the hallway to find Miles standing there. He made her a very low bow, then waved.

"I'll ride off and look for him if he isn't back by morning," he said quietly.

"Thank you."

"Jennifer McKinnon, come inside and shut the door. The draft will do me in, gel!"

She closed the door and took a deep, steadying breath. She'd survived the day. But what would happen when Nicholas returned and found Artane overrun by potential brides?

She supposed she might not know because she probably wouldn't see him.

"To bed, gel," Joanna ordered imperiously. "We've a full day ahead of us tomorrow."

Jennifer closed her eyes briefly, then pasted a polite smile on her face and turned to face her future.

She hoped Nicholas would hurry.

She hoped she would have a reason to want him to.

CHAPTER 25

Nicholas stared at the Black, then reached out and very deliberately held the horse by the bridle. He gave him a look of intense disapproval.

"Bad horse," he said sternly.

The Black only attempted a toss of his head.

Nicholas pulled his head back down. "I *will* ride you, you damned beast," he said, "and this time you will *not* buck me off."

The Black was seemingly very unimpressed.

Nicholas swung up onto his back and gave him no choice. Of course it didn't matter all that much given that he was twenty paces from the drawbridge. Then again, he could have found himself swimming in the moat and that would definitely be worse than having spent the past evening and the whole of the night running from Raventhorpe.

The portcullis was raised. Nicholas lifted his hand in greeting to the guardsmen, then wrestled with the Black until they reached the stables. He swung down gracefully, which was a far different dismount from the last time when he'd found himself pitched off the back of the bloody horse without warning.

That had been yesterday evening. He'd tried to catch the Black, but the horse had run off, then stopped just out of reach and waited for Nicholas to catch up before springing playfully away yet again. And damn the beast if he hadn't been willing to continue the game to the very gates of Artane. Nicholas had alternated between running and walking almost the entire way from Raventhorpe, given that the Black had dislodged him but a league from his sister's hall. It had been a very long night, what with only his curses to keep him warm.

He waved off the stable master and tended the horse himself. He shut the stall door and shot the Black another look of disapproval.

"I will take you out again," Nicholas warned, "but you will be better behaved. If it kills us both."

The Black only snorted and bumped Nicholas's shoulder affectionately with his nose. He snuffled Nicholas's hair for good measure.

"Apology accepted," Nicholas muttered as he walked away. "I think."

He looked at the sky as he walked across the courtyard. It was growing light in the east, but just barely. There was still time to get inside, have a wash, and be standing at

Jennifer's door before she awoke.

He was halfway across the courtyard before he realized that there had been more horses in the stable than usual and that there were several wagons placed next to the stables.

Had his grandmother returned?

He dashed up the steps and burst into the great hall. The hall was empty save a pair of serving lads, stirring the fires. Nicholas ran up to his chamber only to find Montgomery and John snoring happily in his bed. Obviously, they had been displaced to make room for heaven only knew who.

He stripped, washed, and dressed again in clean clothes, then left the chamber and went to stand in front of Isabelle's chamber. With any luck, Jennifer would be the first one out and he could spirit her away for the day before anyone else was the wiser.

He didn't wait long. The door opened soon after he'd taken up his post and so quietly that he knew it had to be his love, sneaking out because she'd felt his presence.

Only it wasn't.

It was his grandmother.

"Ah," Nicholas said, scrambling for something to say.

"Aye, ah," Joanna said, taking him by the arm and pulling him toward the stairs. "Escort an old woman to breakfast and discuss with her why you were not here to greet your potential brides yestereve."

"My horse threw me," Nicholas managed.

"I'm sure you'll teach him manners." Joanna looked up at him and smiled. "How have you been, love?"

"Are you asking about my travels last night, or before that?"

"Either."

"Wonderful." He paused. "Well, save last night. Too much time to think about what I might be missing at home."

"The arrival of six of the most privileged, powerful women in England is what you missed," Joanna said. "They've come with the express purpose of being inspected by you. Blood may be spilt with this lot, I fear." She looked up at him. "Was that what you feared you might be missing at home?"

"Nay, Grandmère," Nicholas said seriously. "Not that."

"I suppose not," Joanna said, studying him thoughtfully. "She has warm feet, you know."

Nicholas looked at her in surprise. "Jennifer?"

"Who else? She's not a bad bedmate. Indeed, I likely should have been sharing with a woman of much higher rank, but Robin insisted and you know I can't refuse him his whims. He was especially adamant that she be treated well."

"The saints be praised," Nicholas muttered under his breath. He would have to thank Robin when he saw him next.

"It seems she has no title," Joanna pointed out.

"I couldn't care less."

"Well, we'll see about that. Now, come and eat, love, and I'll tell you who I've brought with me."

"I'm not interested."

"You'd damned well better be interested, Nicholas," she said sharply, "or at least feign a bloody great bit of interest after all the trouble I've gone through to get this lot all the way north."

He managed to get his ear out of her reach by escaping down the stairs in front of her. He turned and waited for her at the bottom. He made her a low bow, then smiled his most charming smile.

"You are a remarkable woman."

"Flattery will not facilitate your escape from this," she said. "You'll be polite because I demand it."

"Of course," Nicholas said. "And surely you know how much I appreciate your efforts upon my behalf. Now, let me escort you to the table, then I'll go see if Cook is awake."

"So you can then escape by another way and return upstairs?" Joanna asked with a snort. "Absolutely not. Take me to the kitchen and make me something yourself. I understand you're a fair chef."

"Grandmère, I have business upstairs."

"You have business with me in the kitchen.

You may go upstairs when I'm finished with you."

Nicholas considered arguing, but decided that there was no point. The sooner he humored his grandmother, the sooner he could be about his own affairs. She was nothing if not tenacious.

"Very well," he said with a sigh.

He then took his grandmother to the kitchen, prepared porridge, chose fruit, meat, and bread for her, then sat at the worktable and ate right along with her.

"You know, your ladies would be appalled to see either of us here," he remarked.

"I know," she said unrepentantly, "but I'm an old woman and can do as I please."

"And what of me?"

"You can do as I please, as well."

Nicholas reached out, took her hand, and kissed it. "Grandmère, I love her."

Joanna pursed her lips. "I'll need to look her over for several more days before I'm ready to give you my opinion."

"The saints preserve us all."

She smacked his hand. "Disrespectful chit," she said. "You need my permission before you wed her."

"Do I?"

"If you want any of my gold upon my death, you do."

Nicholas took both her hands in his and looked at her affectionately. "I don't need your gold, Grandmère, but I do need your love. You may look her over."

"But you'll wed her if I like her or not, is that it?"

"You always told me to trust my own heart."

"My mistake," she said. Then she smiled and squeezed his hands. "You look happy."

"I am. I would be happier still if I could see her this morning."

"I wouldn't count on that. I've a full day's activities planned for you already."

"Grandmère!"

"Humor an old woman who's nearing the end of her days."

"You'll live forever."

"Well," she said, with a modest smile, "that is the plan, but ofttimes plans go awry." She dabbed her mouth delicately. "A fine meal. You would have made a very fine cook, my love, but perhaps you are better as you are."

"I think so," he agreed.

"Let's have a turn about the garden now, then you'll escort me to mass. I'll tell you of your day whilst we're there."

"Friar Osbert doesn't like it when we don't pay attention."

"I dare him to chastise me. Now," she said, rising, "come along like a good lad."

"Grandmère, I want to see her."

"Miles will watch after her."

"I don't *want* Miles to watch after her."

419

"Why not?" Joanna asked. "She doesn't love him."

"Grandmère," Nicholas said seriously, "I *will* see her this morning."

"After," Joanna said with a glint in her eye. "After you've been polite to all the very rich, *very* powerful women I've brought for you to look over. And you'll do it for no other reason than you don't want to make me look like a fool."

Nicholas looked heavenward, then sighed deeply. "I'll be polite. No more. And only a fool himself would think of you thus."

"Aye, I know," she said with a smile. "I'm just bringing you to heel as quickly as possible."

He rose and frowned down at her. "You are a terrible old woman."

"Whom you love dearly and don't want to disappoint. The garden, Nicky my love, before we are overrun by unpleasant women bent on prodding you to the altar whether you like it or not."

"The morning," he said. "I'll give you that, but no more."

She considered, then nodded. "Done."

Unfortunately, the morning lasted far longer than he would have liked. His grandmother had been telling the truth about the tenacity of the women she'd brought for him to look over. He found himself besieged on all sides

420

by women and their parents who had come, apparently not just to sit at Artane's table and partake of fine meals once or twice, but to become part of the family. He was subjected to lengthy discussions with pompous fathers and scheming mothers. The ladies in question, the ones meant for him, were of the highest quality; even he would admit that. They were also six of the coldest, most calculating horrors he'd ever seen. He wouldn't have dared be interested in any one of them if his heart had been free.

He was definitely not interested now that his heart was taken.

He caught sight of Jennifer periodically. She was never alone. Miles was always there and either Anne or Isabelle was with her as well. She caught his eye a time or two and smiled gravely, but each time he tried to get through the press to get to her, his grandmother would present him with another cluster of people he had to be nice to.

It was enormously frustrating.

It was also exhausting. He hadn't slept since two nights prior and even that night had not been a good sleep. Add that to his irritation over not being able to at least go and touch the woman he loved, and he was finding himself increasingly short-tempered.

As noon came and went, he realized that Jennifer was no longer in the great hall. Montgomery was, however, standing in the passageway that led to the kitchens. Nicholas excused himself and elbowed his way through the crowd to reach his brother.

"Where is she?"

"Through there," Montgomery said under his breath, nodding down the passageway.

"Come with me." Nicholas walked toward the kitchens, but was forced to stop because two of his potential brides were blocking the way. They were standing there with their backs to him.

"Her hair is ghastly," said Sibil of Hansworth. "What think you?"

"A terrible color," Brigit of Islington said coldly. "And did you see the gown?"

"Aye," Sibil said with a laugh. "Is she too stupid to realize that it is ugly? Obviously it was altered for her — and poorly. Why do the de Piagets tolerate her, do you suppose?"

"Perhaps she is their *leman,*" Brigit said cuttingly, "and all the lads share her —"

"Excuse me, if you please," Nicholas said politely.

They turned around. He wasn't surprised, though, to find that neither looked the slightest bit ashamed. They merely stared back at him boldly. Well, Brigit did, and unrepentantly. Sibil of Hansworth, at least, had the grace to eventually look away.

Nicholas walked past them, dragging Montgomery with him.

"Awful wenches," Montgomery whispered.

"Aye." Nicholas put his hand on Montgomery's shoulder. "Go find clean clothing, then meet Jennifer at Isabelle's door and give it to her."

"As you will, Nick," Montgomery said, and turned and ran back up the passageway.

Nicholas continued on into the kitchens where Jennifer was blissfully unaware of what was being said about her. Then again, perhaps she wasn't. Her face was ashen. Miles was whispering furiously in her ear and Anne had her arm around her, but that seemed to accomplish nothing. When she caught sight of him, her expression did not change.

He strode into the kitchen and walked straight over to her. "Montgomery has clothes waiting for you in Isabelle's chamber. Change and meet me in the stables as quickly as you can."

"Are you sure?" she asked hesitantly.

"Sure?" he echoed. "About what? About the disguise?"

"No, sure that you want me —" she began in a very low voice, then she fell silent.

He growled. "Of course I'm sure, damn it." He jerked his head toward the passageway. "Hurry. Anne, would you go with her?"

"Of course," Anne said. She touched his arm briefly, then walked with Jennifer from the kitchen.

Nicholas watched them go, then turned and looked at his father's cook.

"Food, sir, if you please, fit for a saddlebag."

Cook frowned. "For the high and mighty wenches, or the pleasant, gracious one?"

"The latter, surely," Nicholas said.

Cook smiled suddenly. "Aye, my lord. It would be a pleasure to serve her. I'll collect nothing but the finest."

Nicholas nodded in thanks, then turned to Miles. "How has it been?"

"You don't want to know," Miles said grimly. "Where the hell were you?"

"The Black threw me and I had to walk home. From Raventhorpe."

"Oh," Miles said, drawing the word out for quite some time. "You went to talk to Jake."

"Aye, but you could certainly keep that to yourself, couldn't you?" Nicholas said.

"I could."

Nicholas grunted, then waited for Cook to finish his preparations. He gladly accepted a leather pouch full of food and handed it and a bottle of wine to Miles. "Be useful. Go saddle my horse for me and take this with you. If Grandmère sees me with it, I'll never escape."

"It looks like rain outside."

"I couldn't care less."

Miles smiled and left the kitchen. Nicholas thanked Cook profusely, and made his way through the great hall, extricating himself quickly from every conversation that stopped him and avoiding his grandmother with skill even she would have had to admire. He finally slipped out the front door, then made his way to the stables.

Miles had his mount saddled and food stowed in saddlebags. Nicholas took the reins, thanked his brother, and led his mount out into the courtyard. He swung up into the saddle and looked toward the great hall. The door opened suddenly and Jennifer flew out of it and down the stairs with Montgomery hard on her heels.

Nicholas looked up to see his grandmother coming to stand in the doorway. He cursed. He'd given her the bloody morning; he was not going to give her the entire day. He urged his horse forward, leaned over and pulled Jennifer up behind him, then spun his horse around and kicked it into a gallop.

"We're going to die," Jennifer gasped.

"Not today, I vow it," Nicholas said. "Hold on."

Guardsmen and peasants alike scattered in front of him. He earned his share of curses, but he didn't care. He would make amends later. For now, speed was what was needful. It wouldn't have surprised him to have looked over his shoulder to find a contingent of his grandmother's guardsmen trailing him, bent on retrieving him and escorting him back to the hall.

"Where are we going?" Jennifer asked.

"Do you care?"

"No," she said with a laugh.

He smiled, put his hand over hers as she held on to him about the waist. He cut aside before the village, then rode for the shore.

He put his heels to his mount and they flew.

Not far enough or fast enough, but it would do for the day.

CHAPTER 26

Jennifer held on as Nicholas's horse galloped down the beach. It was spectacularly romantic and she wished she'd had music worthy of it playing in the background. But since she didn't, she simply held on and enjoyed the fact that she was out of the viper's pit she'd been living in for the past day and a half. It had made her wish she didn't understand medieval Norman French so well. Heaven help her, but she couldn't go work for any of the harpies Lady Joanna had brought to Artane.

She could hardly bring herself to hope she might not have to.

Nicholas turned his horse away from the water and rode back inland until they reached the edge of a forest. He walked the horse until he found a glade, then reined him in. He slid down, then turned and held up his arms for her.

She fell into them as if she'd been doing it every day of her life.

He clutched her to him and buried his face in her hair. "I missed you," he said in a muffled voice.

She let out the breath she'd been holding and wrapped her arms around his neck. "I missed you, too."

He let her slide down to her feet, then looked at her gravely. "Did you?"

She smiled. "I'm a little afraid to admit how much."

"I'm not," he said. He pulled her hair down, then smoothed his hand over it. "I cursed every moment and every league that separated us. It was dreadful." He bent his head toward her, then hesitated. "May I kiss you?"

She couldn't help a breathless laugh. "Why are you asking?"

"Because I fear that once I begin, I won't be able to stop."

"What of your legendary self-control?"

"I lost it along the strand somewhere."

She smiled. "Then kiss me and we'll just hope for the best."

He did.

In fact, he kissed her so long and so well that she began to wonder if *her* self-control might be on its way out. Finally, he lifted his head and looked down at her. For the first time, his eyes were a dark gray. She reached up to push his hair out of his eyes.

"Your eyes are stormy," she said with a smile.

"I am undone."

"Poor man."

He leaned his forehead on hers. "You've no idea," he whispered.

"Actually," she said with a shaky laugh, "I think I know exactly what you're talking about. We're in trouble."

"I agree. We'd best find somewhere to sit before my knees are no longer equal to holding me up."

She reached up and touched his face. "You look tired. You sit and I'll go look for something green for lunch —"

"Please, nay," he said, laughing. "No salad. I brought food."

Jennifer watched him fetch a saddlebag from his horse. He walked back over to her and led her over to sit on a log. Jennifer sat down gratefully, as she wasn't sure how steady on her feet she was going to be. She'd forgotten, over the past day, just how handsome he was.

And that apparently, in spite of her earlier fears, he was rather fond of her.

Nicholas dug things out of his saddlebag, then slid her a sideways look. "Have you eaten today?"

"I don't think so. I don't remember."

She felt his arm slip around her shoulders. He pulled her close and held her for a moment in silence, then released her and ran his hand over her hair.

"Forgive me that I did not return as I said I would," he said quietly.

"Where did you go?" she asked, then she shook her head. "Sorry. You don't have to tell me —"

"Of course I'll tell you," he said easily. "I went to Raventhorpe, to see to business with my sister and her husband. My father's stallion threw me on the way back. I walked home."

"How far is Raventhorpe?"

"I'd say about twelve leagues."

"Twelve leagues?" she echoed. The man had walked thirty-six miles to get home? "You're a fast walker."

"I ran, mostly."

"Why didn't you just go back and borrow another horse?"

"Because Raventhorpe was the wrong direction."

She felt a little faint. "I see."

"I hope you do." He leaned over and kissed her, then handed her bread. "You had best have that whilst you can. I can think of far more interesting things for you to do than eat."

Jennifer couldn't help but laugh a little. "I suppose I can, too."

Lunch was, as always, up to Artane's usual standards of quality. Jennifer drank from the bottle like any good medieval gal on a picnic would have, then handed it to Nicholas.

"So," she said casually, "how was Amanda?"

He choked. "You know too many of my secrets and I know too few of yours."

"I was willing to tell them, but you wanted a fortnight of silence."

He smiled ruefully. "Aye, I know. And to answer you, Amanda was as she always is — feisty, outspoken, and lovely. She's coming to visit in a se'nnight. I daresay you'll find her to be a kindred spirit."

"Was she happy to see you?"

"I am her favorite brother," Nicholas said, "though perhaps not, of late. I kissed their young daughter, left with good wishes for returning to Artane, and prayed I would find you still here."

"Where else would I go?" she asked lightly.

"The question is," he began slowly, "where else would you go if you could?"

She looked at him in surprise, but he was studying his hands.

"Which is not a good question for today," he said, taking a deep breath, "for I fear I could not bear the answer." He flashed her a weary smile. "Especially if it wasn't the answer I wanted to hear." He rubbed his face with his hands suddenly. "I haven't slept."

"I imagine you haven't slept in a couple of days." She put her hand on his back and rubbed it gently. "Why don't you take a nap."

431

He smiled dryly. "How interesting it will be to watch me sleep."

She stroked his hair for a moment or two, then tucked some of it behind his ear. "Actually, it sounds like a great way to spend the afternoon. I get to ogle you without worrying what you'll think of me."

"Ogle?"

She bit her tongue, then smiled. "Sorry. A word from home. It means to stare at in a lustful way."

"You?" he asked doubtfully, but his eyes were twinkling.

"I'm not a complete prude," she said. "I can appreciate the sight of a good man as well as the next woman. And when the sight happens to be you —" She shrugged. "How can I help myself?"

He stood up and pulled her to her feet. He slowly wrapped his arms around her and smiled down at her.

Then he kissed her.

By the time he lifted his head, she wasn't sure she was ever going to catch her breath.

"Are you going to actually manage to sleep now?" she gasped.

"I doubt it," he said, then rested his forehead against hers. "By the saints, Jennifer McKinnon, you have vanquished me. If only I had the strength to allow you to vanquish me a bit more."

She pulled away and took off Montgomery's

cloak. She laid it on a patch of ground near the log that was fairly free of rocks and roots and, thanks to the trees, free from the drizzle she could see had started up.

"Take a nap."

"So you might ogle?"

She smiled. "Of course."

He hesitated. "I think —"

"Too much. Lie down, Nicholas, and get some sleep. I can keep watch over you. Trust me, I *really* don't mind."

He drew his sword. He stretched out on Montgomery's cloak and laid his sword down beside him.

"Wake me if you hear anything."

"I will." She sat down on the log, put her elbows on her knees and her chin on her fists, then watched him.

He smiled, then his eyes closed. Within moments, he was sound asleep.

Jennifer indulged in her lusting with reckless abandon. It was dangerous, but she didn't care. He was just perfection, from the flawlessness of his face, to the manly set of his boots. She could hardly believe that three months ago she had been in Manhattan, fighting off a groping attempt by Michael McGillicuty and thinking that life was just not going to get any better.

Now, she was sitting on a log in medieval England, still tingling from the kisses of a legendary medieval knight, and starting to truly believe he had feelings for her.

She looked for quite a while longer, then sighed and turned to stare at the shore she could see in the distance. She wondered if Megan was looking at that same view. Was her mother? Had her family flown over only to waste time and money looking for her? Would they figure out there was a gate at Ledenham's abbey and try it only to have it never bring them to the right place?

She sighed. They would be frantic and there would be no way at all to find out what had happened to her.

And what would happen to her? Would the handsome knight propose to the scullery maid and turn her into a lady? Or would she live and die in obscurity, forced to serve one of the complete shrews currently inside Artane's hallowed halls?

"Jennifer, you're thinking again."

She dragged her sleeve across her eyes and looked at him. His eyes were closed. "I wasn't."

"You were. I could tell."

"I thought you were asleep."

He opened one eye and looked at her. "I sleep very lightly."

"Too lightly, apparently."

He opened both eyes and looked at her blearily. "What is it?"

She shrugged. "I can't help but think a little, but it wasn't about . . . well, it wasn't about our fortnight."

He held out his hand. She put her hand in his and let him pull her down to sit next to him.

"Tell me what, then," he murmured.

"Later," she said, leaning against his side. "When you wake back up."

"I should argue. I will, when I can keep my eyes open."

"You do that," she said with a smile.

For a while he stroked her back and smiled sleepily. She couldn't stop herself from leaning over now and again to kiss his cheek, his mouth, his closed eyes.

He opened those beautiful gray eyes at one point and looked at her. "Lady," he said seriously, "my self-control is almost to the breaking point."

She smiled. "I'll leave you alone, then."

He caught her about the waist as she pulled away. "Stay," he said. "But . . ."

"But stop kissing you?"

"If you have any pity in you at all, aye," he said with a smile. Then he shook his head. "Truly I am unwholesomely weary. I can scarce believe what I'm saying."

She stroked his cheek. "I'll leave you alone until you're more yourself. But I will look."

She did, for most of the afternoon. Eventually, she crawled to her feet and stretched the kink out of her back. She took Nicholas's saddlebag back to his horse, then wandered over to sit on her log. She sighed deeply, enjoying the sound of the sea and the smell of the rain.

Until a twig snapped behind her.

She wasn't quite sure what happened after that, but one minute she was in the middle of turning around to see what was behind her, and the next, Nicholas was on his feet and she'd been pulled behind him. He was fully awake, with his sword in his hand and his body completely tensed for battle.

Jennifer shivered. He had been, just the moment before, deeply asleep. She had forgotten for a moment just what he was capable of.

"No threat, mate," said a male voice.

"Is that so?" Nicholas asked quietly.

Jennifer peeked around him. A very large, very scruffy man stood there, a knife in his hands and a rotten-toothed smile on his face.

"Then again," the man said, drawing his sword and grinning, "per'aps there is. Yer lassie there is quite fetching. I think I'd like to 'ave 'er."

"I don't think you'll manage that," Nicholas said mildly, "for you'll need to go through me first."

"With pleasure."

Jennifer backed away as they engaged each other. She snatched up Montgomery's cloak once Nicholas was off it, then bumped into something behind her. She whirled around and found herself facing another man the same size as the first.

"I believe I'll be havin' ye first," the man said, drawing a knife.

Jennifer realized immediately that Nicholas couldn't take care of both of them at once. Well, actually he probably could have, but she didn't want to test it when she might be able to help.

Though her first instinct was to shout at the man and try to make him think she was too feisty for the effort, she had the feeling it was the wrong choice. The man facing her was obviously not one to be discouraged so easily.

She dug deep for her best acting emotion and began to weep piteously. The man laughed and started to loosen his belt. Jennifer cowered until he was close enough, then she kicked the knife out of his hands. She flung Montgomery's cloak into his face, then kicked him as hard as she could in the groin. When he was doubled over, she grabbed him by the hair and yanked his head down. She brought her knee up as hard as she could into his nose.

He stumbled away, howling.

"Jennifer, my horse!" Nicholas shouted.

Jennifer grabbed Montgomery's cloak, then ran for Nicholas's horse and swung up into the saddle. She held the reins and watched as he fought the first man ferociously, giving their attacker no choice but to hold up his sword like a shield. Nicholas punched the first man in the face. Jennifer heard the man's nose break from where she sat. Nicholas backhanded the second, sending him sprawling, then resheathed his sword and ran for the horse. He pulled himself up behind her.

"Go!" he shouted, kicking his horse into a gallop.

Jennifer hung on to the reins and hoped they wouldn't fall off.

"I should have killed the whoresons," he growled into her ear.

She shook her head. "Not worth it," she shouted into the wind.

He wrapped his arms around her waist. "You were magnificent."

"No," she said, with a shaky laugh, "I was terrified."

He was silent until they reached the village, then he took the reins from her and slowed his horse to a walk. "I fear there was more to it than a simple assault by ruffians."

"What do you mean?"

"I suspect Ledenham."

She turned her head to look at him. "Really?"

"It wouldn't surprise me," he said grimly. "We won't go out again without guardsmen."

They rode through the village, through the barbican gate, into the inner bailey, and on to the stables. A stable lad came over to take

Nicholas's horse as Nicholas swung down.

"Nay, lad, I'll see to it, but thank you."

"Of course, my lord Nicholas," the boy said with a smile. "A good e'en to you."

"And to you, lad," Nicholas said, reaching out to ruffle his hair. He turned and held up his arms for her.

Jennifer let him set her on her feet, then followed him into the stable and watched while he tended to his horse. She thought about the first time she'd watched him do the same thing. So much had changed. She never would have imagined, on that particular evening, that she would be sitting in the stables at Artane, watching him tend his horse, and waiting for him to turn around and look at her.

Affectionately.

As he was doing now.

Jennifer watched him lean back against the stall door and look at her for a moment. Then he held open his arms.

That was invitation enough. She jumped up and threw herself at him. He laughed as he caught her, then he smiled down at her purposefully.

"Heaven help me," she managed before he proceeded to kiss her.

She put her arms around his neck and held on. When she finally had to break away to breathe, she was light-headed and laughing.

"Meet me here after supper," he cajoled.

"Do you have to ask?"

"Tomorrow, too?" he asked.

"Yes."

"And the next day? And the day after that?"

She buried her face in his neck. "That is starting to sound serious."

"We have another se'nnight," Nicholas whispered against her ear, "and then we will have serious speech indeed." He pulled back and looked at her. "Until then," he said kissing her briefly, "let me woo you."

"Anything you say," she said.

"What I would like to say is farewell to the madness inside, but I fear it may go on for a bit yet." He tucked her hair behind her ear. "I will begrudge my grandmother every moment that is not spent with you. We'll make do for the next day or two, then see if my grandmother won't start for home. Until then, just ignore the wenches she brought. I certainly intend to."

"Do you?" she mused.

He shook his head wryly. "Jennifer McKinnon, if I kiss you any more in an effort to convince you of that, I'll be unable to walk back to the hall and you'll be forced to carry me. Instead, believe my words as we seek out supper and a chaperon. It may be our only hope."

He took her hand and Montgomery's cloak, then led her from the stables. She walked with him across the courtyard toward the great hall. He looked up and stopped still. "Damn."

"What?"

"My father," he said, "and he wears a particularly paternal mein."

"Is he going to lock me in Isabelle's chamber for keeping you out too late?"

"I imagine he'll lock *me* in Isabelle's chamber for a like reason."

"Let go of my hand then," she said, trying to pull away.

"Nay," he said cheerfully.

He pulled her up the steps with him and stopped a pair of steps below his father. "Papa," he said pleasantly, with a small bow.

Jennifer bobbed a curtsey for good measure.

"I daresay," Rhys said sternly, "that 'tis a trifle late to have a lady of breeding out of her hall, wouldn't you agree, son?"

Nicholas rolled his eyes. "Father, I am a score and eight. I daresay I am old enough to determine what is suitable or not. Wouldn't *you* agree?"

Jennifer found herself the recipient of Rhys de Piaget's gaze, but when turned her way it became quite a bit friendlier. He held out his hand and gave her that devastating de Piaget smile that all his boys seemed to have mastered. She put her free hand in Rhys's and allowed him to pull her away from Nicholas as if she hadn't a competent thought in her head. Rhys de Piaget was stunning. It was obvious where Nicholas had come by not only his looks but his charm.

Rhys tucked her hand under his arm and smiled at her in a way that made her want to agree to whatever he wanted before he even asked.

"Daughter, since your own father isn't here to keep you safe, and demand that you be wooed properly," he added with a dark look thrown Nicholas's way, "allow me the honor of doing so."

"Of course, my lord," she said, mesmerized beyond reason.

"Jennifer!" Nicholas exclaimed.

Rhys turned a stern look on him. "And you, whelp, will treat her with the respect and honor she deserves. She should be chaperoned. She should be wooed in plain sight."

"We *were* in plain sight!" Nicholas bellowed. He paused. "Well, we would have been if anyone had been passing." He glared at his father. "Nothing happened!"

"She's wearing your brother's clothes."

"It was a disguise."

Rhys pursed his lips, then turned to Jennifer with a smile. "Come with me, Mistress McKinnon, and let me put you in the care of my sweet wife."

"Father!" Nicholas protested.

"I understand there will be music for dancing tomorrow night," Rhys said, turning to look at him coolly. "Bathe beforehand, and perhaps this lovely maid will favor you with a turn." He turned Jennifer around and walked up the stairs. "I assume my son has fed you today, or are you hungry?"

She smiled up at Rhys. "He did feed me, my lord, and he was very chivalrous and solicitous."

She thought it was probably best not to mention anything about swords.

Or kissing.

"It is fortunate for him that his chivalry was in full flower, else I would be forced to meet him in the lists. And believe me, my girl, when I tell you that I can still best all my sons."

"I believe it, my lord. And it is obvious to me that your blood flows through their veins. Nicholas has shown me sword skill that has left me breathless."

Nicholas grunted, but said nothing.

Jennifer followed Rhys into the hall and saw, to her dismay, that it was full of the usual suspects milling about, listening to music being played. She hesitated in midstep thanks to the glares she caught the moment she was noticed.

What she tried not to notice, however, was how Rhys smoothly and unobtrusively put himself between her and the company in the great hall. He put his arm around her and walked with her along the left side of the hall and down the passageway to the kitchen.

He made her a place at the worktable, allowed Nicholas to sit next to her, then chatted pleasantly with Cook while a private supper was prepared for them. Jennifer looked at Nicholas.

"Hello."

He smiled wryly. "Aye and that may be as close as we come to a friendly greeting." He reached under the table and took her hand. "My father, your protector."

"He's very kind."

Nicholas grunted. "Aye, I suppose so. If it means we might avoid dining with the full company in the hall, then I might just have to agree with your opinion of him."

But he scowled at his father just the same as he served them supper.

Jennifer smiled as she ate with one hand and held Nicholas's hand under the table with the other.

"The lengths we must go to," Nicholas grumbled.

She smiled at him. "It could be worse."

"Aye, my father could be sitting between us."

"Don't give him any ideas." She paused. "Nicholas?"

"Aye, love?"

She smiled reflexively at the term. "I was just thinking I wanted to learn to use a sword. Better than just a few swings on the beach."

He looked at her gravely. "Today was

frightening, no doubt."

"Weren't you frightened?"

"For myself? Nay. For you? Aye, terrified. But you managed quite well."

She nodded. "You'll help me?"

"Always."

"Where?"

He considered. "The tower chamber. Perhaps we'll steal Robin's page to keep watch for us."

"Does Robin have a page?"

"Aye, Christopher of Blackmour. It will give the lad a respite from Robin's dawn-to-dusk training regimen. Perhaps we'll even invite him in whilst we work, so he can see good technique."

She smiled. "You're terrible."

"Robin deserves it, wouldn't you say?" Nicholas asked. "Keep Montgomery's clothes. When I have a sword secured, I'll send Christopher for you. No one will be the wiser."

"Thank you," she said quietly.

"Surely not," he said, handing her a cup of wine. "Yet another reason to pass time in your sweet company? The pleasure, believe me, is all mine."

"What time? What pleasure?"

Jennifer looked up to see Rhys leaning on the table and peering intently at his son.

"Time for bed, wouldn't you say?" Nicholas said cheerfully. "I'll walk my lady up-stairs."

"We'll go together."

Nicholas protested, but it was in vain. Jennifer soon found herself being escorted by both men. She managed to get through the great hall with a minimum of fuss. There was a bit of elbowing between the two men as they went up the stairs, but eventually Isabelle's door was reached. Nicholas looked at his father.

"Isn't Grandmère enough of a chaperon?" he complained.

"I daresay she isn't," Rhys said pointedly. "Now, kiss your lady's hand and be off with you."

Nicholas swore at his father, then turned and gave Jennifer a look that would have made her want to fan herself if he hadn't had hold of her hand. He bent over that same hand and very chastely kissed it.

"Meet me later on the roof," he said in Gaelic.

"You forget that I speak that tongue as well," Rhys said in the same language. "And nay," he said, removing Jennifer's hand from his son's and continuing on in French, "she will not meet you on the roof."

Nicholas glared at his father. "Did I ask for your aid in this?"

Rhys pointed down the passageway. "Go, whelp, before you force me to remind you who is the superior warrior."

Nicholas pursed his lips, then looked at Jennifer. "Tomorrow, then, my lady." He patted his sword meaningfully. "Our only hope." He handed her Montgomery's cloak. "You might need this as well."

Rhys took Jennifer's face in his hands and kissed her on the forehead. "A good sleep to you, my dear."

"Thank you, my lord."

He shooed her inside. She smiled at Nicholas, then went inside and shut the door.

She wanted to laugh, but she thought it might be best to just go to sleep. She wished desperately for a journal. Her entry would have included an afternoon with a magnificent man, a brush with death, and being adopted by a powerful medieval lord.

It had been a fairly good day.

She wondered briefly whether or not Nicholas was right about Ledenham being behind their little attack, then put it out of her mind. If nothing else, she would gain some sword skill. She supposed in the Middle Ages, that could only be a good thing.

And that would give her more time with Nicholas.

And that was the best thing of all.

CHAPTER 27

Nicholas left his chamber early the next morning, intent on first visiting the blacksmith to see how Jennifer's sword was coming along, then moving on to the seamstresses to see if her gowns were finished. He had scarce walked three paces down the passageway, though, before he found his father's page standing there.

"Aubrey," he said with a smile. "What is it, lad?"

"Your father wishes to see you in his solar first thing, my lord," Aubrey said with wide eyes. "Before you break your fast, he said."

Nicholas put his hand on the lad's shoulder. "Run on ahead, if you like, and bear the tidings that I follow hard on your heels. It will please him."

"Aye, my lord!" the lad said happily and scampered off.

Nicholas considered a brief pause at Isabelle's door, then dismissed the idea. He would humor his father, then bargain with his grandmother. One thing he was certain of: the day would not end without time alone with his lady. The fortnight was passing too quickly and he had wooing to accomplish.

He made his way to his father's solar, knocked, then entered. Rhys was sitting behind his table, waiting. Nicholas shut the door behind him, walked across the chamber, and sat in the chair opposite his father.

"You summoned me?"

Rhys only looked at him for a ridiculously long time in silence, then lifted an eyebrow. "I spoke to Miles yesterday about your lady."

"I'll kill him," Nicholas growled.

"He was particularly loath to reveal any-thing he might or might not have known about her," Rhys said. "I have, however, seen what lies in my trunk. I can only assume that is her gear."

Nicholas nodded.

"Is your lady of Jake's ilk?"

There was no point in denying it. "Aye."

"And you love her."

Nicholas took a deep breath, then sighed. "Desperately."

Rhys seemed to consider that for quite some time, then he leaned forward with his elbows on his table. "Where were you the day before yesterday?"

"Talking to Jake." He paused, then cast cau-tion to the wind. After all, his father knew much more about Jake's past than he himself did. "Jennifer's gate did not work for her. I thought it necessary to ask Jake the location of one that did."

"What did she say when you told her that?"

Nicholas paused. He stood up and walked over to stare out of the window. He found himself incapable of meeting his father's eyes. The subterfuge did not sit well with him; it wouldn't sit well with his father, either.

Then again, Rhys had kept his own secrets over the years, so perhaps he had no room to judge.

"I haven't told her," Nicholas said, finally. "I don't intend to tell her, either."

Rhys made a noise of astonishment. "But why not?"

Nicholas turned around. "Because I don't want her to know."

"Son, that's lying."

"I'm not lying. I'm simply avoiding discussing the truth with her."

"I see the difference," Rhys said dryly.

"I'm avoiding discussing it for the *moment*," Nicholas clarified. "I will. Later."

"Later? When?"

"In a fortnight's time."

"Why a fortnight?"

Nicholas pursed his lips. "If you must know, I begged her for a fortnight in which no secrets were to be revealed because I hoped that if I wooed her thoroughly enough, she would fall in love with me and when I finally told her about Jake's gate, she wouldn't want to use it. Satisfied?"

Rhys bowed his head briefly. "I am sorry, Nicholas," he said quietly, looking back up at him. "I should have known you had your reasons for secrecy. But what of your lady? She seems not opposed to you."

Nicholas shrugged, but he felt anything but disinterested. "I do think she harbors some fond feelings for me. But what will happen when she realizes that she can go home —"

"And that you knew as much, but neglected to tell her."

"Aye," Nicholas said, nodding. "Now you see my dilemma."

Rhys leaned back in his chair. "Aye, you have one, at that. You also have the complication of a keep full of beautifully garbed asps who would sooner stick a knife between your lady's ribs than speak kindly to her. We must provide her with weapons of her own."

Nicholas looked at his father in surprise. "You like her?"

"I like what I've seen of her," Rhys said frankly. "I also assume you wouldn't love her without reason."

"Nay," Nicholas said quietly, "I daresay I wouldn't."

"Then let us be about our strategy. There's no hope of ridding my hall of those women Joanna brought, so we'll simply have to arm your lady against their venom. She is stunning, but her looks won't aid her. She'll need proper clothing."

"I'm having gowns made for her."

"Are they finished?"

"I was going to check this morning to see. You should note, however, that the gown she is wearing is something I altered with my own two hands."

"Saved her wearing her gear in my trunk, I suppose," Rhys said. "Or Montgomery's clothes."

"Aye."

Rhys drummed his fingers on his table. "She'll need those new gowns, new shoes, and she'll want to be properly coiffed. Your mother likes that sort of rot, you know, when we go to court. I imagine 'tis much like carrying a fine sword — which in your mother's case is not exactly the safest thing to do."

Nicholas smiled. "I suppose not."

"Odd, isn't it," Rhys mused, "that Amanda seems to enjoy court so much."

"Amanda is a hard-hearted wench," Nicholas said affectionately, "and loves to ply her acid tongue on whomever she can. Accompanying Jake to court gives her opportunity to do so and feel as if she's bettering the world at the same time."

Rhys looked at him sharply. "Did you make your peace with her? About Jake?"

Nicholas gaped. "Have I no secrets at all?"

"You have a father who loves you enough

to watch you closely. Do the same for your own sons. I assume you and Amanda see eye to eye now?"

"Aye," Nicholas said quietly.

"Good. Now, in addition to garbing your lady properly, make sure you treat her as you should. Woo her where all can see."

"I have been —"

"In *plain* sight," Rhys interrupted. "Joanna will give you no peace else and you *know* how irritating that can be."

"Very well," Nicholas sighed. He rose. "I'll go make certain her gowns have been finished. And I'll see how her sword is coming."

"You made her a sword?" He laughed. "You poor lad. What will you think of next?"

"I'm desperate for the pleasure of her company and I was willing to cross blades with her to have it." He paused at the door and turned. "You should see her, Father. I have no idea what they teach those wenches in the Future, but she took out one of the lads yesterday with her bare hands."

Rhys froze. "The lads yesterday?"

Nicholas cursed, then sighed. "Aye. A pair of lads accosted us near the shore. I think they were in Ledenham's employ."

"I think you should tell me everything."

"Briefly."

"Take what time you need."

Nicholas sighed, returned to his chair, and told his father everything that had happened with Ledenham from the time Jennifer had arrived in the past. By the time he had finished, his father's frown was very severe.

"He'll have to be watched."

"I was a fool yesterday," Nicholas said. "In my defense, I hadn't slept in a pair of days. I'd walked home the night before from Raventhorpe. That damned horse of yours threw me."

"The Black?"

"Aye," Nicholas said shortly.

Rhys lifted one eyebrow. "Want him?"

Nicholas smiled. "Of course."

"He's yours, though I wouldn't take my lady on his back any time soon."

"I won't," Nicholas said, rising. "I'm off to the blacksmith."

"I imagine you are. Where are you training?"

"The tow—" Nicholas stopped short. He scowled. "Damn you."

Rhys stretched with a smile. "I'll fetch your lady and meet you there."

"Father, a bit of peace," Nicholas pleaded.

"In plain sight, son."

Nicholas rolled his eyes and turned for the door. "Very well."

"I'll make sure your technique is as it should be."

"No doubt," Nicholas muttered and shut the door behind him. Well, if it was what he had to do to have the pleasure of Jennifer's company, he would do it.

But the day would come . . .

He sighed and made haste to the blacksmith's.

An hour later, he was sitting in the northeast tower chamber with two swords and breakfast. Jennifer opened the door and he jumped to his feet.

Unfortunately, she was followed by his father, Robin, Miles, Montgomery, and John.

He glared at the men. "Is there enough room in here for all of you? I think not."

Rhys tucked Jennifer's hand in the crook of his arm. "Here's something to look forward to: you may kiss her after you've worked."

Nicholas looked at Jennifer. She was dressed in Montgomery's clothes with her hair braided down her back, looking gloriously beautiful. It was all he could do not to haul her into his arms and never release her. He took a deep, steadying breath. "And what think you of this madness?"

She smiled. "I'm afraid I asked for it, didn't I?"

"I hadn't planned on so many chaperons."

"It is a little intimidating," she admitted.

"No reason to fear," Robin said. "I'll see to your training and be gentle. Trust me, though. By the time I'm finished with you, you'll be able to best Nick handily."

"All she has to do is walk into the chamber and she's bested him," Miles remarked.

"I don't deny it," Nicholas said fervently. He fetched her sword, then handed it to her. "Try this."

She took it gingerly. "It's beautiful. Where did you find it?"

"In the smithy," he said. "Apparently, it was made for you."

She looked up at him quickly. "You're kidding."

He shook his head with a small smile. "I'm not."

"But, Nicholas," she said, holding on to it gingerly, "it's so beautiful."

"I imagine 'tis also damned sharp," Robin said, looking at it with interest. "And that is the part that is beautiful."

Nicholas had to admit the sword was lovely. The hilt was worked with silver and gold with a lovely pattern of roses and trailing vines. And it *was* very sharp.

"It's so light," she said, drawing it from the sheath and holding it up.

"Then let us see what you can do with it," Robin said. "Nick, have a seat and stay out of our way. Come, Jennifer, and let us begin."

Nicholas balked, but his father gave him a hearty shove toward the empty bench. He shot his sire a glare, but sat down just the same. Miles, the twins, and his father joined him there. Nicholas watched as Robin stood

456

side by side with Jennifer and showed her the rudiments of swordplay.

He readily admitted that she was a very, very quick study.

After several minutes of the most basic instruction, Robin looked at her in surprise. "Have you trained?"

She smiled faintly. "I must admit I have, but with very thin swords called rapiers, and only for use on the stage." She paused and looked a little uncomfortable. "As an actor."

"A jongleur?" Robin asked with interest. "Fascinating. Let us move on, then. Engage me."

"I'll help," Miles said, leaping to his feet. He stood behind her and put his hands over hers. "Allow me to show you how 'tis done, sweet lady."

Nicholas would have leaped to his feet as well, but his father shot out his arm and pinned him back against the wall.

"Don't," Rhys commanded.

"I'll kill him."

"Do it later."

Nicholas growled, but remained seated.

He forced himself to concentrate impassively on the work that was going on. He had to admit that Robin was a very good teacher. Jennifer was a very good student.

And Miles was going to be very dead come sunset.

His younger brother was obviously enjoying

himself far too much. He was just too damned close to Jennifer, what with his arms around her and his hands clutching hers. After the third time Miles looked over his shoulder and winked at Nicholas, Nicholas rose to his feet. He looked at his father.

"Are you going to stop me?"

"Not this time," Rhys said with a smile. "He deserves whatever you do to him."

Nicholas took Miles by the nape of the neck and removed him from Jennifer's person like a tick. He looked at his brother. "Make your peace with your Maker."

"But I have so much to live for."

"You should have thought of that earlier."

Robin rested his sword on his shoulder. "I daresay we should think on something to eat. Lads, let Jennifer have first choice. Either that, or, Montgomery, you go fetch something else."

"Why must I always do the fetching?" Montgomery grumbled.

"Because you were born last," Robin said reasonably. "Complaining won't change that, but running to the kitchens and back quickly will earn you an hour a day with me in the lists for the next fortnight."

Montgomery bolted from the chamber.

Nicholas shoved Miles off the bench to make a place for Jennifer. She sat down and blew her hair out of her eyes. She smiled at him.

"Thank you for the sword," she said softly. "I've never had anything so beautiful."

"I pray you never need to use it," he said seriously. "Or the knife that matches it."

"Nicholas," she said, looking stunned. "That was too generous."

He lifted one shoulder in a shrug. "A small thing."

She looked at his sire. "Might I thank him, my lord?"

"Will I want to avert my eyes?" Rhys asked, his own eyes twinkling.

"That might be best."

Rhys waved her on. "Just keep in mind, the boy needs to keep his wits about him if he's to cross blades with you later this morning."

"It will be just a small thank you, my lord."

Nicholas steeled himself for a proper bit of gratitude. His father had it aright; too many of her kisses and he would be rendered useless for the rest of the day. He closed his eyes just the same, anticipating something quite wonderful.

He felt her kiss his cheek.

Robin burst out laughing.

Nicholas opened his eyes in surprise. Then he felt his eyes narrow. He removed Jennifer's sword from her hands and handed it to his father. Then he pulled her to her feet and across the chamber. He drew her out into the passageway, then slammed the door shut. He looked down at her. "My lady?" he said, fold-ing his arms across his chest.

She laughed up at him. "I was teasing you."

"Aye, I noticed."

She unfolded his arms and put them around her, then leaned up upon her toes and kissed him properly.

He wondered, after a moment or two, if he should have been satisfied with a peck on the cheek.

She sank back down on her heels and put her hands on his chest. "You do have to be steady on your feet."

"I haven't been steady on my feet since I first set eyes on you."

"Haven't you?" she asked wistfully.

"Nay."

"Neither have I," she whispered and went back into his arms.

Nicholas held her for several minutes in silence, then he sighed. "They'll come fetch us if we linger," he said. He took her hand and drew her inside the chamber. He scowled at his father. "Here she is, unmolested."

"I never worried about that," Rhys said mildly. "It is her reputation I worried about."

"Well, that is unmolested as well." He looked at Jennifer. "Lunch?"

"That would be lovely."

Nicholas sat with her and the men in his family and couldn't help but smile. It was truly more than he could have asked for.

Truly more than he deserved.

■ ■ ■ ■

Unfortunately, though he thought he deserved the whole day with her, he only managed the morning and the morning didn't last as long as he would have liked. He'd spent quite a bit of it facing his love over swords, though he would have preferred to have been kissing her.

Desperation drove men to mad deeds, apparently.

Rhys clapped his hands on his knees eventually. " 'Tis time," he said.

Nicholas looked over in surprise. "So soon?"

"There will be dancing tonight and your lady must prepare. Your mother and Anne are awaiting her in Isabelle's chamber. You, however, may keep her sword."

Nicholas sighed. "Very well." He looked at Jennifer. "Until tonight, then, my lady."

"Kiss," Rhys said, waving him on.

Nicholas handed his sword to his father, handed Jennifer's sword to Robin, then pulled her into his arms and kissed her with every desperate feeling he had in his soul. If he could have crawled inside her and kissed her soul, he would have.

By the time he released her, tears were streaming down her face.

Nicholas blinked in surprise. "Did I

hurt you?"

"Of course not," she said, clinging to him. "Damn you."

Nicholas smoothed his hand over her hair. He looked at Robin to see his brother wearing a look of profound pity. He closed his eyes briefly, then kissed Jennifer's hair.

"You deserve to be wooed in plain sight," he said.

She pulled back and smiled. "Thank you."

"Aye, I am a chivalrous soul, aren't I?" he said heavily. "And today I'm damned for it." He sighed and released her. "Father, she's yours. Briefly," he added. "And tell Grand-mère that I plan on dancing with her all night."

"Do you indeed?" a voice said imperiously from the door.

Nicholas looked to find his grandmother standing there, watching him with a neutral expression. She held out her hand and smiled at Jennifer.

"Come, love. We found a gown or two for you. You'd best try them on and see what suits."

Jennifer squeezed his hand briefly, then went to throw herself into the talons of his grandmother the dragon. He watched Jennifer until the door was shut behind her, then he turned and looked at the men in his family. "Well?"

"Keep her," Robin advised. "I like her."

"So do I," Montgomery said enthusiastically. "She puts me in the mind of Amanda, actually. Or perhaps Jake," he said pointedly.

"No doubt," Miles said dryly. He heaved himself to his feet and shoved Montgomery toward the door. He put his hand on Nicholas's shoulder in passing. "I was teasing you this morning."

"Prettily said," Nicholas groused, "but it will not save you from my sword."

Miles slapped him on the back. "See to me later, when your knees are a little steadier underneath you."

"That will take time, no doubt," John said, hopping up and making for the door. "What I want to know is when someone will love me enough to make *me* a sword so fine."

"I shouldn't wait that long, were I you," Miles said, pulling him out the door with him. "Best see to it yourself."

Nicholas listened to his younger brothers leave the chamber, then sat down on the bench with Robin on one side and his father on the other.

"You must tell her," Rhys said quietly.

"I know," Nicholas sighed.

"What did Jake tell you when you went to Raventhorpe?" Robin asked. "Oh, wait, I know. A great many things you should have listened to whilst you had the chance before."

"You are a great horse's arse," Nicholas said distinctly.

Robin only laughed. "You should have asked Jake about the Future."

"I did. And I only wanted to know one thing."

"So did I," Robin said. "And he obliged by telling me that I truly *did* go down in history as the greatest swordsman England ever knew."

Nicholas snorted. "He flattered you because you gave him a blacksmith."

"You'd like to believe that, wouldn't you?" Robin grinned. He sat back and shook his head. "I imagine there are many things we would be surprised to learn about the Future."

Nicholas sighed. "It would be marvelous to see."

"You'd want indoor plumbing."

Rhys leaned in. "Indoor plumbing?"

"Water that runs when you turn a lever," Robin said enthusiastically. "And then there is water in the garderobe that carries the cesspit contents away to somewhere where someone else does aught with them."

"Marvelous," Rhys sighed.

"I can see why a girl wouldn't want to give it up," Robin said lightly. He clapped Nicholas on the shoulder. "But you're fairly attractive as well. You can build her something like to what she's accustomed to. Or maybe you can just kiss her so often she forgets about indoor plumbing." He rose and started toward the door. "It may be your only hope," he threw over his shoulder.

Nicholas watched his brother leave the chamber. He bowed his head for several moments, then looked at his father.

"What do you think?"

"What I always think," Rhys said mildly. "That my sons are worthy of the finest women and that not a man in existence is worthy of my daughters." He paused and smiled. "With the exception of Jake Kilchurn, perhaps."

"I like him," Nicholas admitted. He looked at his father. "He didn't smirk once."

"My opinion of him only improves."

Nicholas smiled, then sighed. "Perhaps I should go bathe."

"Do it in the kitchen where you can be seen by all," Rhys advised. "Best give those harlots downstairs a reason to feel that their journey here hasn't been wasted."

"Father!" Nicholas said with a half laugh.

"Damned hussies," Rhys grumbled. "They've eaten through half my larder already. Wed this Jennifer of yours and retreat to your own hall before I've nothing left for the winter."

Nicholas rose and collected his weapons. "I'll do my best."

"Nick?"

Nicholas stopped at the door to the tower chamber and looked back. "Aye?"

"You're happy."

It hadn't been a question. "Very."

"Then I wish you good fortune," Rhys said quietly. "I daresay you'll need it."

Nicholas had no reply. He nodded and made for his chamber. He would leave his gear, then head for the kitchens. His sire had it aright. Perhaps if the six strumpets procured for his pleasure saw more of him than they wanted, they would run off in a fright.

Then again, knowing the women lying in wait for him, he suspected not. Well, at least he would be presentable that night and perhaps have a dance or two with his lady. It wasn't enough, but it might be all he could have that day.

But tomorrow was another day entirely and he would arrange it to his liking.

His grandmother, and her asps, be damned.

CHAPTER 28

Jennifer stood in the middle of Isabelle's room and knew exactly what it felt like to be Cinderella.

Only her fairy godmothers were the relatives of the man she loved.

Joanna had brought her back to Isabelle's bedroom where Jennifer had found Isabelle, Anne, and the lady Gwennelyn waiting for her. She had been plunked right into a tub and scrubbed from head to toe. She'd briefly considered being embarrassed, but they seemed to think it a perfectly normal thing to do, so she didn't bother.

Once she was dried off and swathed in a shift of something so soft it felt like the finest of modern cotton, she was placed in front of the fire, where Anne combed out her hair. Once that was done, Joanna motioned to Gwen.

"Bring out the gowns, love, and let us see what suits her."

Jennifer sat next to the fire and watched as

several gowns were produced and held up for her inspection. She assumed they were Gwen's since they were in the style of what Jennifer had seen her wear. There were four dresses that were very simply made but quite lovely. Joanna waved them away and called for the fancier ones. Jennifer stared in fascination at the remaining four dresses the women held up for her to look at.

There was a gown of vivid red, one of emerald green, one of a soft peach, and yet another of a deep blue. All were worked with embroidery and pearls and heaven knew what else. Jennifer looked at Gwen and struggled for the right tone.

"My lady," she said seriously, "I appreciate the offer, but I couldn't wear any of them."

Gwen looked at her in surprise. "But why not?"

"Because they are too nice," Jennifer said honestly. "If you want to loan me something to wear tonight, I'd rather have it be something less expensive."

"Loan?" Gwen said, looking confused. "But these are your dresses, Jennifer."

"Mine?" she echoed faintly.

"Well, of course, gel," Joanna said briskly. "Dresses, shifts, shoes — everything needful and many other things not needful and extremely luxurious that a woman might want in order to feel beautiful."

Jennifer blinked. "I don't understand."

"Nicky had them made for you," Gwen said, with a gentle smile. "Didn't you know?"

It was amazing how quickly one could go from baffled to overcome. Jennifer felt her eyes begin to burn. That didn't last long because her tears began and eased that burning. She felt an arm go around her shoulders and a cloth be put into her hands. She wiped her eyes, then looked at Anne who was kneeling next to her. Anne smiled.

"Nicky has exquisite taste. He has spared no expense here."

"You could purchase a small castle with what the blue one cost him," Joanna noted impassively. She looked at Jennifer. "He must be very fond of you, indeed."

Gwen laughed softly. "Mother, you know he is. And why not? She's a lovely girl. Come, Jennifer, and have a closer look at your dresses. Anne has it aright. Nicholas has very fine taste. These will all suit you beautifully."

Jennifer rose unsteadily and walked across the chamber. She reached out hesitantly to touch the embroidery on the blue gown that Gwen was holding.

"Do you mind?" she asked quietly.

"Mind?" Gwen echoed with a smile. "That he loves you?"

"I don't know that he does," Jennifer said with a half smile. "I meant that he had been so generous." She paused. "To someone you don't know."

Gwen smiled. "Jennifer, my son is a man full grown. I trust him to know his own heart. If it would ease your mind about my opinion of you, let us take tomorrow and spend it together in my solar. We'll stitch in peace and talk."

Jennifer nodded, because she could do nothing else.

I'm asking you to stay with me and see if this life might suit you.

Nicholas's words came back to her. She was beginning to believe he might just be serious, if he was willing to lay out a small fortune to see her clothed properly.

She put her shoulders back and smiled at Gwen. "Aye, my lady," she said in her best medieval Norman French, "that would be lovely."

"Now we've settled that," Joanna said, "let's be about preparing this miss for the evening. Isabelle, bring over that light-colored gown. Anne, bring the green. I will take this daring red business myself, then we'll hold them up to her and see which one suits her best. Jennifer?"

"Aye, my lady?"

"Don't weep on these gowns. You'll ruin them."

Jennifer sniffed a final time. "I'm fine."

Gwen smiled. "Aye, you are at that. Now, Mother, what do you think? I think we should save the blue for another time. It is the finest of the four."

"I agree," Joanna said. "Anne, come over here and give your opinion."

Jennifer held each of the three remaining gowns up to herself and found herself being scrutinized by four medieval women of high rank.

She was enormously grateful they liked her.

"The red is breathtaking," Gwen said. She smiled at Jennifer. "Not many women could wear it. Nicholas chose well."

"Aye, but I say this pale one is the one for tonight," Joanna said. She took the red gown away and handed Jennifer the peach dress. "Not another woman in the keep would dare wear such a color for fear it would make them look as pale as death." She looked at Anne. "What do you think, love?"

Anne nodded. "You have it aright, Lady Joanna. Isabelle, what do you think?"

Jennifer found Isabelle smiling at her. "I think she's beautiful in all of them," she offered, "but this is especially lovely. I know I could not wear it."

"I would hesitate as well," Anne said. "But Jennifer's hair compliments it and her skin is flawless." She smiled. "As I said before, Nicholas has exquisite taste. But you gave him an equally lovely woman to dress." She reached out and fingered a sleeve. "He will be pleased."

Jennifer watched them put away the other

gowns in a trunk, then she stood and let them dress her. She was then given a chair and Anne and Isabelle worked on her hair.

Joanna and Gwen drew up chairs and conversed about the families camping all over the keep, hoping their daughters would make a match before they left. Jennifer tried to ignore what they were saying, but it wasn't easy. The women were, from what she could tell, enormously wealthy and very well connected.

Joanna took her hand suddenly. Jennifer looked at her, surprised.

"My lady?"

"Are you listening?"

"I'm trying not to," Jennifer said honestly.

Gwen laughed. "I can't blame her."

"I can." Joanna looked at her frankly. "These are the families who make up Nicholas's world. You'd best know their names, at least. You won't be able to ignore them if you choose to wed him, you know."

"Wed?" Jennifer echoed weakly. "My lady, I don't think he's thinking —"

"Well, of course he's *thinking,*" Joanna interrupted. "Do you honestly believe he would clothe you with gowns of this quality if he weren't thinking about marriage? Or make you a sword — though the advisability of that is still in question in my mind. A man does not clothe his mistress so richly." She patted Jennifer's hand. "Learn the names of the

472

families who will be there tonight."

"Of course," Jennifer murmured. She smoothed down her dress. She supposed Nicholas's grandmother had a point, but then again, Nicholas's grandmother didn't know all her secrets.

Give me a fortnight . . .

Well, maybe that included giving the same to his family. Jennifer clasped her hands in her lap and looked at Nicholas's grandmother.

"I'll listen this time."

"As you should," Joanna said approvingly. "Now, we'll begin with the least powerful and work upward. Ida of Louth is the daughter of William of Louth and the cousin of that worthless and penniless Gavin —"

Jennifer listened. She got all the names right when Joanna quizzed her on them two hours later. She didn't cry and ruin her gown.

A good afternoon, by anyone's standards.

And the peach silk felt glorious against her skin. The only thing she could have wished for was a mirror. Anne and Isabelle had changed her hair twice, but finally seemed satisfied with the result. All four of Nicholas's relatives took a final look at her and pronounced her perfect. Jennifer supposed she had no choice but to take their word for it.

"Remember," Joanna said finally, "that Nicholas is the lord of Wyckham and the Count of Beauvois. He has more wealth than any gel's father below. When you wed him, you will sit higher at the table than everyone below save Brigit of Islington, though you will equal her in station. Comport yourself accordingly."

"Of course, my lady."

Joanna clapped her hands and rose. "Off to supper, then. I think we're late."

Jennifer rose as well, then looked at them all. "Thank you," she said simply. "You've been very kind."

"You've made my son smile," Gwen said gently. "How can we not repay that kindness with one of our own?"

"Besides," Joanna said with a conspiratorial smile, "I like the way you look at my grandson. I've never seen a gel look at him quite that way and believe me, I've seen my share of gels staring at him."

"No doubt you have, Mother," Gwen said with a laugh.

"Don't you agree, dear?" Joanna asked Gwen. "She looks at him as if she likes him despite all his flaws."

"Does he have flaws?" Jennifer asked, then bit her lip and laughed. "I suppose he does."

"He doesn't," Anne said. "None that I've ever seen."

"Nor have I," Isabelle agreed. "I think Nicky is perfect."

"You think he's perfect, little one, because he brings you home very expensive presents every time he goes abroad," Joanna said dryly.

"And because he's kind to her," Gwen added. "He's a good man. But I might be biased."

Jennifer only smiled as she walked to the door and listened to the women discuss Nicholas's good points, of which there seemed to be many.

Of course, she had to agree.

"Now," Joanna said, pausing at the door, "let us see if my Nicky manages to put one foot in front of the other once he sees his lady." She drew Jennifer's arm through hers and led her from the chamber. "Follow along, gels, and note every expression you see. We'll discuss them all at length later."

Jennifer smiled. It was such a normal thing to do, to plan to scope out others at a party, that she almost felt at ease — and ease was not something she had yet to feel in the company of all the nobility Joanna had brought with her. She let Joanna go down the stairs first and hoped to heaven she wouldn't trip and go rolling down them after her. She bumped into Nicholas's grandmother at the bottom.

"Sorry," she said nervously.

Joanna turned around. "Jennifer," she began, "let us discuss your entrance. You will walk out into the hall, go before the high table, and curtsey to Rhys."

"I can do that."

"Then you will come and take your place next to me. Let Nicholas gape at you all he likes. Trust me, I'll be marking his every expression to describe to you in the greatest of detail tonight whilst we're abed. First you will dance with Robin, then Miles. Then, and only then, will I allow Nicholas to approach. You may dance with him once."

"Once?" Jennifer asked with a light sigh.

"He must dance with the others," Joanna said with a smile, "but then I suppose you may dance with him as many times as you like."

Jennifer blinked hard. She took Joanna's hands, then bent and kissed her wizened cheek. "Thank you."

Joanna pulled her out into the great hall. She released her hand. "Rhys, first."

Jennifer wasn't unaccustomed to being in front of an audience. After all, playing Paganini in New York City wasn't a walk in the park. She was just performing in front of people she didn't know and didn't care about.

She put her shoulders back and stepped forward confidently, as if she had every right to be in a medieval hall, clothed by a medieval lord, and preparing to take a medieval household by storm.

There was absolute silence as she entered. She imagined she might have heard a gasp or two.

She walked to the front of the high table,

turned to face Rhys, and made him her most elegant curtsey. She straightened and looked at him. She had to admit that she also stole a brief look at Nicholas.

He was gaping at her as if he'd never seen her before.

Rhys got up, walked around the table, and made her a bow. He then offered her his arm and escorted her to her place. She sat down and was grateful for it. She didn't think she would have managed to stand up much longer.

"Nicely done," Joanna said. "Was Nicky smiling?"

Jennifer took a deep breath. "I don't think so."

Joanna leaned forward to look down the table, then sat back. "You have that aright. I daresay he looks as if he's trying not to leap over his father and have you right here."

"My lady!" Jennifer gasped.

Joanna waved her hand dismissively. "The purview of the elderly. I can be as offensive as I like and no one cares."

Jennifer smiled affectionately. "I like you very much."

"Good. I'll live forever so plan on me visiting your hall for decades to come."

"I could only hope," Jennifer murmured.

"Eat, gel. You'll need your strength."

Jennifer ate, but tasted little of it. She was too busy running over dance steps in her head. They weren't difficult, but she wasn't exactly at her best. When Robin asked for a dance, she took a deep breath and hoped she wouldn't make a fool of herself.

"I loathe dancing," he said happily as he led her out into the middle of the hall.

"Then why do you do it?"

"All for Anne," Robin admitted.

Jennifer found it in her to smile. She was grateful for Robin's muttered curses as he concentrated on his feet. One thing she could say for him: at least he kept them from plowing into the other dancers. His complete disgust with the whole activity, which she mentally contrasted with his joy in the lists, was enough to make her laugh.

One dance was all he could muster before he turned her over to Miles. Miles offered her his arm and smiled at her.

"You are stunning," he said honestly.

"Blame the women of your family," she said easily. "I had nothing to do with it."

"Well," he said with a dry smile, "it wasn't as if they were trying to make something from nothing. The gown is lovely, but you are luminous. I'm jealous as hell of my brother."

"You aren't," she protested.

"I am," he said honestly. "Are you sure you wouldn't rather have me? I have no money, no keep of my own, and only modest sword skill, but I vow I would obtain all three in abundance if you would be mine." He paused.

"I would ask Nick if you could keep that dress."

She smiled and squeezed his hand. "I am not the woman for you, Miles, but I appreciate the offer."

"So you say," Miles said with a frown, "yet you will not wed with me —"

"Count yourself fortunate," came a shrill voice from next to them. "I daresay you wouldn't wish to align yourself with a woman of no rank at all."

Jennifer looked over her shoulder. It was Brigit of Islington, the most beautiful of the lot, and the most powerful. Jennifer inclined her head.

"Forgive us," Jennifer said politely. "We've danced into your space."

"You've done more than that," Brigit said in a cold voice. "And trust me, *demoiselle,* all the beautiful clothes in the world cannot make up for the fact that you are nothing. I've never heard of you and I know *everyone* of rank."

"I'm sure you do," Jennifer said with a mildness she certainly didn't feel.

"You'll never have him, you strumpet," she hissed. "I'll see to it."

Jennifer backed up a pace, but found that she'd bumped into someone. She turned around to find Nicholas standing there. His eyes were so cold, she flinched. She was very, very grateful she wasn't the recipient of his glare. Apparently Brigit was tougher than she looked because she didn't give any sign of distress. She only curtseyed to Nicholas and gave him a welcoming smile.

"My lord. You have come to dance."

"Aye," Nicholas said simply. He put his hand on Miles's shoulder and sent him away.

Miles, to his credit, went without hesitation.

Nicholas looked at Jennifer. "My lady, if you would excuse me a moment?"

"Surely longer than a mere moment," Brigit protested. "My lord, you have more sense than this. A peasant dressed in fine clothes?" She laughed scornfully. "And so she will always be."

Jennifer wasn't unaccustomed to venom. After all, one didn't get to the top of the heap in music without a little backbiting. But she was completely out of her element here. Was Brigit going to pull out a little dirk and stab her next?

"Wait for me," Nicholas said to her in Gaelic, then he looked at Brigit. "Now, my lady," he said with a pleasant smile, "if you will allow me?" He offered her his arm with a small bow.

Brigit shot Jennifer a look of supreme triumph and put her hand on Nicholas's arm as if it was nothing more than her due.

The dancers stopped to watch. Even the musicians stopped playing to watch them walk across the floor. Jennifer bit her lip. Was that the sort of woman he was supposed to marry? Likely so, if Joanna had brought her to market. Jennifer shook her head at the thought. To think of Nicholas stuck with that shrew for the rest of his life . . . well, she couldn't imagine it.

Nicholas escorted Brigit over to her seat. Jennifer had no idea what he said to Brigit, but she sat immediately. Brigit looked around Nicholas and shot Jennifer a look of absolute loathing.

Jennifer gulped in spite of herself. Well, there was someone to keep an eye on.

Then Nicholas turned, nodded to the musicians, and walked across the floor. Jennifer took a deep breath as he stopped in front of her and held out his hand.

"That was interesting," she said in Gaelic.

"Wasn't it, though," he agreed. "Dance with me?"

"I would love to," she said, and they began. "I have to tell you that I'd give my right arm to be anywhere but here right now. I'd suggest we bolt for the stables, but I don't want to ruin my dress."

"Ignore them all," Nicholas said with a nonchalant shrug. "I plan to."

"You didn't make me a friend in Lady Brigit," she noted.

"She overstepped her bounds. No one insults my lady," he said lightly, though she could hear an edge in his voice. "No one."

"Watch your back, then. And mine," she added with a shiver.

"You watch my back," he said with a smile, "and aye, I will watch yours. It will mean we must spend more time together."

She had to smile at that. "If we must."

"Did I tell you that you are breathtaking?"

"It's the dress. It was made for me by a wonderful man."

"I don't think he did the stitching."

"He did the choosing, though, and he has flawless taste." She smiled. "Thank you. It was very generous."

"If the gowns please you, then I'm satisfied."

"Please me?" she echoed. "You can't be serious. Your grandmother said you could buy a small castle with what the blue one cost you."

" 'Tis possible," he conceded. "Save it for a special time, then."

"I will." She smiled. "I think we need to stop talking. I can't remember the steps. Don't look at me that way, either."

"How am I looking at you?"

"Like I'm a veal you'd like to carve up for supper."

He laughed. "Forgive me. I'll be quiet, I won't ogle you, and I won't tread upon the hem of your gown. I likely shouldn't kiss you here, either, should I?"

"Likely not," she said.

"Will Grandmère allow me to walk you up to your bedchamber?"

"Definitely not," she said. "But there's always tomorrow. I still have Montgomery's clothes."

"I'll think of a plan. Silently."

She nodded with a smile, then she was forced to concentrate on what she was doing. Dancing was not her forte, though Miles and Montgomery had done a very good job teaching her the steps. What she didn't know, she faked as best she could. Nicholas was very good at keeping her from making a complete fool of herself, silently and without stepping on her dress.

And when the song was finished, he looked at her with a very small smile.

"I must dance with the others," he said gravely. "Once. Then I will return for you."

"I'll be waiting."

"I hoped you'd say that."

Several hours and several more dances later, Jennifer was in bed, enduring Joanna's ice-cold toes on her shins. She didn't dare shiver.

"Well?" she asked.

"He couldn't take his eyes off you," Joanna said promptly. "He put that strumpet from Islington in her place, didn't he? Did you watch him dance with her? He the epitome of good manners and she looking as if she still planned to besiege him with the tenacity of a seasoned warrior. He was utterly unmoved." Joanna chuckled. "She isn't overfond of you, is she?"

"Apparently not," Jennifer said with a smile.

"Aye, well, forget her. I imagine Nicholas has. Now, what of you? Did you enjoy yourself?"

"I felt like a princess," Jennifer said with a half laugh. "It was magical."

"Being in love will do that for a gel," Joanna said philosophically. "Now, I thought I should take the opportunity to enumerate all of my sweet Nicky's finer qualities for you. Shall I begin in his youth and describe how he developed them, or simply list them from one end to the other?"

"Whatever will take longer," Jennifer said with a smile.

Joanna patted her cheek. "What a good gel you are. Now, when he was but a wee lad of six summers . . ."

Jennifer listened happily to a recounting of Nicholas de Piaget's history that would have impressed even the family historians at Artane.

Maybe they were descended from Joanna.

She wouldn't have been surprised.

She spared a brief thought for Lady Brigit, then decided she wasn't worth the effort. It was obvious Nicholas wanted nothing to do with her. Maybe she would find herself of-fended enough to leave right away.

Well, whatever she did, it wouldn't affect them. Jennifer tucked her hands under her pillow and listened with pleasure to what promised to be hours of details about a man who had given her a Cinderella evening.

How could she not love him?

CHAPTER 29

Brigit of Islington stood in the second-finest chamber in the keep and looked out the window. It wasn't enough that Robin and Anne had been displaced for her. It also wasn't enough that she had enjoyed that brief moment of triumph the night before when she'd held on to Nicholas de Piaget's arm and considered how it might feel to be the Countess of Beauvois.

There was someone in her way.

Someone who needed to be removed.

She muttered vile curses under her breath. Who was that Jennifer McKinnon? Brigit knew every woman of rank in England and France and she simply could not place her. Was she some brat of Scots breeding? Obviously so, though Brigit was somewhat surprised to find such beauty coming from a country of barbarians.

Why Nicholas would allow himself to touch an unwashed wench from the north was beyond her to understand. Obviously, he'd been bewitched.

Brigit paused. Bewitched?

It was no secret that all manner of strange things happened in Scotland. Who knew but that the McKinnon wench had exerted some sort of otherworldly power over the good lord of Wyckham. And who knew but that he might be eternally grateful for a rescue from that unholy influence. Perhaps he might reward his rescuer with something far more precious than his gratitude.

Perhaps a place as mistress of Beauvois.

Brigit smiled at the thought. She had been to that lovely keep on the coast of France several years ago whilst traveling with her father. Nicholas had been younger then, not more than three-and-twenty, and so beautiful, she'd been almost more in love with him than with his castle on the edge of the sea. He'd been involved with some wench from the French court, though she'd known his heart was not in it.

She'd begun then to plan out how she might have him.

Lady Joanna had corresponded with her for months, trying to get her to come to Artane and present herself to Nicholas. Brigit had refused, knowing that she was truly the only woman of rank worthy of that beautiful castle in France. Nicholas would have known it as well, which was no doubt why he'd never chosen any of the other women Lady Joanna had brought for his inspection.

She'd known, however, that Joanna had been saving the finest for her final attempt at seeing her grandson wed. Brigit had let Joanna know that she would be pleased to come, now that the rabble had been swept away. And so she'd traveled north, fully aware that it was far away from where she truly wanted to be but that it was the only direction she could take to find herself in France.

And at Beauvois.

There was simply nothing not to like about that castle. Nicholas had bought himself the keep and the title by some means — she supposed by tourneying. It spoke well of his skill with the sword. It spoke more about his taste for fine things. In that brief se'nnight she'd spent there with her sire, she had seen more luxury than even her father could ever hope to boast of in a lifetime. She could only speculate how truly spectacular the place might be now. Gold seemed to flow into Nicholas de Piaget's coffers without him having to do much. At least she supposed he didn't do much. He likely slept half the day away, raised a finger now and again to order his servants about, then spent the rest of the time eating fine food and drinking fine wine. Bastard though he might have been, at least he knew how to live like a lord.

Fortunately for him, she knew how to live like a lady.

She would have considered that further, but the conversation going on behind her distracted her. She would have bid the women be silent, but one was her mother and the other Sibil of Hansworth. If nothing else, Sibil was one for gossip that no one else seemed to ferret out.

"I don't like him," Sibil said with a hearty shiver. "He's too tall. Too intense. Did you see the way he looked at Lady Jennifer last night whilst they danced? I vow he almost set her afire with his glances."

"She is no lady," Gytha of Islington said mildly. She shot Brigit a look, then turned back to Sibil. "But I can understand your revulsion, my dear. Lord Nicholas is a very strong man. He certainly wouldn't be for just anyone."

"He has a murky past as well," Sibil pointed out. "And he lives here in the north instead of in London where things are as they should be." She leaned in toward Gytha. "Did you hear the tales Nigel of Ledenham told of what goes on here? I wouldn't live here for even Nicholas de Piaget's wealth."

Brigit came to sit down next to her mother. "Ledenham?" she said intently. "You know he's mad, of course. But what did he say?"

"He spoke of witchcraft," Sibil said, lowering her voice. "You know he accused Lady Amanda's husband of it. That's why the king is making him build that abbey. As penance."

"Ridiculous," Gytha snorted, "yet interesting, in the way of a frightening tale told at bedtime. Tell us more, Sibil. Ledenham is no friend of the de Piagets, is he?"

"Not at all," Sibil continued. "Hates them with a black passion, I'd say. You would think he wouldn't want to be anywhere near here."

"You would think," Gytha said. She paused. "Why do you say that?"

"Because I could have sworn I saw him in the village when we arrived." Sibil smiled. "Perhaps he is looking for witches. But that isn't possible, is it?" She paused. "Witches don't really exist, do they?"

"Only in Scotland," Brigit muttered.

Gytha squeezed her hand so hard, it hurt. "Of course not, Sibil. There are no such things as witches." She yawned delicately. "Brigit, I daresay the walls of the keep are pressing in on you. Perhaps we should leave Sibil here to have a rest whilst you and I have a small walk. To the chapel, perhaps."

"Of course, Mother," Brigit said.

She rose, nodded to Sibil, then followed her mother out of the chamber.

Gytha shut the door firmly behind her, then paused in the passageway. Her eyes glittered in the torchlight. "I see our salvation."

"*My* salvation," Brigit corrected.

"And you don't think I'll come along when you wed with him and settle in that lovely keep in France?" Gytha hissed. "Why do you think I'm here helping you?"

"He'll wed me on *my* merits, Mother."

"He'll wed you with *my* help, ungrateful chit," Gytha said, "and he'll not do it unless we dispose of Mistress McKinnon." She looked at Brigit. "Be grateful for my aid."

"I am," Brigit said, through gritted teeth. "But you won't be mistress of that keep, Mother."

"I don't want to be mistress; I want to travel without your father. You owe me that much. Now, let us go down into the village and see if our good Ledenham is lurking about. You'll offer to be his eyes here in the keep. And when the time comes, he'll remove our good Scot from our midst and the way will be clear for you to take the place you were destined to have." She paused. "You'd best not make any missteps."

"I can win him, thank you, Mother," Brigit said coldly.

"You'd better," Gytha said, just as coldly. "Now, come. Let us away."

Brigit walked with her mother down the passageway and wished she'd had the guts to simply push the woman down the stairs. A horrible accident and she would have been free of her schemes.

Well, no matter. She would make her own bargain with Ledenham, see Jennifer McKinnon disposed of, then find herself wed to Nicholas de Piaget before the year's end.

491

Who knew that her mother might meet her end then as well?

An unfortunate accident, of course, but accidents did happen.

She decided to save that delicious thought for another time. Now, she had to concentrate on ridding herself of that McKinnon wench. She thought about that entertaining possibility all the way through the hall, through the courtyards, and under the barbican gate before she dismissed it as the wrong solution.

If the wench died, Nicholas would grieve. Perhaps it would be better that he see her for what she was: a witch. Then he would count himself well rid of her and look for the kind of woman of station and rank who could stand by his side at his lovely keep in France.

Aye, far better that Jennifer McKinnon be branded as a witch.

And far better still that Ledenham do the branding.

After all, it was what he did best.

"I think I see him," Gytha murmured. "Put on your best smile."

Brigit was already wearing it.

She closed her eyes briefly, imagined she was standing in the midst of Beauvois's luxurious great hall, then put aside the thought as one to enjoy later.

After her work was done.

CHAPTER 30

Nicholas paused in the passageway. It was the first bloody rest he'd had in three days. Unfortunately, he hadn't passed those days with Jennifer and that was wearing on him.

He didn't want to think about it, but the fortnight was finished after another day and he was dreading more with every hour the moment when he would have to tell Jennifer what he knew. If his current subterfuge hadn't weighed on him so heavily, he would have taken the secret to his grave.

He leaned against the wall and closed his eyes. His chivalry was becoming very inconvenient. It demanded that he entertain his grandmother's guests. Good manners demanded that he at least speak to the women.

All except Brigit of Islington. He made it a point to look through her as often as possible.

He'd had another morning in the tower chamber with Jennifer, but with not only his sire and his brothers, but his grandmother as well, watching and calling him on the slight-est misstep. And damn them all if he hadn't actually had to work at training with Jennifer.

He hadn't seen her yet that morning, though he had spent the evening before star-ing at her, simply breathtaking in a red gown that set her hair and his heart on fire.

She'd looked tired, though. No matter the weapons of her clothes and bearing, it was plain that the company was wearing on her. He would have given much to have simply collected her in the stables and ridden off with her, but even he had come to terms with the wisdom of wooing her where all could see. If nothing else, it would silence those in the company who might have been tempted to disparage her.

He supposed she endured enough of that as it was.

The only thing that had eased him in the past three days was the sight of his family be-ing so kind to her. Anne, Isabelle, his mother, and even his grandmother had rallied around her and protected her. His brothers had been even more protective than the ladies, and his father had watched over her with a paternal eye.

But to have one afternoon of simply sitting with her, without eyes watching them, with-out someone watching for the first mis-step . . .

His father's page, Aubrey, appeared in front

of him. Nicholas groaned silently, then fixed a smile to his face.

"Aye, Aubrey? Where am I needed?"

"Your mother's solar, my lord."

"So early?" Nicholas asked wearily. "It isn't even noon."

" 'Tis urgent, my lord," Aubrey said, wide-eyed.

Nicholas took a deep breath and let it out slowly. "Of course. You needn't go with my reply. I'll go myself."

Aubrey bowed. "As you will, my lord," he said, then he scampered off.

Nicholas pushed off the wall and wandered down the passageways to his mother's solar. He put his hand on the latch, resigned himself to enduring whatever his mother had in mind for him, then opened the door.

Gwen was there, as he had expected. Next to her sat Joanna, dozing in her chair. Anne was there as well, as was Isabelle.

And so was Jennifer.

There was an empty chair next to her.

"Come in and shut the door, Nicky, my love," Gwen said with a smile.

Nicholas looked at his mother. "I love you."

"I always suspected you did," she said pleasantly.

Nicholas shut the solar door behind him, collapsed into the chair next to Jennifer, and smiled. He took her hand and kissed it. "Bliss," he said.

She smiled. "You're very sweet."

"He is," Gwen said, "especially when he gets his way."

"Get my way?" Nicholas snorted. "If I'd had my way, I would have spent time with no one but this woman for the past several days instead of enduring the mindless twits downstairs."

"I chose very carefully," Joanna said between soft snores.

"Then they duped you, Grandmère," Nicholas said, "but no matter. We'll be rid of them soon enough."

"You haven't chosen a bride, Nicholas," Joanna said, opening her eye and looking at him sternly. "And since another lady of breeding has been added to your list, your days of being polite are not over."

"Another!" Nicholas groaned. "By the saints, what wench now?"

"The one you're sitting next to, you bad-mannered lout," Joanna grumbled. "By the saints, children these days are so ungrateful."

Nicholas looked at Jennifer with wide eyes. "Is that so?"

"Apparently," she said, with the faintest of smiles.

"And what do you think?" he asked, as casually as he dared.

She reached for his hand and held it very tightly with his own. He was surprised to see her eyes welling up with tears. He leaned forward.

"Jen," he said quietly, "what ails you?"

She shook her head. "Nothing. I'm terribly flattered that your grandmother would consider me for you."

"Is that all?"

"Yes. I'm just tired."

He rose and held out his hands. "Come with me. We're going to have what privacy can be found. Mother, excuse us. Grandmère, with your permission?" He didn't wait for an answer, but pulled Jennifer to her feet and led her over to a wooden bench set into an alcove under the window. He sat down, then pulled her down onto his lap.

"Nicholas!" Joanna exclaimed from across the solar. "Such impropriety!"

Nicholas fixed his grandmother with a steely glance.

"Are you not here to chaperon me?"

"Aye, whelp, and that means stopping you from doing anything untoward."

"My hands will be in plain sight at all times. You may come and check as often as you like."

She threw a bobbin of thread across the room at him. Fortunately, he had very quick hands and caught it.

"All my work!" she said, shaking her head.

"Has been greatly appreciated, but my lady is very weary. I vow I will be the epitome of all knightly virtues."

"Save the one that says you should allow your lady her own chair," Joanna grumbled.

"I'm wooing her."

"Woo her in her own chair."

Nicholas grunted at her, set aside the thread, then wrapped his arms around Jennifer. "Well?"

"Shocking," she said with a small smile.

"I know," he said, with an answering smile, "but the last few days have been endless and my patience for the niceties of wooing anyone but you is completely exhausted. I'll play for you later. I'll read to you. I'll wind your yarn. For now, just allow me to hold you."

"You don't think I'm going to argue, do you?"

"You look like you might weep instead," he said with a sigh.

"Oh, Nicholas," she said, pressing her face against his neck. "I can't help it."

"The fortnight isn't over," he whispered.

"I wish it would never end," she murmured.

"My thoughts exactly." He tipped her face up and kissed her.

And once he started, he couldn't seem to stop.

He didn't want to stop.

"Nicholas!"

He held his hands out.

"I cannot see Jennifer's."

Jennifer opened her eyes and looked at him. She put up one hand and waved.

"And the other?"

"He's pinning it to the wall behind him, my lady."

"Nicholas, release her!"

Nicholas smiled ruefully. "Forgive me, love. That can't be comfortable. Here, come and sit beside me instead."

Jennifer rose, then sat down next to him. She slipped her hand into his and leaned back against the wall. "Did I thank you properly for the dresses? And everything else to go with them? Nightclothes, shifts, shoes. I don't think I've managed to get to the bottom of that trunk yet." She smiled. "It was too much."

"In truth, it was nothing."

She looked down at their hands together, then brought his hand up and kissed it softly. "It was something to me. You made me feel beautiful."

He suspected that over the course of his very long, very weary existence, he had never once had a woman kiss his hand.

He thought he just might weep.

And he wasn't one to weep.

He turned, slipped his hand under Jennifer's hair, and leaned forward to kiss her. He felt her arms slip up around his neck. He was almost certain, at some point, that he felt her tears on his cheek. He opened his eyes, pulled away but a handsbreadth, and saw that he had it aright. He wiped away her tears with his thumbs, then kissed her again, softly.

"I have never wanted a fortnight to pass so desperately," he whispered, "but I dread its ending. I fear what stands between us." He managed a wan smile. "How do we survive it?"

She hugged him tightly. "I don't know," she whispered against his ear. "I don't know."

"More kissing?"

"I don't think that will help." She paused. "I don't think it will hurt, either."

He smiled at her. "Do you think?"

She reached up and stroked his cheek. "I try not to," she said with a smile. "It lands me in the cesspit every time."

"Did I say that?"

"I think you might have. I'm beginning to agree with you." She settled herself back against the wall and rested her head on his shoulder. "Forget the future, Nicholas," she said softly. "I'm tired enough today to do just that."

Forget the future.

He couldn't have agreed more.

He propped his feet up on the opposite bench and took her hand in both his own. "Are you too weary to talk?"

"I'm not. Especially if it has nothing to do with the future."

He smiled faintly. "Then tell me of the past. Your past. What did you do each day? What did you love? What made you smile?"

500

"I loved my family," she said quietly.

He looked at her quickly but she shook her head.

"I won't cry. I miss them, but I won't cry."

"You may, if you like."

She shook her head. "I won't. But I will tell you of them, if you like."

"I'd like it very much. I should have asked you about them sooner."

"I don't think I could have talked about them sooner," she said quietly. "But I'd like to now."

He closed his eyes briefly. He could hardly bear the grieved tone in her voice. By the saints, he didn't want his days of bliss to be over. When she learned the truth . . .

She told him of her father and mother whose lives had revolved around their children. She told him of her grandmother who sounded a great deal like his own. He discovered she had two older sisters and an older brother, and a niece and a nephew. Her brother built things, her sister and her husband were players, and her next-oldest sister was married to the son of an earl.

He wanted desperately to ask who that earl might be, but he didn't dare — though he was somewhat relieved to know that they still had nobility in the Future. There had to be someone to see to the upkeep of a well-preserved castle.

"And what of your life day to day?" he

asked. "You saw what I do; tell me what you did."

She shrugged. "I played music and designed and sewed clothes for babies with my mother." She smiled up at him. "It doesn't seem a very exciting life, does it?"

He squeezed her hand. "And mine is? I tramp about in the mud half the day with my sword, and spend the other half brawling with my brothers."

She laughed softly. "Point taken. Then, since we both have lives of simplicity, let's trade likes and dislikes."

"Agreed. You begin."

"All right," she agreed. "I love children, but I don't like snakes. I love firelight on a cold evening, but not the intense heat of summer. I love the shore, but I'm not very fond of a hall filled with too many people."

"Aye, well, I can agree with the last," he said with a smile. He considered her list for a moment, then cleared his throat. "Is there anything else you love?" he asked casually.

She looked up at him. Then she put her free hand around the back of his head and pulled him down where she could kiss him.

"Hmmm," she murmured against his mouth.

He supposed that was all the answer he deserved.

"Your turn," she said, leaning her head back against the wall and smiling at him. "Likes and dislikes."

"I love the rain, but hate soggy lists," he said. "I like a sharp sword, hot porridge, beautiful music, but not roofs that leak, boats that leak, and boots that leak."

"I can understand that. And?"

"I love sitting here with you, dancing with you, knowing that 'tis only just after noon and my day with you might potentially stretch far into the evening, but not anything that pulls me away from such a day."

"I couldn't agree more," she said softly. She rested her head against his shoulder. "Please let this day never end."

Nicholas sighed deeply, then leaned his head back against the wall and closed his eyes.

Aye, he wished the same.

Fortunately for his heart, the day lasted as long and was passed as happily with Jennifer as he could have wished.

Save the fact that he feared that it might be the last he would enjoy.

He didn't think on that often. Instead, he played for her. He read to her and the other women in his family as he sat on the floor next to her chair. Periodically he looked up at her, and each time he found that she watched him with a small, intimate smile, as if she loved him.

He wound yarn that didn't need to be

wound. He combed Jennifer's hair despite vociferous protests from his grandmother. He braided it for her not because he especially liked it that way but because it allowed her to sit in front of him, captured conveniently between his feet, and it meant he could touch her for a few more moments.

At one point, he leaned forward with his arms around her shoulders and rested his cheek against her hair. He held her as she talked with his mother, his grandmother, his sister, and his sister-in-law. Kendrick eventually wandered into the solar and found Jennifer to his liking, for he put his two-year-old self into her lap and fell asleep.

Nicholas supposed it was unkind to loathe a small boy, but he couldn't help himself.

He straightened finally, only because his back would have broken otherwise. He unbraided Jennifer's hair and simply ran his fingers through it, marveling at the deep fire of it and the fact that it curled around his fingers of its own accord. He leaned over.

"I'm jealous of Kendrick," he whispered into her ear. "Why don't you push him onto the floor and let me take his place?"

"That's awful," she whispered in return.

"Can you blame me?"

She reached up and stroked his cheek, then put her hand over his. "No, I can't."

"If I pinch him, will he wake up and move?"

She laughed and simply held his hands

crossed over her. "I'm sure you don't mean that."

"I'm sure I do," he grumbled, but he refrained.

In time, though, he had to sit back in his chair, Kendrick woke and wanted his mother, and Joanna noted that the afternoon had waned.

Nicholas looked with alarm at the shadows forming in the chamber. He looked at his mother. "Is there any hope of hiding in father's solar?"

"Impossible," Joanna said.

"Grandmère," Nicholas said evenly, "when is it you will invite your ladies to depart? You know I've no interest in any of them."

"The only thing that will save you is a plighting of your troth to someone," Joanna said.

Nicholas cursed silently. He couldn't. He couldn't ask Jennifer to wed with him until she knew the truth and he wasn't ready to tell her the truth.

"I brought women with the stamina to eat through your father's entire larder. They won't leave until there is a reason to and a mere *nay* from you will not do it."

"I think I feel a fever coming on," Nicholas said. He wasn't opposed to lying at this point. He was at his wits' end.

"Rubbish," Joanna snapped.

"Is there dancing?" he asked wearily.

"A play," Joanna said. "You may thank me later for providing such fine entertainment."

His next-to-last night with Jennifer, taken up with foolishness he couldn't have cared about, with women he never wanted to see again. He picked Jennifer up off the stool in front of him and pulled her into his lap. He wrapped his arms around her.

"I can't bear the thought of it," he whispered into her ear. "I just can't."

"I know," she murmured. She sighed, then got to her feet and held out her hands for him. She pulled him up, then curtseyed to him.

"Until tonight, my lord," she said with a grave smile.

Nicholas watched her leave with Joanna, Anne, and Isabelle. He sat down with a gusty sigh, then looked at his mother to find her watching him.

"Aye?" he asked with a weary smile.

"Why don't you propose marriage to her?" Gwen asked gently.

He sighed deeply. "Because she is of Jake's ilk, Mother."

"I know."

Nicholas blinked. "Did Father tell you?"

"No one told me, love," Gwen said. "I just knew."

Nicholas looked at his mother with a new respect. He'd known, of course, that she was quite possibly one of the most perfect women ever created. She had, after all, given birth to Amanda and Isabelle and managed to endure five sons as well. All his chivalry, all his love for beauty, all his delight in fine things had come from her. But that she not only believed Jake but could recognize someone from his particular world, well —

"I've been at Raventhorpe quite often this past year," she continued with a smile. "And I had no reason to dislike Jake, nor disbelieve him."

Nicholas smiled. "You could have told me I was being a fool about him, you know."

"I assumed you would come to that realization on your own," she said with a deep smile. "Perhaps I was too gentle."

"Perhaps you were."

"Interesting, isn't it, that you should love someone from his time."

"Interesting doesn't begin to describe it," Nicholas said dryly.

"I would like to hear her entire tale at some point," Gwen said. "Though she has no title, she carries herself like a noblewoman. Perhaps in her time titles are done away with and a woman is judged on her merits alone." She paused. "It must be wonderful."

"I fear it is," Nicholas said. "I fear many things, actually." He paused and looked at her gravely. "She thinks she cannot return home." He took a deep breath. "She doesn't know about Jake's gate, or that I know about

Jake's gate, or that I know where she comes from."

"Oh, Nicholas," Gwen said, looking grieved. "My love, why haven't you told her?"

"I didn't want her to leave." He paused. "I fear that when she learns she can go home, she *will* go home."

His mother said nothing. In time, he finally gathered the courage to face what he was quite certain would be a look of disappointment on her face. Instead, she merely regarded him fondly.

"You know that she loves you dearly, don't you?" she asked.

"At first, I hoped that would be enough. Now . . ." He took a deep breath. "Now, I don't know. I'm competing against the bloody Future, Mother." And it wasn't just the Future, it was her family as well. That thought was awful enough that he couldn't even give voice to it.

Gwen smiled, rose, and walked over to lift his face up. She kissed his forehead.

"What can the Future have that could possibly be more desirable than the love of a wonderful man? I think you underestimate yourself and your lady both."

Nicholas only sighed. "Perhaps."

She released him. "Come downstairs. Even if you cannot touch her, you will know she is there. Perhaps that will be enough."

Nicholas nodded. "I'll follow."

One last night.

It wouldn't be enough. He supposed if he had an eternity full of nights and days it wouldn't be enough.

He dragged his hand through his hair, then rose with a sigh. One last night then he would tell her the tidings he'd been dreading.

He could hardly bear the thought of it.

Chapter 31

Jennifer sat on the front steps of the hall and looked out over the courtyard. It probably wasn't ladylike, but today she didn't care. The last of the fortnight had been yesterday.

She had to tell him that day.

The day before had been a complete waste. She'd spent her entire day passing Nicholas while he was at the beck and call of his father, his mother, and his grandmother. She had watched him from afar. He'd waved. She'd waved back.

It had sucked.

Today, though, she would talk to him if it meant dragging him to the stables or seeking sanctuary in the chapel. One way or another, she had to get it over with. She had to tell him the truth. Then she would tell him she loved him.

And hope he loved her in return.

Miles sat beside her. Montgomery and John sat in front of her. In fact, it felt so much like the day when Nicholas had gone to Raventhorpe that she had to look at her clothes to put herself in the right time. She was wearing another of the simpler gowns Nicholas had had made for her. It fit perfectly and was long enough and for that alone she was grateful.

The door behind them opened.

"Move off the stairs, if you please," said an imperious voice. "We're off for another hunt and you're in our way."

She rose and hurried down the stairs with Montgomery, John, and Miles. Miles tucked her hand under his arm and put his hand over hers as many very finely dressed noblemen and women tromped down the stairs and headed for the stables.

Brigit of Islington looked at her and smirked.

Jennifer wondered what in the world that was supposed to mean, but she found that she simply didn't care. She looked back at the other woman impassively and waited until the entire company had passed before she let out the breath she then realized she'd been holding.

"The saints be praised," Miles muttered. "I could not see the last of them too soon. Perhaps they will leave today."

"We could hope," Jennifer said quietly. "Is every lord's daughter so horrible?"

"I wouldn't say all," Miles said thoughtfully. "Some are simply stupid, others vain, still others shrewd and calculating. But a woman who is open and artless? Nay, you are the only woman, outside of my family, who I know to be that." He looked down at her seriously. "You truly do love him, don't you?"

"Yes," she said softly. "I do."

"Damn it," he grumbled.

Suddenly the front door was jerked open and Nicholas came bursting out of the hall. He tossed a blanket at John, saddlebags at Montgomery, and two bottles at Miles.

"Run," he said, taking Jennifer by the hand and pulling her along with him.

"Run?" she asked, holding up her skirts and fleeing with him. "Why?"

"The company has gone hunting and my grandmother is sleeping. We must away if we want any peace today."

She didn't have to hear that twice. She fled with him out the gates and toward the ocean.

By the time they reached the beach, she was winded and unsure if she should laugh or cry. John spread out the blanket, Montgomery dumped his bags on the ground, and Miles carefully set the bottles down. Jennifer fell to her knees, gasping for breath. She looked at Nicholas, who had cast himself down as well and laughed in spite of herself.

"I hope this was worth the stitch in my side," she wheezed.

Nicholas unbuckled his sword belt and laid his weapons aside. He sat up with his arms resting on his bent knees and looked at her with a smile. "Consider it all again in half an hour," he said. "Just think on it. An entire day with nothing but the sight of the strand and the sound of the ocean."

"What about the company back at the keep?"

"I couldn't care less," Nicholas said. "I am finished with humoring my grandmother. I have wasted a se'nnight I could have spent with you by humoring her. I am finished," he said, his words clipped. "Finished."

"I understand," she said with a nod. And she did. Unfortunately, that didn't mean she could put off what she had to do that day.

It only took a few minutes before she'd caught her breath. Well, it was now or never. She turned her back on the lads, took off her shoes, and rolled down her stockings. She looked back at Nicholas.

"I'm going for a walk."

"Do you care for company?"

She smiled, but it felt a little sad. "Yes, if it's yours."

He stood, put on his sword belt, stuck his knife in his boot, then pulled her to her feet.

He didn't kiss her.

Jennifer tried not to read anything into it. She held his hand and walked down to the water's edge.

"North or south?" he asked.

"Either. Both. I don't care."

He put his free hand on her shoulder and turned her toward him. He put his arms around her and held her to him for what felt a little like eternity. She rested her head against his chest, her ear pressed over his heart. It beat steadily, as if nothing would disturb it. Jennifer held on tightly, not regretting for a moment having given him her heart.

"Jen."

She pulled back and looked up at him. "Aye, my lord?"

He smoothed his hand over her hair, then looked into her eyes. "I love you," he said quietly.

She closed her eyes briefly. They burned. When she opened them, tears spilled down her cheeks. "I love you, too," she whispered.

He bent his head and kissed her. It was a simple kiss, quite different than any of his other kisses. His self-control was firmly in check. When he lifted his head, she smiled at him.

"No ravishing today?" she asked with half a smile.

He sighed. "There is aught I must tell you. I will ravish you later, if you'll still allow it."

She hugged him tightly. "I didn't want this fortnight," she said into his shirt. "I wanted to tell you all two weeks ago. Now," she said, pulling back to look at him with tears streaming down her cheeks, "I don't want to talk at all."

"Then let us walk," he said, putting his arm around her and drawing her arm around his waist. "Let us walk."

Jennifer didn't see much. It was hard when all she could do was cry.

"I'm not a weeper," she said, her words coming out in a half sob.

"I know," he said, reaching over to dab her eyes with a cloth he produced from some part of his person.

"Did you bring that for me?" she asked.

"Nay, for myself."

She managed a laugh through her tears. "You didn't."

"Nay," he said softly, "I didn't."

They walked for a very long time in silence. Finally Nicholas stopped. He took her hands and turned her toward him. "Well?" he asked softly. "Shall we have our speech together?"

She bowed her head. "We no doubt should." She looked up at him. "Are you going to tell me you're secretly wed?"

He smiled sadly. "You know I'm not. But what of you? Are you secretly wed?"

"I only have one heart to give," she said, blinking hard. "And it's yours."

He pulled her off her feet and into his arms. He held her so tightly, she almost couldn't breathe. She wrapped her arms around his neck and hugged him back as tightly as she could.

"I don't want to let you go," he said against her ear.

She shook her head. "I don't want you to."

He held her for another eternal moment, then let her slide slowly down to her feet. "Then come and let us be about it. You have aught to tell me and I have aught to tell you. Shall we walk or do you prefer to find somewhere to sit?"

"Where would we go?" she asked, looking back down the beach. "The boys are down there — wait." She frowned. "Is that Robin?"

"Bloody hell," Nicholas cursed. "Have we not enough to endure without more of my family hounding us?"

"Nicholas, now Montgomery's running this way." She looked up at him, feeling a sudden panic. "Maybe something's wrong. Let's go find out."

He nodded, then took her hand and ran with her down the beach. They met Montgomery, who looked wide-eyed and astonished.

"Jenner," he said, hunching over with his hands on his knees, "you won't believe it."

"What?" she asked, willing to believe just about anything.

After all, it had been that kind of year so far.

He heaved himself upright. "Your kin are here."

She staggered as if he'd struck her. *What?*

516

"Robin says so. Your sister and her husband." He looked at Nicholas. "I wonder how they found her?"

"Montgomery, you can't mean it," Jennifer said, clutching Nicholas's hand. "Robin has to be mistaken."

"He isn't. He said the man was a Scot. MacDougal was his name, I think. Is that right?"

Jennifer could hardly believe her ears. She thought she might start to hyperventilate soon. She clutched Nicholas's hand and started to run back toward the castle. She stumbled in the sand and Nicholas pulled her upright. She looked up at him and felt a laugh burst from her in spite of her tears.

"My sister," she said in amazement.

She pulled him forward again, then realized that he looked a little green. She stopped.

"Nicholas?"

" 'Tis nothing," he croaked. "I'm overjoyed for you."

"I can't believe it," she said, still stunned beyond measure. "Can we hurry?"

"Of course," he said. "Let us make haste. But you're missing your shoes. I'll fetch them and catch up with you."

She nodded, but found she couldn't move. She stood there, staring at Artane, trying to put it in the right century. Vic and Connor? It just wasn't possible.

Within minutes, Nicholas had come back

to her. He waited for her while she put her stockings and shoes back on, then hurried with her back toward the castle. It wasn't easy running while holding hands, but she didn't dare let go of him. She stumbled several times and each time he caught her before she went sprawling.

By the time they reached the barbican gate, she had to stop. She leaned against the wall and sucked in deep breaths. When she thought she could go on, she pulled Nicholas up the way with her. She couldn't run anymore, though. She wasn't all that sure she could walk.

But by the time she made it to the great hall, the butterflies in her stomach were fluttering so violently, she thought she might be sick. Nicholas opened the door for her and she walked inside. Once her eyes adjusted to the gloom, she realized that the hall was not empty. Rhys was standing next to one of his fireplaces, talking with a man and a woman dressed in medieval Scottish garb.

Connor MacDougal and her sister Victoria.

"Vic!" Jennifer cried out. She sprinted across the hall and threw herself into her sister's arms. She pulled back. "I can't believe it's you! How did you get here? *When* did you get here?"

Vic looked at her with a frown. "What?"

Jennifer realized then that she was speaking in French. She threw her arms around her sister again and spoke in her ear in English. It felt very strange on her tongue.

"How did you get here?"

"How do you think?"

Jennifer pulled back, looked at her sister again, then burst into tears.

Victoria put her arms around her and held on. "I thought I'd never see you again, you nitwit. What in the world were you thinking?"

"I *wasn't* thinking," she managed. "It just happened."

"I'll say."

Jennifer cried until she couldn't breathe anymore. Then she pulled away and used Nicholas's handkerchief to dry her face off and blow her nose.

She froze.

Nicholas.

She turned around to find him. He was standing near his father, watching the whole scene with a grave expression. She smiled, then turned back to her sister.

"I want you to meet someone."

"Someone?" Victoria echoed.

"Shut up and be nice," Jennifer warned.

"I'm always nice."

Jennifer pulled Victoria over and took Nicholas by the hand. "Nicholas, this is my sister," she said in Gaelic, "Victoria McKinnon Mac-Dougal. That's her husband, Connor, laird of the clan MacDougal. Vic, this is Nicholas de Piaget."

Nicholas took Victoria's hand and bent low over it. "You look very much alike."

"We might look alike," Victoria agreed with a smile, "but I promise that Jenner's nicer."

"She is very kind," he agreed.

Jennifer felt him squeeze her hand before he released it to extend his hand to Connor.

"My laird," Nicholas said formally. "Welcome to Artane."

Connor took his proffered hand. "My lord," he said, just as formally. "Thank you for the welcome."

Then he looked at Jennifer and jerked her over and into his arms. He slapped her back a time or two, kissed her on both cheeks, then deposited her back where he'd taken her from.

It was very awkward and very, very Connor. Jennifer had to laugh. The only woman Connor seemed able to handle gently was her sister.

"We worried," was all he said.

"Laird MacDougal," Rhys said in Gaelic, inclining his head, "perhaps you and your lady would care to take your ease in my solar."

"How fortunate that you speak my tongue," Connor said, sounding pleased. "And that is an impressive sword you have there, my lord."

Rhys grinned. "We'll examine the possibilities of both later. First, though, I'll have your gear brought in from off your horses. We're overrun at present by guests of my wife's mother, but my solar is quite comfortable and we will see you installed there immediately." He looked down. "Lady Victoria, might I carry that large sack for you?"

Victoria shook her head. "Thank you, my lord, but it is for Jennifer. She may prefer to carry it herself."

Jennifer looked at what Victoria was picking up. She found a large rectangular rucksack thrust into her arms. The moment she put her arms around it, she knew what it was.

She looked at her sister in astonishment. "My violin," she whispered.

Victoria raised one eyebrow, then walked off with Connor and Rhys.

Jennifer watched her go. She couldn't believe she was watching her sister walk through medieval Artane with her medieval husband who was now a brilliant Shakespearean actor, along with she herself, in New York. She couldn't believe that in her arms was her $60,000 Degani.

She paused.

Just what in the hell was Victoria thinking, to bring a violin that rare hundreds of years back in time?

She stood there in the hall for quite some time, trying to digest it all, then she remembered. She turned. Nicholas was standing in the same place, looking very, very lost and more serious than she had ever seen him. She attempted a smile.

She failed.

"That was my sister," she whispered. "And her husband."

"I know."

"They came to find me."

He nodded gravely.

"Do you want to come visit with them?" she asked hesitantly.

"If you would like me to."

"Of course I would," she said.

She wrapped one arm around her violin, then held out her hand for his. She started across the great hall, but it felt as if she were floating.

She was in medieval England; she knew that. But holding on to something from the future while holding on to Nicholas at the same time was about to tear her in two. She clutched his hand.

"Can you help me?" she whispered. "Suddenly I don't feel very well."

He swung her up into his arms. She started to cry again and this time she couldn't stop. By the time they reached Rhys's door, she knew she was in the process of losing it. She couldn't see anymore for the tears and she couldn't breathe. She reached up and touched Nicholas's face.

"I can't go in," she wept. "I need to go somewhere private. Somewhere empty. Please."

He tightened his arms around her and started to walk again. Jennifer had no idea where he was taking her. Maybe he thought she'd completely lost it and he was going to dump her and the Degani both into the dungeon. It might have been a good place for them.

He climbed stairs. That had to have been a delicate maneuver, what with her and the violin both in his arms. She lost count of the twists and turns. Finally, Nicholas walked into a very chilly chamber. He set her down carefully. Jennifer realized it was the tower chamber where she'd had her lessons in swordplay. She knew it wasn't much past early afternoon, but the sky had suddenly become full of clouds, which made the room very gloomy.

"Wait," he said quietly.

It wasn't very long before he returned with two torches. He set them into sconces, then stopped. He looked at her gravely.

"What else can I do?"

"Can you tell them I need a bit of time?"

He nodded.

She took a deep breath. That was a little calming, but not much. "Come back," she said. "Please."

He nodded, his expression bleak. "I will."

She watched him go, shutting the door behind him, then stood in the middle of a medieval tower room and tried to find a way

523

to ground herself in reality.

It was altogether impossible.

She took the long bench that the de Piaget men had sat on to watch her train and pulled it into the middle of the room. Then she found two stools and set them nearby. She opened the drawcords of the sack and pulled out her violin case. She set it down on the bench and opened it.

She couldn't bring herself to touch it.

She had never thought to see it again, yet there it was. She had never thought to see her family again, yet her sister and brother-in-law were sitting downstairs in Rhys de Piaget's solar. She'd never thought to ever have a chance to go home again, yet now she knew there existed a gate that worked. Jamie would never have let Connor and Vic come through something that he hadn't been convinced would bring them back home again.

That meant she could go with them.

But to do so, she would have to leave Nicholas in the past.

She buried her face in her hands and wept.

CHAPTER 32

Nicholas walked on shaking legs down the stairs and along passageways until he reached his father's solar. He wasn't one to give in to feebleness, but he supposed when one was dealing with extraordinary circumstances, a little weakness in the legs might be permitted.

Jennifer's sister and brother-in-law had come for her.

She would leave.

He shoved the thought away. He would face that possibility when he had to. First, he would deliver his message, then return to her and see if he could offer her aid.

He found all his brothers standing in a little cluster outside the solar door. He sent Montgomery and John scurrying off with a glare. Miles and Robin were not so easily dislodged.

"Her sister and that sister's husband," Robin said, his eyebrows going up in an annoying fashion. "Interesting."

"Oh, aye," Nicholas said grimly. " 'Tis fascinating."

"He looked to be Scottish."

"He is. Laird of the clan MacDougal," Nicholas said shortly. "I'm certain Father would let you in to offer your greetings if you could stop gaping like a slack-jawed idiot long enough to do it."

Robin looked at him narrowly. "Your distress speaks."

"Does it?" Nicholas snapped. "I hadn't noticed."

Robin exchanged a look with Miles, then turned back to Nicholas. "Why are you here?"

"Jennifer is unwell," Nicholas said shortly. "I took her upstairs. I'm here to deliver those tidings, then return upstairs to see to her. Alone," he added pointedly.

Robin put his hand on Nicholas's shoulder. "I am desperate to go inside and visit but I will find Grandmère and keep her occupied for the next hour or two. *That* is how much I love you."

Nicholas bent his head briefly, then looked at his brother. "My thanks, Rob," he said quietly. " 'Tis more than I deserve."

"Aye, that's why I'll enjoy it so much," Robin said, giving his shoulder a bracing pat or two. "I come out, yet again, smelling like a rose."

He walked off, humming. Nicholas looked at Miles, who regarded him steadily.

"And you?" Nicholas asked. "What do you want?"

"To be of service to you and your lady," Miles said simply. "What might I do?"

Nicholas shook his head slowly. "Truly, I am fortunate to have brothers such as you."

"Your suffering has made you maudlin," Miles said with a small smile, "but I will accept the compliment just the same. Where did you take Jenner?"

Nicholas flinched. Victoria had called her the same thing. If he hadn't believed her before, that name would have convinced him. Unfortunately, he'd believed what she had told him without any aid and he was damned for it.

"To the northeast tower chamber. Where we've been training." He looked at Miles seriously. "Guard the steps, but I beg you not to go up." He paused. "She is not herself."

"My solemn vow," Miles said, putting his hand over his heart. He clapped Nicholas on the shoulder as well as he walked past him and disappeared down the passageway.

Nicholas faced the door, took a deep breath and gathered his thoughts, then entered. His father, Victoria, and Laird MacDougal were sitting comfortably in front of the hearth, chatting as if they'd known each other for years. Of course his father had no reason not to like them. They weren't coming to take away his love.

527

And perhaps they hadn't come to take Jennifer away.

Though he couldn't imagine any other reason.

He smiled as best he could and made Jennifer's kin a low bow. "There is no cause for alarm," he began in Gaelic, trying to sound reassuring, "but Jennifer I think is overcome with joy at seeing you. She was unwell and asked that I take her upstairs. I think a moment or two alone will restore her to her normal self."

He watched Connor assess him, rapidly and without mercy. The man then folded his hands together and rested his chin on his steepled fingers, but said nothing.

Victoria turned to look at him. "She's not feeling well?"

"Nay, my lady."

Victoria frowned. "Are you returning to check on her?"

"Aye."

"She asked specifically to be left alone?"

"Aye."

"And for you to return?"

"Aye."

"Well," she said, apparently softening a bit, "if you don't mind taking care of her, I would be grateful for it."

"It would be my honor."

Victoria rose and came to look up at him. Nicholas had no trouble seeing the familial resemblance. Victoria was very beautiful as well, but she never would have been for him. Jennifer had a sweetness to her that he could see was hers alone, a sweetness much like a song that wouldn't leave his mind but continued to captivate him long after the playing of it had ceased.

"You took care of her."

Nicholas pulled himself back to the matter at hand. "From the beginning," he said.

Victoria took his hand and held it for a moment. "Thank you," she said quietly. "That eases my mind."

Nicholas wished desperately that his mind could have been eased so quickly and with such little fanfare. He bowed over Victoria's hand, then took his leave. Before he shut the door, he looked at his father briefly.

His father's expression was very grave.

He supposed his might have been as well.

He turned and walked back down the passageway, up the stairs, and wound through other passageways until he ran bodily into his brother.

"Sorry," Nicholas said. "I forgot I asked you to come."

Miles smiled briefly. "Not to worry."

"Is she weeping?"

"She was at first. She isn't now."

Nicholas pushed Miles out of his way and sprinted up the steps. He came to a teetering halt in the doorway. He was quite sure he would never forget the sight that greeted his eyes.

Jennifer was sitting on a stool. Laid out on the bench was some sort of viol, by the look of it, in a box the likes of which he had never before seen in his life. She was staring into space as if she no longer lived. Indeed, she was so still, he wondered if that were the case.

"Jennifer," he said, stepping into the chamber.

She turned her head and focused on him with an effort. "Nicholas," she whispered. "Shut the door, will you?"

He shut it.

"Bolt it."

He did so.

She rose unsteadily to her feet. "Now, come hold me."

He wasn't about to refuse. He strode over to her and gathered her carefully into his arms. In truth, he was afraid she might break.

She started to weep.

It was a terrible thing to listen to.

She wept until he thought his heart would break right along with hers. She clung to him as sobs racked her body. He was quite certain he had never heard such sorrow. Ever.

He knew he never wanted to hear it again.

He let her weep. And when the waves of grief that washed over her seemed to lessen, he started to attempt what poor means he had of comforting weeping women. He rarely had the need to use them, but he wasn't a dullard, either. He rubbed her back. Then he stroked her hair. When the time came that she was merely clinging to him, he began to occasionally kiss her hair and murmur soothing words.

It was a very, very long time that he stood there with her. Indeed, he saw that the afternoon had faded and the sky was losing the light of day. He didn't let go, though, because she hung on to him as if he were the only thing that stood between her and an abyss of grief.

He couldn't imagine it.

Finally, she was simply standing in his arms, breathing raggedly. He would have thought she slept, but for the way she periodically wiped her face with his cloth. Finally, she took a deep breath and let out a shuddering sigh.

"Thank you," she whispered.

"Of course," he said quietly. "Of course."

She didn't move. "Nicholas?"

"Aye?"

"I love you."

He closed his eyes. Damnation, was he going to weep now as well? "I love you, too," he said hoarsely.

She shivered and sighed again. "I think I need to sit."

He released her and helped her sit upon one of the stools. He drew the other one close to her, then sat and looked at her.

She looked dreadful. Her eyes were bloodshot, her nose was red, her face was blotched.

He loved her to distraction just the same.

"That bad?" she asked with a grave smile.

He couldn't lie.

Not anymore.

"Aye," he said honestly. "But it matters not."

She looked down at her hands. "Seeing Victoria was a shock."

He imagined it was.

"I thought I would never see her again," she added.

"What a fortunate, joyful reunion, then," he said. There, that hadn't come out as garbled as he'd feared.

She nodded, but she didn't look up.

He could only imagine what she was thinking, what she was planning to say. He didn't want to hear it. He wanted to blurt out that he didn't give a damn what century she was born in or if her bloody sister had come to fetch her. He loved her and he wanted her to stay with him and be his wife.

No matter the cost.

"Nicholas?"

He wrenched his gaze to hers. "Aye?"

"You were swearing."

He blew out his breath. "I'm going daft. Robin mutters under his breath as well. That I should be taking on his characteristics is a very unwholesome turn of events."

She smiled faintly. "Yes, it is." She sobered. "We need to talk."

He sighed. "Aye, I suppose we must." He paused. "You first?"

She got to her feet and walked around the chamber, then came and sat back down. "I'm not sure how to begin," she said uneasily. "You won't believe any of it."

You would be surprised.

But he didn't say as much.

"Is it the truth?" he asked, because he could think of nothing else to say. What was he to say? *Jenner, my love, I already know it all because I was a bastard and didn't tell you what I knew from the beginning.*

He supposed that would not start things off very well.

"It is the truth," she said seriously.

"Then begin at the beginning," he said. "Or, begin with that bit of business there." He nodded toward the viol. "I've never seen its like before. What is it?"

"A 1908 Degani violin." She looked at him seriously. "1908."

"1908," he repeated. "Those numbers are unfamiliar to me. What do they mean?"

"It was the year the violin was made. The Year of Our Lord one thousand nine hundred and eight. It was made in Venice by a man named Degani."

He'd understood, of course, and expected

something of that sort, but still, hearing the numbers come from her lips was unwholesomely unsettling. He had to take a deep breath.

"Venice," he said, grasping desperately for something familiar. "I love Venice."

"Have you been to Venice?" she asked in astonishment.

"Of course," he said. "Rob and I traveled there before he was wed. There are parts of the city that are quite new but still very lovely."

"New," she whispered. "Yes, I suppose so."

He met her eyes. "But that year you mentioned. How is it possible that you have something from that unfathomable date?"

"It is possible because I was born after that date. In the Year of Our Lord's Grace 1978."

He wasn't surprised, but again, the numbers were a hard, unyielding reality.

"Is that so," he rasped.

"Yes, it is so," she said quietly. "My father's mother died and left me enough money to buy the violin. It was almost ninety years old when I bought it."

"1978," he managed. He met her eyes. "Seven hundred and fifty years from now."

"Yes."

He took a very large breath. "I see."

"There is more." She paused. "Do you believe me?"

"I have no reason not to," he said. "Go on."

She took a deep breath herself. "I had come to England to visit my sister Megan. She is married to Gideon, the second son of the current Earl of Artane, Edward."

"Your sister is wed to a de Piaget lad?" Nicholas wheezed.

"Yes and I had come here to see her."

"Here at Artane."

"Yes. I was out wandering the countryside, stepped into Ledenham's abbey, and *voilà,* I was in 1229 and you were rescuing me."

Well, it was a little startling to think that her sister was wed to what had to have been one of his nephews, dozens of generations removed, but he supposed he could accept the truth of that in time. He managed a nod. "I see."

She frowned at him. "You're being very calm about all this."

"I have a strong stomach."

"Well, then here's some more. Apparently, and according to my, um, grandfather James MacLeod, who knows about these sorts of things, there are gates all over England and Scotland where you can go from one century to the next. And back again," she added, "though that didn't work for me. That's what I tried to do when I went back to the abbey, and when I went north of Seakirk, and at the rocks near Artane." She paused. "None of those gates through time worked."

She fell silent. Nicholas clasped his hands

together and thought furiously. Unfortunately, all his thoughts went in circles and landed in precisely the same spot. It was the same spot he'd been avoiding for a solid fortnight, since the very moment he'd begun to hope that if she fell in love with him, she wouldn't want to leave.

He'd known that when she discovered what he knew, she would be angry. But now, hearing the anguish in her voice, he suspected she would be feeling something quite a bit stronger than anger.

She would never forgive him.

"But now Vic and Connor are here," she said softly, "I know I can return home."

Nicholas couldn't look at her. He was afraid if he looked at her, he would weep. He sat there for far longer than he should have, but it was simply beyond him to speak. Finally, he gestured toward the violin.

"Will you play for me?" he asked.

"What?"

He looked up at her then. "Will you play for me?"

She looked completely taken aback. "Is that it? Aren't you going to say anything else?"

"Play for me first," he said quietly. "I beg you."

He wanted to hear her play. Not only that, it would give him time to get his feet back underneath him — though he didn't hold out much hope for that anytime soon.

He watched her slender fingers as she picked up a long stick. There were strands of something down one side. He frowned. He would have sworn it was horse hair, but what did he know of Future gear?

"It's called a bow," she said softly.

"Why?"

"I haven't the foggiest idea right now," she said shakily. "I'll think about it later."

Later. If there was a later.

She rubbed something on the bow, then picked up the violin itself. She ran the bow over the strings and tuned them. That much he knew from his own playing of something with strings.

But then her skill with playing and his took a radical parting of the ways.

He listened to a jaw-dropping number of notes and sounds that seemed to fly from her fingers like magic. He gaped at her, more astonished than he ever had been in his life — and he was by no means unlearned or innocent. He had traveled far and wide and seen a great many things. But he had never seen or heard anything like this before.

She stood up, plucked at her strings absently, tried a few melodies before she stopped. She took the violin and tucked it under her arm and bowed her head. He wondered if she was finished, then he watched her put the violin under her chin again, lift her bow and begin.

It was, he realized with sickening clarity, the beginning of the end for him.

The song was simple, but it held a beauty that left him completely overcome. The notes continued to sweep along, like a stream that had captured him and had no intention of letting him go. The music drew him in, wrapped him in an intimate embrace, warmed him and soothed him. He wanted it never to end.

And when it did, he bowed his head.

He knew what he had to do.

It was what he had feared from the beginning, what he had ignored for weeks, what he had dreaded from the moment he'd clapped eyes on her. Her song had convinced him he had no choice.

He would have to let her go.

CHAPTER 33

Jennifer finished the Schubert, then put her violin under her arm. She could hardly believe she had her instrument in her hands again. The pleasure that playing had brought her was almost more than she could stand. After weeks without modern music, the sound of Schubert's notes coming from under her fingers was something she thought might take a very long time to get over.

She realized, with a start, that it was the same piece she'd played for Lord Edward that night she'd been at Artane. Well, perhaps *played* was being generous. It was the same piece she hadn't been able to get through.

Was this why?

She looked at Nicholas. He was sitting on his stool with his hands clasped, his forearms resting on his knees, his head bowed.

She walked over to him. "Nicholas?"

She saw the tears glistening as they fell onto the floor.

She put her violin in the case and the case

onto the floor. She put her bow on the bench, then sat down and put her hands over his.

"Nicholas?" she whispered.

He lifted his head. His eyes were red and tears were streaming down his cheeks.

"I've never heard anything so exquisite in all my life," he said hoarsely. "You play . . . you play so beautifully."

"Thank you," she said reflexively. She attempted a smile. "Thank you."

He lifted her hands and kissed them. Then he put them back in her lap and rose.

"I must tell you the real reason why I went to see Amanda."

Jennifer blinked at the non sequitur. Then, as she realized what he'd said, she gasped, unable to catch her breath. She couldn't catch her breath because the wind had just been knocked out of her. All right, so she had no reason to be jealous of Nicholas's sister, but there was something about knowing that the man she loved had once loved someone else. Now that he was going to tell her why he had gone to visit that someone, it was just a little breath stealing.

"Go on," she said, but there was no sound to her words. Just a little squeak.

A pitiful little squeak.

Nicholas walked to the window, then turned and walked back to his stool. He sat down slowly. "I actually went to see her husband."

"Oh," Jennifer said, feeling suddenly quite

a bit better. "Her husband?"

"Jackson Alexander Kilchurn IV."

"He sounds like nobility," she said, attempting a smile. "Or someone in line for the throne."

"He is neither, though the sentiment would flatter him." He paused for several minutes. "There is another of those gates you speak of."

Jennifer opened her mouth to ask what he meant, but then the import of his words sunk in. "Another gate? Another time gate?"

"Near Artane," Nicholas said. He took a deep breath and then let it out slowly. "It goes to the Future."

"And how in the world would you know that?" she asked incredulously.

"Amanda's husband used it to get back and forth from here to his home in 2005. More than once, if the truth is to be told."

"Amanda's husband?" Jennifer asked incredulously. "The one you went to . . . oh," she said. "The one you went to see."

Nicholas nodded.

"Did you go to see him . . . about . . ."

He nodded.

"You went to see him to find out about a *time gate?*"

He bowed his head. "Aye."

She had to wait a moment to catch her breath. "You knew? About me?"

He lifted his head and looked at her. "From

the moment I saw you."

She almost fell off her stool. "You *knew?*"

"I told you I had something to tell you."

She had to get up and pace. There was a part of her that was afraid that she would keep saying those two words indefinitely, or at least until she could wrap her mind around the reality of them. She stopped and looked at him.

"You knew. About me."

"Aye."

"You knew about me from the *start?*"

He nodded grimly.

"Does this other gate work? The one your brother-in-law used?"

He closed his eyes briefly. "Aye."

"Let me understand this," she said, feeling herself start to shake. "You knew I was from the future the moment you met me, you watched me try to get back there three separate times, you knew where a working gate to the future found itself, yet you didn't tell me."

He winced. "Aye."

She could hardly catch her breath. When she did, she could hardly use it to breathe out words. "You lied to me?" she whispered.

He jumped to his feet suddenly. "I didn't want you to go," he said, glaring at her.

"You lied to me!" she exclaimed.

"Aye, I lied to you, damn you to hell," he shouted. "I lied to you and I would lie again

542

the same way, time and time again."

She recoiled. She wasn't sure what surprised her more: that he would purposely withhold the one fact that could have spared her all the agony she'd gone through for the past two months, or that he'd shouted at her.

"You lied to me," she whispered.

"Aye, I did," he snarled. "But it matters not *one whit* now, does it, because now that you have a way to return home, you'll leave with your sister and her husband and go your merry way without a backward glance."

She blinked. "But —"

"I'll be *damned* if I'll watch you leave with them and vanish into nothingness."

She gaped at him.

"And if you think I'd ask you to stay after listening to that —" He pointed at her violin.

His hand was trembling.

"After listening to that," he said, taking a deep breath, "then you're mad as well as damned and I'll have no part of you."

And with that, he turned and strode out of the chamber.

He slammed the door shut behind him.

Jennifer stared after him, more stunned than she'd ever been in her life. She wanted to sit, but she couldn't. She wanted to pace, but she was frozen in place.

He'd known that another gate existed.

She paced around the room, then found herself looking down at her violin. It was tempting to just put her foot through it, run after Nicholas, and tell him that if that's what was going to keep him from asking her to marry him, then it was a nonissue.

Assuming he'd ever wanted to ask her to marry him.

She knelt down — actually she collapsed to her knees, but since no one was there to watch, she supposed she could call it what she liked — and mechanically started to put her violin away. She cleaned the rosin off the strings. She loosened the bow and tucked it back into its place in the lid. She secured her violin inside the case, then shut the whole thing up, put it back into the medieval bag Victoria had so thoughtfully provided, and set it all on the bench.

She had to set herself on the bench as well.

Amanda's husband was from the future?

She wondered who else knew that. How many members of Nicholas's family knew that Jackson Kilchurn — and she remembered Montgomery telling her that his name was Jake and thinking at the time that it was a very strange name for a medieval guy — was from the future?

Did they all know?

Did they know about her?

She thought suddenly of her jeans rolled up in Lord Rhys's study. Had he examined them? Did he know his son-in-law was more than he seemed?

And why had Nicholas traveled all the way to see Jake Kilchurn about the gate if he'd never intended to tell her?

She shook her head. He probably *had* intended to tell her — after their fortnight moratorium was up.

She looked out the window at the darkened sky and considered other things.

He'd had gowns made for her, he'd had a sword made for her, he'd wooed her for a fortnight. He had to have known she wanted to tell him where she was from, yet he'd begged her not to. She frowned. That was what didn't make sense. If he'd known she was from the future, why wouldn't he have wanted her to admit it? What in the world had he thought fourteen days of delay would accomplish?

Well, other than her falling in love with him. She froze.

Was that what he'd intended? Had he *wanted* her to fall in love with him? He had hoped that if she did and he told her the truth, she wouldn't *want* to go?

She rubbed her forehead. She had a headache from crying and that was making it incredibly difficult to remember what he'd said. All she knew was he had shouted at her, he had wept when she'd played, and he assumed now that Vic was there, she would go home.

Was it possible he didn't want her to go?

Was it possible she could stay in the past with him?

She closed her eyes briefly. If she did, that meant never seeing her family again, never seeing her nieces and nephews grow up, never again having ice in her drinks. No chocolate, no junk food, no indoor plumbing. No television, no iPod, no front-row seats at the New York Philharmonic.

She started to pace. No career as a soloist, no more Manhattan lifestyle, no more great roast beef sandwiches at DiMaggio's deli down the street from Victoria's apartment. No more Thanksgivings, or Christmases, or Easters at her parents' house. No more family reunions. She would never see Megan again, or her parents, or her grandmother.

She wondered, absently, if Vic had brought a camera. At least her parents would get to see what Nicholas looked like.

Then again, he looked a lot like Gideon, so maybe they didn't need a picture.

She paced for a very long time. In the end it came down to one simple choice: her family, or the chance for a family of her own with Nicholas.

When looked at in that light, the choice was no easier, but it was much clearer.

She picked up her violin, took a torch off the wall as easily as if she'd been doing it her whole life, then left the tower room. Miles was standing at the bottom of the stairs, looking up at her. She stopped in front of him and shoved her violin into his arms.

"Don't lose that."

"I won't."

She started to walk away, then turned and looked at him. "You knew, didn't you?"

"About what?" he hedged.

"About me."

He hesitated, then sighed. "Aye."

She wagged her finger at him. "You'd better be careful. You might find one dropping onto your front door someday."

"If only I could be so fortunate," he said quietly.

"Where did Nicholas go?"

"He thundered off down the passageway. He forbade me follow him, which I wouldn't have done anyway since my task was to guard you." He paused. "Are you going after him?"

"Of course."

Miles smiled. "I hoped so."

"Well, we'll see what he thinks," she said, then she turned around and walked away.

Yes, who knew what he would think indeed. She was almost afraid to find out.

CHAPTER 34

Nicholas strode through the crowded great hall, ignoring everyone who spoke to him. He didn't usually tremble and he never wept. That he had done both in the past several hours was surely a sign that things were gravely amiss in his life. All the more reason to put those things — or that one thing named Jennifer McKinnon — behind him as quickly as possible.

He would go back to Wyckham and help Petter. Stone masonry was a goodly work. He could spend a pair of years rebuilding his castle, then turn his mind back to the things he'd been considering when a certain red-haired angel had dropped into his life and turned it upside down: grumbling whilst going to fat in his chair before the fire, complaining about the rain, grousing about the fare.

Aye, a future to look forward to indeed.

He loped down the steps and walked swiftly across the courtyard to the stables. He considered, then decided he would saddle the Black. After all, his father had given him to him and it was past time the beast was taught a few manners. Nicholas took the saddle from his other mount's stall and slung it over the Black's door, just to let him know what was coming and that Nicholas had no intention of running away from the confrontation.

He paused.

It didn't set well with him that'd he done just that with Jennifer, but damnation, what else was he to do? Watch her disappear? Turn and wave at him before she —

"What are you doing?"

Nicholas put his hands on the saddle to steady them. "Why do you care?"

"I suspected you were on the verge of making a complete fool of yourself, so I came to rescue you. From yourself, apparently."

"Go away," Nicholas said flatly.

"Nick," Robin said sharply, "what are you doing?"

Nicholas looked at his brother. "I am leaving before I have to watch *her* leave."

"Brave of you."

"I don't want her to make a choice she'll regret," Nicholas growled. "I'm thinking of *her.*"

Robin snorted. "Of course you are. So kind, so thoughtful. Such a bloody great display of *chivalry* —"

Nicholas couldn't help himself. He punched his brother in the face. Why Robin wasn't expecting it, he didn't know.

It took quite some time before his fury was expended, but by then, he felt as if his horse had kicked him in the gut. He lay on the hay-strewn floor of the stable, staring up at the ceiling, and concentrated only on breathing. That was task enough for the present.

"Why do you think she'll go back?" Robin asked, hunched over on all fours next to him.

Nicholas sat up with a groan. "Because she is an angel, she plays an instrument made for an angel, and I won't be the one to take that away from her."

"You idiot," Robin said. "Why do you think it's your choice? Have you considered that she might *want* to stay?"

Nicholas looked at him grimly. "You didn't hear her."

"Actually, I did," Robin said. "I came to the bottom of the stairs to check on you and heard her up in the tower chamber. It was . . . well, I've no words for it. But music is fleeting, brother." He looked at Nicholas seriously. "Love lasts forever."

"And if I die?" Nicholas asked with a wince. "What do I leave her then?"

"Saints, Nick, you're richer than the bloody king. Fix your damned hall, or move to France. Buy her beautiful fabric, give her wonderful children, import musicians and artists until you're sick of tripping over them. If all you give her is a year of bliss, then she won't curse you. Chances are you'll live longer than Grandmère and by your end, she'll be longing for you to lay your moldy self down in your grave."

Nicholas considered, then shook his head. "I dare not."

Robin blew out his breath in frustration. "Then you deserve every moment of misery you'll experience during every day of what will no doubt be an unnaturally long life. I, for one, will refuse to listen to you complain. I will also refuse to brawl with you ever again." He heaved himself to his feet and looked down. "I don't know what's happened to you. The brother I grew to manhood with and loved more than my own sweet self never would have sat in the bloody hay and given up." He walked away.

"I haven't given up," Nicholas bellowed after him.

"Of course you have, you coward. Oh," Robin said. "Finally. Help has arrived. You deal with him."

"Why?"

Nicholas closed his eyes briefly. It was Amanda.

"Because he's made an arse of himself and I can't watch anymore. You'll have to ask him what he plans to do next."

"I will indeed," Amanda said, sounding

interested. "But first tell me what he's done already."

"He's run away."

"I did *not* run away," Nicholas said, crawling to his feet with another groan and turning around. "I am allowing Jennifer to return to the life she should have."

"Perhaps she doesn't want that life!" Robin exclaimed. He threw up his hands. "I can't talk to him."

"It looks as though your fists have tried," Jake remarked.

"Aye, but they lost patience as well."

Nicholas watched Robin walk from the stables, cursing loudly. He turned to look at his sister and her husband. Amanda was regarding him thoughtfully. Nicholas scowled at her.

"What?" he snapped.

She pursed her lips. "You needn't snarl at me. I'm not the one who just made an arse of myself. And what do you mean, you're allowing her to return? Did you send her away?"

"Nay," Nicholas said darkly. "I told her that I wanted nothing to do with her."

"Nicholas," Amanda said faintly. "Have you lost all sense?"

Nicholas looked at his sister bleakly. "I can't watch her leave, Mandy, and I know she will."

Jake shook his head. "What a waste," he said. "And here I spent the past week making

552

you a ring." He opened his hand.

Nicholas, against his better judgment, walked over to look. He took the ring from his brother-in-law and caught his breath at the sight.

"Medieval tools," Jake said quietly, "but modern gems. I'm still working on my technique."

"The saints preserve us all if you find any more of it than you have already," Nicholas said with feeling. " 'Tis perfect as it stands."

And it was.

Diamonds and rubies — that much Nicholas had learned at Jake's table. The stones were square, set in gold, and went all the way around the ring, like a flame that burned forever. It was so perfectly Jennifer, so sparkling and fiery, that Nicholas almost couldn't see it for the sudden mist in his eyes.

He looked up at Jake and found that he had nothing at all to say.

"Like it?" Jake asked.

Nicholas blinked, hard. "Aye. Very much. What do I owe you for it?"

"Nothing," Jake said. "Brotherly affection and all that."

Nicholas smiled and bent his head. "Thank you. It's exquisite."

"Yes, it is," Jake said. "Now, give it back, since you apparently don't have a use for it."

Nicholas felt his eyes narrow of their own accord. He found that his fists were clenched and he had no memory of clenching them.

"Nay!" Amanda said quickly. "Not you two as well. Nicky, stop being a fool. Don't you love her?"

He sighed and dragged his hand through his hair. "Aye."

"Then, imbecile, go and propose to her. What are you waiting for?"

He looked at Amanda, pained beyond measure. "She can go home," he said quietly. "Home to the Future."

"So could Jake, at any moment. But he doesn't because he loves me. Why is it so impossible to believe that your Jennifer could feel the same way about you?"

"You didn't hear her play her violin," he began, but he looked down at the ring in his palm and considered truly for the first time just what Jake had given up. He'd seen some of the baubles Jake had made in his time and brought back to give to the ladies of Artane. He had to look no farther than Amanda's ring, which was so beautiful, it hurt the eyes to gaze on it overmuch, to see what Jake had traded for Amanda.

He looked at his brother-in-law and took a deep breath. "I shouldn't ask this with my sister standing here —"

"No, you shouldn't," Jake said with a smile, "but you could because the answer would be the same if she weren't. No, I don't miss anything. Well, outside of indoor plumbing, but I'm working on that." He put his arm around Amanda. "I would do it all over again a million times and count myself the most fortunate of men every time."

"Jennifer will lose her family," Nicholas said quietly.

"And gain one with you," Amanda said, reaching out to put her hand on his arm. "Nicky, why don't you just go ask her what *she* wants to do? What have you to lose but your pride?"

"I don't have any pride left."

"Apparently you do, or you would have proposed already," Jake said dryly.

Nicholas sighed, then looked at Amanda. "Is my face bruised?"

"Not overmuch, thankfully," she said. She reached up and picked hay out of his hair, then brushed it with her fingers. "There you are, freshly groomed and ready to ask for her hand."

Nicholas stood there for another moment or two, then smiled at his sister. "Thank you."

"My pleasure," she said softly. "Now, beat it."

"Beat it?"

Jake laughed. "It means get on with it. Nick, there really are a few words you should learn if you're going to be married to that girl."

Nicholas found that he could smile. "Aye," he said. "I suppose so."

He kissed Amanda on the cheek, clapped a hand on Jake's shoulder, then hurried back toward the hall. Aye, he would rush back upstairs and hope Jennifer was still there where he could fall to his knees and grovel properly in private. He would tell her that he adored her, promise her untold luxuries, and hope to hell she would be willing to give up everything she had to stay behind with him.

He ran up the steps, had to rest for a moment and damn his brother for so many fists to the ribs, then pushed open the hall doors and strode inside.

And then he came to a skidding halt.

The hall was, not unexpectedly, full of his grandmother's offerings. They were also, unfortunately, all at table, leaving him a very large space in the middle of the hall that he would have to cross on his way to the stairs.

And they were all looking at him.

He started inside only to realize that he wasn't going to have to go all that far.

Jennifer was walking out of the stairwell.

He realized the precise moment she caught sight of him because she froze in place. He couldn't decide if she was pleased to see him or sorry because now he would disrupt her flight toward Jake's time gate.

He decided, suddenly, that it was perhaps better if he just didn't think at all.

He cast caution and pride to the wind and strode across the hall toward her. He stopped

556

in front of the lord's table, a pace away from her. He wanted to drop to his knees right there, but he wasn't sure he dared, so he simply stood there and looked at her.

"My lady," he managed.

She returned his look, her expression very grave. "My lord," she said softly.

"Ah," Nicholas began, then he fell silent. He could feel every eye in the hall fixed upon him. He took a deep breath, but that did not aid him.

"I thought you were leaving," Jennifer said quietly.

Well, that was something he could address easily enough. "I am," he said distinctly, "a horse's arse."

She tilted her head and studied him. "Are you?"

He winced. "I should just hand you my sword and invite you to use it."

She almost smiled. "That seems a little counterproductive, doesn't it? I don't think I want you dead."

"Do you want me at all?" he said quietly.

She clasped her hands in front of her. "I could ask you the same question, couldn't I?"

He swallowed with an alarming amount of difficulty. What he wanted to do was haul her into his arms. Whether she would want him to was something he couldn't guess. He took a deep breath and supposed all he could do was begin at the beginning.

"Forgive me," he said.

"What terrible thing did you do?" she asked.

"I lied to you."

"Well, yes, I suppose," she agreed. "In a way, though no more than I did to you." She paused. "You also yelled at me."

He closed his eyes briefly, then looked at her. "I will never do either again."

"Forgiven," she said.

He looked at her in surprise. "So easily?"

"I'm not one for holding grudges. But you could tell me why you did it." She paused. "You could tell me why you did quite a few things, actually, but I suppose this isn't really the place for it."

"Likely not, since the answers you'll want require privacy," he agreed.

She looked at him for a moment or two in silence, then smiled. "Well? Are we going somewhere to talk?"

He considered, then shook his head. "Nay, I think not."

"You think not?"

"I want to ask you something."

"What? To agree to another fortnight, now that all the secrets are out?"

"Nay."

She blinked in surprise. "Really?"

He took a deep breath. "I daresay, my love, that a fortnight won't suffice."

"Really," she repeated, sounding a little breathless.

He looked about him, just to see how many witnesses he might have for what he was about to do. There were all his grandmother's ladies, of course, with their parents. Some of them were standing, gaping. The rest were whispering frantically. There were a few mothers weeping already.

He supposed those weren't tears of happiness.

Nicholas looked at the high table. His entire family was there. His father, his mother, his grandmother, his brothers and Isabelle. Jake and Amanda had come inside and were standing with their daughter. Even Jennifer's kin, Connor and Victoria, were watching.

Those souls, at least, were smiling.

Nicholas turned back to his lady. He took a step backward, started to bend down, then winced.

"What happened to you?" she asked.

"Robin," he gasped, putting his hand to his side. "Bruised ribs."

"I'll kill him later."

He shot her a brief smile, then went down fully on one knee, gasping at the pain. When he could see again, he reached out and took her hands.

Her ring clinked on the stone.

"Damnation," he said. He found it, fortunately, without having to dig through too many rushes, then he looked up at her. "Now, I'll try this again."

She was smiling as tears streamed down her cheeks. "Try what again?" she asked.

"Something that I would really prefer to do in private and I imagine I will when the rabble is cleared from the hall. Something I should have done in the tower chamber an hour ago. Something I should have done the very moment I saw you." He looked up at her seriously. "I know what you will give up for me if you say me yea. I know I am selfish to ask it of you —"

"Why don't you just ask me whatever it is you're going to ask and let me decide that?" she said softly.

"I vow I will see that it is worth it," he promised.

"Did I ever tell you that you talk too much?"

He managed a laugh. "I'll be about my business, then. Now, what are all your names? I'd best get that part right or your sister will make it known."

"There's a MacLeod in the middle there," she said with a smile. "And you're right. Vic will tell on you."

He bent his head and kissed her hands, then looked up into her glorious eyes that were full of tears. "Jennifer MacLeod McKinnon," he said loudly, "here before this company, I pledge myself to you, vow to shield you with my body and my name, and ask you to plight your troth with me." He paused. "Will you?"

"Aye," she said, just as loudly.

Then she smiled and hauled him back up to his feet.

He got there with a gasp, which was covered nicely by the amount of noise his family was making. Cheers, clapping, whistling: there was not a smidgen of dignity to spread between the lot of them. Nicholas noted that the rest of the hall was clapping politely, but that clapping wasn't enough to cover the howls of outrage from his grandmother's offerings.

He wondered if he and Jennifer should retreat to his father's solar and bolt the door.

But instead, he did what he had been longing to do for a solid se'nnight. He pulled Jennifer into his arms in front of the entire company and, as she would have said, kissed her silly.

She finally pulled away from him laughing, then hugged him so tightly that he gasped again, in spite of himself.

"Did he have to break your ribs to bring you to your senses?" she asked in surprise.

"I would have gotten there eventually on my own," he wheezed. "Robin just sped up my thinking. I suppose 'tis fitting, since I did the same for him once upon a time."

She looked up at him and smiled. "Did you

really just ask me to marry you?"

"Let us retire somewhere private and I'll ask again," he said. "I might spend the rest of the evening asking you in a dozen different ways. Then I'll tell you all the reasons I love you and all the things I'll do so you don't regret having stayed with me."

"Don't I have to do anything in this relationship?" she asked wryly.

"Love me in return," he said, bending his head to kiss her again. "Play for me," he whispered against her mouth. "Forgive me."

"I already forgave you," she said honestly. "I think I understand."

"Do you?" he asked with a smile. "That I loved you from the moment I set eyes on you and that the thought of you leaving fair killed me?"

"Something like that," she said with a smile of her own. "Tell me again later, when I'll remember what you've said. I don't think I'll remember anything now."

"Remember that I love you," he said. "For now, perhaps we might sit at the table together. Think you?"

"Ask your grandmother."

He put his arm around her and led her behind the high table. He stopped behind his grandmother who turned around to look at him with raised eyebrows.

"Aye?" she said, a smile playing around her mouth.

"I wooed her in plain sight. I bloody well asked her to wed me in plain sight. *Now* may I sit with her at the damned table?"

Joanna's eyes brimmed suddenly with tears. She stood up and hugged the half of him where Jennifer wasn't standing. "Well done, Nicky, my love," she said. "Well done, indeed."

Then she pinched his ear.

He pulled back with a scowl. "What was that for?"

"For making her cry, whelp. Best spend the rest of your days making up for it." She slid a pointed look down the table. "And you'd best go see if her sister's husband will allow it. I don't imagine you asked his permission, did you?"

Nicholas wished his side didn't hurt so damned much. He looked down at Jennifer. "Why do I suspect he'll want to meet me in the lists to settle this?"

"Because I imagine he'll take any excuse to cross blades with a legend."

Nicholas sighed and led her over to where Connor MacDougal was now standing behind Victoria's chair. Victoria's expression was one of satisfaction. Connor's wasn't.

Nicholas made him a low bow, catching his breath as he did so. He straightened, winced, then looked at Jennifer's brother-in-law.

"Since her sire is not here, I should have accorded you the respect due him and asked your leave before I asked for her hand."

Connor folded his arms over his chest and frowned a most impressive frown. "Aye," he said with a curt nod, "I daresay ye should have."

"I'm asking now."

"I'll leave my answer until I've seen ye in the lists. Dawn suits me."

Nicholas nodded gravely.

"But ye can take yer ease with her tonight," Connor conceded. "You might not be able to on the morrow."

Nicholas didn't dare smile; he suspected Connor was all too serious about that. So he made him a small bow, then turned to Victoria. She was almost smiling.

"You didn't ask *me* anything," she said pointedly.

"Your mother is rather whom I should be questioning," Nicholas said with another hitching bow.

"Why?"

"I would ask her how she managed to produce two such exquisite daughters."

Victoria gaped at him, then laughed. "Oh, Jenner, he's good."

Jennifer tugged on his hand. "Stop. It'll go to her head. Nicholas, I'd like to sit down now between you and my sister."

Nicholas stood back and watched as Robin went about settling everyone into new places. He caught his brother's eye in passing. Robin only winked. Nicholas soon found himself standing next to his sire.

"Well?" Nicholas asked.

His father clapped him on the shoulder. "Congratulations."

"Thank you." He smiled gravely at his sire. "And my thanks for your wise words, as well."

"I'll continue to offer my support as chaperon until you're wed," Rhys said smoothly.

Nicholas opened his mouth to protest, then caught sight of the twinkle in his father's eye. Rhys laughed, clapped him on the shoulder, then moved out of the way to make room for his family, who seemed to be determined to swarm his love.

Nicholas realized then that he was holding Jennifer's ring in his hand. He waited until all his family had taken an inordinate amount of time to either congratulate her, or, in the case of his elder brother, offer her condolences. Nicholas shoved Robin out of the way before he warmed overmuch to his topic, sat down next to her, and smiled.

"Finally."

She smiled. "I couldn't agree more."

"I have something for you."

"More than your heart?"

He slid the ring onto her finger. Her reaction was all he could have wished for. She looked up at him, clearly stunned.

"It's gorgeous."

"I should have saved it for the ceremony,

but I've already dropped it once. You'd better keep it." He looked down at the ring on her finger, then saw that she was looking at it with tears in her eyes. "What is it, love?"

"When did you do this?"

"I asked Jake to make it for me when I was there," he admitted. He stared down at it for a moment, then back up at her. "I hoped."

"Didn't you know?" she murmured gently.

He shook his head, then lifted her hand to kiss it. "We must have speech together," he said quietly. "About a great many things."

"Later," she suggested. "Perhaps a very long walk along the shore with just us two."

"If Connor MacDougal leaves anything of me, we'll do it tomorrow," he said with a smile. "But tonight, perhaps we might retreat to my father's solar with your family and mine and simply be at peace."

She nodded, her eyes sparkling with tears. "Yes."

He suspected that she would grieve that her parents weren't there, as well as her other sister and brother. He sighed to himself. There were things that he would never be able to ease for her, things he could never make up.

But he would try, just the same.

He found that he simply couldn't look away from her. He supposed in time they would both digest the events of the day, discuss what had been said in the tower chamber, come to their own peace about it all. For now, he was simply grateful she had said him aye.

And that he could hold her hand on *top* of the table for a change.

CHAPTER 35

Jennifer sat on a very cold stone bench pushed up against the wall of the lists and watched the skirmish going on in front of her. Blades screeched, men swore in a manly fashion, grunts and exclamations of appreciation and irritation mingled in the air in a very medieval fashion.

"He's nuts."

Jennifer looked at her sister sitting next to her, watching her husband with disgust.

"He's loving it," Jennifer corrected with a smile. "How often does he get to do this for real in Manhattan?"

"More often than either of us would like to think about," Victoria said with a sigh. She linked arms with Jennifer. "I have to tell you, this feels a little surreal."

"A little?" Jennifer echoed. "Vic, we're sitting in Artane's lists, in 1229 no less, watching your fourteenth-century Scottish laird of a husband and my thirteenth-century medieval lord of a fiancé hack at each other with very sharp swords. Of course it's going to feel a little surreal!"

Vic leaned her head back against the wall and smiled. "I'm going to miss you."

"You might not," Jennifer said, striving for a light tone. "Connor might thrash Nicholas so badly that he'll have to concede, then Connor won't let him marry me."

Victoria snorted. "Do you actually think your Nicholas is going to take no for an answer?"

Jennifer looked at him and smiled. "Probably not."

And she doubted he would. He'd held on to her hand or touched her in some other fashion from the moment he'd dropped to his knee in front of an entire collection of medieval nobility and proposed. He'd held her hand at dinner. He'd held her hand while they'd visited in his father's solar far into the wee hours. He'd put his arm around her as they'd walked up the stairs to Isabelle's room.

And then he'd proceeded to kiss her for quite some time.

He'd told her that he grieved for what it would cost her to give up her family. Though she'd reassured him she thought it was worth it, she supposed he still wasn't completely comfortable with the thought. In all honesty, she couldn't say she was either. It was one thing to stay when she had no choice. It was another thing to willingly and knowingly make the choice to leave her family behind.

Ahead.

Whatever.

She looked at Nicholas fighting with Connor and thought, though, that while the decision was wrenching, it was the right one. He was everything she'd ever looked for but never found. He was tall, strong, handsome, and so unabashedly a man that he made every other man she had ever come into contact with look like a seventh-grade boy. She'd never thought to even meet someone who could hold his own with the men in her family. Now she realized that she had found a man who could not only hold his own, but stand out in every way.

He was standing out against Connor presently with only a minimum of effort and Connor was simply terrifying. And she was fairly certain that Nicholas had cracked ribs. Jennifer elbowed Vic.

"It's impressive, isn't it?"

"Yours or mine?"

"Either," Jennifer said with a smile. "Both."

"It's unsettling," Victoria admitted with a slightly nervous laugh. "I'm used to watching it on stage, but you know how that goes. This is just one step away from the real business. I wouldn't want to meet either of them in a deserted alley."

"Trust me, I understand," Jennifer agreed. She watched for another minute or two, then turned to look at her sister. "All right, now that we have some privacy, I want details. What happened after I left?"

Victoria pursed her lips thoughtfully for a moment or two before she answered. "Do you really want the truth?"

"Don't I?" She sat up with a start. "Did something happen to Mom and Dad? Granny?"

Victoria waved her back. "No, nothing like that."

She sat back and let out a deep breath. "Then tell me what happened. Who found my car? And my Kit Kat and Lilt? I bet Megan found all of it and *ate* the Kit Kat, just in case I came back too quickly."

Victoria laughed. "Well, I suppose that might have happened. All I can vouch for is that Megan did worry, of course, when you didn't come home. She and Gideon went looking for you and found your car near Ledenham Abbey."

"Did everyone panic?"

Victoria shifted. "Well, they probably would have, but Ambrose, Hugh, and Fulbert were sitting on top of a quaking, half-crazed pickpocket. The police came, but not before Ambrose had told Megan that you'd popped through a time gate." She paused. "I get the feeling he was taking credit for planning that."

"No doubt," Jennifer said, feeling a little breathless. "They've planned everyone else's weddings; why not mine? But tell me what happened then? Did everyone fly over? Oh," she said, sitting up quickly, "your run of the *Shrew*. Who finished it for you?"

"We finished it ourselves," Victoria said gingerly.

Jennifer blinked, then smiled dryly. "Thanks a lot."

"You said you wanted all the facts, so hang on before you get irritated with me. Of course when Megan called us we were frantic and were busily thinking of how awful the show would be with our understudies —"

"Were you brilliant?" Jennifer interrupted.

Victoria smiled. "Connor has been absolutely riveting. Even Marv Jones from the *Pillar* has raved about him."

"And what about you?"

Victoria smiled modestly. "He has gushed. More than once."

"Wow."

"I thought so, too."

"All right, so you were preparing to hop right on a plane, and then what?"

Victoria looked at her seriously. "You're sure you want to know?"

Jennifer felt her smile falter. "This is awful. You're beginning to convince me I don't want to."

"Buck up," Victoria said, patting her on the knee. "Megan *was* panicked until Gideon's uncle, Kendrick, pulled out the family history tomes."

"Tomes?" Then she paused. "Kendrick? That's a very interesting name. You know, Nicholas's nephew is named Kendrick."

Victoria looked at her briefly, open-mouthed, then shut her mouth with a snap. "Nah," she said, "it's not possible. This guy is the Earl of Seakirk and he has six kids. It couldn't possible be the same person. Anyway, apparently they're pretty big on genealogy, those de Piagets, so Kendrick looked up the marriage record of Nicholas de Piaget and everyone relaxed."

"Why?"

"Because, silly, he married *you*."

Jennifer laughed uneasily. "You scared me."

"Yeah, well, the antics of your kids scared us, so we're even."

Jennifer froze, then turned slowly to look at her sister. "What do you know?"

"What *don't* I know?"

Jennifer bowed her head and let out a shuddering breath. "I'm not sure I want to hear any of this." She looked at her sister. "I assume I remain in the past."

"You're not going to be having kids with the guy if he's here and you're there."

"I suppose so," Jennifer laughed weakly. She took a deep breath. "Anything else I should know?"

"You live happily ever after," Victoria said. She smiled. "You can't ask for more than that, can you?"

Jennifer looked at Nicholas who was still sparring with Connor with the energy of a man who'd just stepped out onto the field ten minutes earlier, not three hours ago. "No," she said slowly, "no, I can't."

"He *is* spectacular," Victoria said. "And it's obvious he's head over heels in love with you."

"Do you think so?" Jennifer asked wistfully.

"Get real," Victoria said with a laugh. "You know he is. He can't keep his eyes off you, he can't keep his hands off you, he wields a sword as well as my husband so he'll keep everyone else from getting their hands on you. What else do you want?"

Jennifer sighed and looked at her sister. "Family reunions?"

"I brought a map from Jamie, if that's the case."

Jennifer gaped at her. "You talked to Jamie?"

"Well, of course," Victoria said, exasperated. "How do you think we got here at the right time?"

"I was assuming you asked Thomas."

"What does he know?" Victoria scoffed. "Maybe he has time traveled, but not nearly as much as *I* have. He's a rookie."

"And you're such a pro," Jennifer said dryly.

"I take what glory I can," Victoria said with a smile. "And yes, we did talk to Jamie. We flew over after the run, got our things together, then drove all over Northumberland with him, trying to figure out just what gate would work best. Apparently Jamie knows your future brother-in-law, Jake. Jake's gate is the most reliable, but I brought you lots of choices just in case you and Nicholas want a little vacation in the future. *In* the Future, as it were. Or any number of other centuries."

"Jamie should open up a travel agency."

"I suggested that. Elizabeth said no."

"I'm not surprised," Jennifer laughed. Then she sobered. "A map," she said slowly. "I'm not sure I want it."

"Keep it," Victoria said. "It's part of your dowry. I have the feeling your guy might like a turn in a nice, red Ferrari someday."

"Heaven help us," Jennifer said weakly. She took Victoria's hand and clutched it suddenly. "Are we happy?"

"So the annals say," Victoria said with a smile. "Genealogy doesn't lie." She squeezed Jennifer's hand. "But even knowing you'll be blissfully happy doesn't make it any easier. I keep trying to convince myself that we probably would have never seen each other again if we had been pioneer settlers or Pilgrims or something like that. But this," she began with a shake of her head, "I have to admit that this seems a little more final."

"What do Mom and Dad think?" Jennifer

asked hesitantly. "Is Dad completely freaked out?"

"He's resigned," Victoria said. "He's the one who keeps working the pioneer angle." She paused. "He misses you."

Jennifer sighed deeply and rubbed her hands over her face. "That's the only thing that bothers me. I wish I could see them just one more time." She looked at her sister. "Did you bring a digital camera?"

"Are you nuts? I thought your violin was pushing it." Then she winked. "Of course I did."

"I need to think about the Degani," Jennifer mused. "You probably should take it back with you when you go."

Victoria shook her head. "I think you should keep it. They can bury it with you and I'll dig it up when I get home."

"Vic, yuck," Jennifer said with a shiver. "That's disgusting."

"Too much time travel does that to a person."

Jennifer thought about her violin, about the absolute joy of playing it. "I wonder how safe it is."

"I'll tell you this much," Victoria said seriously. "Wyckham becomes the cultural capital of the north. You rival Queen Eleanor's patronage of the arts. You may want to keep it."

"Maybe so," she said thoughtfully. She

looked at her sister. "How many kids do we have?"

"Too many."

"Vic!"

Victoria laughed. "You have lots, they raise lots of hell, and you both live to a ripe old age. At least as far as the stories go. Who knows? It could be all made up and you have a dozen girls who bankrupt you because of what it costs to provide dowries for them, so you come back to Artane and live in the stables."

"Vic?"

"Yes?"

"Shut up."

Victoria laughed, put her arms around Jennifer, and hugged her tightly. "You'll have a great life, sis. If I didn't know it was going to be such a great life, I'd have a much harder time leaving you back here."

"Will you stay for the wedding?"

"That's why we're here. When is it, by the way?"

"You would know."

Victoria smiled. "So, I imagine, would you and I also imagine it's not going to be nearly soon enough to suit your groom. Oh, look, they're finished. Who do you think won?"

Jennifer looked. Nicholas and Connor were clasping hands. Robin was hovering on the edge of the field like a carrion bird, looking for the spoils.

"I think it was a draw," Jennifer said. She looked at her sister. "Do you like him?"

"I like that he loves you," Victoria said, "and I like my first impressions of him. Let me get to know him and then I'll tell you. Not that it will change your mind."

"Too late for that," Jennifer murmured, watching Nicholas and Connor walking toward them. "Far too late now."

They stopped in front of them. Connor put his hand on Nicholas's shoulder.

"I said him aye," Connor said. "If you want him."

"I do," Jennifer said, with a smile.

Connor looked over his shoulder. "There's another one over there that looks as though he wants a bit of exercise." He lifted an eyebrow. "Do you mind, my love?"

"Help yourself," Victoria said, waving him away. "Enjoy."

Connor wasted no time in turning and bounding back onto the field.

Victoria smiled at Jennifer. "It's like a buffet for him. So many swordsmen, so little time to sample them all."

"Robin will keep him busy for quite a while," Jennifer said wryly. She looked up at Nicholas. "You walked a fine line, my lord."

"Did you notice?" he said. He stretched and winced. "I couldn't grind him into the dust, lest he say me nay, and I couldn't let him grind me into the dust, lest he find me lacking. Robin, however, will have no such compunction. I think I might change and return to watch the carnage."

"Do," she said with a smile. "I'll be waiting."

His smile almost burned her where she sat. "I'm glad you will be," he said. He bowed to her, bowed to Victoria, then smiled at her one more time before he walked from the lists back to the house.

Jennifer watched him go.

"He has it bad," Victoria said with a low whistle.

"I recognize the symptoms," Jennifer said a little breathlessly, "suffering from them quite badly myself." She looked out onto the field to find Robin and Connor already going at it enthusiastically. "You know, Vic, Connor may have met his match here. Robin's very, very good. And he has no reason to be nice."

Victoria shrugged nonchalantly. "He'll survive. He's a little out of practice, but he loves this. I probably won't get him out of the lists at all while we're here."

"You'll have to come back and visit," Jennifer said quietly. "It would be good for him, I'm sure."

Victoria squeezed her arm, but didn't answer.

Jennifer understood. It was too tender a thought to discuss, so she simply sat and enjoyed her sister's company.

It *was* surreal.

She contemplated that for quite some time, then noticed a movement to her left. Nicholas was walking along the wall toward her.

She supposed there would come a time when she was used to the sight of him, but it hadn't happened yet.

She stood up, then went into his arms.

"You're still here," he whispered.

She lifted her head and smiled up at him. "And just where else would I go?" she asked. "You're here."

"Thank you."

"You don't have to keep saying that."

"Oh," he said, looking at her seriously, "I must. Every day. Each and every day I'm fortunate enough to have you in my life." He smiled. "Especially since I have Laird Mac-Dougal's permission. Odd, isn't it? That they arrived at just such a time."

Jennifer hesitated. "Nicholas . . ."

He froze. "Should I sit down?"

"You may want to. Here, come sit with us. We'll keep you from embarrassing yourself by falling over."

He then took her hand and sat down on the bench next to Victoria. Jennifer sat down next to him, then put her head on his shoulder.

"Here is the tale," she said with a smile. "You see, they have this book at Artane —"

"Several books," Victoria interrupted.

"*Several* books," Jennifer amended, "at the Artane that stands eight hundred years in the future. Books about the history of the de Piaget family."

"The saints preserve me," Nicholas said faintly.

"Hold on, bucko," Victoria said. "It's going to be quite a ride for you."

"Bucko?" Nicholas whispered to Jennifer.

She squeezed his hand. "Term of affection. So, in this book they have at Artane, apparently there is a record of all the marriages of all the descendants of the first lord of Artane, Rhys de Piaget."

Nicholas shivered. "Indeed."

"And, as you might expect, they have a record of the marriage of his second son, Nicholas."

Nicholas shivered again.

Jennifer smiled up at him. "To me."

"In a fortnight?" Nicholas asked.

"Actually, yes."

He put his hand on her cheek, bent his head and kissed her softly. "The saints be praised." He looked at her. "So this is how they knew."

"It is."

He froze again. "But that would mean that they knew . . ." He looked at her with wide eyes. "They knew when they came yesterday. Before . . ."

"Yes," she said softly. "Before."

He shuddered this time. "It is too strange,"

he said quietly, "to know that my actions are already known to souls living centuries after I'm dead."

"Well, they're still going to be a surprise to me," she said with a smile. "Do you want to know anything else?"

He laughed uneasily. "I'm not sure. Do I?"

Victoria leaned forward. "Tell him about your kids."

"Kids?" Nicholas wheezed.

"Children," Jennifer said. "We have several. Vic won't tell me how many."

"The saints preserve me," Nicholas said faintly.

"Don't worry," Victoria said. "In the annals of Artane, you are known as a perfect knight. Chivalrous, kind-hearted, talented, wealthy." She smiled at him. "You don't think I'd leave my sister with you otherwise, do you?"

"Thank you," Nicholas said faintly.

Jennifer smiled. "Maybe that's enough of the future for now. I think I'd like to just enjoy the present." She closed her eyes, ignoring the sounds of swords and curses in two languages, and smiled to herself. It would be a good life.

"Jen?" Nicholas asked finally.

"Aye, my lord?"

"Will you wed me in a fortnight's time?"

She lifted her face to him. "Wasn't that your plan?"

"I would have preferred tomorrow," he said,

kissing her, "but my grandmother told me nay." He paused. "I half fear she will never go home."

"Oh, she'll go," Jennifer assured him, "but only after you've been properly wedded and bedded. She told me so herself. Then she looked me up and down to assure herself that I might be equal to the task."

He laughed. "What a dreadful old woman."

"She loves you."

"And why not?" he said archly. "After all, 'tis written in the annals of Artane that I am a knight with peerless chivalry."

"You're starting to sound like Robin."

"Oh, please stop me before I truly do," he said with an uneasy laugh. Then he paused. "Will you play for me tonight?"

"Of course, but don't you think I should wait until everyone leaves?"

"The ladies are all on their way," he said with a smile. "I bid farewell to them all in a clump not ten minutes ago. The castle is ours. Well," he paused, "with the exception of Brigit of Islington. She wasn't feeling well."

"We'll ignore her."

"Perhaps she'll remain in her chamber with her mother. I daresay we'll have peace enough."

After supper Jennifer pulled out her violin and tried not to let the feeling of déjà vu distract her. It was just what she'd done that night for Lord Edward. It was the same high table that she laid her case on. It was the same hall she prepared to play in. The only thing that kept her grounded was looking at Nicholas. He knew what she was thinking because she'd told him about her earlier performance.

He smiled gravely.

Jennifer took a deep breath and wondered about the advisability of what she'd been asked to do, what with Brigit still running around. Playing her violin in front of the de Piagets would have been one thing; playing in front of Brigit and her mother would not. But since they were upstairs and the servants had been dismissed for the evening, she supposed she was safe enough.

She took out her violin, tuned it, then made Rhys a curtsey.

She looked once more at Nicholas, then began.

She played several of her favorite pieces, some difficult, some merely beautiful. Victoria didn't seem surprised, nor did Connor, but she noticed that the rest of Nicholas's family, including Jake, were overcome in various ways. Nicholas's eyes were very red. The women in his family were weeping. Jake was gaping. Nicholas's brothers were watching silently, their mouths hanging open.

Finally, she played her favorite Schubert.

She watched Nicholas periodically while she was about it. He was sitting in his chair with his head bowed, his arms resting on his knees, his hands clasped, much as he'd sat the first time she'd played for him. But when she finished, he looked up.

And he smiled, an intimate smile that she knew was just for her.

She tucked her violin under her arm and took her bows. Rhys had leaped up from his chair and strode over to her, clapping enthusiastically. "Beautiful. Simply beautiful."

She curtseyed to him. "Thank you, my lord."

He beamed at her. "For that, Mistress McKinnon, you must have something special from my household." He nodded toward Nicholas. "Perhaps that lad there."

"I will have him gladly, my lord," she said, with another curtsey. She put her violin away, handed the case to Miles for safekeeping, then went to sit with Nicholas. She would have sat down next to him, but he pulled her into his lap instead. He wrapped his arms around her.

"You are spectacular," he whispered into her ear. "Unbelievably spectacular."

She smiled at him. "It's just music."

"Well, that was good, too."

She laughed and put her arm around his neck. "I love you."

"I love you, too." He paused. "I don't suppose I can kiss you here."

"I imagine not," she agreed.

"A fortnight," he said, shaking his head. "What was I thinking?"

"I have no idea," she said honestly. "Tomorrow's probably too late."

He smiled and held her close. "I daresay, my love, that a lifetime will not be long enough to love you."

"I couldn't agree more," she said, resting her cheek against his.

She spent the rest of the evening listening happily to conversations in Gaelic and French, loving the fact that Victoria and Connor had been so easily and happily welcomed into the de Piaget family circle, and wishing that it could go on forever.

She enjoyed it enough for several lifetimes.

CHAPTER 36

Nicholas stood in the lists and sparred happily with Connor MacDougal. The man was ferocious, but in an entirely different way from Robin. It was a pleasure to exercise with him, as much of a pleasure as it had been to come to know him and his lovely wife. He knew he would never miss Connor and Victoria in the same way that Jennifer would when they left, but he would miss them just the same.

It had been a se'nnight of pleasant days spent with Jennifer, Victoria, and Connor either walking along the strand, riding about the countryside, or merely sitting in his father's solar, talking of things he had considered and considering things he most definitely had not. Sometimes his family had been with them, sometimes only one or two members of his family, sometimes just Jennifer and her kin.

Sometimes it was Jennifer's kin and Jake, with Jake being caught up on what for him should have been current tidings. It was then that Nicholas began to have some sympathy for what Jennifer must have gone through, for it was difficult to follow their modern English save for the words he had learned, most notably *whatever.* They did go on quite often in Gaelic, in deference to him, but it was obvious to him that he was going to have to learn modern English. Amanda could babble in it quite happily, so he knew he had no excuse not to —

The scream reached his ears before he realized it was someone calling his name.

He turned to see Victoria running across the lists toward him.

He was running toward her, his heart in his throat, before he knew he intended to move. He sheathed his sword and caught her by the shoulders.

"What?" he demanded.

She hunched over. "Violin," she wheezed. "Stolen."

"What?" he said, stunned.

She forced herself upright and held on to his forearms. "Jenner and I were going upstairs," she managed. "To make sure it was all right." She gasped for breath. "Montgomery and John were unconscious. Someone hit them. The violin was gone. Jenner turned and ran down the stairs." She looked at him, her visage very pale. "I ran after her, but she was already gone. One of the women, that last one who's still here, said she'd seen someone leaving with a long box. She said she thought it was Ledenham."

"Ledenham!" Nicholas exclaimed.

"Do you know him?"

"Aye," Nicholas said grimly. He took her arm and pulled her with him toward the stables. "Tell me what else you know."

"The woman said she'd seen Ledenham heading for the beach. I think Jenner must have grabbed a horse —"

"How long ago?" Nicholas demanded.

"As long as it took me to find you. The woman said you were in your father's solar. It took me a few minutes to get there, then realize you and Connor were in the lists."

Nicholas released her and sprinted for the stables. He skidded to a halt in front of the Black's stall, grabbed a bridle, and put it over the horse's nose. He led the beast out, swung up onto his bare back, and thundered out of the stables. He rode for the front gates.

By the saints, what was Jennifer thinking?

He followed the tracks up over the dunes and down onto the strand. The Black bucked then, but Nicholas kicked him as hard as he could and the horse shot off like a bolt from a crossbow. Nicholas had to fight him to keep him going the way he wanted, but once he gave the Black his head, they flew.

Not fast enough, though.

He saw the little cluster of souls far ahead

of him on the shore. When he reached them and leaped from his horse, he realized that Jennifer was standing in a circle of men, men who were each obviously hardened warriors.

Nicholas drew his sword and his knife and threw himself into the fray.

He killed two immediately, leaving four plus Ledenham. He was hard-pressed to keep the four at bay. It left him absolutely no time or energy to see to Jennifer and he hoped she had the good sense to keep herself out of Ledenham's hands. He tried to keep all four men in front of him, but he found that almost impossible. First one slipped behind him, then another.

He killed the third, then again tried to slip out of the noose. He engaged them all, but couldn't deny that he was in trouble. He saw, out of the corner of his eye, a sword coming down in a ferocious chop toward his head.

It met another sword suddenly thrust into its arc.

A sword that was not his.

"Och, that isn't fair, is it?" Connor demanded. "Why don't ye come after me instead, little man."

Nicholas had never been so grateful for anyone as he was for Connor MacDougal at that moment. Ledenham's man turned and attacked Connor. Connor only laughed. Then he sang what Nicholas could only assume was a Scottish battle song.

That alone, he noted absently, should have been enough to finish the other man off.

He suspected that he wouldn't say anything to Connor about the fact that he could not sing on key. Instead he applied himself to the remaining two men. In time, he realized that he had other help in the persons of Robin, Miles, and Jake.

"We'll just watch," Robin called helpfully.

Nicholas would have cursed at him, but he didn't have the chance. Robin threw himself suddenly into the fray. He made short work of his lad, then finished Nicholas's as well.

"I didn't need help," Nicholas snapped.

"Aye, you did." Robin pointed with his sword. "Look."

Nicholas ignored Connor's continued battle with the last man and turned to see what had inspired Robin to intrude where he hadn't been wanted.

Ledenham stood there with his knife across Jennifer's throat.

Nicholas thought he just might be ill.

He heard, faintly, Connor's man fall with a sigh.

Then all was silent, except for the noise of the sea endlessly roaring and the sound of birds crying in the air.

"Choose," Ledenham said coldly. "The woman or her devil's instrument."

Nicholas forced himself to breathe evenly. He slowly resheathed his sword, then folded his arms over his chest as if he actually struggled to make a choice. He saw Jennifer's violin case lying on the ground at her feet. There was a crossbow bolt sticking out of it. He wondered, with another sickening lurch, if that bolt might have been meant for him. Perhaps Jennifer had been forced to leap too close to Ledenham in order to save him.

He looked up slowly and met Jennifer's eyes.

She merely regarded him serenely, as if she walked in a pleasant garden, enjoying the flowers. In his garden at Wyckham, perhaps, where she had weeded out so many things that didn't belong.

He supposed he needed to do his own bit of weeding now.

"Well," Nicholas said thoughtfully, "that is a choice indeed. Which would *you* prefer?"

Ledenham cursed. Jennifer flinched as the knife tightened across her throat.

"I don't care," Ledenham spat. "You choose. But know that one way or another, the choice will damn you."

"Will it?" Nicholas asked calmly. "How so?"

"Save her lute and I'll do with her what I will. Save her, and I'll take the witch's lute to the king and ruin you." Ledenham sneered. "One way or another, you suffer."

"And you think that taking this lute to the king will redeem you?"

"Of course it will —"

"He didn't believe you before," Nicholas interrupted.

"I didn't have *proof* before, damn you," Ledenham snapped. "I have it now. Brigit of Islington has heard the witch play it. She says 'tis the devil's music. She has agreed to be my witness."

Nicholas was unsurprised. "Very well, then. Give me the woman, take the lute to the king, and I'll dangle from a noose outside your front gates within the month. Or, better still, keep the woman, kill me, then you'll have both her and the lute."

"What manner of fool do you think I am?" Ledenham asked scornfully. "Kill you whilst all your brothers stand there? And the warlock? And that bloody Scot as well?"

Nicholas unbuckled his sword belt and threw it and one knife to Robin. He pulled another knife from his boot and tossed it to Jake. He took off the leather jerkin he'd trained in and handed it to Miles. Then he opened his arms wide, standing in only a tunic, hose, and boots.

"I am unarmed," he said easily. "Kill me if you like. I suppose you could kill the wench as well, but that would leave you without any sport after I'm gone. She and the lute together would make powerful proof for the king, don't you think?"

Ledenham hesitated, then frowned. "Why are you doing this?"

"Because she shouldn't have left without telling me," Nicholas said. He found that it had a ring of truth to it and the irritation was genuine. "And damn her if she didn't take my horse as well. Here, here's a better idea. I'll beat her first, then you tie her up, kill me, then you do with her what you will. What do you think?"

Ledenham stared at him in surprise.

His arm relaxed just enough that Jennifer moved.

"Nay!" Nicholas shouted, but it was too late.

She had shoved away Ledenham's arm and elbowed him so hard in the ribs that he bent over double in spite of himself. She leaped away, but tripped over a corpse and went sprawling.

Nicholas started after her, but there was apparently no need. Robin jerked her up and out of harm's way and deflected with his sword the knife Ledenham threw at her.

"Pitiful," Robin said, shaking his head.

Nicholas shot his brother a look of thanks, then turned back to Ledenham. "You have your sword. I have nothing. I would say that matches us quite evenly, wouldn't you agree?"

Ledenham cursed him viciously, then drew his sword and attacked with a bellow. Nicholas leaped out of the way as he thrust, ducked to avoid losing his head, then jumped aside as Ledenham charged. Robin threw him his sword. Nicholas caught it, then waited patiently as Ledenham turned.

Ledenham pulled up short. "You vowed you would fight without your sword."

Nicholas shrugged. "I lied."

Robin burst out laughing. Nicholas might have smiled as well, but there was the matter of a furious Nigel of Ledenham yet to face. He wasn't sure if he should simply kill the man, or hope he cursed himself into a frenzy and died of madness. Nicholas actually wouldn't have been surprised to see the latter happen. Ledenham was beginning to froth at the mouth.

The man *was* mad.

He was also not completely unskilled. Nicholas fought him for quite some time, avoiding corpses and trying to ignore the comments Robin was making about Ledenham's swordplay. In fact, all the men in his family, as well as Connor, had taken up a rather spirited discussion of Ledenham's faults. After those had been discussed to their satisfaction, they turned to Nicholas's technique. The combination French and Gaelic that wafted toward him was almost a little distracting.

Ledenham tripped suddenly. He stepped on Jennifer's violin, slipped backward, and landed full on the sword of one of his dead knights.

He died with a gurgle.

Nicholas stared at him in surprise, then let

out the breath he'd been holding. He jammed his sword into the sand, then stepped over the corpses and yanked Jennifer away from his brother. He clutched her to him.

"Damn you," he said, finding that he was shaking far more than he should have been. "What were you thinking?"

"I'm not sure," she said, her teeth chattering.

"Don't ever go out without me again," he said in a very low voice. *"Ever."*

She looked up at him, her visage very pale. "I think I like it better when you shout at me."

He jerked her against him again. "Damn you, Jennifer McKinnon, the sight of you with his knife across your throat almost finished me. The violin isn't worth it."

"I didn't care about the violin," she said, her voice muffled against his shoulder. "I was afraid he would show it to someone and we would both burn at the stake."

"That would never happen," Robin put in.

Nicholas glared at his brother. "Are you involved in this conversation?"

"Just being helpful, as is my wont. Nick, I don't think your lady realizes who she stands to give herself to." Robin smiled at Jennifer. "You'll notice he fought the lion's share of the lads here, for one thing. Secondly, had Ledenham made an accusation, no matter the evidence, the king would not have accused Nicholas. And as Nick's wife, you would have been safe as well." He paused. "At least I think you both would have been safe. Perhaps you'd best find a better hiding place for that thing than behind Montgomery's back."

Jennifer pulled away and looked up at Nicholas. "I think I should send it back with Victoria."

Nicholas didn't need to consider the thought. "Nay, love, 'tis right that you have it. We'll find a better way to see to it."

Jennifer looked over her shoulder at the cluster of corpses, then buried her face in his neck. "I'm sorry," she whispered. "I didn't know what else to do."

"Aye, I know," he said with a sigh. "I can't say I would have chosen differently. But I vow I almost died of fright, seeing you that way."

She nodded, then looked up at him. "Hey," she accused, "you said it was okay for him to kill me. That's a pretty big bluff."

"I knew him well," Nicholas said. "It did not serve him to have you dead, but I will tell you that I *never* want to do that again. I can see now that my only choice is to sew you into my clothes."

Robin snorted loudly. "Oh, by the saints, let us leave them here. Who knows what else he will suggest to soothe his delicate nerves."

Nicholas glared at his brother, then released

Jennifer long enough to take all his gear back. He put on his jerkin, his swordbelt and sword, stuck his knives back where they were supposed to go, then fetched Jennifer's violin. He looked at the corpses cooling around him, then met Robin's eyes.

"I'll see to these lads," Robin said. "You see to your lady and her gear. I'd get both home sooner rather than later."

Nicholas nodded. He led Jennifer over to his horse, boosted her up into the saddle, then handed her the violin. He swung up onto the Black and looked at her.

"Can you hold that and ride at the same time?" he asked.

"Do I want to give it to you?" she countered. "Isn't that the same horse that threw you?"

"He's much better behaved today."

Jennifer smiled. "I'll manage, thanks just the same. You could ride with me if you'd rather."

"I would," he said honestly, "but I fear if I let this demon go by himself, I'll never see him again. I daresay he'll be a fine addition to our stables. Let's go see how Montgomery and John fare, then we'll pass a very quiet, uneventful afternoon in Mother's solar. I think it may rain soon. I imagine we can convince Connor and Victoria to join us in a game of bridge."

Jennifer smiled at him. "They've corrupted you."

"It helps pass the time," he said with a grimace. "And we need time to pass."

"Only a week until the wedding, but I don't know what you were thinking. It feels more like a year." Then she paused. She looked down for several moments before she glanced over at him. "Thank you for the rescue."

"I'll scold you about it later," he began lightly, but he saw immediately that she was more affected than she'd seemed. He considered, then swung down off the Black and pulled himself up behind her. The Black be damned. He wrapped his arms around her and took the reins. "Hold your gear, my love," he said, clucking his mount into a trot and leaving the Black to follow. "I won't say anything else."

"Oh, you can," she said, her voice quavering the slightest bit. "I deserve it. It was colossally stupid. I didn't know what else to do and I forgot that swords are very sharp."

"I still think sewing you into my clothes is the best thing for you," he said with a smile. "At least for the first little while."

"Will you hold me when we get back to Artane?"

"Aye."

"For the rest of the day?"

"And far into the night, if you like. Grand-mère can chaperon."

She nodded, but said nothing else.

He threw Brigit of Islington and her mother out the front gates half an hour after he returned home. He told them that Ledenham was dead and if they didn't wish to be there for the inquest and confess their part in the scheme, they should leave. It wasn't his habit to threaten women, but he felt compelled to remind them that Ledenham's interest in Jennifer's instrument had been a very deadly one.

They departed without protest. Or comment.

He watched Jennifer for the rest of the day, holding her when she seemed to need it, holding her hand otherwise. She didn't seem to be suffering ill effects from her adventure, but he knew it was only a matter of time before it occurred to her just how close she had come to dying.

It took until supper, which said much about her stamina.

He'd barely begun to cut meat to share with her before she'd begun to shake. He watched, silent and grim, as tears streamed down her face. He thought, at one point, that she would be ill.

She sat for quite some time, her face buried in her hands, simply breathing in and out.

Nicholas looked over her head and met Victoria and Connor's eyes. Victoria winced.

Connor only nodded knowingly. Finally, Jennifer took a deep, shuddering breath and put her shoulders back.

"Better," she said, attempting a smile and failing. She looked at him and shivered. "I never want to go through that again."

"Sword skill, my love."

She shook her head. "It wouldn't matter. I couldn't have killed any of them. I couldn't even use my usual self-defense moves." She looked at him, her visage pale. "I've never had a knife across my throat before."

"May you never again," he said, with feeling. "Perhaps you should hang your sword over the hearth and concentrate on your knife. You cannot be without some sort of protection, no matter how useful your hands might be."

She nodded uneasily. "You're right."

"Of course, you could agree to that stitching idea I had."

"I don't even think I can make a joke about this."

He put his arm around her. "You've seen the worst of it," he said quietly. "I beg you, though, not to leave without me. If ever I must go to war, I'll leave men behind in the keep to protect you. Not even Amanda leaves the keep without Jake." He paused. "Well, perhaps she does, but not often. She has also trained with Robin. There is a ruthlessness to her that you do not have."

"I think I could learn to use a knife."

He nodded and sat back in his chair. "Aye, you could. But let us put it aside for now. Forget today. Your instrument is safe, you are safe, and there is your family to be enjoyed. Jake says he has a new card game he thinks I will enjoy."

"I hate to ask which one."

"Go Fish, 'tis called. He said 'tis just my speed, whatever that means. What do you think?"

She laughed. "I think you'll want to meet him in the lists in the morning, but maybe not." She let out a shaky breath. "I think I'll be okay."

"I daresay you will," he agreed. He took her hand and kissed it. "I will keep you safe, Jen."

"I know."

Nicholas poured her wine, then saw to her meal. He caught Connor's eye at one point. Connor nodded shortly, obviously satisfied.

Nicholas was satisfied as well. Perhaps Connor would carry a good report to Jennifer's father and yet another mind would be at ease.

And his would be as well, as soon as he was able to rid it of the sight of Jennifer with a knife across her throat. He could admit to nothing but relief that Ledenham was gone. Perhaps he would buy the abbey ground himself as a token of good will and see the place finished. He supposed neither he nor

Jennifer would ever want to go there, but then again, they might. At least they would know the time gate there had ceased to exist. It would save several monks an uncomfortable trip into a world that was not their own.

He pushed aside his thoughts and concentrated on his meal.

She was safe.

Nothing else mattered.

CHAPTER 37

Jennifer stood in Gwen's solar and allowed herself to be made over into a medieval Cinderella ready for the grand ball. It reminded her a little of the first time the women in Nicholas's family had played fairy godmother. She'd had a bath, had her hair fixed by Anne and Isabelle, and had looked over her gowns with Joanna, Gwen, and Amanda to decide which one would suit. Only this time it was a little different. Victoria was there as well, watching with tears in her eyes, and her Prince Charming was, from all accounts, pacing in the chapel, worrying that she would change her mind.

That message had come by way of Isabelle who had gone to check, then returned to deliver her report in a tone that suggested that she very much wanted Jennifer to assure her that such a thing wouldn't even have crossed her mind.

Jennifer had been happy to reassure her.

She looked down at her dress. It was the

royal blue gown, encrusted with pearls and gems and embroidered with all manner of flowers and vines. It was simply stunning and Jennifer hoped she could do it justice.

Then Victoria came over to her with something behind her back.

"I thought you might need these," she said with a smile.

"What?" Jennifer asked.

Victoria handed her her glass slippers. "For you."

Jennifer looked quickly at her sister, then started to cry.

"Nay," Joanna scolded, "no more of that. You'll blotch the dress and ruin your face. Nicholas will think 'tis my doing and frown at me."

Jennifer shook her head, but she also dried her eyes. She stood there in clothes truly fit for a princess, then smiled.

"Well?" she asked. "What do you think?"

"Beautiful," Gwen said, coming to take her hands and kiss her cheek. "We'll go downstairs and wait for you. I thought you might want a few minutes with your sister."

Jennifer found herself hugged in turn by Nicholas's grandmother, his mother, his sister-in-law, and both his sisters. She watched them shut the door behind them, then turned and looked at Victoria. "Well?"

"Well, you've had a brush with death, completely overwhelmed an entire clan of medieval nobles with your music, and now you're going to marry a man who they still talk about reverently at Artane eight hundred years from now." Victoria shrugged with a smile. "How can you top any of that?"

Jennifer hugged her sister. "I'm so glad you came."

"Trust me, I wouldn't have missed it for the world." She pulled back and fussed with Jennifer's hair. "I told myself I wouldn't cry, but I don't think I'll manage not to. You look just gorgeous." She smiled wistfully. "Are you happy?"

"Deliriously."

"You look like it. And he's wonderful." She smiled. "I know what the annals say, but there's nothing like getting to know the legend in person."

"Genealogy doesn't lie?" Jennifer teased.

"Not in Nicholas's case," Victoria said honestly. "He is, amazingly enough, everything he was reputed to be. And he plays a mean game of Go Fish."

Jennifer laughed. "At least he has a sense of humor."

Victoria hugged her again. "I think you'll be blissfully happy with him. Now, we probably should get going before he wears out his boots pacing. Or will he be wearing those fancy medieval shoes with the pointy toes?"

"Would Connor?"

"Are you kidding?" Victoria said with a

laugh. "No way."

Jennifer smiled. "I can't imagine Nicholas would, either, unless his grandmother has insisted. No, even then, I think it will be boots. You'll have to tell me. I don't think I'll notice."

"You'd notice those shoes."

Jennifer laughed. "I probably would. I imagine he's safe from that indignity." She took a deep breath. "Will I suit?"

"Of course," Victoria said. "But let me take a picture of you by yourself. Go stand over there by the fire."

Jennifer did, ignoring the sensation of being pulled in two every time something from the future collided with the past. She supposed that in time that would cease. Even the De-gani might start to feel normal.

She blinked away the spots in her eyes and made Victoria show her the picture.

"Wow," she managed. "Is that me?"

"Miss Medieval," Victoria said with a smile.

Jennifer could hardly believe it. Admittedly, it had been a while since she'd looked in a mirror, but she'd almost forgotten what she looked like. Her hair was piled on top of her head with a few tendrils curling down the back of her neck. Gwen had unearthed a tiara of sorts from some trunk or another and placed it lovingly on her head.

But the dress . . . the dress was stunning.

"He has good taste," Jennifer murmured.

"He does," Victoria agreed. "He picked you, didn't he?"

"I suppose he did," Jennifer agreed.

"I'll take a picture of you and Nicholas together later."

"He'll flip."

"I think he's flipping as it is," Victoria smiled. "We'd better go save him from himself."

Jennifer nodded, then linked arms with her sister and left Isabelle's room.

She walked down the hallway, then down the stairs to the great hall. It was empty, which would have unnerved her, but it still had its medieval trappings and she was sure everyone was waiting in the chapel. She did have to take several deep breaths just the same.

"Are you okay?" Victoria asked.

Jennifer smiled weakly. "I'm not sure what century I'm in."

Victoria laughed uneasily. "You know, I think I understand that. This is a little spooky. Let's go outside. I'm sure the sight of the stables will reassure us."

Jennifer nodded and continued with her sister across the hall. A servant bowed and opened the front door for her. Jennifer walked down the steps, then realized that the way had been strewn with flowers. She smiled at her sister.

"Wow."

"I'll say," Victoria said with a smile. "I don't think I had anything this fancy."

Jennifer blinked. "You *were* married at Artane, weren't you? I'd forgotten."

"Thanks," Victoria said dryly.

"It looks different in the future."

"Not much," Victoria said. "So, if I get a little misty, that's why. Now, come on and hurry. Someone's opening the chapel door."

Jennifer watched her feet as she crossed the courtyard. It had been a while since she'd worn heels and the last thing she wanted to do was fall on her face five minutes before she was supposed to get married. She made it to the chapel steps, then looked up.

Her father stood there.

Jennifer had to clutch Victoria's hand. "Dad?" she said, more surprised than she'd ever been in her life.

He smiled and held open his arms. She threw herself into them and hugged him tightly.

"Oh, Dad," she said, starting to cry. "You came."

"Do you think I'd miss this?" he asked gruffly. "Damn it, Jen, this makes a trip across the Pond look like a jaunt down the street to the Mini Mart."

"Oh, Dad," she said, pulling back and sniffing hard to keep from ruining her dress. "I can't believe you came. And I'm sorry —"

He shook his head and kissed her cheek.

"No, don't start that. We'll have a good long talk later. Right now you need to go marry that poor man at the front of the church who looks like he'd like to throw up. But first go give your mother a hug. Then you can come back and I'll walk you down the aisle."

She hugged him for a few more minutes in silence, then let him dry her eyes. She smiled, then went inside. Her mother and grandmother were standing just inside the door, waiting for her.

She hugged her mother tightly. "When did you get here?" she whispered in amazement.

"About an hour ago," Helen said. "Long enough to meet your groom and have your father attempt to terrify him." She pulled away and smiled. "Granny and I translated for him."

Jennifer turned to her grandmother and hugged her. "Granny, you came, too."

"I'm a veteran time traveler," Mary said, looking fabulous in a medieval ensemble that rivaled anything in the chapel. "I thought I'd better figure out how to get here so I can come visit now and then."

Jennifer laughed. "I certainly hope so." She smiled at her grandmother, then turned and held on to her mother for quite a long time. She pulled back finally.

"Thanks, Mom," she said quietly.

Helen kissed her on both cheeks. "I wouldn't have missed it for the world. Now, go rescue your future husband from his nerves."

Jennifer nodded, then went back to stand next to her father. He held out his arm. Jennifer took it and smiled up at him.

"Thank you."

He cleared his throat roughly. "Children leave home. Some go farther away than others. If he's who you want, I'm happy."

"Dad, he's wonderful."

"Damn well better be."

"Have you really frightened him?"

"Yes. Repeatedly. I'll frighten him some more after the ceremony. But now, let's get this show on the road. I don't think your Nicholas really wants the memory of his wedding day to include his having puked on the priest."

Jennifer laughed. "I imagine not." She turned and walked down the very short aisle. She smiled at Nicholas, who was indeed looking much worse for the wear.

Her father put her hand in his with a growl. Nicholas smiled weakly, then heaved a small sigh of relief. He made her father a small bow, then looked at Jennifer.

"You're here."

"Of course," she said with a smile. She squeezed his hand. "I love you," she whispered.

"The saints be praised," he murmured, with feeling. Then he smiled at her. "And I you."

The priest cleared his throat pointedly. Jennifer winked at Nicholas, then did her best to put on a more serious expression.

It was hard, when all that joy was threatening to burst out of her.

She tried to listen to the ceremony but it was hard to concentrate on mass in Latin, which she understood very little of, and it was hard to concentrate when she was so overwhelmed by the fact that she was marrying the man she loved and her parents had come to witness it. So she held Nicholas's hand, said what she was supposed to say when she was told to say it, and hoped she was marrying him.

"Translate for me later," she whispered.

"I will," he promised.

The priest called for a recounting of what the parties would bring to the marriage. Jennifer supposed hers wouldn't take long and she wondered if she should mention her violin. The priest looked at a sheaf of paper in his hands.

"A trunk full of valuables from her sire," he muttered, "and Wyckham keep." He looked up. "Wyckham?"

Jennifer looked up at Nicholas. "Wyckham?"

He shrugged with a smile. "I made it part of your dowry a fortnight ago. I thought that even if you changed your mind, it would be yours. Finished, of course. Petter is building you a gallery for musicians to play in. The music will waft down to the great hall in a pleasing fashion." He paused. "The roof won't leak this time."

"Oh, Nicholas," she said, stunned. "That's too much."

"That roof isn't finished yet," Robin put in from where he was standing on the other side of his brother. "I wouldn't praise him over-much for it. Besides, wed him and he has it back again, so —"

Nicholas elbowed Robin in the ribs so hard, Robin doubled over with a grunt. Robin straightened, clapped a hand on Nicholas's shoulder, and pointed at the priest.

"Write this down, though he doesn't need it and doesn't deserve it. Garrison knights, a squire or two, and I've even found him a page willing to brave his sour self. Father is sending him a decent steward."

"And a cook," Rhys put in. "As well as a seamstress or two. His mother thinks it important that he continue to dress his lady as she deserves."

Jennifer smiled up at Nicholas and heard nothing else. Whether or not Wyckham was his again was immaterial. He had given her security when he hadn't had to, he had clothed her when it would have been easier to let her carry on with a hem that didn't match, and he had put his life on the line to spare hers.

It was so much more than she'd ever expected.

The priest cleared his throat. Jennifer looked at him.

"What?"

"You must sign the marriage contracts, my lady," he said.

Jennifer signed. Nicholas signed. Then he turned her to him, pulled her into his arms, and kissed her.

Quite chastely, actually.

She looked up at him. "Is that it?"

"Your father's standing not ten paces away."

"But we're married."

He frowned. "You're taller."

"It's the shoes and you're digressing."

He smiled, though he still looked a little queasy. "I've never had a father-in-law before. I'm doing my best."

She put her arms around his neck, leaned up and kissed him instead. But not for too long. Her father was watching, after all.

"What now?" she asked.

"Supper," Joanna announced. "A fine feast has been prepared. Jackson, come translate for Jennifer's father. I can hear that her mother and grandmother speak Scots, which I find very pleasing, so perhaps Jennifer and Nicholas will translate for me."

Jennifer watched Nicholas's family gather up hers and escort them out of the chapel. She realized only then how many people had come. Jake had taken her father in hand and was leading him, rather wide-eyed, out of the chapel as he chatted with him in English. Montgomery had made her mother and grandmother low bows and offered his services to translate for them with Joanna. Amanda and Victoria were leaving arm in arm, chatting happily in a bewildering mixture of Gaelic and English with Connor trailing along, holding Amanda's daughter and trying not to wince as she alternately tugged on his hair and tried to chew on the enormous brooch that pinned his plaid to his shoulder. Robin collected Anne and his sons and escorted them and his younger brothers out into the sunshine.

Jennifer stood with Nicholas until they'd all gone out, including the priest, then looked at him.

"Weren't we supposed to go first?" she asked.

"They were distracted by the thought of lunch," he said solemnly.

"I suppose so." She turned to him and took his hands. "Privacy at last."

"Jennifer," he said, sounding shocked, " 'tis the chapel."

She laughed. "I wasn't suggesting anything untoward, my lord. But you could kiss me properly."

He let out a long breath. "Are we wed? In truth?"

"I think I signed something that said we were. You were supposed to be understanding the Latin bits."

"I didn't listen. I was too busy wondering if your father would plunge a blade into my back at an inopportune moment."

"You were not," she said with a laugh.

"Actually, I was," he said honestly. "He had stern words for me about the care and keeping of his youngest child."

"And what did you tell him, my lord?"

"I used the first English word I learned."

"And that was?"

"Whatever."

She laughed and clasped her hands behind his neck. "You didn't."

"I didn't," he said with a smile, putting his arms around her waist. "I told him, through Jake whom I thanked profusely for his aid, that I loved you beyond reason, that I would spend every day making certain that you felt cherished, and that you would lack for nothing that I could possibly provide you in the way of luxuries. Then I showed him my sword."

She smiled. "Was he impressed?"

"It seemed to satisfy him."

"He's not watching now, you know."

"Jennifer," he said with a laugh. Then he paused and shrugged. "I suppose I'm within my rights to kiss my wife, aren't I?"

"I suppose so. But don't mess up my hair."

"I won't. I hate to think of what my grand-mother would do to me if I did."

She smiled as he drew her closer and kissed her properly. He kissed her until she thought perhaps that he should stop. He lifted his head and looked down at her.

"Food?"

"Why?"

He laughed and kissed her again. "Because, my love, it is a reason to sit with our families as long as is polite. And it will save your father a trip out here to look for us."

She nodded, took his hand, and walked with him from the chapel. "I can't believe they came."

"They love you," he said gently. "How could they not?"

"My father doesn't even like to fly," she said. "This was really something for him."

"Fly?"

She smiled. "We have several things to discuss, my lord."

"Later."

"Much later."

He smiled and held open the hall door for her.

Jennifer walked in and paused to take in the sight. The high table was empty. Instead, one of the lower tables had been placed in front of the fire and everyone was gathered around it. She saw Jake sitting next to her father, chatting amicably. Her mother and

617

grandmother were sitting with Joanna and they were smiling and nodding as Montgomery translated for them. Victoria and Connor were sitting with Rhys and Amanda, who seemed to be translating for Robin and the rest of the lads. Jennifer smiled to herself. Though she missed Thomas and Megan, it was enough for the day.

"Nicholas! Jennifer!"

"We're being summoned," Nicholas said, smiling down at her. "I think Grandmère wants more translation than Montgomery can provide."

She followed, smiling, grateful, and happy beyond belief.

Nicholas and her family, in a hall that was firmly grounded in the thirteenth century.

It was bliss.

CHAPTER 38

Nicholas sat near the fire in the great hall and did his best to concentrate on what was going on around him. He wasn't one to be distracted, but he supposed he had cause. After all, it wasn't every day that he wed a woman he adored, entertained her family from the Future, and plotted ways to kill his elder brother and brother-in-law all at the same time.

Robin and Jake were, of course, doing all they could to quietly suggest to him that a standing up might be called for.

"When hell freezes over," he'd said to Robin as Robin had brought him wine. "I'll see you in hell first," he'd remarked calmly to Jake as Jake had refilled his cup.

They'd only smirked and returned to their seats where they whispered together and smirked a bit more.

Standing up, Nicholas snorted. As if he would actually allow them to strip him, one, or strip Jennifer, two. He imagined that her knees did not knock. If they did, he didn't care. He wasn't going to repudiate her, so it was best that Robin and Jake merely retreat to the lord's solar for a quick game of fish.

Nicholas scowled. Jake had quite a bit to answer for, actually.

"You're frowning," Jennifer said sweetly.

He turned to her and smiled. "Happy thoughts, actually."

"I think you have Robin's demise on your mind," she said, her eyes twinkling. "Perhaps Jake's as well. I don't think anyone else has dared tease you."

"They haven't," he agreed.

"I think they're trying to distract you," she said solemnly. "You look a little nervous."

"Me?" he echoed. "Never. Never mind that your father continues to glare at me and your grandmother has nodded knowingly several times in my direction."

Jennifer laughed. "It serves you right for all the times your grandmother sized *me* up."

He took her hand in his. "I suppose it does. But 'tis torture just the same."

"I don't think the torture's going to end anytime soon," she remarked. "I understand your grandmother has a full afternoon planned. Music. Dancing. Perhaps a play. My sister and Connor are very famous actors, you know. They might do something to entertain us. At your grandmother's behest, of course."

"I am unsurprised," he grumbled.

Jennifer laughed and patted his hand. "I'm sure the day will just speed by. You'll see."

What he would see is someone's head on a pike outside the gates. Or perhaps two someones. He decided on that after the wedding feast had been accomplished and other chairs set up by the fire for relaxing and conversing. His family seemed perfectly content. Jennifer's family seemed perfectly at ease. Jake was translating for Father McKinnon. Jennifer translated for her mother and grandmother. Nicholas saw that his parents were doing their best to make Jennifer's parents feel at ease. Anne, Amanda, and Isabelle were their gracious selves, adding beauty and charm to the afternoon.

Still, the day dragged on like a cart with a broken axle.

Nicholas found that he was as nervous as a cat. Between Jennifer's father looking at him as if he was about to bed his daughter, and Robin and Jake occasionally coming close to make suggestions on how soon he should retreat upstairs to his chamber which they had made ready for him so he could do just that, Nicholas was tempted to do damage to someone.

"Dancing, now," Joanna announced. "Robin, go fetch the musicians. Everyone else, make ready for a lovely afternoon."

Nicholas would have complained, but he

found himself suddenly pulled to his feet.

"I must speak with you," Jennifer said seriously. "Come with me now."

Nicholas followed her across the hall whilst the rest of the company was in confusion trying to sneak food from where it had been laid on the high table, or flee out the front door before Joanna could catch them. He was unwholesomely unsettled by Jennifer's tone. Had she changed her mind? Had she decided that she might prefer Wyckham without him?

She pulled him into the stairwell and turned around.

He steeled himself for the worst.

She took off her shoes. He looked at her in surprise. Was she now going to clout him over the head with those terrifying bits of business?

Then she leaned up and kissed him.

He blinked. "I'm confused. I thought you wanted to speak to me."

"Not really," she laughed. She took his hand and pulled him up the stairs. "Come on, Nicky."

"Nicky," he repeated. He followed her up the steps and down the passageway. "Where are we going?"

"We're going to bolt ourselves in your chamber, of course. Miles has done us the favor of supplying enough food and drink that we won't need to unbolt the door until at least tomorrow morning. Also, the trunk my father brought along is inside." She smiled up at him. "Future marvels, my lord."

"Ah," he said, realizing what she was about. "Are you avoiding Robin and his ideas of standing up?"

"Damned right," she said, pulling him down the passageway.

He followed her into his chamber. In this, at least, his brothers had not done poorly. There was a fire in the hearth, wine on the table and candles lit for their pleasure. His brothers were noticeably absent.

That was perhaps the best gift of all.

Jennifer shut door, then bolted it. She set her shoes on the floor, then turned and looked at him.

"Well?"

He smiled weakly. "I'm unaccountably nervous."

"Why? It's just me."

"Your father's downstairs."

"I promise, he won't come tuck us in."

He laughed and took a step closer to her to pull her into his arms. "I certainly hope not." He looked down at her. "I still cannot believe you're here."

"Neither can I," she with a tremulous smile. "But I don't regret it." She pulled his head down and kissed him. "Where is your self-control, my lord?"

"I left it with your father."

"I'm sure he appreciates it. Now, why don't

you kiss me? I don't think you have to stop today. But be sure you do a thorough job."

He smiled, pulled her into his arms, and obliged her.

Thoroughly.

Nicholas woke quite late, for him. Of course, it made a difference when he had spent most of the night not sleeping.

Blissfully so.

He sat up. The sun was already up and streaming through the window. It fell upon the figure of a flame-haired woman who was kneeling in her shift in front of her trunk, peering into it.

"You said you'd wait," he chided.

She turned and smiled at him. "I did wait. I was just peeking."

He clucked his tongue and rolled from the bed, wrapping a sheet around his hips. She looked up at him.

"Cute."

"Cute?"

She pointed to his sheet. "Attractive."

"Is it?"

"Actually, it's distracting, just like the rest of you. Now, do you want me to concentrate on the trunk or not?" she asked, with one raised eyebrow.

He smiled. "Well, now that you ask, nay. Not exactly."

She laughed and held up her arms to him.

It took another several attempts at investigating the trunk whilst doing so in various states of dress before Nicholas found himself the next morning sitting with his wife in front of the trunk, both of them fully clothed. Nicholas looked at Jennifer and sighed lightly.

"I suppose we'll manage this this time."

She laughed. "I suppose so. But don't worry. I sent a message to my father that we wouldn't be down until dinner. You have all afternoon for a very, very long nap."

"The saints preserve me."

"I think you said that a lot last night. You might say it again this morning." She opened the trunk. "Here you go. The Future brought right to your lap."

Nicholas peered inside with the same care he might have used whilst looking into a trunk full of asps. He frowned. There were books, but of no sort he'd ever seen before. He looked for quite some time without touching, then finally sat back on his heels and looked at Jennifer.

"I must admit it," he said slowly. "I have no idea where to start."

"I'll start for you. Maybe I'll make piles for me, piles for you, then we'll see what's here to share." She reached in the trunk. "Oh, look. Some chocolate. Definitely for me."

He looked at the shiny gold box. It looked

like a holy relic, but what did he know? "Chocolate?"

"It's food."

"You should share."

"Maybe. You can have half of one of the smallest pieces and I'll have all the rest." She smiled. "It's Godiva. It's powerful."

"I'm a knight of legendary prowess. Your sister said so. I daresay I'll survive."

She opened the box and took out a small brown ball. She closed the box back up reverently and put it down. Where he couldn't reach it, he noted. She bit into the ball.

Her eyes rolled back in her head.

He reached out to catch her only to have her straighten and wink at him.

"Just kidding. You try."

He accepted what was left of the small ball she had eaten. He sniffed. He had, he could say with all honesty, never smelled anything like it. He considered just a small taste, but decided that was cowardly. Instead, he popped the entire thing in his mouth and chewed.

He understood the eye rolling.

He swallowed and smiled. "How much is left?" he asked, trying to see around her.

"Not as much as we'd like. I think they have chocolate in Spain. Did you never have any?"

"Nothing that tasted like that," he said, with feeling.

"Yeah, well, this box has my name on it, so

don't try anything funny."

He frowned at her, but she only laughed at him. She reached out and smoothed her hand over his hair and smiled.

"I'm teasing. I'll share. Maybe. Let's see what else is in here."

Nicholas watched as she pulled things out of the trunk and set them on the floor.

"Violin strings, lots of rosin, a book on restringing my bow. Very important. Some music which I'll look through later. Knitting needles, though yours were nicer. Lots of yarn. My granny's doing, obviously." She held a ball of pale yarn up to her cheek, then held it against his. "Cashmere. Lovely, isn't it?"

"Wonderful," he said honestly.

She peered again into the trunk. "Here we have washable, organic feminine protection products, thank you, Mother. A book on natural childbirth." She shot him a look. "I imagine that's from my grandmother. She likes to be prepared."

He watched with wide eyes. "So I see."

She pulled out a gray, flat box and opened it. She smiled and looked at him. "For us both, I imagine. Surgical needles for sutures."

"Smaller than mine."

"Much. Let's hope we never have to use them. Plus a book on herbal medicine. Very useful."

"Any more chocolate?"

Jennifer poked around in the trunk. She flashed him a smile. "Several boxes of Godiva, a couple of Kit Kats and a six pack of Lilt."

"Good?"

"Very good." She pulled out a pair of what looked like soft gauntlets. "Leather gloves. For you. Cashmere socks. For you again. Oh, and Nicholas look, here's a chess set." She smiled. "It must be from my father. He's the only one who plays chess."

He smiled. "Perhaps he isn't opposed to me after all."

"I imagine he's not," she agreed.

He watched as she continued to remove things he supposed he would learn the use for at some point. Then she pulled forth the books he'd peered at before; they were nothing like he'd ever seen.

"Books," she confirmed. "There's a tag on them with your name, so I assume they're for you." She smiled. "They'll blow your mind. We have geography, history, Shakespeare, all sorts of other literature. You'll love it."

"These are books?" He shivered. "I've never seen anything so fine."

"Well, it's entirely possible that we should feed the fire with most of them after you've read them," she admitted, "but I think you'll enjoy them until then." She looked inside the trunk, then froze.

"Jen?"

She pulled out two small, gray boxes. They

were similar to her cell phone, which she had shown him the night before. She looked at him.

"Music," she whispered.

"In there?" he asked, stunned.

Tears rolled down her cheeks. "In here. And solar battery chargers as well. I'll show you how it all works, but not now. Now I think I just have to sit and think."

"And eat more Godiva?"

She laughed. "When it's gone, it's gone."

"Then let's eat it now, before Robin finds it. Though the books are tempting as well."

"I have competition," she murmured.

He hauled her into his lap and wrapped his arms around her. "You most certainly do not. But I'm tempted to agree with what you said." He took an unsteady breath. "All this could truly see us at the stake."

"What should we do?"

"Lock it well," he said with feeling.

"We could burn it."

"Not the chocolate," he said immediately. He paused. "Not the books." He looked at her in wonder. "And I thought I could provide you with luxuries. I daresay I cannot equal —"

She kissed him softly, interrupting him. "You clothed me when I had nothing. You made me look like a princess when I could have looked like a peasant. You married me, when you could have had anyone."

"I *wanted* you," he said. "I would have waited dozens of lifetimes for you —"

She put her hand over his mouth, then put her mouth over his mouth. "Don't even say it. This stuff is just stuff and nothing compared to what I feel for you." She reached over and shut the trunk lid. "Let's leave the rest for later. Now, I think we have better things to do."

He couldn't have agreed more.

It occurred to him, at some point during that long, luxurious afternoon with Jennifer McKinnon in his arms, that he'd known the truth of the matter long before he'd seen what the trunk contained.

The true marvel from the Future was what he held in his arms.

Chapter 39

A fortnight later, Jennifer sat in front of the hearth in Nicholas's bedroom and let her hair dry by the heat of the fire. She watched her husband as he padded about the chamber, wearing hose and boots but looking for a tunic and cursing while he was about it. Then he stopped and looked at her. He put his hands on his hips.

"What?" he demanded.

She shrugged with a smile.

"Are you ogling me?" he asked archly.

"I might be."

"Jennifer de Piaget, your parents are leaving today," he began with mock sternness, then he sobered. "I'm sorry. That isn't fodder for jest."

She held up her hands as he walked to her. He pulled her to her feet and into his arms. She rested her head against his bare chest, his heart beating strongly beneath her ear, and put her arms around him.

"You know what makes it bearable?" she

asked softly.

"I daren't imagine."

She looked up at him. "You. Once they leave, you'll come back here and make love to me, won't you?"

"Will it make you feel better?"

"I'm not sure. Let's try several times and see."

"Jenner," he said with half a laugh, then he shook his head. "Your self-control, my lady, is sadly lacking."

"I'm trying to distract myself."

"Let me offer my services in that endeavor."

She smiled and hugged him. "You, my lord, are full of chivalry. How is it I was so fortunate to win you?"

"You felled me the moment you looked at me," he said, then he paused. "Nay, that isn't true. You felled me the first time I set eyes on you. I've been drowning in love ever since." He held her tightly to him. "By the saints, Jen, I don't think I'll ever accustom myself to having you." He took a deep breath. "You sacrificed —"

"My family," she said, looking up at him, "but no more. They will read about us and know we were happy. And who knows that they won't try the gates again at some point and come for a visit."

"Your granny would worry me with a map in her hand," Nicholas admitted.

"Isn't she wonderful?"

"She is," he agreed. "I'd keep her, but I think your sire might begrudge me two of his women."

"My mother would miss her," Jennifer said. "But it wouldn't surprise me to see her at some point in the future." She patted his back, then slipped from his arms. "We should go." She dragged her sleeve across her eyes. "But we'll return here."

"Aye. And then the shore."

She blinked. "The shore?"

"It is a very, very empty strand."

"Ha," she snorted. "Your brothers would find us."

"Robin has a tent. We'll borrow it."

She nodded, though she couldn't think past what was going to happen in the next hour. She knew her family had to go. She had made her choice and she had no regrets.

But that didn't mean it was going to be easy.

At least she'd had a decent amount of time with them. Victoria and Connor had been there for well over a month, long enough to merit a room of their own. Her parents and grandmother had been there for almost three weeks, long enough for her father, Jake, Rhys, and Nicholas to become attached at the hip. Nicholas had done his best to pick up as much English as possible in that time and gone out of his way to woo her father as thoroughly as he had her. Jennifer had watched her father fall under his spell. John had even spent his share of time laughing with him.

That boded well, to her mind.

She had spent all her time with her mother and grandmother, followed by a contingent of armed Artane males and more guardsmen than needful each time they dared poke their noses out of the gate. She couldn't remember anything specific that they'd done, outside of many pleasant afternoons in Gwen's solar with all the ladies and equally as many wonderful mornings walking along the beach. Other than that, all she knew was that she had spent every moment possible with them during the days.

Well, except for a few naps.

"You're ogling me again."

She smiled and shook her head. "Sorry."

"Don't be," he laughed. "Have I complained?"

"No, you haven't," she agreed.

She watched as he found a tunic and yanked it down over his head. He took her hand and led her from the chamber. He fitted a newly made key to the newly installed lock, put the key into the purse at his belt, then led her down the hallway.

Jennifer took several deep breaths as they walked. She blinked several times as she followed Nicholas down the steps. He paused on the bottom step, then turned and looked at her.

"Will you be all right?" he asked quietly.

"I can't cry," she said, trying to smile. "That isn't the sight I want them to carry away. I'm happy, damn it."

"So I see by your tears."

She wrapped her arms around his neck and held on to him tightly. "I *am* happy. I'm just not happy about this."

He rubbed her back soothingly. "I know, my love," he whispered. "And I'm sorry for it."

She stood there in the comfort of his arms for several minutes, then sighed and pulled away. "I'm okay now. Let's go see them off. I'll definitely need to be distracted this afternoon, though."

He took hold of her hand. "I am at your service."

She smiled and followed him out into the great hall. Her family was gathered near one of the massive fireplaces, talking quietly with Nicholas's family. Jennifer quickly memorized the scene so she could replay it again later. She had a family picture upstairs in the trunk, obviously taken with the whole crew before Vic and Connor had come back to find her, and she supposed that would be a comfort.

Nicholas hesitated.

Jennifer looked up at him. "Don't you dare."

He smiled grimly. "Sorry."

"If you aren't a rock right now, I will crumble. I've made my choice."

"I know."

"If you ask me if I'm sure right now, I'll clunk you over the head with your sword."

He smiled. "Perhaps you are fiercer than I suspected."

"It's an act," she said softly. "But I'm going to go with what works right now."

She continued across the hall with him, then hugged her mother. She kept one arm around her and one around Nicholas's waist and simply soaked in the companionship of so many people she loved.

Bittersweet took on an entirely new meaning at that moment.

"Tell Megan I love her," she said, looking at her mother with a smile. "And Thomas. Gideon and Iolanthe as well. I'll miss them all."

"I'll make sure they know," Helen said with a smile. "Anything else?"

"Apologize to Charles Salieri. No, wait," she said with a frown. "What *are* you going to tell him?"

"Certainly not the truth," Helen said with a half laugh. "What do you want me to tell him?"

"You could tell him part of the truth," Jennifer said slowly. "Tell him I fell in love with an English lord and I won't be coming back to New York."

"He'll have apoplexy. And he'll camp out on my doorstep until I give him your phone number."

Jennifer winced. "I imagine he will. He'll get over it. Maybe Mr. Bourgeois will be out of the nuthouse by the time you get back. I wonder what happened to him in the first place?"

"I understand Hugh McKinnon took up the violin and paid him a little nighttime visit to display his proficiency." Helen smiled deeply. "Apparently, it was a memorable concert."

"Poor man," Jennifer said with a laugh. "Well, do what you think you should, Mom."

"I will, honey."

Jennifer watched as her mother smiled at Nicholas.

"Take care of my baby," she said with a smile. "Though perhaps I don't need to say that."

He shook his head. "You're right to, my lady. And I will. I will do all I can to see she never regrets her choice."

"How could she?" Helen said with a smile. "You were worth the trip."

Jennifer smiled, patted Nicholas's back, and went to have a few quiet words with her sister. She hugged Victoria tightly.

"I'll miss you."

Victoria shook her head. "Don't start or I won't make it through the morning." She kissed Jennifer on both cheeks. "I'm glad we came. I'm glad I got to see you get married. I'll tell Megan and Thomas all about it and we'll think about you often."

Jennifer nodded, hugged Connor briefly, then turned to her father. She went into his arms and found that she couldn't say anything. So she stood, trying to breathe evenly and feeling him struggling to do the same. Finally, she pulled back.

"You like him?"

John nodded. "He's worthy of you. And believe me, the bar was set extremely high."

"Thank you, Dad."

"For what?"

"For coming all this way. For leaving me behind. For not minding."

"Never said I didn't mind," John said gruffly. "But you're happy."

"It's the pioneer lifestyle," she said lightly.

He grunted and hugged her again. Then he stepped back. "We need to go. Nicholas has your granny well in hand. Why don't you walk with me to the stables?"

"All right."

The walk there was far too short. Jennifer did her best to imprint on her heart the memory of walking across Artane's courtyard with her father. She stopped and watched as her family exchanged embraces and kind words with Nicholas's relatives. Horses were sorted out and saddled. Jennifer watched

Nicholas boost her grandmother up into the saddle. Mary leaned over and patted his cheek affectionately. He saw to her mother as well, then took a deep breath and walked over to where she was holding the reins of his horse.

"Ready?" he asked.

She nodded.

"Will you ride with me?"

"Of course. But you knew that already."

He swung up onto his horse, then pulled her up into the saddle in front of him. "Aye," he said quietly. "I knew."

Jennifer sat in the security of his embrace as they left the castle and rode through the village. It took far too little time to reach what Jake indicated was the time gate. It was only then that she realized he had come with them. But he didn't dismount with the rest of them.

Jennifer looked at him in surprise. "Aren't you staying?"

He shook his head. "The gate will work. See you at dinner."

Jennifer felt Nicholas jump off his horse, then let him help her down. He squeezed her hand, then went to help her mother and grandmother.

He came back to her side, though, and looked a little uneasy.

"What?" she asked.

"I'm spooked," he said honestly. "There is

an odd feeling here."

Jennifer smiled. "I won't let you fall through the gate."

"I'm not concerned for myself."

She squeezed his hand briefly, then gave final hugs to her family. Then she stepped back, took Nicholas's hand and put on her brightest smile.

The little group of five turned and led their horses onto the invisible X.

Her mother turned and waved.

And then they were gone.

"Merciful saints above," breathed Nicholas, swaying a little.

She shivered. "I agree."

"And we could do the same."

She looked at him in astonishment. "You don't mean that."

"Your granny instructed me to think on it. She said I should always keep my options open."

"It means to keep an open mind."

"If my mind were any more open, it would fold back on itself like a book with a broken spine."

She looked up at him and smiled, then put her arms around him. "Let's go to the shore."

"Are you sure?" he asked gravely. "You don't want to stay here a bit longer?"

She shook her head. "Distraction, my lord, is the order of the day."

He wrapped his arms around her and held

her close for a very long time in silence. Then he pulled back to look down at her. "The strand?" he asked gently.

She nodded. "Please."

"Without the tent?"

She smiled. "Perhaps just for a ride. And a walk. We could stay there all day." She shrugged. "Who knows what might happen when the sun sets?"

"We will become lost," he said with a smile. "That's what happens when the sun sets." He looked at the innocent spot of ground once more and shook his head. "I wonder how many unsuspecting souls have found themselves in a century not their own?" he mused.

"Too many to count, probably."

He ran his hand over her hair. "Will you be well?" he asked guardedly.

"I'll cry."

"I'll hold you."

"I'll be fine."

"I'll distract you if you are not."

She smiled and tugged on his hand. "The shore, my lord. It will soothe me."

He walked with her to his horse and swung up into the saddle. He pulled her up behind him.

Jennifer wrapped her arms around his waist and leaned her head against his back. She closed her eyes and was grateful for a moment or two to let her tears run down her face unobserved.

In time, she managed to blink them away. She watched the scenery as it passed by and realized that this was exactly what she had wanted, but it had come true in a way she never would have expected. No cell phones. No stereos — well, except for the iPods, but she could turn those off. No street noise. Just peace and unobstructed sky and beautiful English countryside that stretched out forever. She had unimaginable luxuries by medieval standards and she had something she never, ever would have found in Manhattan.

A knight in shining armor who loved her.

Half an hour later, she was walking down the beach with that knight, talking of nothing, and wondering if her heart would break.

He stopped and looked at her. "Distraction?"

"I'm not crying over my family," she said, blinking hard. "I'm crying over you."

"Nay," he said with a half laugh, "that isn't how it is supposed to be. 'Tis my duty to make you smile."

She put her arms around him and held him tightly. "Thank you," she whispered. "Thank you for loving me and making me your wife. I'm so happy, I think my heart really will break."

He was silent, but clutched her so tightly to him that she finally had to wheeze out a request that he allow her to breathe. He let her slip down to her feet. She looked up and blinked in surprise.

His eyes were very red. He shrugged helplessly and smiled.

"My heart broke the first time I saw you," he said. "I thought it had healed, then you agreed to wed me. I'm toast."

She smiled. "You've been talking to Jake."

"Aye." He paused. "What is toast?"

She laughed and pulled him back down the beach. "I'll tell you later. Didn't you say there was some privacy somewhere here?"

"One could hope," he said cheerfully.

Several hours later, she rode with him up the cobblestone road, under the barbican gate, and into the courtyard. She sat on a bale of hay while he stabled his horse, then took his hand and walked with him back to the great hall. He looked at her with a smile.

"You are gorgeous," he said frankly.

"And so are you," she returned. "But you have sand in your hair."

"So do you," he said with a smile.

She smiled and went inside Artane's great hall with him.

She played for them in Rhys's solar that night, then simply sat next to Nicholas and enjoyed the company of his family.

She forced herself not to think about her own.

643

In time, Nicholas rose, said good night to his family, and picked up her violin case. He led her from his father's solar, then shut the door and looked at her.

"How are you?"

"In need of another distraction," she said honestly.

"Let me see what I can do."

"I was hoping you would say that."

She walked with him up the stairs and down the passageway to his chamber. He led her inside and over to a chair, then went to bolt the door. He lit a candle, stoked the fire, then gently pulled her up and into his arms.

"Now, to my work," he said bending his head to hers.

Jennifer smiled.

"What?" he asked.

"I was just thinking."

"Of what?"

"My mom said that she put her favorite song on one of the iPods. It's called 'When I Fall in Love.' "

"And?"

"The song claims it will be forever." She reached up and touched his face. "I don't know if forever will be enough for me," she said softly.

"Then we'll ask for eternity," he whispered against her mouth. "But I don't think that will be long enough, either."

■ ■ ■ ■

It was the middle of the night when she woke. The candle was still burning and she allowed herself the luxury of watching Nicholas, unobserved. His hair was like pale, spun gold, his face beautiful in sleep. She smiled to herself. Obviously those de Piaget historians had known what they were talking about.

For all she knew, *she* had been the one to pass on tales of his perfection.

That gave her a headache, thinking about time running around in circles, so she let that thought slip right on by and concentrated on what was there in front of her. It was captivating enough for several lifetimes.

She looked behind his head and saw on the little table on the far side of the bed a stack of books and another stack of paper. He'd begun making himself notes the very first day he'd seen the history books. She'd watched him thumb through the books, flinching now and then, but seeming to handle it fairly well.

He'd asked her, during the moments when they'd come up for air since their wedding, countless questions about English. He had also, during the odd moment when she'd tried to eat, begun to sound out the texts in French and Italian. She imagined the onslaught of questions about music and art wasn't far behind.

She hadn't played the iPods yet. She had to save something for the future.

She smiled. Nicholas's appetite for knowledge was as voracious as his appetite for her. She half wondered if she would manage to keep up with him in either.

She reached out and brushed his hair gently out of his eyes before she could stop herself. He opened his eyes and looked at her with a smile.

"You weren't asleep," she said in surprise.

"I watched you until you stirred," he admitted. "I can't seem to help myself."

"Then we're both toast."

He smiled and pulled her closer. "I daresay I've fallen so far with you that there is no longer any hope for me." He closed his eyes. "When I fall in love," he murmured.

Jennifer leaned over, blew out the candle, and returned to Nicholas's embrace.

It will be forever . . .

Chapter 40

Wyckham
Summer 1231

Nicholas stood in the gallery of Wyckham and looked down into the great hall. Truly Petter had outdone himself. The arch that held up the roof was enormous and the gallery that encircled the walls one floor up was spectacular. He could hardly wait to put musicians there and hear their sweet tones floating down to please his lady's ears.

He leaned on the railing and stared at the lady in question. She was below, running after a lad of a year who seemed determined to lead his mother on a merry chase. Jennifer caught him, swung him up in her arms, and laughed as he burrowed into her neck.

Nicholas shook his head in silent wonder. How different his life was than he had ever expected it to be. He had come to Wyckham that particular spring certain he would rot in an unstable chair before his hearth, complaining and muttering about the misery that was his life.

Now, he looked down into his great hall and smiled at the sight. Who knew how long the keep would last after his death? Jennifer had admitted to him, quite a while after they were wed, that Wyckham had not stood the test of time. He hadn't cared. If it stood long enough for them to live and love in it, what did the Future matter? His life was full of music, beauty, and a woman who was both.

She paused, then looked up at him.

She smiled.

Nicholas was happy to be holding on to something sturdy. They had been wed two years, yet still she could fell him with a smile alone.

Though, he supposed he was not alone in that. They had passed a goodly portion of the past two years in France. It had been wonderful, and Jennifer had made it so. Everywhere they went, she made it wonderful. She put people at ease, drew music out of them, appreciated even tremendously bad lays sung to her beauty.

He supposed she wasn't completely adverse to the lays he sang to her.

Now she stood in the midst of her hall, with his son on her shoulder, and looked up at him with an expression of love.

Nicholas was lost.

Completely, totally, irretrievably lost.

He made his way quickly down the stairs, strode across the floor, and stopped in front of her.

Baby James reared back and howled.

Jennifer looked at him and laughed in spite of herself. Nicholas could see now that her hair was escaping its braid, her dress had been gummed by a very small mouth, and she looked, as she would have said, a bit frazzled.

"I've tried everything," she said, with a weary smile. "I nursed him. I rocked him. I chased him. He needs a nap but he refuses to take one."

"Let me try," Nicholas said. He took James in one arm, took Jennifer by the hand, and led them both to his bedchamber.

A fire was burning in the hearth. He put Jennifer into a chair before it, then began to pace. James was most definitely not satisfied, but the sheer motion seemed to be enough for him. In time, Nicholas was no longer pacing, but merely standing in one place, holding the lad against his shoulder and rocking ever so slightly. He turned to see if Jennifer was still awake.

She was watching him, smiling as if he pleased her in some way. He lifted an eyebrow.

"Aye?" he whispered.

"I love you."

"Because James is asleep?"

"That, too."

"Do I dare put him down?"

She held up her hands. "I can't be responsible for what might happen then, because you *know* he'll wake back up. But," she added with a smile, "I would be up for an afternoon nap if you could manage to get him down."

"Would you sleep?"

"Hopefully not."

He would have laughed, but even a small snort made his son stir. He sat down in the rocker next to his lady and hoped it would encourage a deep sleep in the lad. Jennifer leaned on the arm of her chair and watched him.

"I love you," she said with a smile.

"Do you?" he asked.

"You know I do. Oh, by the way, I'm pregnant again."

"What?" he exclaimed.

James lifted his head, bellowed his displeasure, looked about himself sleepily, then put his head back on Nicholas's shoulder with a thump. Nicholas stroked his back and looked at his lady who was grinning madly.

"Are you, in truth?" he whispered.

"I am." She smiled. "You can't be surprised."

"I'm not surprised," he said, reaching out for her hand. "But I am thrilled beyond measure."

She brought his hand up and kissed the

back of it, then held it to her cheek. "It is a very great gift, my lord," she said softly. "Thank you."

"I did nothing," he said modestly.

"Well," she said with a twinkle in her eye, "I wouldn't say *nothing*. But what I would say is that we should decide where we'll have this one. Here? Beauvois?"

"Are you interested in another sea crossing?" he asked.

"Not particularly, but you know I love it in France. Perhaps it would be fitting for this child to be born there."

Nicholas nodded with a shiver. Wyckham might not have stood the test of time, but Beauvois certainly had. And apparently his second son, John, would make it even more spectacular than Nicholas had managed to.

The Beauvois Guide Book said so.

He had the Beauvois Guide Book because Jennifer's mother and grandmother had brought it with them, along with an additional supply of chocolate and some wine, when they'd come to be midwives for James's birth.

"Too much knowledge," Jennifer murmured. "It's dangerous."

He smiled, feeling slightly queasy. "Aye. I would have to agree."

"We should go to France."

"We should."

She looked at him with a grave smile. "Is it

spooky to have read about your children before they're born?"

"You know it is." He squeezed her hand. "I'll think on it more later. For now, I think I must digest these mind-blowing tidings of your pregnancy."

She laughed softly. "I love it when you do that."

"The Future-speak thing?"

"The Future-speak thing," she said softly. She leaned over to kiss him. "Mind-blowing, indeed. Put the baby in the crib, Nicky, and let's go have a nap. I think morning sickness is going to start up again in the next week or so. We'd better take advantage of its absence."

Nicholas obliged, in more than one request, then found himself, an hour later, sitting in the rocker with his lady in his arms, rocking gently. He wasn't sure if she slept or not, though he imagined she did. He would have closed his eyes, too, but he couldn't bear to.

He might have missed something otherwise.

He shook his head in wonder again at the absolute miracle that had become his life. A woman who had given up everything because she loved him. A child and another one yet to come. A trunk full of marvels that never failed to amaze and astonish him.

Both batches of Godiva — the wedding present and the additional gift on the occasion of James's birth — were, unfortunately, gone, but they had made them last as long as possible. He'd told Jennifer, at one point, that it might be worth testing out the Xs on James MacLeod's map for more of the stuff, but she had informed him that being a chocoholic was not necessarily a knightly characteristic he should be striving to develop.

He wasn't sure he'd agreed.

The wine her grandmother had brought had been too strong and Jennifer had much preferred what was to be found at Beauvois, though the Kit Kats had been lovely and the Lilt surprising.

But what had continued to astonish beyond measure had been the books.

He supposed he would never accustom himself to knowing the things he now knew about the Future. Cars, telephones, televisions, aeroplanes, rocket ships. The list was endless and staggering in its implications.

Then there was the art, the music, the plays. He found himself murmuring Shakespeare under his breath as he trained, Dante whilst he mucked out stables, Wordsworth as he walked through his garden. So many words, so many thoughts, so many images he never would have dreamed of.

Mind-blowing, indeed.

He was sorely tempted, deep within the recesses of his soul where he didn't venture often, to take Jennifer and his son, and try one of the gates.

"No."

He blinked. Then he looked to find Jennifer leaning her head on his shoulder, looking up at him. "What?" he asked.

"No. You have things to do here."

He felt his jaw drop. "What are you talking about?"

"You're thinking about using the gates and I'm telling you that you have things to do here. Children to produce. A legend to create. Musicians and artists to import."

He pursed his lips. "I wasn't thinking anything of the sort."

She smiled as she reached up and stroked his cheek. "You know, my lord, you mutter when you think too hard. It's worrisome. And you're a terrible liar."

He kissed her softly. "A brief visit."

"Nicholas, no," she said with a laugh. "Really." She put her arm around his neck and kissed him firmly. "Really."

"Why not?" he asked with a smile.

"Because I think if you actually got behind the wheel of a car, I'd never get you back to your family," she said. Her smile faded. "And I'm serious about that, Nicky. I think you've seen too much."

"Should I burn the books?" he asked grimly.

"More than likely."

"I'll think about it."

"There's a lot to be said for peace and good earth and endless skies. And your exceptionally lovely keep on the sea."

"Aye."

"Burn the books, Nicholas," she said solemnly. "And stay here with me."

"Of course," he said, gathering her close. "Of course."

"The music, too."

"Jennifer," he said in a low voice. "You jest."

She shook her head. "Honestly, I think we would be better off to burn it all. Well, except a few necessities my mother provided for me and that book on natural childbirth. And the needles. And the chess set."

"And my socks," Nicholas said. "I will not burn my socks."

She laughed and rested her head against his shoulder. "Not the socks, my lord. A man needs his comforts."

"You are my comfort and in truth the rest of it means nothing in comparison," he said quietly.

And it was true. The Future with all its marvels held no allure for him when compared to the woman in his arms. She had given him love, music, beauty, a child.

And another yet to come.

He lifted her face up and kissed her softly. "I love you."

"I love you."

"I'm keeping the map."

"I imagined you would."

He smiled and hugged her tightly.

When I fall in love . . .

It was more than he could have hoped for, more than he deserved, more than he would ever accustom himself to.

And it was all because of Jennifer.

He closed his eyes and smiled.

CHAPTER 41

Megan MacLeod McKinnon de Piaget sat with her baby in her arms in the lord's solar at Artane and listened with half an ear to the goings on around her. Gideon and his uncle, Kendrick, the earl of Seakirk, were playing chess and laughing. Kendrick's children were making mischief as surreptitiously as possible. Lord Edward and Kendrick's wife, Genevieve, were discussing the proper pruning of rosebushes. Megan smiled to herself and wondered if her sister was at that very moment in her own time sitting in the lord's solar, watching her own husband play chess with one of his brothers. Perhaps she was at Wyckham, making it lovely. Perhaps she was in France, walking along the beach.

Her parents and Victoria and Connor had returned the week before from their trip back in time to see Jennifer marry Nicholas de Piaget. Victoria had said they were content.

Megan didn't doubt it. Nicholas sounded like a wonderful man and she had no trouble believing that her sister was gloriously happy.

Still, it would have been nice to know for sure.

The earl rose and stretched. "Children, I'm off. Kendrick, lad, stay out of my Schnapps."

"Of course, my lord," Kendrick said with a grin.

"I'll take the lads up for you, if you like," he offered. "And your wee girl. She's a lovely thing, that Mistress Adelaide."

"Brilliant," Kendrick said. "Lads, go with His Lordship and don't pester him about things in glass cabinets. Addy, Mum and I will be up in a moment to tuck you in, aye?"

Megan watched her father-in-law tromp out with Kendrick and Genevieve's rambunctious brood, waited until the solar was completely devoid of all youthful ears, then turned to look at Kendrick.

"Okay," she said firmly, "spill it."

"Spill what?" he asked innocently.

"All the details you've been hunting up since my family left last week," she said. "Gen and I watched you do it."

"I was just reading," he said with a shrug. "I'm a reader, you know."

"Right," Megan said wryly. "Come on, Kendrick. You know you want to tell us."

Kendrick tipped his king. "I must admit, I've learned a few interesting things."

"Things that you didn't already know?" Genevieve asked dryly. "After all, you did squire for Nicholas, didn't you?"

Megan gaped first at Genevieve, then at Kendrick. "You did *what?*"

"In another life," Kendrick agreed. "Aye, I did."

"Then you knew Jennifer."

Kendrick smiled gravely. "Very well."

Megan felt tears spring to her eyes. "You didn't tell me?"

"I couldn't, now, could I?" he asked gently. "Not then. Not before Jennifer even knew what the future had in store for her. And I didn't dare until your parents had come back from the past with a good report. You never know how history might find itself changed."

Megan sighed. "You're right, of course. But you could make me feel better *now* by giving me an eyewitness account of her life."

He sat back in his chair. "Gladly. What will you know?"

"Was she happy?"

"She was. Deliriously." Kendrick smiled. "My uncle loved her to distraction. I was forever stumbling upon him kissing her in darkened corners. Actually," he said, scratching his head, "now that I think on it, he kissed her in lightened corners as well."

Megan smiled. "I'm glad to hear it. But did you ever know who she was? What she was?"

He shrugged. "I thought she was a fairy.

That was my uncle Montgomery's doing, as you might imagine, what with his being the source of all information on fairies. He was convinced she was of Jake Kilchurn's ilk. And so she was."

"But, Kendrick," Genevieve asked in surprise, "what did you think when you first met Megan?"

"That I was seeing a ghost," Kendrick laughed. "I covered it manfully by gaping at Gideon instead."

"Tell me more of Jennifer's life," Megan urged. "They lived at Wyckham?"

"Part of the year. The other half they went to France. Nick had Beauvois, of course, and Auntie Jen loved the ocean."

"How many children did they have?"

"Ten, including two sets of twins."

Megan gaped. "You're kidding."

"I never kid," he said solemnly. "It was all that kissing. I daresay it led to other things."

"Heaven help her," Megan said, with feeling.

"Aye, she said the same thing. Often." He smiled. "She had a few who were definite handfuls."

"Who?" Genevieve asked. "The ones who were willing to throw in their lots with you and see what sorts of adventures they could give their father gray hairs over?"

Kendrick winked at Megan. "She knows me too well."

"Ten children," Megan said, shaking her head. "I'll bet she wished for a midwife, at least."

"She had one. Two, generally, for most of her children." Kendrick smiled. "A couple of Scottish ladies. Helen McKinnon and Mary MacLeod, I believe. I met them a time or two."

Megan gaped at him. "My mother? My *grandmother?*"

Kendrick smiled. "So it would seem."

Megan looked at Gideon and felt a little shaky. "I think it's going to take me a while to get used to all this wandering through time that I never knew about."

"Trust me," Gideon said, looking a little green himself, "I feel the same way."

Megan took a deep, steadying breath, then looked at Kendrick again. "All right, I can handle some more now. Did she play her violin much?"

"I heard her play countless times," Kendrick said. "Most often in France, where new music was not so strange and the servants more discreet. The peasants enfeoffed to Wyckham were convinced there was a spirit who played music to break a heart inside the keep. In France, they just smiled and went about their work. But," he added, "she did manage to keep a full compliment of other musicians at Wyckham. Nicholas had built a gallery there and music was played every night.

661

Nicholas loved to dance with her."

"I imagine that led to more kissing," Megan said dryly.

"And more children," Genevieve laughed.

"I daresay my uncle planned it thus," Kendrick said with a twinkle in his eye. "All I know is that he cherished her more than life itself and not a day went by that I didn't see him do something special for her. Flowers, a walk at sunset, music, a beautiful gown. He lavished gifts and love and attention upon her." He smiled at her. "You can rest easy knowing she was adored throughout their life."

"When did she die?"

Kendrick shifted. "She was still alive when I was killed."

Megan looked at him closely. "And?"

He returned her look, but his eyes were wide with feigned innocence. "And what?"

"You know something you're not telling."

Genevieve laughed at her. "Megan, you know him too well. Kendrick, we can all tell you're bursting to say something else. Spill the beans."

"They're fairly considerable beans."

"Spill them," Megan warned, "or Gideon will take you out and thrash you in the lists."

Gideon looked up quickly. "Megan, I could run him over in the lists with the Range Rover. I think the thrashing would be limited to that."

Kendrick laughed and reached over to clap a hand on Gideon's shoulder. "You're coming along nicely with your swordplay. Never my equal, of course, but you're holding your own."

"He needs to go to Jamie's medieval boot camp," Megan said.

"I've considered it," Gideon said with a grin, "but I fear that it would lead to all sorts of adventures that you might not want."

"Blame it on me, why don't you," Megan laughed uneasily.

"I'll share the blame," Gideon said with a smile. "I think Artane Enterprises would fall apart without me there to micromanage it." He winked at Megan. "Though a little vacation up north might not be such a bad idea. Who knows where a trip to James Mac-Leod's land might truly lead?"

"All I know is that it's leading me away from what I want to know," Megan said. She looked at Kendrick. "Spill those substantial beans. How old was Jennifer when she died and what happened to the Degani?"

Kendrick seemed to consider his words. "Their graves are inside the church gates. You could go look, if you liked."

"Did they bury the violin with her?" Megan asked in surprise.

Kendrick looked at her, clear-eyed. "I never said that."

"Husband, what *are* you saying?" Genevieve asked faintly.

"I said their graves are inside the church gates," Kendrick said. "Whether the violin, or anything else, finds itself inside those graves is anyone's guess."

Megan gaped at him, stunned. Then she looked at Gideon. He was gaping at Kendrick in a similar manner.

"Kendrick, old man, what are you saying?" Gideon said.

Kendrick fished a key out of his pocket and slid it across the table to Gideon.

"You should put that somewhere."

Gideon picked it up as if it had been a live snake. "Whyever for?"

"Someone may come looking for it someday."

"What is it?"

"The key to the little cottage adjacent to Wyckham."

"Why do you have the key?" Gideon asked.

"I own the cottage."

Megan frowned. "Why?"

"Because it came with the castle."

"You own the castle, too?"

He smiled. "It seemed like a good idea at the time."

"Kendrick," Genevieve said seriously, "what in the world are you talking about?"

Kendrick smiled. "I am saying that there was a very interesting map in my uncle Nick's trunk. I saw it the first time I picked the lock

664

to see what he kept inside there. The map had all sorts of red Xs on it." He looked at Megan. "I wonder what those were?"

"It sounds like a Jamie map."

"Aye, I would say so . . . now. At the time, I had no idea. All I'm suggesting is that maps are very interesting, graves may or may not be filled with their owners, and that a very expensive, very rare violin really doesn't belong in a tomb."

"Kendrick!" Genevieve exclaimed.

He held up his hands. " 'Tis but a bit of conversation." He looked at Megan. " 'Tis only that. But, all I can tell you is that I caught my uncle Nicholas studying that map more than once." He paused. "You can make of that what you will."

Megan looked at Gideon, then she began to smile. She smiled in spite of the single tear that rolled down her cheek.

"Well," she said. "We should probably buy a bigger house with a guest room. Who knows when we might have guests?"

"Someday," Kendrick said. "Just someday."

Megan took a deep breath. "I won't think about the possibility now, then. It's enough to know that he loved her. Then."

"He did, very much," Kendrick agreed. "You will be pleased, I think, with him. I mean," he said with exaggerated haste, "you would have *been* pleased with him."

Genevieve rose and pulled him up out of

his chair. "You, my lord, have an overactive imagination. Come for a walk with me. I think I saw a darkened corner not far from here."

Kendrick laughed and followed her toward the door.

"If I were you, I would buy that bigger house," he whispered to Megan on his way by. "You'll never know when you might need it for an unexpected family visit."

Megan smiled as they left the lord's solar, then looked at her husband who was sitting in the chair across from her. "Well?" she asked.

"Let's put that baby down, woman, and find our own darkened bit of hall," he said, getting to his feet and coming to stand in front of her. He held down his hand.

Megan took it and let him pull her up. She looked up at him. "I think she's happy."

"It sounds as though she is," Gideon said. He put his arm around her and turned her toward the door. "Is your mind at ease?"

"What, after all those appalling hints Kendrick dropped?" she asked incredulously. She paused. "Do you think he's kidding?"

"I don't think he kids."

"He's a terrible tease."

Gideon kissed her softly. "I daresay, Megan my love, that we had best be prepared just in case. Who knows how many extra bedrooms we should have. She had ten children, after all."

Megan nodded with a smile, then walked with him out of the lord's solar and across the great hall. Well, she supposed she would know in time whether Kendrick was teasing or not. And in the end, maybe it didn't matter. One way or another, Nicholas and Jennifer had lived happily ever after.

It was the perfect fairy-tale ending.

That was enough for her.